LEONIBUS
BOOKS

An Imprint of
TWO BRIDGES PRESS
www.twobridgespress.com

ALSO BY C.W. GORTNER

The Last Queen

The Spymaster Chronicles

C. W. GORTNER

TWO BRIDGES PRESS
San Francisco

Leonibus Books
An Imprint of Two Bridges Press
1563 Solano Ave # 325
Berkeley, CA. 94707
www.twobridgespress.com

Copyright© 2006 by Christopher Willis Gortner
All rights reserved, including the right of
reproduction in whole or part in any form.
Brief passages may be quoted for review purposes.

Two Bridges™ and logo are registered
trademarks of Two Bridges Press, San Francisco

Manufactured in the United States of America
Second Edition 2006

This book is a work of fiction.
All the characters are either products of the
author's imagination or are used fictitiously.

Designed by Studio P

Library of Congress Control Number: 2006906898

ISBN–13: 978-0-9723947-1-0
ISBN–10: 0-9723947-1-0

For Erik

HOUSE OF TUDOR

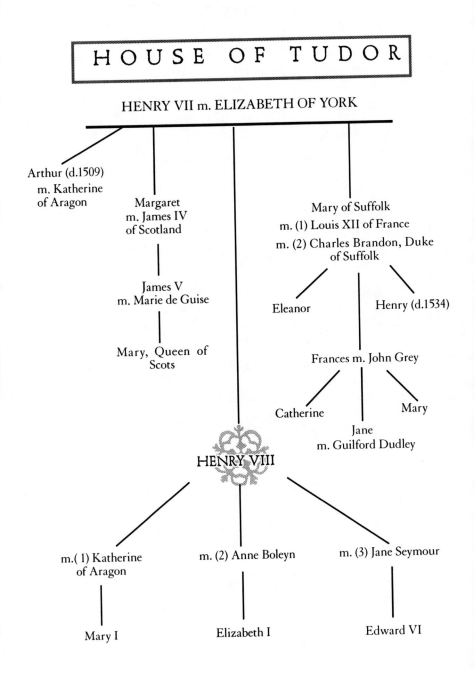

HENRY VII m. ELIZABETH OF YORK

Arthur (d.1509)
m. Katherine
of Aragon

Margaret
m. James IV
of Scotland

James V
m. Marie de Guise

Mary, Queen of
Scots

Mary of Suffolk
m. (1) Louis XII of France
m. (2) Charles Brandon, Duke
of Suffolk

Eleanor

Henry (d.1534)

Frances m. John Grey

Catherine

Jane
m. Guilford Dudley

Mary

HENRY VIII

m. (1) Katherine
of Aragon

m. (2) Anne Boleyn

m. (3) Jane Seymour

Mary I

Elizabeth I

Edward VI

1602

Everyone has a secret.

Like the oyster with its grain of sand, we bury it deep within, coating it with opalescent layers as if that could heal our mortal wound. Some of us devote our entire lives to keeping our secret hidden, safe from those who might pry it from us, hoarding it like the pearl, only to discover that it escapes us when we least expect it, revealed by a flash of fear in our eyes when caught unawares, by a sudden pain, a rage or hatred, or an all-consuming shame.

I know all about secrets. Secrets upon secrets, wielded like weapons, like tethers, like bedside endearments. The truth alone can never suffice. Secrets are the coin of our world, the currency upon which we construct our edifice of grandeur and lies. We need our secrets to serve as iron for our shields, brocade for our bodies, and veils for our fears— they delude and comfort, shielding us always from the fact that in the end we, too, must die.

"Write it all down," she tells me, "every last word."

We often sit like this in the winter of our lives, chronic insomniacs in outdated finery, the chessboard or the game of cards neglected on the table, as her eyes—alert and ever-wary after all these years, still leonine in a face grown gaunt with age—turn inward to that place where none has ever trespassed, to her own secret, which I now know, have perhaps always known, she must take with her to her grave.

"Write it down," she says, "so that when I am gone, you will remember."

As if I could ever forget . . . .

Whitehall, 1553

CHAPTER ONE

Like everything important in life, it began with a journey—the road to London, to be exact, my first excursion to that most fascinating and sordid of cities.

We started out before daybreak, two men on horseback, destined for a fate I could not have foreseen. I had never been further than Warwickshire, which made Master Shelton's arrival with my summons all the more unexpected. I scarcely had time to pack my few belongings and bid farewell to the servants (including sweet Annabel, who'd wept as if her heart might break) before I was riding from the castle where I'd spent my entire life, unsure as to when, or if, I would return again.

My excitement and apprehension should have been enough to keep me awake. Yet I soon found myself nodding off to sleep, lulled by the countryside and my roan Cinnabar's amble. Master Shelton's gruff announcement started me to attention.

"Brendan, lad, rouse yourself. We're almost there."

I sat up in my saddle. Blinking away my catnap, I reached to my cap only to find my unruly thatch of light auburn hair. Master Shelton had frowned at its length, grumbling that Englishmen shouldn't go unshorn like the heretic French.

He wouldn't be pleased by the loss of my cap, either.

"Oh, no." I looked at him.

He regarded me impassively. A puckered scar ran across his left cheek, marring his rugged features. Not that it mattered. Archie Shelton was not, and had probably never been, a handsome man. Still, he had impressive girth and rode his steed with authority, his cloak, emblazoned with the ragged bear and staff, denoting his rank as the Dudley family steward. To anyone else, that granite stare would have inspired trepidation. I had known him all my life, and had long grown accustomed to his taciturn manner.

"It fell off about a mile back." He extended my cap. "Since my days in the Scottish wars, I've never seen anyone sleep so soundly on horseback. You'd think you'd been to London a hundred times before."

I heard rough mirth in his rebuke. It confirmed my suspicion that he was secretly pleased by this precipitous change in my fortune, though it wasn't in his nature to discuss his personal sentiments regarding anything the Duke or Lady Dudley commanded.

"You can't go losing your cap about court," he went on as I clapped the red cloth hat back on my head and peered to where the sun-dappled road veered over a hill. "A squire must be attentive at all times to his appearance." He eyed me. "My lord of Northumberland and her ladyship expect much of their servants. I trust you still remember how to behave with your betters."

"Of course." I squared my shoulders, reciting in my most obsequious tone: "It's best to remain silent whenever possible and to always keep your eyes lowered when spoken to. If uncertain as to how to address someone, a simple 'my lord', or 'my lady,' will suffice." I paused. "See? I haven't forgotten."

Master Shelton snorted. Again, I caught an amusement in his eyes he would never admit to. "See that you don't. You'll be squire to his lordship's own son, Lord Robert. It's an opportunity I'll not have you squander. If you excel in this post, who knows? You could rise to chamberlain or steward. The Dudleys reward those who serve them well."

As soon these words were uttered, I realized I should have known. It wasn't as if I had a range of options to choose from, and it went a long way toward explaining Master Shelton's efforts on my behalf.

Even after Lady Dudley had joined her family year-round at court, her steward had returned twice a year to the castle where I remained with a skeleton staff. Master Shelton came ostensibly to oversee our upkeep, but it seemed he'd had other plans, as well.

My duties had been confined to the stables. Master Shelton assigned me other household chores, as well, and paid me, for the first time, a

4

modest sum. He even took in a local monk to tutor me—one of thousands who begged and bartered their way through England since old King Henry abolished the monasteries. The staff at Warwick deemed her ladyship's steward unnatural, a cold and solitary man, but Master Shelton had always shown me kindness.

Now, I knew why.

He was grooming me as his successor, once old age or infirmity demanded his retirement. It was hardly the role I aspired to, filled as it was with all those tiresome domestic obligations Lady Dudley had neither time nor inclination for. Though it was a far better future than someone in my shoes ought to expect, I'd rather remain a stable hand than become a privileged lackey dependent on sufferance. Horses, at least, I understood, whilst the Duke and his wife were strangers to me in every sense of the word.

Still, I shouldn't appear ungrateful. Master Shelton clearly expected my appreciation of his trust in my abilities, and so I bowed my head with as much gravity as I could muster.

"I would be honored if I were deemed worthy of such a post."

A cragged smile, all the more startling because of its rarity, lightened Master Shelton's face. "Would you? I thought as much. Well, then, we shall have to see, won't we?"

I offered a wan smile in return. Serving as squire to Lord Robert would prove challenge enough without assuming the worries of a potential stewardship. Though I had not seen the Duke's fourth-born son in years, he and I were of age, and had dwelled together in Warwick during our childhood.

In truth, Robert Dudley had been my bane. Even as a lad, he'd been the most handsome and talented of the Dudley brood, favored in everything he undertook, be it archery, music, or dance. He had also been inflated with pride in his own superiority—a rogue who delighted in leading his four brothers in rousing games of 'thrash-the-foundling.'

No matter how I tried to escape, or how fiercely I struggled, Robert always managed to hunt me down. He directed his walloping gang of brothers to duck me into the scum-coated moat or dangle me over the courtyard well, until my shouts turned to sobs and my beloved Dame Alice rushed out to rescue me. I spent the majority of my time scrambling up trees or hiding, terrified, in the attic. Then Robert was sent to

5

court to serve as a page. After his brothers were likewise dispatched to similar posts, I discovered a new-found freedom.

Now I found myself on my way to serve him, at his mother's command, no less. Startling as the appointment was, I had always known noble families did not foster unfortunates like me for charity's sake alone. A day had to come when I'd be called upon to pay my debt.

My thoughts must have shown on my face, for Master Shelton cleared his throat and said, "No need to fret. You mind your manners and do as you're told, and all will go well." In another rare display of sensibility, he reached over to pat my shoulder. "Dame Alice would be proud of you this day. She always thought you would amount to something."

I felt my chest tighten. I saw her in my mind's eye, wagging a finger at me as her pot of herbs bubbled on the hearth and I sat entranced, my mouth and hands sticky with fresh-made jam.

You must always be ready for great things, Brendan Prescott. We never know when we'll be called upon to rise above our lot.

I averted my eyes, pretending to adjust my reins. The silence lengthened, broken only by the steady clip-clop of hooves on the cobblestone and baked-mud road.

Then Master Shelton said. "I trust your new livery fits. You could stand to put some meat on your bones, but you've good enough posture. Been practicing with that quarter stave like I taught you?"

"Every day," I replied. I forced myself to look up. Master Shelton had no idea of what else I'd been practicing these past few years at Warwick.

It had been Dame Alice who first taught me my letters. She had often told me the only limit on our minds is the one we impose, and after her sudden death, I vowed to pursue my studies. I lavished the sour-breathed monk Master Shelton hired with such fawning enthusiasm that before he knew it, he was steering me through the intricacies of Plutarch. I often stayed up all night, pouring over books I pinched from the Dudley library. Learning, I discovered, had a passion all its own. There were even times when I found occasion to combine two passions, reading aloud from a volume propped on Annabel's buttocks as she giggled that she understood not a word of what I said. I needn't detail here the punishment I imposed for such delightful ignorance.

I repressed my smile. Master Shelton was literate, of course. He had to be in order to balance the household accounts. But in his stolid opinion, no servant, no matter how assiduous, should be conversant on the philosophies of Erasmus or Thomas More, much less fluent in French and Latin. He never presumed to more than his station in life, nor would he tolerate such presumption in others.

We rode on in quiet, cresting the hill. As the road threaded through a treeless vale, the emptiness of the landscape caught my attention, used as I was to the unfettered woodlands of Warwickshire. We weren't that far away, a two-day ride at the most, and I felt as if I were entering a foreign domain.

Smoke smeared the sky like a thumbprint. I caught sight of twin hills, then a rise of massive walls, surrounding a sprawl of tenements, spires, riverside manors, and endless latticed streets— all divided by the emerald Thames.

"There she is," said Master Shelton. "The City of London. You'll miss the peace of the countryside soon enough, if the cutthroats or pestilence don't get to you first."

I could only stare. London was as dense and foreboding as I'd imagined it would be, kites circling overhead as if the air contained carrion. Yet as we drew closer, abutting the serpentine walls, I spied pasturelands dotted with livestock, herb patches, orchards, and prosperous hamlets. It seemed London still had a good degree of the rural to commend it.

We reached one of the seven city gates. I took in everything at once, enthralled by a group of overdressed merchants perched on an ox-drawn cart, by a singing tinker carrying a clanging yoke of knives and armor, and a multitude of beggars, apprentices, officious guildsmen, butchers, tanners, and pilgrims. Voices collided in argument with the gatekeepers, who had called a halt to everyone's progress. As Master Shelton and I joined the queue I lifted my gaze to the gate looming overhead, its massive turrets and fanged crenellations blackened by grime.

I froze. Mounted on poles, staring down through sightless sockets, was a collection of tar-boiled heads—a grisly feast for the ravens, which tore at the rancid flesh.

Beside me Master Shelton muttered, "Papists. His lordship ordered their heads displayed as a warning."

Papists were Catholics. They believed the Pope in Rome, not our sovereign, was Head of the Church. Dame Alice had been a Catholic. Though she'd raised me in the Reformed Faith, according to the law, I'd watched her pray every night with the rosary.

In that instant, I was struck by how far I was from Warwick. There, everyone turned a blind eye to the practices of others. Here, it seemed, a man could lose his head for it.

An unkempt guard lumbered to us, wiping greasy hands on his tunic. "No one's allowed in," he barked. "Gates are hereby closed by his lordship's command!" He paused, catching sight of the badge on Master Shelton's cloak. "Northumberland's man, are ye?"

"His lady wife's chief steward." Master Shelton withdrew a roll of papers from his saddlebag. "I have her safe conducts here for me and the lad. We are due at court."

"Is that so?" The guard leered. "Well, every last miserable soul here says they're due somewhere. Rabble's in a fine fettle, what with these rumors of His Majesty's mortal illness and some nonsense of the Princess Elizabeth riding among us." He hawked a gob of spit into the dirt. "Idiots. They'd believe the moon was made of silk if enough swore to it." He didn't bother to check the papers. "I'd keep away from crowds if I were you," he said, waving us on.

We passed under the gatehouse. Behind us, I heard those who had been detained start to yell in protest. Master Shelton tucked the papers back into the saddlebag. The parting of his cloak revealed a broadsword strapped to his back. The glimpse of the weapon riveted me for a moment. I surreptitiously reached a hand to the sheathed knife at my belt, a gift from Master Shelton on my fourteenth year.

I ventured, "His Majesty the King, is he dying?"

"Of course not. His Majesty has been ill, is all, and the people blame the Duke for it, as they blame him for just about everything that's gone wrong in England. Absolute power, lad, it comes with a price." Master Shelton's jaw clenched. "Keep an eye out. These streets are rife with knaves."

I could believe it. Instead of orderly avenues lined with shops, we traversed a tangle of crookbacked lanes piled with refuse, side alleys snaking off into sinister darkness. Overhead, dilapidated buildings leaned against each other like fallen trees, their ramshackle galleries colliding, blocking out the sunlight.

Master Shelton pulled to a halt. "Listen."

My every nerve went on alert. A muted sound reached me, seeming to come from everywhere at once. "Best hold on," warned Master Shelton, and I tightened my grip on Cinnabar, edging him aside moments before an onslaught of people came pouring into the street.

Their appearance was so unexpected that despite my grip, Cinnabar started to rear. Fearing he would trample someone, I slid from the saddle to take hold of his bridle.

The crowd pressed around us. Motley and smelling of sweat and the sewer, they made me feel like I was a new and rare kind of prey. I started to angle for the dagger at my belt before I noticed that no one was paying me any mind. I looked at Master Shelton, still mounted on his massive bay. He barked an undecipherable order at me. I craned my head, straining to hear him.

I was almost knocked off my feet. The multitude surged forward as if by some unseen, collective cue. It was all I could do to scramble onto Cinnabar as we were propelled by the mob through the streets and onto a riverbank.

I yanked Cinnabar back not a moment too soon. Before me, algid as liquid jasper, ran the Thames. In the distance downstream, rimmed in haze, a stone pile bullied the landscape.

The Tower.

I went still. I couldn't believe I was seeing that infamous royal fortress. Master Shelton cantered up behind me. "God's blood, I thought I'd lost you. Come. This is no time for dalliance."

I forced myself to pull away and check my horse. Cinnabar's flanks quivered, his nostrils a-flare, but otherwise he seemed well enough. The crowd had rushed ahead to a row of tenement houses and swinging tavern signs. As we moved toward these, I belatedly reached up to my brow. I had to chuckle. By some miracle, my cap remained firmly in place.

The crowd had come to a stop. They were fewer than they had seemed, an impoverished group of common folk. I watched, bemused, as barefoot urchins tiptoed among them, skulking dogs at their heels.

Master Shelton scowled. "Lad, go see if you can find out what this lot is gawking at."

9

I handed over my reins, dismounted again, and wedged into the crowd, thankful for once for my slight build. I was cursed at, shoved and elbowed, but I managed to push to the front. Standing on tiptoes to see past the craning heads, I made out a narrow dirt thoroughfare ahead, upon which rode an unremarkable cavalcade of women and men on horses. I was about to turn away when a portly woman beside me shoveled her way forth, brandishing a wilted nosegay.

"God bless ye, sweet Bess," she cried. "God bless ye!"

She threw the flowers into the air. A leaden hush fell. One of the men in the cavalcade heeled close to its center, as if to shield something—or someone—from view.

It was then I noticed a dappled charger hidden among the larger horses. I had a keen eye for horseflesh. With its arched neck, lithe musculature, and prancing hooves I recognized it for an Arabian, a breed rarely seen in England, and more costly than the Duke's entire stable.

Then, I looked at its rider.

I knew at once it was a woman, though the hood of her cloak concealed her features and leather gauntlets covered her hands. Contrary to custom, she was mounted astride, toned legs sheathed in riding boots displayed against her embossed saddle—a mere sliver of a girl, without apparent distinction, save for her horse, riding as if intent on reaching her destination.

She must have felt the crowd watching her and heard the woman's cry, for she turned her head. To my astonished disbelief, she pushed her hood back to reveal a fine-boned face, framed by an aureole of coppery hair.

And she smiled.

CHAPTER TWO

E verything around me receded. I recalled what the guard at the gate had said, some nonsense of the Princess Elizabeth riding among us, and I felt an actual pang in my heart as the cavalcade quickened around the corner and disappeared.

The crowd began to disperse, though one of the urchins did creep onto the road to retrieve the fallen nosegay. The woman who'd thrown it stood transfixed, hands at her breast, gazing after the vanished riders with the gleam of tears in her weary eyes. I reached out and lightly touched her arm. She turned to me with a dazed expression.

"Did you see her?" she whispered and though she looked right at me, I had the impression she did not see me at all. "Did you see our Bess? She's come to us at long last, God be praised. Only she can save England from that devil Northumberland's grip."

I stood immobile. Was this how the people of London felt about John Dudley, Duke of Northumberland, whose son I would soon serve? In my isolation, I had believed the Duke was a powerful but benign lord, the King's guardian and protector. How had he incurred such hatred?

Disconcerted, I turned about. Master Shelton had ridden up behind me, and sat, glowering, on his bay. In a low voice he said, "You are a fool, woman, to speak thus of our lord duke."

She gaped. When she caught sight of the badge on his cloak, she staggered back. "The Duke's man!" she gibbered. She stumbled away. Those who remained took up the cry as they, too, fled for the safety of the tangled alleys or the nearest tavern. On the other side of the dirt thoroughfare, a group of decidedly coarse men paused to stare at us.

When I saw the glint of blades being jerked from sleeves, my stomach somersaulted.

"Best mount now, lad," Master Shelton said, without taking his eyes from the men. "Blood could be spilt this day."

He did not need to tell me twice. I vaulted into my saddle. Master Shelton swerved about, scanning the vicinity. The men started to cross the road toward us, blocking the route the cavalcade had taken. I waited with my heart in my throat. We had two equally disagreeable options. We could go back the way we'd come, which led to the riverbank and the maze of streets, or plunge into what looked like an impenetrable row of decrepit timber-framed buildings. Master Shelton appreciated our dilemma, whirling his bay back around on its hindquarters, gauging the approaching men.

He gave a ferocious grin, dug his heels into his bay and spurred it forth—straight at them.

I followed at a break neck pace, certain that blood, and brains and entrails, would indeed be spilt. The men froze in mid-step, eyes popping as they beheld the charge of solid muscle and hooves coming toward them, before they threw themselves to either side like the clods of dirt our horses tore from the road. As we thundered past, I heard a gut-wrenching scream. I glanced back.

One of the men lay face down on the road, a pool of red seeping from his mangled head.

Master Shelton plunged us between the ramshackle edifices. All light extinguished. The miasmic smells of excrement, urine, and rotting food were overpowering. Overhead, balconies formed a claustrophobic vault, festooned with dripping laundry and slabs of curing meat. Night soil splashed as our horses bolted through overflowing conduits that emptied the city's filth into the Thames. I held my breath, the torturous passage seeming to go on forever, until we burst into open expanse.

I pulled Cinnabar to a halt. Everything had gone by in a whirl. As my pulse ebbed, I took note of the sudden, verdant silence. We had crossed into another world.

About us, oaks and beeches swayed. Underfoot, stretched a carpet of meadow as far as my eye could see. I might have marveled at the peculiarity of such a place in midst of the city, had I not been trying to make sense of what had just transpired.

If I was not mistaken, we had witnessed the arrival incognito of the King's younger sister, the Princess Elizabeth, and nearly been assaulted by a gang of ruffians, one of whom we'd killed as we made our escape. Adding to my bewilderment was that Master Shelton seemed a different man altogether, as if he had turned to stone. I'd never seen him behave so oddly, and curiosity was always my weak spot. I could not help myself if I tried.

I took a moment to collect my thoughts. Then I said carefully, "That woman, she said the Princess was here. She called her Bess. Was she, the Princess Elizabeth?"

Master Shelton's voice matched his face, hard and remote. "If it was, then it can only mean trouble. It follows her wherever she goes, just like her mother. The Boleyn witch compelled many good souls to their deaths."

Never had I heard him speak thus. I did not dare pose another question, though now, of course, I had a hundred.

I knew about Anne Boleyn. Who did not? I'd thrilled while growing up to lurid tales of Henry VIII and his six wives. I knew his son, our current king, Edward VI, had two half-sisters, the ladies Mary and Elizabeth. In order to marry his second wife, Anne Boleyn, Henry had cast aside the Lady Mary's mother, Katherine of Aragon, and made himself Head of the Church. But Anne did not enjoy her crown long. Reviled by the people as a whore and heretic, only three years after giving birth to Elizabeth, she was accused of adultery and treason, and beheaded.

That Anne Boleyn was despised even after death did not perturb me. I was unnerved by the way Master Shelton spoke of his hatred. His was the tone of a man with a vendetta.

As I struggled to make sense of it, he directed my attention toward a silhouette etched like thorns against the afternoon sky.

"His Majesty's Palace of Whitehall. Come, lad. It's late."

We rode across the vast open park, into streets that fronted walled manors and dark medieval churches. I saw a large stone cathedral standing like a sentinel on a slope and marveled at its stark splendor, but as we came closer to the palace itself, I surrendered to awe.

I had seen castles before. Warwickshire abounded in fortresses replete with ramparts and battlements, while the Dudley estate where

I'd been raised was reckoned one of the most impressive in the realm. But Whitehall was unlike anything I'd seen. Nestled by a curve in the river, Henry VIII's royal residence rose before me—a multicolored hive of fantastical turrets, curved towers, and galleries sprawling like somnolent beasts. From what I could discern, two major thoroughfares dissected it. Every square foot teemed with activity.

We entered under the Clock Gate, cantering past a crowded forecourt into an inner courtyard crammed with jostling menials, officials, and courtiers. Taking our horses by the reins, we started to make our way on foot to what I assumed would be stables when a trim man in a crimson doublet came purposefully toward us.

Master Shelton stopped and bowed stiffly. The man likewise inclined his head in greeting. Light blue eyes assessed us, a spade-shaped russet beard complimenting lively features. Even then he defied any approximation of his age, appearing both impossibly youthful and sage at the same time.

As I lowered my gaze in deference, I spied crescents of dried ink under his fingernails. I heard him say in a cool, modulated voice, "Master Shelton, her ladyship informed me you might be arriving today. I trust your trip was not too arduous."

Master Shelton said quietly, "No, my lord."

The man gave a courteous nod, his gaze shifting to me. He had the penetrating look of someone who sees far more than he ever lets on. "And this is . . .?"

"Brendan. Brendan Prescott. To serve you, Your Grace." On impulse I executed a bow that demonstrated hours of painstaking practice.

To my dismay, he let out a hearty laugh. "A youth of unforeseen talents. You must be Lord Robert's squire, newly brought from Warwick." His smile widened. "Your master may require such lofty address from you in private, but I am content with a mere 'Master Secretary Cecil' or 'my lord', if you do not mind."

I felt heat rush to my cheeks. "Yes, of course," I murmured. "Forgive me, my lord master secretary."

"The lad is tired, is all," Master Shelton said. "If you would inform her ladyship of our arrival, we'll not trouble you further."

Master Secretary Cecil arched a brow. "I'm afraid her ladyship is not here at the moment. She and her daughters moved to Durham Manor on the Strand, in order to free up room for the nobles and their retinues. As you see, his lordship has a full house this evening."

Master Shelton stiffened. My gaze darted from him to Master Secretary Cecil's unrevealing smile and back again. In that moment I understood Master Shelton had not known, and had just been put in his place, so to speak. Equals, these men were not. It seemed I had an entirely new and unfamiliar level of hierarchy at court to master.

Cecil continued. "She did leave word she has need of your services and you are to proceed to Durham forthwith. I can provide you with an escort, if you like."

In the background, pages raced about with flambeaux, lighting iron sconces mounted on the walls. Dusk slipped over the courtyard, and Master Shelton's face. "I know the way," he muttered and he motioned to me. "Come, lad. Durham's not far."

I made a move to follow. Cecil reached out. The pressure of his fingers on my sleeve was unexpected, light but commanding. "The lad will lodge here with Lord Robert, also at her ladyship's command." He turned to me. "I will take you to his rooms."

I had not counted on being left on my own so soon, and I must confess it made me feel like a lost child. I searched Master Shelton's face, hoping he'd insist I go with him to report in person to Lady Dudley. He only said, "You've your duty to attend to. Go. I'll look in on you soon as I'm able." Without giving Cecil another glance, he strode off, leading his bay back to the gate. Taking Cinnabar by the reins, I started after Cecil.

As I passed under an archway, I looked over my shoulder.

Master Shelton was gone.

I barely had time to gawk at the immensity of the hammer-beamed stables, populated by a multitude of steeds and hounds. Entrusting Cinnabar to a young dark-haired groom with an avid palm for a coin, I shouldered my saddlebag and hastened after Master Secretary Cecil, who led me across another inner courtyard, through a side door, and up a staircase into a series of interconnecting rooms hung with enormous tapestries.

Turkish and Venetian carpets muffled our footsteps. The air was redolent of wax and musk, sweat, and musty fabric. Candles dripped in candelabra. The strains of a disembodied lute wavered from some unseen place as courtiers drifted past us, the glitter of jewels on claret satins catching the light.

None so much as glanced at me, but I could not have been less at ease than if they had stopped to ask my name. I wondered how I would ever succeed in finding my way about this maze, much less steer a clear route to my master's rooms.

"It is overwhelming at first," Cecil said, as if he could read my thoughts, "but you'll adjust to it in time. We all do."

"Am I that obvious?" I asked, eyeing him. He'd seemed prepossessing in the courtyard, but here in the gallery's length, dwarfed as we were by grandeur, I thought he more resembled one of the middle-class merchants who came to sell their wares at the Dudley Castle, men who had carved for themselves a comfortable niche, having learned not to take life's vicissitudes to heart.

"You have a certain look," Cecil said. "I find it refreshing." He chuckled. "It won't last long. The novelty fades all too quickly. Before you know it, you'll be complaining about how cramped everything is, and how you'd give anything for some fresh air."

A cluster of laughing women in dazzling headdresses glided toward us, aromatic pomanders clanking from cinched waists. I gaped. I had never seen such artifice before, and, when one of them glanced at me with seductive eyes, I returned her invitation, so entranced by her exquisite pallor I completely forgot myself. She smiled, wickedly, and turned away as if I had ceased to exist. I stared after her, crushed. At my side, I heard Cecil laugh under his breath as we rounded the corner into another gallery, this one surprisingly empty of people.

Mustering my frayed nerve, I inquired, "How long have you lived here?"

I knew he might think me too forward, but I reasoned I couldn't be expected to learn anything if I did not ask. He was still a servant. Regardless of his rank over Master Shelton, Lady Dudley had given him orders.

Again, I received his curious half-smile. "I don't live here. I have my own house nearby. Rooms at court, such as they are, are reserved for those who can afford them. If you seek to ask me my business, I will tell you that I am master secretary to his lordship the Duke and the Council.

So, in a manner of speaking, we eat from the same hand."

Once again I found myself muttering, "Forgive me. I didn't mean to offend, my lord, I mean, Master Secretary."

"A simple 'Master Cecil' will suffice. There's ceremony enough here, without us adding to it." A mischievous gleam lit his pale blue eyes. "You needn't ask my forgiveness. It's not often a courtier has the privilege of conversing with someone untainted by pretense."

I kept quiet as we mounted a flight of steps. The corridor we entered was narrower than the galleries, devoid of tapestries and carpets, revealing functional plaster walls and plank flooring.

He came to a stop before one of several doors. "These are the apartments of the Duke's son. I'm not certain who is in at the moment, if anyone. They each have their duties. In any event, I must leave you here." He sighed. "A secretary's work never ends, I fear."

"Thank you, Master Cecil." I bowed with less effect due to the saddlebag in my hand. My misgivings notwithstanding, I was grateful to him for his kindness. It was apparent that he'd gone out of his way to make me feel less uncomfortable.

"You are welcome," he said, and he paused, regarding me in pensive silence. "Prescott," he mused. "Your surname has Latin roots. Has it been in your family long?"

The question caught me off guard. For a moment, I plunged into panic, unsure as to how, or if, I should answer. Would it be better to brazen an outright lie, or to take a chance on a possibly newfound friend?

I decided on the latter. Something about Cecil invited confidence, but even more compelling was the possibility that he already knew. He had, after all, been aware I'd been brought to court to serve Lord Robert. It stood to reason that Lady Dudley, or perhaps the Duke himself, had shared other, less palatable truths about me. It was not as if I was worthy of their discretion. And, if I spoke an outright falsehood to one who had their trust, it could ruin any chance I had of furthering myself.

I met his placid stare. "Prescott," I said, "is not my real name."

"Oh?" His brow lifted.

Another wave of anxiety engulfed me. There was still time. I could still offer an explanation that would not stray too far from reality. I had no idea why I didn't, why I felt the pressing, almost overpowering, need to speak the truth. I'd never willingly imparted the mystery of my birth to anyone. From the time I had discovered that what I lacked could make me the brunt of cruel taunts and even crueler suppositions, I decided that whenever asked I would admit only what was necessary. No need to offer details no one cared to hear, no need to invite any more speculation than was already there.

The quiet perceptiveness in his regard made me think he would understand, perhaps even sympathize. Dame Alice had sometimes looked at me like that, and she had not balked at telling me even the most difficult of truths. I trusted that quality in others.

I took a deep breath, and added, "I am a foundling. Dame Alice, the woman who raised me, gave me my name. In olden times, those called Prescott lived by the priest's cottage. That's where I was found. In the former priest's house near Dudley Castle."

"And the name Brendan?" he asked. "Was that her doing, as well?"

"Yes. She hailed from Ireland. She had a deep reverence for St. Brendan."

A moment ensued, laden with a silence that was no silence at all. The Irish were despised in England for their rebelliousness, but until now my name had never roused undue curiosity. As I waited for Cecil's response, I began to fear I'd made a mistake. Illegitimacy was a handicap an industrious man could turn to his favor. Lack of any lineage, on the other hand, was a liability few could afford. It usually sentenced one to a lifetime of anonymous servitude.

At length, Cecil said, "When you say 'found', I assume you mean you were abandoned?"

"Yes. I was a week old, at best." Despite my attempt to sound nonchalant, I could hear the strain in my voice. "Dame Alice had to hire a local woman to nurse me. As fate would have it, a woman in town had just lost her babe. Otherwise, I might not have survived."

As another uncomfortable silence descended, I heard myself rushing to fill it, as if I had lost control of my own tongue. "Dame Alice used to say the monks were lucky I wasn't dropped on their doorstep. I'd have eaten their larders dry, and what would they have had to weather the storm old Henry brewed for them?" I started to laugh, seconds before I realized I had brought up the subject of religion, not the safest subject at court. Dame Alice, I almost added, had also said my appetite was exceeded only by the size of my mouth.

Cecil remained silent. I was beginning to despair that I had done myself in with my indiscretion when he murmured, "How dreadful."

The sentiment's compunction failed to match the scrutiny of his eyes, which remained fixed on me as if he sought to engrave my face in memory. "This woman who raised you, this Dame Alice, might she have known who your parents were? Such matters are usually local in origin. An unwed girl got in the family way. It occurs all too frequently, I'm afraid."

"Dame Alice is dead," I said. My voice was flat. Despite my previous honesty, some hurts I would not willingly reveal. "She was beset by thieves while on the road from Stratford. If she knew anything about my parents, she took it with her to her grave."

Cecil lowered his eyes. "A pity. Every man, no matter how humble, should know from whence he came." He suddenly inclined to me. "You mustn't let that dissuade you. Even a foundling can rise high in our new England. Fortune often smiles on those least favored."

He stepped back. "It's been a rare pleasure, Squire Prescott. Please, do not hesitate to call upon me should you require anything. I'm easily found."

With that simple offer, which was anything but, he gave me another of his cryptic smiles, turned heel, and walked away.

CHAPTER THREE

I watched him disappear down the gallery before I steeled my nerve, sucked in a deep breath, and turned to the door before me.

I knocked. There was no reply. After another knock, I tried the latch.

The door opened.

Stepping in, I found that the apartments, as Cecil had called them, consisted of an undersized chamber dominated by a bed with a sagging tester. Scarred wainscoting adorned the lower half of the walls, the lone small window glazed with greenish glass. A lit candle stub floated in oil in a dish on the table. Across the floor were strewn matted rushes, soiled articles of clothing, and assorted utensils and dishes. The stench was nauseating.

I dropped my saddlebag on the threshold. Some things never changed. Rooms at court or not, the Dudley boys still lived like hogs in a sty.

I heard snores coming from the bed. I edged to it, my heels crunching on slivers of meat-bones embedded in the rushes. I avoided a pool of vomit by the bedside as I grabbed hold of the tester curtain and tugged it aside. The rungs rattled. I leapt back, half-expecting the entire howling clan to lunge at me, brandishing fists.

A lone figure lay on the bed, clad in wrinkled hose and shirt, his tangled hair the color of dirty wheat. He exuded the unmistakable stench of cheap beer: Guilford, the fair baby of the clan, all of fifteen years old and in a drunken stupor.

I pinched the hand dangling over the bedside. When all I roused was another guttural snore, I grabbed his shoulder and shook it.

He swung out his arms, rearing a sheet-lined face. "Pox on you," he slurred.

"Good eve to you as well, my lord Guilford," I replied. I took a prudent step back, just in case. Though he was the youngest of the five Dudley sons, against whom I'd won more battles than lost, I was not about to risk a thrashing my first hour at court.

He gaped at me, his saturated brain trying to match identity to face. When he did, Guilford scoffed. "Why, it's the bastard orphan. What are you—" He choked, doubled over to spew on the floor. He groaned, fell across the bed. "I hate her. I'll make her pay for this. I swear I will."

"Did she spike your ale?" I asked innocently.

Guilford glared and clambered out of bed. He had the Dudley height, and I knew that if he hadn't consumed his weight in alcohol he'd have pounced on me like a cub with a boil. Instinctively, I slid my hand to the sheathed dagger. Not that I could have ever used it. A commoner could be put to death for so much as verbally threatening a noble.

Still, the feel of its worn hilt was reassuring.

"Yes, she spiked my ale." Guilford swayed. "Just because she's kin to the King, she thinks to snub her nose at me. I'll show her who's master here. As soon as we're wed, I'll thrash her till she bleeds, the miserable—"

A voice lashed across the room. "Shut your miserable trap, Guilford."

Guilford blanched. I turned about.

Standing in the doorway was none other than my lord and master, Robert Dudley. In spite of my apprehension at our reunion after ten years, he was a sight to behold.

I should have envied him. Whilst mine was an unremarkable face, so commonplace it was as easily forgotten as rain, Robert was a superlative specimen of breeding at its best. Impressive in stature, broad of chest and muscular of shank like his father, with his mother's chiseled nose, thick black hair, and long-lashed, dusky eyes that had certainly made more than a few maidens melt. He had everything I did not, including years of service at court and, upon Edward's ascension, prestigious appointments leading up to a distinguished, if brief, campaign against the Scots, and the wedding and bedding, or vice versa, of a country damsel of means.

Yes, Lord Robert Dudley possessed everything a man like me could desire. And was everything a man like me should fear.

He kicked the door shut with his booted foot. "Look at you, drunk as a priest. You disgust me. You have piss for blood in your veins."

"I was"—Guilford had turned white as canvas—"only saying . . ."

"Don't." Robert spoke as if he hadn't seen me standing there. He swerved, his eyes narrowed. "I see the stable whelp made it here intact."

I bowed low. Our association, it seemed, was to take up where we'd left off, unless I could prove I had more to offer than a body he could pummel.

"I have, my lord," I said in my finest diction, "and I am honored to serve as your squire."

"Is that so?" He flashed a brilliant smile. "You can start by cleaning this mess. Then you can dress me for the banquet." He paused. "On second thought, just clean. Unless you learned how to tie a gentleman's points while mucking out horseshit." He let out a high laugh, finding, as ever, great pleasure in his own wit. "Never mind. I can dress myself. I've been doing it for years. Help Guilford, instead. Father expects us in the Hall within the hour."

I kept my expression neutral as I bowed again. "My lord."

Robert guffawed. "Such the gentleman you've become. With those fancy manners of yours, I'll wager you'll find a wench or two willing to overlook your lack of blood."

He turned back to his brother, stabbed a finger circled by a silver ring. "And you keep your mouth shut. She's but a wife, man. Bridle her, ride her, and put her to pasture as I did mine. And, for mercy's sake, do something about your breath." Robert gave me a tight smile. "I'll see you in the Hall, as well, Prescott. Bring him to the south entrance. We wouldn't want him to spew all over our guests."

With another callous laugh, he strode out. Guilford stuck out his tongue at the departing form, and to my disgust vomited.

It took every last bit of patience I had to accomplish my first assignment in the time allotted. As far as the room was concerned, I threw everything I couldn't fold or stuff into coffers under the bed. I then went in search of water, finding an urn at the end of the passage.

I ordered Guilford to strip. The water ran brown off his flaccid skin, the raw bites on his thighs and arms indicating he shared his clothing with a thriving colony of mites and fleas. He stood naked and shivering, cleaner than he'd probably been since he'd arrived at court.

Unearthing a relatively unstained chemise, hose, doublet, and damask sleeves from the clothing press I extended these to him. "Shall I help my lord dress?" I inquired. He scowled, ripping the clothes from my hands.

I left Guilford to wrestle with his garments. From my saddlebag I removed a fresh pair of hose, my new gray wool doublet, and good shoes.

As I held these, I had an unbidden memory of Dame Alice smoothing animal fat into the leather, "to make them shine like stars," she'd winked. She had brought me the shoes from one of her annual trips to the Stratford Fair. Two sizes too large at the time, to accommodate a still-growing boy, I'd proudly sloshed around in them, until one dark day, months after her death, I tried them on and found they finally fit. Before I'd left Warwick, I'd rubbed fat into the leather, as she would have. I'd taken it from the same jar, with the same wood spoon . . . .

My throat knotted. In Warwick, I could pretend she was still with me, a benevolent presence. The mornings spent in the kitchen that had been her domain, the fields where I'd ridden Cinnabar in the afternoon, the turret library where I'd read the Dudleys' forgotten books, it felt as if she were about to come upon me at any moment, remonstrating it was time I put away my studies and eat something before I wasted away to skin and bone.

Here, it seemed she was as far away as if I'd set sail for the New World. For the first time in my life, I had the post and means to gain a better future than the one to which my birth had condemned me, and I was skittish as a babe at a baptism.

Recalling this favorite saying of hers, I smiled. She had always believed I could do anything I set my mind to. If only out of respect for her memory, I had to do more than survive. I had to thrive. Who knew what the future held? Ludicrous as it might seem at this moment, it wasn't inconceivable that one day I might earn my freedom from servitude.

I slipped off my road-soiled hose, careful to keep my back to Guilford as I washed with the last of the water and dressed. When I turned about, I found Guilford entangled in his doublet, shirt askew, and hose about his knees.

With an obsequious nod, I went to assist him.

CHAPTER FOUR

Though Guilford had been at court for years, presumably engaged in more than the satiation of his own vices, he got us lost within a matter of seconds. I imagined being discovered centuries later, two skeletons with my hands locked about his throat, and took it upon myself to ask directions. With the aid of a gold coin secured from a grumbling Guilford, a page brought us to the Hall's south entrance, where four of the Duke's sons waited in their ostentatious finery. Only the eldest, Jack, was absent.

"Finally," declared Ambrose Dudley, the second eldest. "We'd begun to think Brendan had hog-tied you to the bed to get you dressed."

Guilford scowled. "Not bloody likely."

The brothers laughed. I noticed Robert's laughter didn't reach his eyes, which kept shifting to the Hall, as though in anticipation of something.

Henry Dudley, the shortest and least comely of the brothers, and therefore the meanest-tempered, clapped my shoulder as if we were the best of friends. I was pleased to discover that if mine was only a moderate stature, I still stood a head taller than he.

"How fare you, orphan?" he jibed. "You look as if you haven't grown an inch."

"Not where you can see," I replied, with a tight smile. Matters could be worse. I could be serving Henry Dudley, who as a boy had enjoyed drowning kittens in the Avon just to hear their piteous mewling.

Henry's lips curled. "Ho! Does the mongrel now fancy himself a purebred?"

My smile widened. "Not every dog needs a pedigree."

"No," spat Henry. "But even a dog can tell who its mother was. Can you?"

He eyed me, avid for a tussle. His attacks on me had always been edged with more than derision, but this wasn't anything I hadn't been subjected to before, or indeed contemplated in the loneliness of the night. I would not rise to the bait.

"Given the chance, I rather hope I could."

"No doubt," Guilford sneered. "I'd say the same if I were you. Thank God I'm not."

Robert glared at his brothers as they burst into laughter. "God's teeth, you sound like a gaggle of women. Who cares about him? If I were you, I'd be more concerned about what's going on around us. Just look at the Council, hovering about the royal dais like crows."

I followed his stare to where a group of somber men stood close together, the black of their outfits blending like paint. They were gathered before a dais draped in cloth of gold, upon which sat a throne embroidered with the Tudor rose. It now struck me that I could see the King himself tonight.

My gaze shifted to the Hall itself.

It was luminescent, the painted ceiling offset by a black and white-tile floor over which nobles moved as though on an immense chessboard. In the gallery, minstrels strummed a refrain, while lesser courtiers streamed through the open doors, some moving to trestle tables laden with victuals, subtleties, and decanters of wine, others assembling in knots of finery to whisper, stare, and preen.

If intrigue had a smell, Whitehall reeked of it.

I heard a footstep behind us. Turning about, I caught a fleeting look at the tall, lean figure in iron-colored satin, and then I bowed as low as I could.

John Dudley, Duke of Northumberland, said in a quiet voice, "Ah, I see you are all here. Good. Ambrose, Henry, see to the Council. They look in dire need of drink. Robert, I've just received word that there is need for someone of authority to see to an urgent matter at the Tower. Pray, go and attend to it."

Even with my head bowed I heard the stunned incredulity in my master's reply. "The Tower? But I was there this afternoon and all was in order. There must be a mistake. Begging your leave, my lord father, might I see to it later?"

"I'm afraid not," said the Duke. "As I said, the matter is urgent. We've imposed an early curfew tonight, and nothing can occur that might unsettle the populace."

I could almost feel the fury emanating from Robert. With a curt bow, he said tersely, "My lord," before he turned heel and strode off.

The Duke addressed his remaining son. "Guilford, find a chair by the hearth and stay there. When their Graces of Suffolk arrive, attend them as befits your rank."

Guilford skulked off. With a pensive sigh, the Duke turned his passionless black eyes to me. "Squire Prescott, rise. It's been some time since I last saw you. How was your trip?"

I had to crane my head to meet Northumberland's gaze.

I had been in his presence only a handful of times, his service at court having required lengthy absences from Warwick, but he was still an imposing figure. John Dudley had retained the lean build instilled by a lifetime of military discipline, his height complimented by his knee-length brocade surcoat and tailored doublet. The thick gold chain slung across his shoulders testified to his success. Few would have looked beyond it to the hint of insomnia under his deep-set eyes, or the careworn lines wiring his prim mouth in its cropped goatee.

Recalling what Master Shelton had said about the price of absolute power, I said carefully, "My trip was uneventful, my lord. I thank you for the opportunity to be of service."

"Is that so?" Northumberland looked to the Hall. "Well, it is not me you should thank. I did not bring you to court. That was my lady wife's doing, though I hardly think Robert deserves the luxury of a servant." He sighed, returned his gaze to me. "How old are you?"

"I believe twenty, my lord. Or, it's been twenty years since I came to live in your house."

"Indeed." He offered me a smile that barely touched his mouth. "The same age as Robert. Perhaps that can explain my wife's persistence. You are a man, and should be allowed to prove yourself in our service." He motioned. "Go. Attend to my son and do as he says. These are perilous times. Those who demonstrate their loyalty will not go unrewarded."

I bowed low again, about to slip away when I heard the Duke

murmur, "We won't forget those who betray us, either." He didn't look at me as he spoke. Turning away he stepped into the Hall, where a palpable hush greeted his entrance.

Unnerved by his words, I moved in the direction Robert had taken.

The court was a far more sinister place than I'd supposed. The more I considered it, the more I began to question the purpose for my summons. Unlike her husband the Duke, Lady Dudley had been part of my childhood, an aloof presence I'd avoided at any cost. She'd always treated me with disdain, when she deigned to notice me at all. Why would she want me, a nobody, at court, in midst of an exacting time for her family?

I was so distracted by my thoughts I scarcely paid heed to my surroundings. Halfway through a corridor, an arm shot out and grabbed me about the throat. I was hauled into a closed, fetid room. The fecal-spattered hole, and stomach-churning smell, demonstrated the room's function. As I staggered against a wall, I thrust out a hand to avoid fouling my clothes, reaching with my other hand to the dagger I'd stashed under my doublet.

"I could cut off your hand with my sword before you release that paltry blade."

I turned about. "Had I known my lord had such need of me, I'd have come sooner."

A shadow stepped forth. Lord Robert seemed overwhelmingly large in the confined space. "Never mind you that," he said. "What did my father say to you?"

I kept my voice calm. "He said I should attend you, and do as you bid."

He took another step forward. "And?"

"That's all he said."

Robert stepped so close to me, the smell of his expensive musk was overpowering. "You'd best be telling the truth. If you're not, you'd best pray I don't find out." He paused, regarding me intently. "He made no mention of the King?"

"No." I measured the silence. "Though I've heard His Majesty is ill," I added.

He snorted, "No doubt, rumors being what they are." He stepped away. I heard a flint being struck. Moments later, a taper flared in his hand. He set it on the floor. "I'll give you this much. You haven't learned to lie yet."

He looked at me over the wavering flame, misshapen shadows splashed across his face.

"What else have you heard, pray tell?"

I decided it would go easier for me if I feigned naiveté. Looking down to my feet, I demurred, "I try not to heed idle gossip, my lord."

He guffawed. "Aren't you the meek one? I'd forgotten how good you were at fading into the background, never seeing or hearing what didn't concern you. I understand now why Mother was set on bringing you here. You are truly someone who doesn't exist."

His sharp burst of laughter ended as abruptly as it had appeared "Yes," he mused, as if to himself, "the squire who doesn't exist. It's perfect."

I went very still. I did not like the look that overcame his face, a slow calculated malice.

"Yes, why not?" He rocked back on his heels. "Tell me, Squire, what would you say if I asked you to fulfill an errand for me tonight that could earn you your fortune?"

I did not take my gaze from him. The rank air in the room felt like a noose about my throat, cutting off my breath.

"What? Have you nothing to say?" Robert's smile showed a hint of teeth. "I find that strange. A clever weasel like you—I'm offering you the opportunity of a lifetime, a chance to earn your way out of service and be your own man. It is what you dream of, is it not? You don't want to be a servant forever, do you?"

I had to stop from immediately responding to the undeniable truth his words stirred in me.

"Did you know she's coming here, tonight?" he breathed, and it was then I understood of whom he spoke. The Princess Elizabeth.

"No, of course not," he went on, as I struggled to retain my impartial expression. "How would somebody like you know of such events? But I have my ears about court. I know she will appear here tonight, and at my lord father's behest, no less."

His face darkened. It was the first, but not the last, time I would witness that obsessive lust in his eyes, a lust for that which he in his conceit believed he was entitled to possess. When he next spoke, his voice was hot, furious, as if I had, in fact, faded to nothing, an invisible being before whom he need not measure his words.

"He promised that when the time came, I would not be neglected. He said none was more worthy than I. But now it seems he'd heap honors on Guilford, and set me to do his dirty work. By God, I've done everything he's asked, including marrying that insipid Amy Robsart, because he thought it best. What more can he want from me?"

I had never heard Robert, or any of his brothers express anything other than conformity with the wishes of their patriarch. True, he had sent his sons away while barely in their teens to serve in influential households and assist him in his rise to power. True, they had no will other than his. But they'd never known a day of hunger in their lives, and each would reap the appropriate titles and estates. I had no reason to pity any of them, but I could see Robert had long chaffed against the paternal tether that bound him.

What I did not comprehend was why.

"Enough!" Robert hit his fist into his palm. "It's high time I showed my mettle. And you, you skinless rat, you are going to help me. You will take my message to her." He thrust his face at me. "Unless you'd rather I sent you back to that pathetic excuse for a castle in Warwick?"

A rush of excitement ran through me. It was true. The Princess Elizabeth, daughter of Henry VIII and Anne Boleyn, was here, in London. I had witnessed her arrival with my own eyes. Now Robert wanted to send me to her. Master Shelton had said wherever Elizabeth Tudor went, trouble followed, and trouble this certainly seemed. I probably should have said I would prefer to return to Warwick, where life at least was predictable, but instead I replied, "Perhaps my lord can explain what is expected of me."

Robert smirked. "You're smarter than you look." He paused, glancing over his shoulder before he lowered his voice. "The first thing you need to know is that she's apt to surprise you when you least expect it. I've known her since she was a girl, and I tell you, she likes nothing more than to set everyone around her to wondering."

The guarded note in his voice surprised me. Given his comments regarding his wife, the fact that he could feel respect for a woman other than his mother made me all the more curious.

"Take her arrival, for example," he continued. "She steals into the city without prior word or warning, and only once she's at her manor does she send word requesting leave as to when she may visit her brother, as her sister, the Lady Mary, did a few months past."

Robert let out a staccato laugh. "From her manor, which is close enough to the river she can take to it at a moment's notice. Now, there's pure Tudor mischief if ever I saw it. God forbid she should put herself at our mercy, or that her harridan sister should outdo her. And she knows my lord father dares not refuse her, for, just as she planned, rumor of her arrival runs like wildfire through London. The rabble is her protection, for they love her well. She thinks to keep us on our toes, contrary minx that she is."

I felt sick. He spoke as if it were to be expected that a princess should sneak about and request leave to visit her own brother, as if it were the most natural thing in the world that she should fear the Dudleys. Affronted by his disregard, I blurted, "She is sister to His Majesty. Surely she has nothing to fear here."

The moment I spoke, I wanted to bite off my tongue. With a lunge, Robert grabbed me by my doublet collar, his fist twisting the fabric until he was choking off my breath.

"Statements like that," he said, "could get you into more trouble than you're worth. You will fare better if you keep quiet and do as you're told. Or do you think to outsmart me?"

I croaked an incoherent denial. His hand twisted tighter before he let me go. I crumpled to my knees, gasping for air. When I finally raised my eyes to him, his stare was dark.

"You will tell her she must not doubt me. I will arrange a time for us to meet. Then I will have what I was promised. Get up."

I rose to my feet. I had the overwhelming impression I should be doing everything possible to escape this errand, as it concerned affairs I should know nothing about.

Yet even as I hesitated, I was revisited by the image of the smiling girl astride her Arabian, and knew I could do nothing else. I was not enough of a fool to pretend I couldn't see Robert and his father were involved in something dangerous. I was also enough of an opportunist to recognize an advantage, laden with pitfalls as it might be.

I could feel a bruise starting under my collar. I drew in a steadying breath, my voice hoarse. "My lord, forgive me for my indiscretion, yet I can't help but wonder if she will heed me. It's not as if I'm anyone to her."

"You may not be. But I certainly am. I am her truest friend, whom she has never had cause to question. She knows I am not my father. I won't play her false."

He fished under his gauntlet, tossed something at me. I caught it in mid-air. "When you show her that, she'll understand. Do it in private. I don't want anyone at court knowing my business. Tell her I couldn't come, but I hope to send word soon, by the usual route."

He took a menacing step to me. "Answer only what she asks. She can smell duplicity. And don't let her out of your sight if she dismisses you. I want a full accounting of her actions, from the time she enters the palace until she leaves."

Unhooking a pouch from his belt, he dropped it by the taper, which was melting into the floor. "There's more where this came from if you succeed. If you fail, I'll find you, no matter what gutter you crawl into."

He unlatched the door. "The water gate is straight ahead. After you've done as I ask, feel free to enjoy yourself. Elizabeth always retires early. Once you've seen her gone, find yourself a wench. Drink. Eat till you puke. Only don't breathe a word to anyone, and be in my chamber by the stroke of nine tomorrow."

He stalked out.

I opened my palm to look in disbelief at what he had tossed at me. Then I grabbed the pouch and fled that room.

As I stood gulping air in the corridor, I untied the pouch with quivering fingers. It contained more gold than I had ever seen. One or two more like these, and I could bribe my way to freedom.

All I had to do in return was deliver Lord Robert's ring.

CHAPTER FIVE

Robert's directions proved as misleading as he was; and it was only after I had trekked down a bewildering series of corridors that I passed from the palace into sudden night.

Torches mounted on the walls converted Whitehall's bays into opaque eyes. A near-full moon rode in the sky, rimming the knot garden before me in a tarnished glow. Copses of willows and fragrant herb patches, edged by a waist-high yew hedge, led to moss-licked steps and a quay. Three guards swathed in wool stood there, a lit iron brazier beside them casting fiery reflections onto the river.

There was no one else in sight.

The soughing of water reached me. I might have enjoyed strolling awhile, enjoying the unexpected tranquility and the balm of the night, had I not the pressing dilemma of what to do next. I couldn't simply approach and state my desire to speak alone with the Princess. No guard worth his salt would be amenable to a stranger lacking proof of identity, save for the badge on my sleeve, which could be stolen, and a ring I couldn't show.

The opportunity would have to present itself. I tarried under the palace shadow, listening to water shred against stone. When I discerned a distinct, more rhythmic splash, I readied myself.

A canopied barge glided into view.

The guards formed rank. From the garden, a figure materialized. A jolt went through me when I recognized Master Cecil. Then, another man dressed entirely in black emerged to stand beside him. My nape prickled. How many others were nearby, lurking in the shadows?

The barge was secured. I moved closer to the quay, my creeping steps sounding impossibly loud in my ears as I tiptoed through pools of darkness and crouched low behind the ornamental hedge. I was almost at the river's edge. Oddly enough, I felt no trepidation, no fear of discovery, drawn as if by magic to the sight before me.

Three cloaked figures emerged from the barge and mounted the steps to the quay. She was at the forefront, leading a lean, silvery hound on a chain. As her tapered hand cast aside her hood, I caught a glimpse of fiery tresses subdued by silver filigree, framing a youthful, angular face.

Cecil and the stranger in black bowed low. I edged closer, taking advantage of the hedge's shadows. Cecil and the Princess were a pebble's throw away. The watered silence enhanced their voices. I heard Cecil's first, imbued with urgency.

"Your Grace, I beg you to reconsider. The court is not safe for you at this time."

"My sentiments precisely," interposed an officious voice. It came from the shorter of the Princess's two attendants, a stout matron who spoke with impudence. Behind her, the other attendant, who was slightly taller, remained silent, muffled in a cloak of tawny velvet.

"Just as I told Her Grace not an hour ago," said the matron, "but would she heed me? Of course not. She insists on putting her own neck on the block, to no purpose that I can see."

Elizabeth Tudor's voice was crisp. "Kat, pray, do not talk about me as if I were not here." She stared at the matron, who, to my surprise, stared right back. This trusted servant had apparently served her mistress long enough to not fear either reprimand or dismissal.

Elizabeth returned her attention to Cecil. "As I informed Mistress Astley, you fret too much. This court was never safe for me, yet I've weathered it well enough. I'm alive, am I not?"

Judging by the familiarity in her tone, she had more than a passing acquaintance with the Master Secretary, as well.

"Of course, Your Grace," replied Cecil. "I do not question your capacity for survival. But I do wish you'd consulted me before leaving Hatfield. By coming here as you have, you risk his lordship the Duke's displeasure."

"Do I, indeed?" she said, in wry mirth. "Well, unless I'm misinformed, contrary to popular belief, the Duke does not rule here. I don't see why he should be displeased. I'm as entitled as my sister to see my brother." She yanked at her cloak. "If there's nothing else, I must get to the Hall. Edward will be expecting me."

I had to scramble behind the hedge after them, dreading the thought that I might at any moment crunch down on a stray twig and thereby announce my presence. Fortunately, my soft leather soles made no discernible sound on the lawn.

I had eavesdropped on a conversation not meant for my ears, entrusted with a message that had begun to seem like a dangerous ruse. Robert might say he'd never play the Princess false, but Cecil believed the Duke would. I found it all the more unsettling that in my zeal to act the good servant I might cause more trouble than I knew.

"Your Grace," Cecil said as he hustled behind her, for despite her delicate appearance she had an athletic stride, "again, I implore you. You must understand the risk you run. Otherwise, you would not have refused his lordship's offer of rooms in the palace."

She stopped. "Not that I need explain myself," she said coldly, "but I 'refused,' as you say, to lodge in the palace because there are too many people at court, and my constitution is such that I cannot afford an illness."

She held up a hand, preempting his protest. "I won't be dissuaded. I have bided my time in Hatfield long enough. I mean to see my brother, tonight. No one, not even his lordship of Northumberland, will dare stop me."

Cecil's reluctant incline of head showed he recognized the futility of further argument. "At least allow Master Walsingham here to accompany you," he said. "He's well trained, and can accord you the proper protection should—"

"Absolutely not. I've no need for Master Walsingham's, or anyone else's, protection." She gave Cecil an indignant stare. "God's blood, am I not the King's sister?"

She didn't wait for an answer. She turned to continue to the palace, her dog in pace at her side. All of a sudden, it growled and paused, turning baleful eyes to the hedge. I froze, certain it had smelled me. She yanked at it. The dog did not budge, its growl becoming a menacing snarl.

I heard her say, "Who goes there?" and I knew I had no other choice.

34

To the hound's blood-curdling bark, I stood and shifted through an opening in the hedge. I knelt, removed my cap. The moonlight sliced across my face. She went utterly still. The dog snarled again. Cecil snapped his fingers. Then the guards were at me, swords scything in release. In a second, blades surrounded me. If I so much as yawned, I could impale myself.

The dog was straining at its chain, ready to pounce, snout drawn back and fangs bared. The Princess patted its sleek head. "Hush, Urian," she murmured. "Be still." The hound obeyed, amber eyes fixated on me.

Cecil said, "I know this youth, Your Grace."

One of her thin, red-gold brows arched. "You do?"

"Yes. He's harmless, I assure you."

She gave a dry chuckle. "I don't doubt it, seeing as he thought to hide from us in the yew, of all places. Who is he, pray tell?"

"Lord Robert Dudley's squire."

Despite my prostration, I glanced up in time to catch the quick look Cecil cast in my direction. I couldn't tell whether he was displeased or amused. Whichever the case, I had the impression he'd rather I didn't reveal our previous acquaintance.

The Princess motioned. The guards shifted back. I stayed on one knee.

There are moments that define our existence, moments that, if recognized, are pivotal turning points in our life. Like pearls on a chain, the accumulations of these moments will in time become the essence of our youth, and provide solace when our end draws near.

For me, meeting Elizabeth Tudor was one of those moments.

She wasn't beautiful. Her chin was too narrow for the oval of her face, her aquiline nose emphasizing a hollow curve of cheeks and proud brow. Her mouth was disproportionately wide and her lips thin, as if she savored secrets. And, she was too pale and slim, like a fey creature of indeterminate sex.

Then I met her stare. Her eyes were fathomless, over-wide pupils limning her gold irises, like twin suns in eclipse. I had seen eyes like hers before, years ago, when a traveling menagerie had entertained us in Warwick. Then, too, I had been captured by their dormant power.

Elizabeth had the eyes of a lion.

35

"Lord Robert's squire?" she said to Cecil. "How is it I've never seen him before?"

"I'm new to court, Your Grace," I answered. With guarded respect, I added, "Your dog is foreign, is he not?"

She shot me a terse look, for she'd not given me leave to speak. "Italian. You are familiar with breeds?"

I nodded. "I had occasion to learn during my time in the Dudley stables."

She tilted her head. "Hold out your hand."

I hesitated for a moment before warily extending my wrist. She loosened her grip on the chain. The hound thrust his muzzle at me. I almost recoiled as I felt his breath on my skin. He sniffed, a growl rumbling in his throat. Then, to my relief, he retreated.

"You must have a way with animals," Elizabeth said. "Urian rarely takes to strangers." She motioned me to my feet. "What is your name?"

"Brendan Prescott, Your Grace. To serve you, Your Grace."

"You're a bold fellow, Brendan Prescott. State your purpose."

I discovered I was trembling, and I recited in a voice that sounded far too rushed to my ears, "My lord asks that I convey his regret that he could not be here to receive Your Grace. He was called away on urgent business."

It was as far as I dared go. I had the uncanny certainty that if I elaborated further she would know I'd been primed. She was looking at me with an intensity that made me think of tales I'd heard of her late father. It was said Henry VIII had such a piercing stare, he could see through a man's skin to his veins and judge for himself how true the blood ran.

Then she arched her throat and released husky laughter. "Urgent business, you say? That much, I do not doubt. Lord Robert has a father to obey, does he not?"

I felt my smile emerge, lopsided. "He does, Your Grace."

"Yes, and I know better than most how demanding fathers can be." With the laughter still on her lips, she handed Urian's chain to Cecil and gestured with long delicate fingers. "Walk with me, Squire Prescott. You've given me cause for amusement tonight, and it's a quality I value greatly." She cast a pointed look at those behind her. "Considering how little of it I find around me these days."

36

Elation rushed from my head all the way to my feet.

That trouble followed her wherever she went was undoubtedly true.

In that moment, however, I couldn't have cared less.

I moved after her into the palace, taking care not to overtake her. This was just as well, for, at the first opportunity, the matron, Mistress Astley, shouldered her way past me to the Princess's side, muttering something inaudible. I heard Elizabeth say in reply, "No. I said I would walk with him, and walk I will. Alone."

Mistress Astley retorted, "I forbid it. It will incite talk."

"I hardly think a simple walk can incite anything, my Ash Cat," said Elizabeth dryly. "And you're far too short to forbid me anything anymore."

The matron glowered. Cecil said, "Mistress Astley, the lad will do her no harm."

Mistress Astley snorted. With a glare at me, she retreated.

I looked gratefully at Cecil. To my discomfiture, he avoided my gaze, slowing his pace to fall behind us, as if he were of no account. Equally discomfiting was the stranger in black named Walsingham, who moved with the stealth of a cat despite his stony features.

Appraising, mistrustful strangers surrounded me. The only person whose face I had not yet seen was the Princess's other attendant. I assumed she, too, disapproved of my uninvited presence, though the one time I glanced over at her I caught a glimpse of bold eyes looking back at me from within her hood, as if she were amused.

Elizabeth interrupted my thoughts. "I said walk with me, Squire, not dawdle at my heels."

I hastened to her side. When she next spoke, her words were rapid, hushed. "We've little time before we reach the Hall. I would know the true reason for Robin's absence."

"Robin, Your Grace?" I echoed, and I cringed at my ineptness.

"Do you serve another Lord Robert, per chance?" She gave a terse laugh. "Urgent business, indeed. I'd have thought nothing save imprisonment would have kept him this night."

"I . . ." My tongue felt like leather in my mouth. "I fear I cannot say, Your Grace."

"Meaning you don't know." She turned into a gallery. I quickened my step.

"Meaning he didn't tell me," I said. "But he did ask that I give you this."

I reached to my doublet. Her hand shot out, gripping my wrist. Though her fingers were cold, her touch seared like flame. "God's teeth, you are new to court. What is it? Tell me."

"A ring, Your Grace, silver with an onyx stone. My master took it off his own finger."

Color flared in her cheeks. For a second, her regal mask slipped, and I saw the covert flush of a maiden who cannot hide her pleasure. I was so flustered by the revelation that I plunged on, reckless to fulfill my orders. "He said Your Grace would understand, and that he will soon arrange a time for you to meet alone, so he can have what he was promised."

A dead silence followed my outburst. To my dismay, her entire person stiffened.

"Is that so?" She looked at me from a height I could not possibly hope to scale. "Then you may tell him, from me, that I understand perfectly. As usual, he thinks far too much of himself. And, far too little of me."

In that moment, I wanted nothing more than for the floor to open and swallow me whole. From ahead came muffled music and voices, signaling our proximity to the Hall.

"My lady," I ventured, before I lost whatever was left of my courage, "my lord was most insistent I give you proof of his constancy."

She came to a mortifying halt. "And I will not be compromised by your master or any other man," she hissed. Without taking her eyes from me she called out, "Ash Cat," and Mistress Astley hustled forth, shoving me aside so she could remove Elizabeth's cloak.

I had been dismissed. As I stepped back, Elizabeth's other attendant went forth to assist her mistress. I was startled by the revelation of her vivacious face, a knowing sparkle in her honey-colored eyes. I averted my gaze, stung by her delight in my humiliation.

It was then I noticed that Walsingham had slipped away. The guards stood at attention as Cecil bowed before the Princess. "Master Walsingham asked that I excuse him. By your gracious leave, I'll see

Urian to his kennel." He started to turn away.

"Cecil," she said, and he paused. "I must do this," she whispered. "You know I must."

He inclined his head. "I do. I pray Your Grace will come to no harm because of it." He turned and walked away, the hound at his side.

Elizabeth turned to the Hall. Her women flanked her, guards in the foreground. Her chin lifted as the music ceased. A herald warbled her arrival. She descended the steps in utter silence. I inched forward to the shadows by the doors, watching as the Duke came striding forth through the bowing ranks of courtiers, accompanied by the lords of the Council.

"My lord of Northumberland." Elizabeth held out her hand. From where I stood, I saw his lips linger on her skin, his eyes lifted to hers all the while, encompassing and cold.

"It is my pleasure to welcome Your Grace to court," he intoned.

"There's no need. I've been here before," she replied, and her voice lowered a notch. "Though I confess I'd begun to think you would deny me the pleasure indefinitely, my lord."

Something dark passed over the Duke's face. "I only waited for the opportune time. His Majesty will be overjoyed to see Your Grace again."

"As shall I to see him." She set her hand on his sleeve and let him bring her into the Hall. Amid the incandescent flames and sheen of mirrors, the colored satins, and extravagant jewels she stood out like a pillar of alabaster.

My gaze rose to the dais.

A chill crept up my spine. It was as if I were seeing everything for the first time, my senses attuned to a new world of treachery and deceit, populated by well-fed predators, who circled the Princess much as wolves circle a kill.

I fought back the urge to rush in and defend her. She had been breathing this venomous air from the hour of her birth. If anyone knew how to survive here, it was she. Instead of worrying for her, I'd do better to focus on my own troubles. I had yet to deliver the ring, and Robert had made it clear what to expect if I failed. I saw others like me in the Hall, liveried shadows behind their masters, carrying goblet and napkin. If only I could locate one of the Dudleys, I, too, might become invisible, until I found the opportunity to approach her again.

I searched the crowd. As I looked, Elizabeth drifted through the Hall, pausing to tap a shoulder here and offer a smile there. When she reached an enormous hearth situated close to the dais, she paused. Seated upon upholstered chairs were persons of import. All rose and dropped into obeisance at her approach.

As luck would have it, lurking at a sideboard not far from the noble company, was none other than Master Shelton.

CHAPTER SIX

I stepped into a surge of incoming courtiers. Swept aside like so much flotsam, I evaded an onslaught of servitors carrying platters, followed by a cluster of overblown ladies in mammoth gowns, who blocked my way.

Then I felt someone haul me by my sleeve.

"What are you doing here?" demanded Master Shelton. I smelled wine on his breath as he brought me to the sideboard. He also looked to be in a foul temper.

"Well?" he said, eyeing me. "Are you not going to answer? Where is your master?"

I decided the less I said, the better. "His lordship the Duke sent him on an errand."

"Then you should have gone with him," said Master Shelton. "You should never be far from your master's side. It's bad form."

Biting back an impulsive retort, I said, "I understand, but my lord asked that I wait for him here." I didn't look at Master Shelton as I spoke, distracted by a shift in the ebb and flow of the crowd, through which I caught sight of the Princess.

She was talking to a diminutive girl seated in one of the grand chairs by the white stone hearth. This girl wore simple garb that echoed Elizabeth's, as did her coppery hair and pale skin, only hers was freckled. Sprawled in a chair at her side, his complexion flushed from too much wine, was Guilford Dudley.

I glanced at Master Shelton. His face had set like mortar. Curiosity, as usual, got the better of me. Having experienced her considerable magnetism, I could understand how the Princess might rouse strong emotions in those she knew. But I could not possibly see why Master

Shelton, of all people, should feel such antipathy toward her.

"Who is that?" I asked, hoping to draw him into conversation.

He frowned. "You've a poor memory. That's Lord Guilford, of course. Any other Dudley family members you fail to recognize?"

"I mean the girl sitting next to Guilford."

He went silent for a moment. Then he said, "Jane Grey," and there was a pained timbre in his voice. "She is the eldest daughter of their graces the Duke and Duchess of Suffolk. Her maternal grandmother was the French queen, Mary, sister to Henry VIII." His jaw clenched. "Not that it makes any difference to you."

I wondered if this Jane Grey was Guilford's betrothed, who'd allegedly given him the sour ale. I was about to probe further when another figure caught my attention.

It was Elizabeth's other attendant.

She had discarded her cloak to reveal a shapely form in a gown that matched the umber in her hair, which tumbled, loose, to her waist. A striking girl, in vivid contrast to the painted creatures around her, a radiance to her cheeks, and those eyes the hue of bee nectar—eyes I recalled watching me with undeniable mirth.

She prowled the perimeter of the noble company with surreptitious ease. I thought the Princess must be aware of her, though both women acted as though they had never met. I stared.I may not have been at court long, but I knew insolence when I saw it. And it looked to me as if the girl was eavesdropping on her betters' conversation.

As if she could sense my scrutiny, she paused, looked at me. Her gaze met mine. I read defiance, arrogance, and a definite challenge.

I smiled. Besides the obvious attractions, she offered the perfect solution to my dilemma. She had seen me speak to Elizabeth, and try to convey my master's message. Like me, she must have noticed the Princess's covert interest in Robert's offer. Surely, she would be amenable to accepting the ring in her mistress's stead.

All of a sudden, I wanted the errand done with. I wanted to make my excuses to Master Shelton and go to bed. Whether or not I could retrace my steps to the Dudley chamber remained to be seen, but at least I could rest easy knowing I'd done as ordered. After a good night's sleep, I'd be in a better frame of mind to ascertain how best to navigate any future role I might have to play in Lord Robert's schemes.

As I continued to watch, the girl turned to a group of passing women, and in the blink of an eye, blended into their midst. Only when I focused on them as they sauntered past did I spy her among them, a sway to her step. She cast a teasing smile over her shoulder. It was a blatant invitation any man with blood in his veins would be a fool to pass up.

Master Shelton apparently agreed. With a chortle, he remarked, "Now, there's a comely wench. Why not see what she has to offer?" He gave me a rough pat on the back. "Go on," he urged. "Should Lord Robert come looking for you, I'll tell him I sent you away, the Hall being no place for a squire without his master."

I was momentarily flummoxed. I might have been mistaken, but I had the distinct impression he wanted to get rid of me, which suited me fine. Forcing a chuckle, I gave him the appropriate grin, squared my shoulders, and strolled off. When I looked back over my shoulder, I saw he had turned to the wine decanter behind him.

I trailed the girl at a distance, admiring her confident air and that lustrous hair rippling like a banner down her back. I wasn't inexperienced when it came to women, and I thought her far more enticing than any primped or powdered court lady. But I had so taken to her pursuit, I didn't pause to consider she might have another end in mind than facilitating our acquaintance.

She made an abrupt maneuver, and, like smoke, vanished into the crowd. I turned, searching, turned again and came to a stop.

I couldn't believe it. I'd never seen anyone disappear thus. It was as if she'd taken flight.

Only then did I take stock of my surroundings and realize with a belated curse that she had, in fact, brought me around the Hall to the other side. Now I stood closer than before to the royal dais, the company of nobles, and the Princess.

I sought to make myself small. Close up, they were an intimidating group: privileged and glossy, with the air of unassailable primacy that characterized the nobility. Elizabeth had left Jane Grey and sat, bemused, listening to the person opposite her. All I could see of this person was a gross, ringed hand clutching a cane.

I began to sidle backward, wary as a cat, praying the Princess would not catch sight of me. All I needed was for her to single me out, and cast

43

the remainder of my already doubtful future into ruin.

So intent was I on my retreat that I almost failed to see the person bearing down upon me. When I did, I froze in my tracks.

It was Lady Dudley, Duchess of Northumberland.

The sight of her was like cold water flung in my face. Lady Dudley, Lord Robert's mother. Could it get any worse? Of all the people I might have come across, why her? In her world, lackeys always knew their proper place. And mine was certainly not lurking in this Hall.

She was like marble, her austere beauty enhanced by an exquisite garnet velvet gown. As I stood there, paralyzed to my spot, I was plunged back to a day, years ago, when she'd come upon me smuggling a book out of the Dudley Castle library.

I'd turned thirteen, grief-stricken over the loss of Dame Alice. The book was one of French psalms, a favorite of Dame Alice's, bound in calfskin, with a dedication in French on its frontispiece.

A mon amie, de votre amie, Marie.

Lady Dudley had taken it from my hands, told me to remove myself at once to the stables. An hour later, Master Shelton had arrived with a whip. He delivered the strokes lightly, causing more humiliation than pain, but until Lady Dudley departed for court the following year, I never went near the library again. Even after she was gone, it took weeks before the lure of the books won me back, and I only went at night, returning each book to its shelf before dawn.

As for the volume of psalms, it was the one thing not my own that I had taken when I left Warwick. It was now wrapped in cloth and hidden in my saddlebag, an offense whose punishment I dared not imagine.

A burst of caustic laughter came from the chair opposite Elizabeth, jolting me to attention. Lady Dudley hadn't spotted me yet. Left with no other alternative, I started to inch my way to the group, sweat soaking under my doublet.

It was at that precise moment that I stumbled against Jane Grey's chair.

She shifted about, startled. In her gray-blue eyes, I glimpsed a haunting resignation. Then she tensed her thin shoulders. In a tremulous voice she said, "Who are you?"

I felt my entire existence come crashing down around me.

44

At her side Guilford exclaimed, "What, you again!" He sprang to his feet, an accusatory finger pointed at me. "Prescott, you intrude on your betters."

I had made a fine mess of things. I should never have come so close. I should never have followed that girl. Come to think of it, I should have just stayed put in Warwick.

"Prescott?" Jane Grey looked at in confusion. "You know him?"

"Yes, and he's supposed to be serving my brother Robert." Guilford snarled. "Prescott, you'd best have a reason for this."

I opened my mouth. No sound came out. Jane Grey was staring at me. In a jerking motion, I removed my cap and bowed. "My lady, please forgive me if I have disturbed you."

Glancing up through the tangle of hair falling across my eyes, I saw faint color blotch her cheeks. "You look familiar," she said, her voice halting, hesitant. "Have we met before?"

"I don't believe so, my lady," I said softly. "I would remember it."

"Well, you obviously haven't remembered your manners," snapped Guilford. "Go find something to serve us this instant, before I have you flogged."

As I feared, his belligerence alerted the others. Elizabeth rose from her chair and retreated to the hearth. Her disdain was secondary, however, to Lady Dudley's inexorable passage. My chest constricted. I had no excuse to offer, save that I searched for Robert, which sounded contrived even to me. As I bowed low, I feared it was the end of whatever illusions I had of furthering myself in the Dudley service.

"Is something amiss, my dear?" Lady Dudley asked Jane. I imagined her chill green-blue eyes passing over me in utter disregard. "I trust this manservant of ours isn't troubling you. He's obviously misinformed as to his proper place."

"Yes," said Guilford gleefully. "Mother, see to it he doesn't disturb us again."

I peeped up, saw Jane's gaze shift from Guilford to her soon-to-be mother-in-law, and back again. She gnawed her lip. I had the distinct impression she wanted nothing more than to disappear.

"He, he . . ."

"Yes?" prompted Lady Dudley. "Speak up, dear."

Jane crumpled. Darting an apologetic look in my direction she

45

muttered, "I thought I knew him. I was mistaken. Forgive me."

"There's nothing to forgive. Your eyes must be tired from all that reading you do. You really must try to study less. It can't be good for you. Now, please excuse me a moment."

I almost gasped aloud as I felt Lady Dudley's fingers like blades, digging into my sleeve. She steered me a short distance away. Without a slip of that rigid smile, she said, "Where, pray tell, is Robert?"

My mouth went dry as bone. "I thought Lord Robert might..."

It was useless. I could barely talk to her, much less lie. It had always been like this. I often wondered why she'd taken me in, when it was clear she couldn't abide me. I lowered my gaze, bracing for an ignominious end to my short-lived career at court. She'd not forgive my breach of etiquette. I'd be lucky if I spent the rest of my days scrubbing her kennels.

Before she could speak, a strident voice boomed, "Why the fuss over there?" And the ringed hand gripping the cane banged it twice, hard, on the floor. "I would know this instant!"

I recoiled. Lady Dudley went perfectly still. Then a peculiar smile tilted her lips. She motioned to me. "Well, then. It seems Her Grace of Suffolk would meet you."

CHAPTER SEVEN

With a knot in my throat, I followed her. As we neared, Elizabeth glanced at me from her stance at the hearth. There wasn't a hint of recognition in her cool amber gaze.

"Kneel," Lady Dudley hissed in my ear. "The Duchess of Suffolk is of royal blood, a niece of our late King Henry VIII. She will demand your respect."

I dropped to one knee. I caught a glimpse of a spaniel huddled on a massive lap, its red leather collar encrusted in diamonds. The dog yipped.

I slowly looked up. Ensconced on a mound of cushions, constrained by a gem-encrusted bodice and galleon-sail nectarine skirts, was a monster.

"Her Grace Frances Brandon, Duchess of Suffolk," lilted Lady Dudley. "Your Grace, may I present Squire Prescott? He's newly come to court to serve as a squire to my son."

"A squire?" The civility in the Duchess's high voice was brittle as piecrust. "I can't very well see him bowed over like that. On your feet, boy. Let us have a look at you."

I did as she bade. Metallic eyes bore at me. She must have been handsome once, before inactivity and overindulgence had taken their toll. The phantom of her once robust beauty could still be discerned in the tarnished auburn hair coiled under her enormous jeweled headdress, in the line of her aquiline nose, and translucence of her skin, which was taut and white, without blemish or wrinkle.

But it was her eyes that transfixed me—cruel, appraising, and appallingly shrewd eyes, which belied the indifference of her expression, tyrannical as only those born to privilege can be.

I couldn't hold her stare for long, dropped my discomfited gaze to her hem. Her left foot was twisted inward, grossly swollen and squashed into a ludicrously small, square-cut beribboned slipper.

Her mouth twitched. "I was an expert rider in my youth. Are you? A rider, that is?"

I struggled for my voice. My reply issued low, cautious. "I am, Your Grace. I was raised among horses."

"What he means is that he was raised at our manor at Warwick," interposed Lady Dudley, and I thought I heard a perverse note of challenge in her voice, almost like a taunting. "He came to us by accident twenty years ago. Our housekeeper at the time found him—"

A terse wave of the Duchess's ringed fingers cut her off. "I asked the boy." Her stare remained fixed on me. "Have you no family?"

I glanced at Lady Dudley, though I knew I would find no succor. Her lips parted, offering a glimmer of teeth. With a sudden drop of my stomach, I wondered if I was about to be cast off. It happened often enough. Masters transferred, bartered, or exchanged servants for favors, to pay off debts, or to simply dispose of those who had ceased to please. Was this why I had been brought to court? Had all my aspirations been mere fanciful notions?

"No, Your Grace," I said. I couldn't keep the quaver of fear from my voice.

"A pity." The impatience in the Duchess's tone indicated she'd heard enough. She said briskly to Lady Dudley, "Your charity is to be commended. I trust he'll prove worthy of it." Her hand flicked at me. "Leave us."

Overcome by relief, I bowed and started to back away, remembering that one should never turn one's back on a member of the royal family.

And then it happened.

As I retreated with my head lowered, praying I wasn't about to bump into another chair behind me, I heard Lady Dudley's bone-slicing whisper as she leaned close to the Duchess's ear, "Il porte la marque de la rose."

My entire being went cold. It was spoken in French, a language neither woman could have known I had studied these past years with the aid of Robert's own discarded grammar book. The Duchess sat as if

48

petrified. Then her ferocious gaze turned on me. What I saw in those slitted eyes curdled my blood.

He bears the mark of the rose.

I felt as if my belly were full of snakes. Lady Dudley stepped back from the chair, offered the Duchess a brief curtsey. The Duchess still did not move. Behind her, lurking at the fringe of the group, I caught a tawny flicker. I blinked, looked again. It was gone.

A heavy hand came down on my shoulder. I wheeled about.

There was no mistaking the fury on Master Shelton's scarred face. He escorted me to a side door, saying as we went, "I thought I'd seen you off with that wench. Instead, you are getting yourself mixed up in that which doesn't concern you. Is this to be my reward, after everything I've tried to do for you?"

His reprimand had no effect on me. My mind whirled like a mill, though I had the sense not to give voice to my tumult, following Master Shelton without a word, even when he practically threw me through the doorway into a corridor.

"Don't you dare move," he said. "I've some advice for you later."

He returned to the Hall. Catching my breath, I ran my tongue repeatedly over dry lips before I slowly, with almost painful trepidation, slid my hand to the top of my hose. Then, further down, to the inner jut of my hip, near where the points held my codpiece in place. Under the worsted fabric, I could feel it. It took all my strength not to strip away the concealing clothing, and reassure myself it wasn't what I thought, that it couldn't possibly be . . .

The rose. Dame Alice had called it that. She had said it was a sign I was blessed. But how did Lady Dudley know? How could she have discovered something so intimate, something so personal, which I had always thought belonged to a lonely boy, and a laughing, red-cheeked woman, his only friend in a hostile world? How had Lady Dudley found out? And why would she have wielded it like a weapon upon someone who could have no reason to know or care?

Anger flared in me, then. Dame Alice was dead. I couldn't stop mourning or missing her; but in that instant, God help me, I hated her for wrecking the purity of my memories, for having violated our trust by giving Lady Dudley a confidence I'd always kept close to my heart, believing it ours alone.

49

I shut my eyes, invoking strength. Removing my hand and pressing it to my pounding heart, I felt the ring tucked there, in my inner pocket. As if it were a lightening bolt, it jolted me with an unpleasant realization. The Duchess of Suffolk was my enemy. I didn't know why, but I knew it as surely as I could know anything in this menacing place. Whatever Robert planned, whatever Lady Dudley intended, somehow I had a part in it, the Duchess of Suffolk had a part in it, and so did the Princess Elizabeth.

Elizabeth. The thought of her shone in me like a beacon. I could be mistaken. Perhaps she, too, had something to fear here. I could help her. And she might also help me.

Which was why I had to reach her. *Now.*

I bolted forth. Moments later I was slipping back through the door and crouching into the crowd, in time to witness a blast of horns from the gallery and the Duke's march to the dais.

He paused there, raised a hand. The entire Hall went silent. As he began to speak in a resounding voice, I peered through the ranks of courtiers to the hearth, where Elizabeth stood, alone. The Duchess of Suffolk, I saw, had also risen, and was staring toward the door through which I had just come. A knife of fear stabbed through me. I shifted sideways, seeking the camouflage of those around me.

The Duke's speech carried into the Hall. "His Majesty wishes to extend his gratitude to all those who have expressed concern over his health. It is at his request that I make this announcement."

He scoured the courtiers with his stare. "His Majesty is a benevolent prince, but he has been displeased by the rumors that have come to his attention of late. Contrary to those who dare speculate, he is well on his way to recovery. Indeed, at his physicians' advice, he has retired to his Palace at Greenwich, where he can hasten his cure. As a sign of his improvement, he also wishes it be known he has given gracious consent to the marriage of my youngest son, Guilford Dudley, to his beloved cousin, Lady Jane Grey. Said union will be celebrated tomorrow night with festivities at Greenwich, where His Majesty himself will bless the couple. His Majesty commands we toast this joyous occasion."

A page hastened forth to hand the Duke a goblet. He brandished it in the air. "To His Majesty's health. May he long reign over us. God save King Edward VI!"

As if on cue, servitors entered, armed with platters of goblets. Courtiers rushed to snatch these, thrusting them upward. "To His Majesty!" they shouted in unison.

Northumberland gulped down his wine and abandoned the dais, proceeding from the Hall with the lords of the Council scuttling behind like leaves in his wake. From where I hid, I saw Lady Dudley follow, but at a distance, accompanied by the court's fervent applause and the glowering Duchess of Suffolk. The Duchess's daughter, Jane Grey, followed, her tiny hand lost in Guilford's as he strutted proudly, his father's chosen link to the Tudors' royal blood.

The silence that fell at their departure lasted only a few seconds. As the inevitable speculation broke out, and courtier turned to courtier like fishwives in a market, I glanced in sudden, painful understanding at the hearth. Ashen disbelief spread over Elizabeth's face. Her goblet dropped from her hand. Wine splashed across the floor, spattering her hem. Without warning, she stalked out the side door.

The next minutes passed like years as I stood, waiting to see if anyone would follow. The courtiers began to take their leave. No one seemed to pay mind to Elizabeth's exit.

I moved to the door when I spied the Princess's attendant sidling up to a stark figure I failed to recognize for a moment. When I did, my heart lurched. It was Cecil's associate, Walsingham. Even as I watched, he and the girl exchanged a few words and parted, he turning pointedly away while she hastened into the Hall.

Neither showed any intention of going to the Princess's aid.

Their indifference decided the matter for me. I went to the door, determined to intercept Elizabeth and offer my services to her. Before I could exit, Master Shelton blocked my way.

"I thought I told you to stay put. Or haven't you had enough trouble for one night?"

I met his blood-shot stare. He'd never given me cause to mistrust him. Yet he answered to Lady Dudley in everything he did, and in that moment I saw him as a reminder of the power the Dudleys held over me.

"Since you seem to know more about this so-called trouble than I do, maybe it's time you explained it." I was past minding my tone, incensed by the possibility that he had played me for a fool.

His voice turned ugly. "You ungrateful whelp. I don't need to explain anything to you. But I'll tell you this much: If you value your hide, you'll stay away from that one. She's poison. Poison to the core. Just like her mother. No good ever came of the Boleyn witch, and none will come of the daughter."

The words were like filth. It was a sign I knew I should heed, a warning I was about to make a decision I'd not be able to change later.

I didn't care. At that moment, I vowed to follow my own instincts, to not let him, or anyone else, influence my course. Extricating my arm from his grip I said quietly, "Be that as it may, I still have my master's bidding to fulfill."

"If you do this, I'll not be responsible for it. I'll not protect you from the consequences."

"Nor will I expect it of you." I inclined my head and walked around him. I did not look back, though I could feel him watching me. I had the uncanny impression that despite his coarse manner, he understood what I was about to do, that somehow, in some distant past, he had felt the same compulsion, and was trying to save me from it.

Then all thought of him left my mind as I hurried into the passageways in search of the Princess.

CHAPTER EIGHT

At first I despaired that I was too late, and that she had vanished into the labyrinth of halls and galleries and rooms. My heels struck hollow echoes on the floors as I dashed down one corridor, paused, and turned into another. I was following my instincts, avoiding the line of sputtering sconces spaced unevenly on the walls, braving the darker twists and turns with the blind hope that she would not take so easy a route.

I nearly sighed aloud when I came upon her, facing a low arched doorway that led into a courtyard, bunching handfuls of her gown as she waited in the shadows. She'd removed her filigree net, her hair coiled loose, like fire, over her taut shoulders. Her face was deathly white, bright anger in her cheeks. Hearing my approach before she saw me, she spun about. "Kate, you must get word to Cecil at once. We must—"

She stopped, stared. "By God, you are bold. Too bold, by far." She looked past me. Panic colored her voice. "Where are my women? Where are Mistress Astley and Mistress Carey?"

I bowed low. "I haven't seen Mistress Astley," I said, and I heard in my tone that calm inflectionless stance I'd learned to use when dealing with an unpredictable, potentially volatile horse. "If by Mistress Carey, Your Grace refers to your other lady, she didn't seem inclined to follow you. In fact, I saw her go in the opposite direction."

"She must have gone for Ash Cat, and to ready my barge." Elizabeth paused. Her eyes were unblinking, riveted on me as if she could truly divine my purpose under my skin. She abruptly gestured, moving with swift steps into the courtyard, where the shadows were thick.

Glancing back to the doorway, she said in a whisper, "Why are you following me?"

My hand went to my doublet. "I still have my master's orders to complete,"

"Is that so?" she replied. "Have I not endured enough from his kind already, without your adding to it?" In the open air, her indignation echoed a decibel higher than it should. She looked translucent, almost wraith-like. She had come to court to see her brother, and the King, no doubt at the Duke's command, had departed for Greenwich without a word. Now, here I stood, a nuisance, determined to win her favor for my master at any cost.

"Forgive me, Your Grace," I said softly. I took a step back. "It wasn't my intention to cause you more distress."

Robert and his ring be damned. I would concoct an excuse as to why I'd failed in my assignment. If I was dismissed or beaten, so be it. I was literate and able. With some luck, I wouldn't starve.

I started as the Princess spoke again. "It is my lord the Duke's intentions which concern me most at the moment."

I went still. Master Shelton's words spilled in my mind.

She's poison. Poison to the core.

I couldn't turn away. I understood in that moment I had reached a crossroads, one that could shape the rest of my life. Poisonous or benign, here was someone I dared not resist.

"I know nothing of his lordship the Duke's intent," I said. "If I did, I would be the first to tell you. But I have eyes and ears. I saw what happened tonight."

She tilted her head. "You've an able tongue, squire. Let me warn you, I've dealt with far abler in my time. Be careful where you tread."

I met her stare without flinching. "Your Grace, I only state what I see. I learned early in life to look beyond the obvious."

The faintest ghost of a smile passed over her lips. "Is that so? Well, so have I."

"Then we have something in common, if I may be so forward."

She arched a brow. "Forward seems to be something you excel in." She paused. "So, tell me, what did you see to send you scurrying after me as if I were a damsel in distress?"

I didn't disregard the warning in her words. This was treacherous ground, not some fable in which I might play the hero. This was the court, where the only thing that mattered was power. She knew it all too well. She had grown up among its quicksands. She had lived with it since she'd been old enough to learn the truth of her mother's fate.

I marveled at my own effrontery, that I should dare compare my circumstances to hers. But the truth was that whether or not we cared to admit it, we were both pawns in the Dudleys' game. That was why I couldn't walk away. There *was* no walking away. The fact that she stood here, alone, in need, roused an undeniable ardor and loyalty in me.

"I saw," I said, "that you did not anticipate being denied His Majesty's presence. You expected him to greet you tonight, as he surely would have, were he truly on the mend from his illness. Now you are afraid, because you fear the Duke has done him harm."

She was silent. Then she said, "You are perceptive. Eyes such as yours could take you far. But if you can see so much, then God spare me from those with even keener sight, for it's clear that travesty in the Hall was meant as a warning. It is John Dudley of Northumberland, not my brother, who now rules this realm."

I fought the urge to look over my shoulder, half-expecting to hear the Duke padding up to us, his flock of councilors at his heels.

"Did Robin know about this?" she asked. Before I could answer, she lifted her hand. "No, don't tell me. I've never had cause to mistrust him before. I won't start now."

I swallowed. It was on the tip of my tongue to tell her what I thought about her Robin, and, in the process, of what had occurred between Lady Dudley, her aunt the Duchess of Suffolk, and me. But all I had were suspicions, and something instinctual, almost primal, held me back. Some matters, I thought, can only be disclosed in their own time.

"Your Grace," I said at length, "I do not know if Lord Robert can be trusted or not. But if you so command it, I will try to find out."

Without warning, a burst of laughter broke from her lips, wild and uninhibited, and then it vanished as soon as it appeared. Her eyes were dark as garnets, fierce with pride and intelligence.

"I believe you would do exactly as you say. For better or worse, their corruption has not yet touched you." She smiled in sudden sadness. "What is it you want of me, my gallant squire? Don't tell me it is nothing, for I can see it all over you. I can feel it. I am no stranger to longing."

And as if I'd known the answer all along, never knowing when or if this moment would come, I said, "To serve you, Your Grace, wherever it may lead."

She clasped her hands, glanced down. Dry wine soiled her hem. "I hadn't expected to make a friend tonight," she said at length. She lifted her gaze to me. "Much as I appreciate the offer, I fear it would only complicate your standing with the Dudleys, which seems none too firm. I would, however, gladly accept an escort to my barge. My ladies must be waiting for me."

Resisting a profound sense of loss, as if I had been refused something so sweet I would mourn it the rest of my days, I bowed low. She reached out, touched my sleeve. "An escort," she said softly, "to see me safe. I'll lead the way."

Without another word she took me through the courtyard and back into a maze of silent galleries hung with tapestries, past casements shuttered by velvet drapes and embrasures that offered moon-drenched glimpses of patios and gardens. I wondered what she felt, being in this place built by her father for her mother, a monument to a passion that had consumed England and ended on the scaffold. There was nothing in her expression to betray she felt anything at all.

We emerged where we had started, in the mist-threaded garden leading to the quay. Standing there in anxious vigil were her women. Mistress Astley bustled forth, the Princess's cloak in her hands. Elizabeth raised a hand, detaining the matron's advance. Her other attendant, the one she had called Mistress Carey, remained where she stood, enveloped once again in her tawny cape and hood.

I feared Elizabeth nursed a serpent in her midst. But before I could voice my opinion, she turned to me and said, "Look to your own safety now, for I fear the Duke brews a storm that could rend this realm apart. I'd not wish to be associated with the name Dudley then, not considering men have lost their heads for less."

She drew back. "Fare you well, squire. I don't think we'll have occasion to meet again."

She turned briskly and strode to her barge. Her cloak was thrown over her shoulders. Flanked by her women, she stepped down the steps. A few moments later, I heard the boatman's oars strike the water as the

56

craft was plied into the rising tide, sweeping her away from Whitehall, away from the court.

Away from me.

In the wake of her departure, I allowed the pain to come. She had said no. She had said no because she cared for me. Much as it hurt, I prayed it was true. I prayed we would not meet again, that she'd leave London while she still could. This court, I thought, echoing Master Cecil's pronouncement only hours ago in this garden, was not safe. Not for her. Not for anyone.

I passed a hand over my doublet and felt the ring in my pocket. I sighed. I had failed in my first, and probably last, task for Robert Dudley. I should see to my own safety now.

I started back into the palace. After what seemed like hours of aimless wandering, I stumbled upon the stables, where the dogs greeted me with lazy barks, drowsy-eyed amid slumbering horses in their painted stalls. After checking on Cinnabar, whom I found well stabled, with plenty of oats, I located a clean pile of straw in a corner. Divesting myself of doublet and boots, I burrowed in, drawing the straw over me as if it were the finest linen.

It was warm and it was safe, and it smelled like home.

CHAPTER NINE

I awoke disorientated. For a moment I thought I was back in Warwick, and had once again fallen to sleep in the stables while pouring over a tome. I drowsily patted the straw at my side, as if to assure myself I hadn't misplaced the book, before, with a start, the events of the past day and night came flooding back to me.

It was not the most auspicious way to start my career at court, I thought, as I righted myself on my elbows and reached for my boots. I paused.

Crouched at the edge of the hay pile, wrist-deep in my doublet, was a young groom.

I smiled. "If you're looking for this"—I held up the pouch—"you'll be disappointed. I never go to sleep without it. A habit of mine, to dissuade would-be thieves."

The youth started to his feet, his mop of disheveled black curls and wide indignant eyes making him look like an impish seraph. I recognized him now. He was the same lad I'd entrusted Cinnabar to yesterday, the one with the eager palm.

Upon closer inspection I saw that, under his uniform flax and hide, he was spare as a blade, his cocksure attitude implying first-hand experience with penury. A lowly stable hand, perhaps an orphan, as well: London must teem with them, and where else could a parentless, penniless lad seek employment than in the machinery of the court?

I pulled on my boots. "Are you going to explain why you were about to steal from me, or shall I just summon your Master of Horse and be done with it?"

"I wasn't going to steal! I only wanted . . ." The boy's protest faded as he realized he'd not concocted a believable excuse.

I repressed a smile. "You were saying?"

He thrust out his chin. "You owe me money. You paid me to take care of your horse, didn't you? Well, if you want it fed and brushed this morning, you need to pay again. By the looks of it, you're not a noble. And only nobles have the right to board their animal for free."

"Indeed?" I opened up my pouch, taking great delight in the fact that I now had the ability to actually toss out a coin, never mind it might be the last trove I saw in some time.

The boy caught it. His curious green-flecked eyes narrowed as he examined it. "Is this a real gold angel?" he breathed, looking up at me.

"I think so." I retrieved my rumpled doublet. "I certainly hope so."

As I slid my arms into the sleeves, I watched the boy bite the coin, and, with a satisfied nod that would do a moneylender justice, pocket it. I had the suspicion I'd just paid for an entire month of boarding and feed, but suddenly it didn't matter. I knew how it felt to labor without reward. Besides, the kernel of an idea had awakened in me. I had been a boy like this not too long ago, canny as a street cur, and as careful to keep from getting trampled underfoot. Boys like us, we often saw and heard more than we realized.

"There's no need for your Master of Horse to know about this," I added. "Oh, my name is Brendan Prescott. And you are?"

"The name's Peregrine." He perched on a nearby barrel, removed two crabapples from his jerkin. He pitched one at me. "Like the bird."

"Just Peregrine?" I made a grimace. I was in fact famished, seeing as I hadn't eaten since yesterday morning, but still the apple was terribly sour.

"Isn't that enough?"

"Oh, yes. And simple to remember. How old are you, Peregrine?"

"Twelve. You?"

"I'm twenty." Or so I think, I almost added.

"Oh." The boy tossed the apple core into Cinnabar's stall. My roan snorted and began to munch. "You look younger. I thought you might be close to Edward's age."

"Edward." I paused, my heart quickening. "Do you mean, His Majesty King Edward?"

"Who else?" Peregrine frowned. "You're strange. You're not from here, are you?"

This time, I had to grin. Oh, he was an orphan all right. Only someone who'd spent the majority of their life fending for themselves possessed that keen an eye. I hadn't thought to encounter such unvarnished honesty in Whitehall.

"No, I'm not," I told him. "I hail from Warwickshire."

"Warwickshire? Never been there. Never been anywhere outside Temple Bar."

"Yes, well, Warwick's a lovely shire." I contained my impatience, brushing sprigs of straw from my hose. "Do you know His Majesty well?" I asked, off handily as I could.

He shrugged. "As well as you can know any prince. He used to come here a lot. He loves his animals, and he hated being stuck indoors all day. His lordship the Duke always had him studying or writing or meeting people he didn't care about, so sometimes he'd steal away to visit me. Or rather, visit his dogs and horses. I was just someone who cared for them."

I thought of Elizabeth, of the livid fear on her face as she heard the Duke's pronouncements in the Hall, and I had to restrain my overwhelming anxiety.

"And does he still come here, to the stables?" I looked at the boy, then, thinking that if he were exaggerating his association with the king, it would show.

He didn't look abashed or ill at ease at all. He shrugged again with the nonchalance of one who's learned not to pay too much mind to the comings and goings of his betters. "Not in a while. The Duke probably put an end to his visits. Edward— I mean, His Majesty— once told me his lordship had reprimanded him for befriending menials. Or maybe he's just too sick. He coughed up blood the last time I last saw him. From what I hear, no one at court has seen him in weeks. But at least he has his nurse to take care of him."

"Nurse?" I echoed. For no apparent reason, the hair on my nape prickled.

"Yes. She came here with a signed order from his lordship, to fetch one of Edward's spaniels. An old woman, with a bad limp. She smelled sweet, though, like some kind of herb."

Though I stood on firm ground, for a second the stable swayed around me, as if it were a galleon in a storm. "Herb?" I heard myself say, my voice echoing in my ears. "Which one?"

"How would I know?" Peregrine rolled his eyes. "I'm not a spit boy who turns the roast. Maybe she's an herbalist, or some such thing. I suppose when you're the king and you get sick, you get one of those along with all the other doctors and leeches."

I had to consciously remind myself to breathe, to not give in to the irrational urge to grab the lad by his jerkin. Everything that had transpired since I'd arrived had addled my wits. Plenty of women dabbled in herb-lore, and besides, he'd said she was old, with a limp. I was seeing shadows at every turn. Much good I'd be to anyone in this sorry state.

"Did this woman say who she was?" I managed to ask. Considering the circumstances, I could only hope my face didn't betray my profound chagrin at my own foolishness.

"No. She just took the dog and left."

I realized I should probably stop before I roused his suspicion, but I couldn't help myself. I had to probe further. "And you didn't question her?"

Peregrine stared at me. "Now, why would I do that? She knew the dog was Edward's. Why else would she have come? In case you haven't noticed, I'm nobody. I do as I am told. Ask too many questions around here, and you're asking for trouble. I don't want trouble."

"Of course." I forced out a smile, shook my ruminations aside. I would be wise to cultivate this scamp. Given the mystery surrounding the King, it couldn't hurt to have as many ears in as many places as I could.

Peregrine leapt off the barrel. "I have to get back to work. The Master of Nags is due at any moment, and he'll have my hide if I don't have these beasts fed. I also have to crate Her Grace's hound for transport to Greenwich. She's like Edward. She loves her animals. A pretty lady, and nice too, not like some people around here. She pays for my services."

I gaped at him. "Her Grace, the Princess Elizabeth? She was here?"

Peregrine laughed. "The Princess in the stables? You really had too much wine last night, didn't you? No, Brendan Prescott from Warwickshire, her friend Secretary Cecil paid me last night to see to Urian. Now, I have to go. Hope you find your way back to wherever you belong."

He started into the stable. I scrambled in the straw for my cap, calling out, "Wait!" Searching my pouch for the largest coin I could find, I threw it to Peregrine. "I'm afraid I did overindulge last night. I was lucky to make it here. I don't think I could find my way back by myself, and I have to be in my master's chamber soon. Might you show me the way?"

The boy grinned, fingers clamped on the coin. "Only to the gardens. I have work to do."

The sun struggled to break through a pall of cloud. Wind nipped at my face, sharp as teeth, shredding the flowerbeds and showering the air with petals. As Peregrine led me to a tree-lined pathway, he asked, "Is that the Duke's badge on your sleeve?"

"It is," I replied. "Why do you ask?"

He shrugged. "No reason." He pointed down the path to the monolithic bulk of the palace in the distance, rooftops and turrets and gateways a jumbled mass. "Through there and to your left. Once you reach the inner courtyard, you'll have to ask someone else for directions. I've never been inside."

I bowed. "Thank you. I hope we meet again, Peregrine."

His smile lit up his elfin face. In that instant he appeared very much his age, reminding me again with a pang of myself at that age, a precocious lonely boy striving for attention. "If you ever have need of a page," he offered, "or just someone to help you with the odd chore, I'm your man. I can do more than feed horses, you know."

"I'll keep it in mind," I said, and began walking down the path, wind-tossed leaves under my feet. I glanced back. Peregrine stood immobile. I started to wave when a gust snatched off my cap. Cursing, I scampered after it. Lunging to catch it before it blew under a bush, I glimpsed out of the corner of my eye two figures emerging from the trees on either side of the path, dirks in hand. I didn't hesitate. I spun about to bolt back the way I'd come.

The men pounced. Shouting, flailing with my arms, I succeeded in landing a kick in a groin before a fist crunched my jaw and sent me flying to the ground. As everything about me reeled, I heard a cold voice say, "That's enough. I don't want him bloodied."

The men eased back, one of them clutching his groin and letting loose an obscenity. Despite the pain in my head and jaw, I mustered a chuckle. "Too late," I said, to the unseen man who'd called off the attack. "I think I've broken a tooth."

"You'll recover." My cap was tossed at me. "Get up. Slowly."

He stepped into view, his cloak hanging from emaciated shoulders. It was Walsingham, looking even more austere in the dawn than he had under moonlight. He couldn't have been much older than me, judging by the timbre of his voice and unlined sallow skin. Yet he seemed an ancient, who'd never known a moment of spontaneity in his entire, abstemious life. At least I knew now what his training was. Walsingham, it seemed, was an expert henchman.

"You might have asked to speak with me," I said. "I am amenable."

He ignored my remark. "I suggest you not attempt to flee or otherwise resist. My men can yet break a tooth, or other things." He motioned. The ruffians flanked me. There was no way to extract my dagger from my boot.

One of the men grasped my arm. As I spun about to fend off another attack, the other man thrust a sackcloth hood over my head and bound my hands with rope. Thus, blinded and restrained, I was forced off the path, in a direction I assumed led away from the palace.

They took me at an unflagging pace through the hunting park and into winding streets, where the clatter of wheels vied with heels on stone. I smelled the Thames, rank with rot. I heard the cries of vendors, and then I was shoved through a door, protesting, for which I earned a clout.

Pushed through another door, I staggered into a room ripe with the scent of oranges. I'd eaten an orange once, years ago, and had never forgotten it. Oranges were imported from Spain. Those who could afford them had luxurious tastes, and the wherewithal to indulge them.

The rope about my wrists was undone. The door shut behind me. I ripped off the hood. A familiar figure rose from a desk set before a casement window that offered a sweeping view of a riverside garden. I stared, scarcely able to believe my eyes.

"You," I breathed aloud.

CHAPTER TEN

I'm afraid so," said Master Secretary Cecil. "You've been mishandled, and for that I must apologize. Walsingham thought it best if we gave you no choice."

I knew without asking that Walsingham now stood outside the door, preventing any attempt I might make to escape. I clamped down on an angry retort, watching Cecil move to an oak sideboard, upon which sat a platter of victuals, the basket of oranges, and a silver flagon. I was fairly certain this abduction had something to do with last night, which made my curiosity slightly stronger than my trepidation, but only slightly.

"Breakfast?" asked Cecil.

I rubbed my chaffed wrists. "No, thank you. I lost my appetite."

Cecil smiled. "You'll recover it soon enough. A young man like you, with no gristle on his bones, when I was your age, I ate at all hours. I gather by your tone, however, that you are displeased with me. May I ask, why?"

"Besides the fact you dragged me here by force?" I retorted, before I could stop myself. I clenched my jaw, hearing the involuntary flare of anger in my voice. This was not a man I should offend. He needed something from me, and if last night was any indication, he had the Princess's trust. That he also served the Duke only complicated an already complex situation. In the final say, a man can only have one master.

Which did Cecil serve?

He busied himself at the sideboard. "I'm not Her Grace's enemy," he said, "if that's what you're thinking. Indeed, I regret to say I may be her only true friend, with any influence that is. Please, sit." He motioned graciously to an upholstered chair before the desk, as if he were receiving a guest. I sat. Handing me the plate and goblet, which I deliberately left untouched, he returned to his desk, an assured presence in his black breeches and doublet. "I believe Her Grace is in considerable danger," he said without preamble. "But then, I think you already know that."

I disguised my mounting apprehension. I wouldn't be cajoled, graciously or otherwise, into admitting aloud my own thoughts about the Princess's situation.

Cecil reclined in his high-backed chair. "I must say, I find your reticence curious. You were listening in the garden last night, were you not?" He raised his hand. "There's no need to deny it. Eavesdropping is a time-honored rite of passage at court. Only, sometimes what we overhear can be misinterpreted. Especially when we fail to get the whole story."

A bead of sweat trickled between my shoulder blades. What an incompetent I was. What on earth had possessed me to creep so close? Of course Cecil had known I was there. I'd probably made enough noise going through the bushes to alert the entire palace guard. I had another, more unsettling thought. Had I overheard more than was good for me?

Cecil was looking at me. I had to say something. "I was sent there by my master." I sounded hoarse, my voice barely making it past the sudden lump in my throat. I could die today. This man clearly took the business of protecting the Princess seriously. He could have me killed and make my body disappear and no one would ever know. Squires who failed their masters must run away often enough; and just as often were never heard of or seen again.

"Oh, I do not doubt it," said Cecil. He sighed. "What else could you do? And I must admit, you did him honor, gaining Her Grace's confidence without rousing her suspicion, which is no easy feat. I hope Lord Robert paid you well. You certainly earned it."

It suddenly occurred to me that Cecil might wish to know about the message I carried. If so, then feigning ignorance might convince him I posed no threat. I'd best play the part for all it was worth, at least until he revealed his plan for me. For a plan he most certainly had.

"I'm afraid I don't understand," I said.

65

"No," said Cecil. "Why should you?" He had a stack of ledgers to his left, an inkwell rimmed in jewels to his left. "I, on the other hand, am in a position to know a great many things. And what I don't know, my intelligencers find out for me. You'd be astonished at what can be bought for the price of a meal." He met my stare. "Does my candor surprise you?"

Play the fool. Play it for all it was worth. "I'm wondering what any of this has to do with me."

Cecil chuckled. "I should think a clever boy like you would have figured it out. It's not every day you gain Elizabeth Tudor's notice. And I could use someone of your unique talents."

I absorbed this news in silence. Just when I thought matters couldn't get any worse. "What exactly are you saying to me?" No use acting the bewildered rube now.

"Put simply, I wish to hire you. It's a lucrative offer, I assure you. I require someone fresh, outwardly ingenuous, and somewhat forgettable, at least to the undiscerning eye; yet capable of engendering trust even in those as skeptical as the Princess. You did offer to help her last night? She told me so herself after she left you. If you agree to work for me, you will be helping her in more ways than you can imagine."

A tightening in my stomach forewarned me not to expose my burning interest. However I was to proceed, I'd best do it carefully. It could be a trick. It probably was a trick. How could it be anything else?

"Why me? I don't have any training as an . . . intelligencer."

"No. But what you don't know, you can learn. What you do have, however, is something that cannot be taught. Infallible instinct. I should know. I possess it myself. Believe me, it's more precious than you realize. On a more practical note, you serve Robert Dudley, and he obviously trusted you enough, or deemed you innocuous enough, to give you a private message for the Princess. I need to know what he wants from her. Her life may depend on it."

My mouth went dry. "Her life?"

"Yes. I have reason to think the Duke plots against her, and that his son Lord Robert, your master, plays a part of his scheme."

It was a trick, I thought with a sinking in my stomach. I was here because I served Lord Robert. Elizabeth had not revealed my purpose. That was why I'd been dragged here with a sack over my head. Cecil knew I had imparted a message from my master, and the moment I confessed it, I would be silenced.

Forever.

"I regret to hear that," I managed to say, resisting the urge to start shouting, as it would be better to go down fighting than wait for whatever end Cecil had prepared for me. "But as my lord secretary must know, a servant who betrays his master risks having his ears and tongue sliced off." I forced out an arid laugh. "And I'm fond of mine, thank you very much."

"You've already betrayed him," he replied. It was a statement, brisk and impersonal. Though nothing overt changed in his manner, he abruptly radiated cool menace. "Regardless of how you choose to act, your days as a Dudley servant are numbered. Or do you think they will keep you after they get what they want? Lord Robert used you as his errand boy, and his lord and ladyship despise loose ends."

He bears the mark of the rose.

I flashed on the Duchess of Suffolk, saw again those horrid eyes staring through me, into me, and realized that Cecil was right. Whatever Lady Dudley had meant when she whispered those words, it couldn't be good for me. If I stayed Robert's lackey, God knew if I would live long enough to reap the dubious benefits. The time had come to try my luck elsewhere.

"Are you saying they'll murder me once I've done whatever it is they want?" I asked.

"I am, though of course I have no concrete proof."

"And for that, I should leave their service for yours?"

"Not exactly." He steepled his hands at his bearded chin. "Are you interested?"

I met his regard. "You certainly have my attention."

He inclined his head. "Let me start by saying that the Duke and his family are in a precarious situation. They weren't prepared for Her Grace's visit. None of us were, in truth. Yet here she is, determined to see her brother, and so she must be dealt with. She took precautions by letting news of her presence leak out to the populace, which will provide her some safety for the time being. But she makes a grave mistake in assuming the Duke will do her no harm. She's so incensed by what she sees as his refusal to accommodate her that she insists on proceeding to

67

Greenwich and ascertaining His Majesty's recovery for herself."

Cecil smiled wryly. "She's not easily dissuaded once she sets her mind to something, and Northumberland has been thorough. Edward's absence last night roused her suspicion and her anger, as he hoped it would. She is a devoted sister. Too devoted, I fear. She will never leave court until she discovers the truth. Or until the truth finds her."

I was perched on the edge of my chair. "And you think the Duke would . . . ?"

I couldn't finish. I saw in my mind that inscrutable look in Northumberland's eyes and heard his strange murmur, which suddenly adopted a more sinister overtone.

We won't forget those who betray us.

"I wish I knew," said Cecil. "When Edward suffered a relapse, the Duke ordered him sequestered, all access to his person denied. If the Duke has such power over the King himself, imagine how susceptible Her Grace is. Moreover, I suspect His Majesty is far more ill than any of us know. Why else would the Duke have taken such pains to announce his recovery, even as he sent Lord Robert to oversee the munitions in the Tower and the manning of every gate in and out of London? Even if Her Grace could be persuaded to return to Hatfield, she would find her way barred. Not that she will. She believes the Duke holds her brother against his will. My concern is that she not be lured into the same trap."

It was the first time since Dame Alice's death that someone had spoken to me as an equal, and the trust it implied went a long way to soothing my doubts. I had to remind myself that duplicity at court was endemic. Not even Cecil could be immune.

"Have you told Her Grace of your concerns?" I asked, and as I spoke I recalled her stinging admonishments last night. Clearly, Elizabeth wasn't one to take caution to heart.

"I have." He sighed. "To no avail. She will see Edward, she says, if it's the last thing she does. That's why I need you. I must gather irrefutable proof that the Dudleys work against her."

My hands tightened in my lap. All of a sudden I didn't want to hear anymore. I didn't want to be forced across a threshold that, only last night, I would have willingly crossed. The danger he described was beyond anything I could contend.

To risk myself like this would be to court my own death.

But there was a part of me that could no longer be denied. A transformation was taking place. I was no longer an anonymous squire, determined to better my particular lot. It was inexplicable, absolutely terrifying, yet there was no escaping it.

"Her Grace means everything to me," Cecil went on, and I understood by the reverence in his voice that he, too, had felt the force of her. "But more importantly, she is everything to England. She is, in truth, our last hope. Edward became a king too young, and has been under the thrall of his so-called protectors ever since. Now, he could be dying. Should Her Grace fall into the Duke's hands, it will destroy what those of us who love England strive for—a strong and united nation, invincible against the depredations of France and Spain. The Duke knows this. He knows how valuable she is. And, if he is to survive, he must have her under his control. But what can he offer her that will guarantee her participation in whatever he plans?"

He paused, his light blue eyes focused on me as though I knew the answer.

I had to stop my hand from creeping to my doublet. The ring. Robert had given me his ring. He said he would have what he'd been promised.

My mouth went dry as bone. "It's not possible," I said, in a bare whisper. "Lord Robert already has a wife."

Cecil smiled. "My dear boy, one need only look to Henry VIII to see how easily wives can be replaced. Robert's union with Amy Robsart was a mistake he must have come to regret almost as much as his father. She's a country squire's daughter and the Duke now demands higher rewards for his sons. If he could persuade the Council to approve Guilford's union with Jane Grey, why not Robert's to Elizabeth? It would be the ultimate coup, not to mention the means he needs to continue his rule over England. For make no mistake, the Duke intends to rule. He has ever since he gained control of the King's person."

The ring in my pocket felt twice its weight. It was insane, and yet it fit with everything I could expect of the Dudleys. What had Robert said? *Give her this. She will understand.* Had she understood? Was that why she'd refused it? Because she knew what his ring offered? Or did she, in a secret place in her heart not even she dared plumb, desire it? I had seen the ardor in her face. She herself had told me she was no

69

stranger to longing. She had a depth of passion no one suspected. Maybe she wanted him.

I made myself pause, to breathe. Things were happening too quickly. There were too many twists and blind turns. I must concentrate on what I knew and what I'd heard.

"But Her Grace and the King— they have an elder half-sister," I said at length. "The Lady Mary, is she not the heir to the throne? If Her Grace were to wed Lord Robert, she still couldn't rule unless . . ."

My voice trailed off. In the silence, I heard a fly buzzing over the platter of neglected fruit on the sideboard. I could barely contemplate where my deductions had led me.

"See?" Cecil said softly. "You can learn, and quickly, I might add. Yes, Mary Tudor is next in line to the throne. But she is also a Catholic, and the people will never have Rome in England again. Her Grace, on the other hand, was born and raised in the Reformed Faith. She is also eighteen years younger than Mary, and can most certainly produce a male heir. The people would rather see her on the throne than her Papist sister. And that, my boy, is what the Duke can offer: England itself. It's a temptation few could resist."

I reached for my goblet, took a long draught. Religion. The bone of contention. People died for it. I'd seen their heads displayed by the Duke's command.

Was he capable of doing the same to a princess? I couldn't pretend to know the inner workings of a man I'd seen a half dozen times at most, whose values were far removed from my own. Nevertheless, something troubled me, an assumption it took me a few seconds to disentangle and put into words. Once I did, I stated it bluntly, with conviction.

"Her Grace would never condone it, not if it meant the murder of her own sister."

"No," Cecil agreed, to my relief. "She and Mary have never been close, but you are right. She would never let herself be embroiled in treason, at least not willingly. It is, I hope, the one fatal flaw in the Duke's plan. Northumberland underestimates her. He always has. She would have the throne, yes, but only when, and if, her time comes."

Treason. The Dudleys plotted treason, against the King, against his two sisters, against all those whom I had seen gathered to welcome her to London. And then I heard Elizabeth herself, as though her lips

70

were at my ear.

I would not wish to be associated with the name Dudley then, not considering men have lost their heads for less.

I knew why she had warned me. She had divined what the Duke intended, and she didn't want lives risked for her sake. She'd come to court fully aware of what she might incur. Whatever happened, she had resolved no one save her should pay for it.

In sudden decision, I took out the ring. "Lord Robert asked me to deliver this. She wouldn't accept it. I haven't told him yet."

Cecil exhaled a long breath. "Thank God." A smile that had no warmth in it curved his lips. "Your master, it seems, has overstepped himself. That could well explain in part why Her Grace has insisted on staying at court. Now that she knows his weakness, she will exploit it to reach her brother." He regarded me. "I wish you had more time to consider, but, as you can surmise, time is a commodity we lack. We may have only a few days remaining to save her."

I nodded, turned my gaze to the window. I saw a woman enter the garden, leading a child by the hand. She smiled as the boy pointed to something I couldn't see on the river, perhaps a passing boat or flock of swans. She leaned over, tucked a stray curl of hair under his cap.

A profound emptiness opened within me. I was reminded in that moment of Dame Alice, and, less tenderly, of Master Shelton. The steward would never forgive me for what he could only deem as a betrayal of the family that had, strictly speaking, saved me from certain death. But Dame Alice would have understood. Of all the lessons she had instilled in me, the one dearest to my heart was being true to one's self.

Foundling and probable bastard, a servant with nothing to my name, I couldn't deny that I craved anything less than the freedom to be the man I had always dreamed I could be.

I returned my gaze to Cecil. I felt no fear now, no doubt or hesitation. "What do you want from me?"

He smiled. "Perhaps the question should be, what do you want from me? I should think that at the least you'd expect to be paid."

I knew at once what I wanted. What I didn't know was whether I could trust him with it, even if the stark truth told me I couldn't trust anyone else. The question burned inside me, demanding an answer I wasn't sure I should ever voluntarily seek.

"Take your time," Cecil said. "For now, I can promise you freedom from drudgery for the rest of your days, as well as, should you be interested, a permanent post in my service." He reached for a ledger. A brief stillness ensued. Then he said with uncanny insight, "In my experience, men usually hunger for more than material appeasement. Do you? Hunger, that is?"

He looked up. I wondered if he could see my hesitation. I recalled again the words that had passed between Lady Dudley and the Duchess of Suffolk. There was truth there, tangled and twisted. But I wouldn't speak of it. I couldn't entrust everything I knew, everything I was, to this man. In the final say, he was still a stranger to me.

Cecil was silent. When he next spoke, his voice was low. "I make it my duty to study those who cross my path, for weaknesses as well as strengths. You are someone who carries a secret. You hide it well, but I can see it. And if I can, so will others. Take care to guard yourself, lest one day it is used against you when you least expect it."

I nodded, said nothing. I did not realize how prescient his warning would turn out to be.

"I should also tell you that my role in this matter must remain anonymous," he added. "Her Grace's safety must come first, above all else. It goes without saying you must also follow my orders without deviation or question. Do you understand? Any change you make could put you, and consequently our plan, in the gravest danger. You are not the only one working to save her. You will have to learn to trust even those you do not know."

I took in a deep breath. "I understand."

"Good. For now, you will attend Lord Robert. Remember everything he says. You will be advised of how to report your information, as well as any changes in our plans." From his stack of ledgers he took a folder. He opened it before me. "Herein is a scaled map of Greenwich. Memorize it. I'm not certain when, but I believe that at some time during the festivities for Guilford and Lady Jane, the Duke will make his move. Before he does, we must get the Princess away."

I leaned close, taking the map as Cecil delineated my assignment.

CHAPTER ELEVEN

I left the Thames-side manor in a daze. The sounds and sights of the awakening city assaulted me, reminding me I was indubitably late for my appointment with Robert. I quickened my pace. Cecil had assured me that the palace wasn't too far away. He had even offered an escort, which I politely refused. The less I saw of the dead-eyed Walsingham and his henchmen, the better.

The sun drew random fingers of light over the river. A strange, oppressive humidity hung in the air. The day promised to be hot, once the morning dissipated, and merchants and vendors were already about their daily business.

No one seemed to mark me as I passed, but I pulled my cap lower on my brow. I was all too aware of the badge on my sleeve, announcing my affiliation, and it required strength of will not to rip it off. I would have to learn to conceal my newfound revulsion for the Dudleys if I was to convince Robert of my devotion.

A spy. I was going to spy for Master Cecil, to help the Princess Elizabeth. It wasn't a role I would ever have envisioned for myself, even in my wildest moments. Only yesterday, I had been riding into London, a callow lad pondering how to best adapt to my new post. One day later, I was returning to my master with treachery in my heart. I found it difficult to sort out my feelings about my own duplicity, until I thought of the frightened young woman standing alone in a corridor in her wine-splattered gown.

What is it you want of me, my gallant squire?

It wasn't until I'd traversed several crowded, noisy blocks that I realized I was being followed. Once or twice, I caught glimpse of the shadow behind me, and had to resist the impulse to swivel about and confront it. I set my hand on my dagger, now at my hip. With a taut smile I continued on my way, avoiding the dense undergrowth and trees of the hunting park. Rounding into King's Street, which passed under a gateway through Whitehall, I paused, casually, to adjust my cap. When I felt the shadow draw near, I said, "Some fool is courting a knife in his belly."

A stricken pause followed. I finally glanced over my shoulder. "Why are you dodging me?" I asked, and flush-faced Peregrine replied, "You needed my protection."

"I see. So, you witnessed the attack, did you?" I hooked my hands in my belt. "You might have called for help. Or better yet, fetched some. I certainly paid you enough."

"I was going to at first," Peregrine said in a rush, "but I decided to follow you instead, in case they hit you over the head and threw you in the Thames. I used to fish corpses from the river for a living. You're lucky I did, too, because I wasn't alone."

"Oh?" I raised my eyes to scan the vicinity. "Someone fished corpses with you?"

"No, stupid." Peregrine sidled up to me, his voice lowering to an urgent whisper. "Someone else is following you. I saw him come out of the trees in the park after you were taken. He crept around the manor while you were inside, peeking in windows and—Ouch!" Peregrine yelped as I grabbed him by his jerkin and thrust him into a side alley.

He struggled. I clamped a hand to his mouth. "Be still, coxcomb. Whoever you saw back there could be watching at this very moment. Do you want us both to end up in the river?"

His eyes widened. Removing my hand, keeping vigil on the alley's entrance, I said, "Do you know who he is?"

The boy gave a nod, wormed out from inside his jerkin a pocket dirk. I had to grin. I'd had one just like it when I was a boy. "Does he know you?"

"No. I saw him in the stables a few days ago, but didn't attend him. He had two horses stalled. He's wearing a hood and cloak today, but I recognized him. When he left the stables, he kicked one of the mutts. It was just wagging its tail, hoping to be petted, and he kicked it." Peregrine grimaced. "I hate anyone who kicks a dog."

"Me, too," I told him. I took off my cap, wiped the cold sweat from my brow. This mystery man hadn't accosted us, though the alleyway, snaking as it did to a dead end littered with refuse, presented the ideal spot for an ambush. Either he wasn't willing to reveal himself or he wasn't ready to risk it. Neither offered me much consolation.

I opened my pouch to pour coins into Peregrine's palm. "Listen closely. I can't afford to play right now, much as I'd like to. I assume your work can be neglected, seeing as you followed me here, so can you find out where he goes without getting yourself into trouble?"

"I've been tiptoeing around him all morning," said Peregrine, nodding vigorously. "I'll find out everything you need to know. Trust me. I can be sly as a snake when I want to."

"Of that, I'm sure. Here's what we'll do." I explained quickly, then clapped a hand on the boy's shoulder and hauled him back to the street, where I threw him from my side.

"And don't let me see the likes of you again! Next time, I'll feed you to my dog, you thieving knave!"

Peregrine scampered off. Several passersby paused to wag their heads at this evidence of roguery in their midst. I searched my doublet in visible anger, slapped on my cap, and tramped onward, scowling like a man who has narrowly escaped having his hard-earned wages filched.

I was relieved to reach Whitehall unscathed. The main courtyard was full of servants and chamberlains, and I discreetly asked for directions to the Dudley chamber.

Despite my determination to help the Princess, and Cecil's explicit trust, I hadn't been convinced I could look Lord Robert in the face and not give myself away. It was one thing to despise him for using me to his own ends, quite another to know I had to put up an impenetrable front to keep him from achieving them.

Whoever had been following me had learned of my meeting with Cecil. I thought it safe to assume the man's intent was not benevolent. Not only was Elizabeth's future, and that of her sister, the Princess Mary, at stake, but my own life could hinge on my ability to complete this task. All I need do for the moment was convince Robert his cause was not lost, only delayed by feminine caprice. As for what came after, given recent events, it was best not to look too far ahead.

Taking a deep breath, I threw open the chamber door, my excuse ready on my lips.

I came to a disconcerted halt.

The room was empty. Only the stripped bed frame and scarred central table remained. On this table were my saddlebag and cloak.

"Finally," a voice said from behind me. I wheeled about.

Resplendent in scarlet brocade, his slashed breeches cut short to reveal his muscular thighs and enhance the protruding splendor of his curled and patterned codpiece, Lord Robert Dudley swaggered into the room.

I bowed as low as I could. "My lord, please pardon my tardiness. I got lost, and—"

"No, no." He waved his gloved hand. "Your first night at court, all that free claret and food, a serving wench or two, how could you resist?"

His grin was brazen, displaying strong teeth. Not a pleasant grin, certainly, but appealing all the same. Much as I hated to admit it, I could see how any woman, even a princess, might respond to him. The grin also indicated, to my relief, he wasn't inclined to see me grovel.

He arched a brow. "You missed the packing of my coffers, you sly devil, not to mention my good news."

"News?" I repeated. Come to think of it, he did look smug.

His dusky eyes glittered. "Why, yes. I've received word from my father that Her Grace has decided to remain with us to celebrate Guilford's nuptials." He winked suggestively. "It seems she can't resist me. And I owe it all to you." He laughed, slinging an arm about my shoulders. "Who would have known you had such a honeyed tongue? We should consider sending you abroad as an ambassador."

I forced a grin in return. "Indeed, my lord," I managed to quip. "Thus may you take heed of how to woo a lady."

"Bah!" He thumped my back. "You are a live one, I'll grant you, but you've a ways to go before you're fit to woo anything other than a tavern slut. I, on the other hand, will soon pay suit to a princess of the blood."

In his own inimitable way, Lord Robert simply assumed the Princess was going to Greenwich because of her interest in him. But now at least I had proof to take to Cecil. By Robert's own admission, he confirmed his intent. I could scarcely look at his face, thinking that under that enviable façade lay the soul of a villain.

"Does my lord think she'll . . .?" I let the insinuation linger.

"Oblige me?" Robert played with the fringes of his gauntlets. "How could she not? She may be a princess, but she's also Nan Boleyn's daughter. And Nan always had an eye for the gentlemen. But, like Nan, she'll make me wait. It's her way. She'll make me beg before I am deemed worthy. No matter. It'll give me all the more time to bait my snare."

I detested him in that instant, overcome by the urge to wipe that insufferable grin from his face. Instead, I took considerable pleasure in removing the ring from my doublet. I extended it. "I certainly hope so, my lord, because she wouldn't take this from me."

His self-indulgent expression froze. He stared at the ring in my palm. "Did she say why?" he asked in a flat voice.

"She said you thought too much of yourself. Or, too little of her." I realized I shouldn't be saying as much. I was supposed to encourage his delusions, not go about crushing them. But I couldn't help myself. Lord Robert Dudley deserved to be yanked down a notch or two.

To my belated regret, I saw I had succeeded. His jaw clenched. For a moment, I thought he would knock my hand aside, ring and all. Then he gave a terse guffaw. "Well, well. She refused my token. But, of course, she did. The royal virgin, always presuming on her chastity. It's her favorite role. We'll let her have her fun for now, eh?"

The icy mirth in his tone sent a shiver down my spine. Then he gestured magnanimously, all charm once more. "Keep the ring. I'll put a finer one on her finger yet."

Cuffing my shoulder, he sauntered to the door. "Gather up your things. We're going to Greenwich, but not by barge. Leave the river to weaklings and women. We'll ride our steeds over good English soil, like comrades and friends should."

He thought we were friends now, accomplices in his sordid game of deceit. I bowed, turning to the table to hide my revulsion. "My lord," I said in a low voice.

He chuckled. "I'll leave you to change, then. Don't take too long." He paused. "You always were particular when it came to undressing," he mused suddenly, and my heart leapt against my ribs. He shrugged. "It's not as if you've anything I haven't seen before."

With another short laugh, he strolled out, closing the door behind him. I waited until I was certain he wouldn't come barging in before I quickly, almost furtively, divested myself of my rumpled new doublet and good shoes.

I stood in chemise and hose. I had to look. Hooking my hand into my hose, I lowered it to my groin. The large maroon discoloration spilled across my left hip, its edges like wilted petals.

It had been there as long as I'd known my own body, and caused me no end of shame. Though not uncommon, such blemishes were dubbed 'demon bites' or 'Lucifer's paw-print' by the ignorant and superstitious. I'd learned early to conceal my skin from prying eyes, particularly those of the Dudley boys, who'd have tormented me all the more.

Dame Alice had said it was a rose left by an angel while I was in the womb. More practically, as I matured, it had been simple bedmates like Annabel who'd taught me that everyone wasn't as sensitive about it as I was, not giving the mark a second thought, but rather lavishing it, not to mention the rest of me, with caresses.

La marque de la rose, Lady Dudley had whispered.

I shuddered, pulled up my hose, and reached for my worn leather jerkin. Rolling up the doublets, I stuffed them into my saddlebag. I would discover the truth of my birth, no matter the cost. For now, being Robert Dudley's new friend was a fine start. A friend was trusted, relied upon, confided in; a friend was someone one turned to in times of need. And wherever Robert went, there his new friend would be, like a shadow.

I had no doubt that the shadow trailing me wouldn't be far behind.

Greenwich

CHAPTER TWELVE

Greenwich Palace materialized before me in a multitude of turrets and pointed blue slate rooftops, fronted by the southeastern swath of the Thames. From the high slope where Robert and I halted to rest our mounts, I thought it a more graceful sight than Whitehall's colossal sprawl, a secluded palace nestled amid woodlands, removed from the grit of London. It was difficult to conceive of any menace lurking there. Yet Cecil believed it was in Greenwich that the Duke had sequestered the King, and it was there that he would make his move against Elizabeth.

"She was born in Greenwich," Robert said, breaking into my thoughts. "September 7, 1533." He chuckled. "It was quite the occasion. King Henry had been striding about for months, crashing heads, and cutting not a few off, declaring to all who cared to listen that his beloved queen would bear him a son. But when Anne Boleyn took to her bed, all she brought mewling into the world was, as Henry himself put it, 'another worthless daughter'."

I glanced at him. "A beautiful place to be born, my lord. She must be fond of it."

"She is. She even had her own apartments as a babe, at Queen Anne's insistence. Anne wanted her daughter close, regardless of how Henry felt." Robert straightened in his saddle. "I wonder if she's arrived yet. It would be just like her to keep us waiting."

I hoped she did. The longer she delayed, the more time I'd have to appraise the situation. Cecil had said it was likely Edward was lodged in the palace itself, perhaps in the so-called Secret Lodgings, a series of guarded chambers connected to a long gallery, designed to afford the monarch privacy. The more I could discover about Edward's exact whereabouts, the more Cecil could learn about the Duke's plans. I also had to join up with Peregrine, and find out who was following me and why.

"Let us be off," cried Robert. "Last one there has to feed the horses."

With a spirited laugh, he set spurs to his bay. Cinnabar leapt at my gentle nudge, reveling in the opportunity to display his prowess. Habituated to long daily rides in Warwick, my roan was not used to too many hours in the stable. With the wind against my face, and Cinnabar's flanks propelling me forth, I surrendered to the moment, reminded of the days when I'd rode bareback in the fields as a boy, without a care in the world.

The palace sprang up before me, faced in red brick riddled with plaster grotesques, octagonal chimneys breathing roast smoke, and knot gardens a confection of herbs and perennials. Waving his hand imperiously, using his horse as a wedge, Robert steered us through a horde of courtiers amassed outside the main gatehouse. We rode past a ward into a cobblestone courtyard, around which were assembled edifices painted in the Tudor green and white.

Grooms led lathered horses into these stables, the noble owners in leather cloaks peeling off gauntlets as they stalked into the palace.

Robert leapt from the saddle. Unhooking his saddlebags, he raked a hand through his wind-tossed hair. "I won the wager," he declared. "See to the horses. I've a room off the inner court. Wait for me there. I have to report to my father." He strode away, leaving me with the horses panting warmly in either ear.

It was as simple as that. Fate had contrived to leave me to my own devices.

I turned and led the horses into the nearest stable. Harried grooms were running about accommodating a multitude of roans, geldings and palfreys, divesting them of saddles, brushing them down, and stabling them with armloads of fresh oats and hay.

None took notice of another servant among them. I recognized the Duke's own sleek Barbary in a far stall removed from the others, beside an exit gate with a view of a vast hunting park, and I led the horses to it.

Like his son, Northumberland had disdained going by river. I clicked my tongue at the Barbary as I stabled Robert's steed and Cinnabar. "Enjoy it," I told my horse. "There's no predicting where we might lodge next." Cinnabar nuzzled me.

A liveried groom approached. "Will you be requiring any feed?"

I nodded, started reaching into my jerkin for a coin. "Yes, please, and—" I stared. "Where in God's name did you get that green coat? Or should I say, steal it?"

Peregrine grinned. "I borrowed it. These Greenwich stable grooms are easily bribed. They'd strip naked for the mere glint of gold."

"Is that so?" I returned to the horses, lowering my voice. "Did you find him?"

Taking my cue, Peregrine busied himself spreading hay on the floor. "Yes. He's here."

I paused. "In the palace?"

"Yes. After I left you, I followed him to a tavern where he'd tethered his horse. He didn't even stop for a drink. He took to the road and got caught up in the servant transport from Whitehall, which gave me time to hop a cart. He rode beside us but stayed apart, as if he smelled better, though there were ale and songs aplenty. When he arrived, he went to the Queen's Apartments. The guards didn't check his papers at the gatehouse. He must have some clout."

"The Queen's Apartments?" I frowned. "But His Majesty isn't married."

Peregrine shook his head, as if I were hopeless. "That's just what they're called. Old Henry's wives used to reside there. Guess who's lodged there now? Jane Grey and her mother, the Duchess of Suffolk. I think our man is a Suffolk hireling."

I suppressed my disquiet. The Duchess had been the recipient of Lady Dudley's words concerning me, and had, apparently, set one of her men to trailing me. Why? What possible importance could I have to her? I couldn't begin to ponder the answer, but one thing, at least, was clear. She was probably learning at this moment about my enforced visit to Cecil's manor house.

"What does he look like?" I asked. "Big or small? Tall or short?"

"Taller than you," said Peregrine, "but not by much. He has a pointy face, like a ferret."

"A ferret." I gave him a wry smile. "I'll remember that. Excellent work, Peregrine. I'm sorry I can't repay you the coins you used to get that coat, but maybe later, eh?" I ruffled his hair, about to turn away when I heard Peregrine scoff.

"I don't want your money. I can earn extra coins whenever I like. There are plenty of lords and ladies willing to pay me for information. What I want is to work for you. I've had enough of the stables. I think you'd make a good master."

I was taken aback, though upon consideration I realized I should have seen it coming. The boy had clung to me like a clam since we'd met. Regardless of how I might view my circumstances, to him, I was worth clinging to—the personal attendant to the Duke's own son, in his debt for saving me from a potentially lethal stalker, with coins to throw his way. But, of course, this thought led me to another possible reason for his interest, one not nearly as innocent.

I smiled. "I'm flattered, but I can't afford you."

"Why not? I don't cost much, and you must be earning a decent wage. Secretary Cecil always pays his men well, and— Stop that!" He yanked away from my pinch to his ear.

I glanced about the stables. The grooms were still too busy to pay us any mind, and the stalls partially concealed us in any event. Still, someone could be nearby, listening.

I pulled Peregrine close. "I never said who was paying me," I informed him.

He recoiled, inched back. "You didn't? I must have thought . . ." He chewed his lower lip. I could practically see that agile mind conjuring lies out of thin air. "You were taken to his house." He stopped. He didn't sound convincing, and he knew it.

I regarded him without visible reaction. His stare shifted to the stall gate. In the second before he bolted, I registered panic on his face. Jerking forward, I snatched him by the collar. He was stronger than he looked, being little more than gristle and bone, but I got a firm grip to hold him dangling, like an errant pup.

"I think," I said, "it's time you told me who is paying you."

"No one," he squeaked. I tightened my grip, making an overt move for my dagger with my other hand. He sang out in a shrill treble, "I can't say. He threatened to kill me if I did."

I knew this much was the truth. I slackened my grip, letting a moment pass before I let him go. To his credit, Peregrine didn't make a run for it.

"I'm disappointed," I told him. "I thought you were my friend."

"I am your friend. I helped you, didn't I? I warned you that you were being followed, and I followed that Suffolk man here. No one paid me to do that."

"Oh? If memory serves, I believe I paid you. And rather well, I might add."

"I still risked my life." Peregrine puffed out his chest. "And for what? Maybe I was wrong. Maybe you'd not make such a good master, after all."

I gave him a cold smile. "It was Walsingham, wasn't it? He told you to show me to that path, so I could be overtaken. You didn't happen to see it. You knew about it beforehand."

Peregrine started to protest. He shuffled his feet in the straw and lowered his eyes, the portrait of abject misery.

"Then you came after me," I added, "and, according to you, happened to chance upon this Suffolk man. Does he exist? Or is Walsingham setting me up for further trickery?"

That got his attention. He reared his face up, furious. "Of course the man exists. And why would Walsingham want to trick you? You both work for Cecil."

"Perhaps, but then I never thought you'd trick me, either."

"I haven't!" Peregrine's voice resounded through the stables, causing the horses to stomp their hooves and the grooms to look up. Abashed, he dropped his voice. "I didn't trick you," he repeated. "I'm not Walsingham's lackey. He came and ordered me to see you to that path. He knew you were asleep in the hay pile. Don't ask me how. But I don't work for him, and he didn't pay me. He said either I did as he ordered or else. I figured you'd fallen into serious trouble when his men took you, so I decided to follow in case."

"In case, what? So you could fish out my corpse?"

"No." He glared. "In case you needed me. I liked you."

I heard a desperate ring of truth in his breathless avowal. Had I been in his place, I would have done much the same. I knew what it felt like to be scared and have everything to lose. Moreover, Walsingham wasn't one to broach no for an answer, particularly from some urchin

83

he'd just as soon kick as look at.

"You're lucky I believe you," I said at length. "But I can't hire you. I don't have a treasury to draw upon, and who's to say what'll happen the next time someone offers you a few ducats?"

"I'll work for free," he said, "to prove myself. I'm not afraid of anything. I'll go anywhere you want me to, find out anything you need to know. All you have to do is tell me."

I softened my tone. "I'm sorry but the answer is no. This task I'm entrusted with could be dangerous. I'll not put you at risk."

"I've been at risk for all of my life. I can take care of myself."

"I realize that. But I can't allow it."

"You need someone to help you. You can't possibly save the Princess without—" Choking on his own words, Peregrine leapt back from me into Cinnabar's rump.

I rounded on him. "How do you know about that? And don't dare lie to me this time, or I vow you'll rue the day we met."

"I overheard it," he whispered. "At Cecil's house. The window was open."

"And you were there all that time, listening?"

He nodded hastily. "Our man almost saw me. He crept right past the hedge where I was hiding. I could have reached out and grabbed his cloak."

I went still. "He also heard?"

"I don't know. I don't think so, or at least not all of it. He wasn't there long enough. When Lady Mildred, Cecil's wife, and their son came into the garden, they scared him off."

"Cecil's wife and son, were they? Well, aren't you the little snake, slithering about where you're least likely to be stepped on?"

Peregrine tittered nervously. "Yes, yes, I am. See? This little snake can be of use to you."

"Not so fast. What else do you know? Best tell me now. I hate surprises."

"Nothing. I swear on my mother's soul, may she rest in peace, whoever she was."

Whoever she was . . .

I averted my eyes. I should order him back to Whitehall, back to his life of anonymity and opportunism. It had to be safer than whatever awaited me here.

But I couldn't. I saw myself, the child I had been. I, too, had wanted more, had *had* more, at least more than Peregrine. He deserved the same chance. I just hoped neither of us would have reason to regret it.

"I'd expect you to earn your keep," I told him. "And to obey me in all things."

He sketched a clumsy bow. "Say no more, master. I'll do anything you require."

I couldn't contain my sudden laughter. "Don't call me master. My name will do."

Peregrine's smile was so fulsome it warmed my heart. It was certainly an odd way to go about making a friend, but a friend I had made, nevertheless.

CHAPTER THIRTEEN

It turned out Peregrine was well versed with the layout of Greenwich, having been there on several occasions and in various capacities, including as a kitchen scullion. He was able to answer most of my questions concerning the palace, including the fact that Greenwich, like most abodes beautified by the Tudors, had been built using the remnants of the old medieval edifice. I asked about the Secret Lodgings, and how we might access them.

"The Privy Gentlemen watch over those rooms," Peregrine explained as we entered an inner ward. "They're charged with guarding the gallery to the king's chamber and preventing anyone from intruding. Of course, they can be bribed, but it's risky. A Privy Gentleman who betrays the King's trust can lose his post, and his head, if His Majesty gets mad enough."

"Do you know any of Edward's Privy Gentlemen?"

"You do. Your master Lord Robert is one of them."

"I mean someone we can trust."

Peregrine considered. "There is Barnaby Fitzpatrick. He's the King's childhood friend. Sometimes he'd accompany Edward to the stables. He never said much, just stood and watched Edward like a bull. I don't know if he's here, though. I heard that most of Edward's attendants were banished when he fell ill. Something about exposing His Majesty to contagion, though he looked well enough to me until the Duke got hold of him."

"Peregrine, you're a veritable mine of information." I donned my cap. "If you ever do choose to betray me, I won't stand a chance."

He gave me a sour look. "Do you want me to look for Barnaby

or not? He might know a way to get to the King, if that's what you're after."

I glanced over my shoulder. As I did, I realized scouting the vicinity was becoming second nature to me, and I didn't like it. "Keep your voice down," I said. "Yes, that could be useful. Look for this Barnaby. I don't know where I'll be, but . . ."

"I'll find you. I've done it before; and Greenwich's not that big."

I nodded. "Good luck, then. Whatever you do, please try to stay out of trouble."

Clad in the camouflage of his stable clothes, having discarded the green coat, Peregrine dashed across the ward and up a covered staircase. With a whispered prayer for his safety, I went the opposite way, into the wing that housed the nobility. I had, for a reason I could not explain, decided to leave my saddlebag hidden in the straw near Cinnabar, where no one could steal it without getting their guts kicked in. I had removed only my dagger, which I had stashed in my boot, and I moved easily, without visible burden.

The corridors were quiet, with only a stray servant or two meandering about. I confronted a passage lined with identical doors, some shut, others ajar, all indistinguishable. I should have asked Robert exactly which room was his, I thought, as I started trying latches and peeking into the chambers. The rooms were similar in layout: a leather or faded cloth curtain separating a small but adequate front room from a much smaller bedchamber, some of which had primitive garderobes. As in Whitehall, the walls were uniformly whitewashed, the scrubbed wood floors unadorned. What few furnishings the rooms contained—a stool or bench, a table, a battered bed or pallet on rickety legs—were strictly utilitarian. Not luxurious by court standards, but at least they appeared free of louses, rodents, and the ubiquitous, moldering rushes.

It took a few tries before I located Robert's room at the far end, recognizable because of his saddlebags tossed beside a leather coffer brought from Whitehall. His mud-spattered riding cloak was flung across a chair, as if he'd discarded it in a hurry.

He was gone, presumably to report to his father. I debated what to do next. Perhaps I could take advantage of this spare time to search his saddlebags for clues.

I froze in my tracks. There were footsteps coming. I didn't stop to think. Bolting past the curtain into the bedchamber, my breath lodged in my chest as I crouched down and put my eye to a frayed moth-hole in the worn fabric.

I waited. Without a sound cloaked figure appeared in the doorway. For a paralyzing second I feared my shadow had found me. I forced myself to look, my relief overwhelming when I realized that despite the hooded cloak and scuffed boots, this person was shorter than me, and smaller in build. Unless Peregrine had made a mistake, it couldn't possibly be my mystery man.

The figure glanced about the room. Then it withdrew a folded parchment from within its cloak and set it on the table, shifting the pewter candlesticks so as to make it plain to whoever entered.

It didn't linger after that, leaving as quickly as it had appeared.

I counted to ten under my breath before I slipped forth. The parchment was fine, of an obvious costly grain. But it was the seal that captured my attention. That filigreed, embossed E encircled by vine tendrils could belong to no one else. I reached for the missive. I had to stop myself from tearing it open. There could be something in it I needed to know, something that would affect the course of my mission. Still, I couldn't open a letter from the Princess obviously intended for Robert. Not unless . . .

I scratched the edge of the wax seal with my fingernail. To my surprise, it was still tacky and easily lifted. With my heart hammering in my ears, I unfolded the parchment. Two brief lines were inscribed there in an aristocratic hand, followed by an unmistakable initial.

> *My lord, it seems there is a matter of some urgency we must discuss. If it suits your discretion, pray reply in kind by the established route, and we shall meet tonight, after the stroke of twelve, in the pavilion.*
> E

I stood, breathless. I almost failed to hear the staccato footsteps marching down the passage outside, until they were suddenly at the door, sending me diving once more into hiding.

This time, it was my master who strode in, dressed still in his riding gear, his features contorted. "Why must I always be the one he sends off to do his dirty work?" Robert yanked off his gauntlets and flung them aside.

Behind him, poised and immaculate, was his mother, Lady Dudley.

My throat tightened. She clicked the door shut. "I'll not countenance a tantrum. Your father may request your obedience, but I demand it."

"You have it! You've always had it. I even wed that Robsart wench because you and Father thought it best. Everything you've ever asked of me, I've done."

"No one said you haven't been an exemplary son," she replied.

"Oh?" Robert laughed harshly. "Excuse me if I beg to differ. In my experience, exemplary sons aren't sent off on fool's errands."

"It is not a fool's errand." There was something eerie about her inflectionless tone. "In fact, what we ask implies significant trust in your abilities."

Robert scoffed. "What ability? To ride off at a moment's notice to arrest an old maid, which any idiot with half an escort could do? It's not as if she'll put up a fight. I'll wager she has no more than a dozen retainers with her, if that."

"Indeed," said Lady Dudley. I was relieved to hear her voice revert to its familiar severity. "And yet that same old maid could be our undoing." Her eyes fixed on him. "Mary is demanding a full accounting of her brother the King's condition. Otherwise, she threatens to take matters into her own hands. I need not tell you this can only mean she's receiving information from someone at court."

"No doubt," was Robert's flippant reply.

"Yes, and the last thing we need is for her to flee the country to throw herself on her cousin the Emperor's mercy. Mary must be silenced before she does us more harm, and you're the only one we dare send. None of your brothers has your training. You've ridden in battle; you know how to command men to your will. The soldiers will not question your order when it comes time to take her."

I clenched my teeth. Mary, the Princess Mary. They were talking about the King's elder sister. I recalled what Cecil had said about her, about her staunch Catholicism and how she threatened the Duke. I leaned closer to the curtain, slipping the missive into my jerkin. It did not escape me that I was, at that moment, indulging in the very rite of passage of the court Cecil had mentioned. Eavesdropping, it seemed,

89

had its advantages.

"I understand all that," Robert was saying. As he pushed a hand through his tangled hair, he resembled an uncertain youth, caught between his own compulsive desires and the iron will of his parents. "I know how much we stand to lose. But Father and I had agreed that, for now, Mary posed no threat. She has no army, no nobles willing to support her cause, and no money. She might suspect much but she's in no position to do anything about it. Elizabeth, on the other hand, is here, in Greenwich, under our noses. She's a survivor above all else. I know she will recognize the advantages of our proposition. Once we have her agreement, there'll be time enough to hunt down her meddlesome Catholic sister."

I dared not move a muscle. Every nerve was on alert as I awaited Lady Dudley's response.

"My son," she said, and there was a subtle wavering in her tone, as if she sought to repress an emotion that threatened to overwhelm her. "Your father doesn't confide in me these days. But I know he faces tremendous odds. He has overseen this realm since Edward took the throne six years ago, and he hasn't gained in popularity because of it. Though I agree that your proposal is a wise one, we still must contend with the Suffolks and the Council."

"Once we have Elizabeth," interrupted Robert, "we won't need them. That's what I tried to tell Father, but he wouldn't listen. She is the key. She'll get us whatever we require."

"You're impatient," she rebuked. "Without the Council's approval, you cannot hope to have your marriage to Amy Robsart annulled. I need not remind you that, until you're free of her, you cannot hope for anything more than a friendship with Elizabeth Tudor."

Robert's face went bone white. "Father promised," he said in a fierce whisper. "He promised me neither the Suffolks nor the Council would stand in our way. He said the annulment wouldn't be an issue, that he'd force them to sign it at sword-point if need be."

"Circumstances change." Lady Dudley sighed. "Your father can't force further concessions at this time. There's too much at stake. Elizabeth should not have come. In doing so, she's put our feet to the flames. If she should take into her head to petition the Council to see her brother, or, God forbid, demand it of us in public. . ." She paused, the unspoken consequences of this calamitous possibility hovering between them.

Then she said, "Your father needs time, Robert. If he's decided it's best to not approach her yet, you must trust his judgment. He never does anything without a purpose."

As she spoke, I saw her eyes lift a fraction, past Robert to the curtain. My blood iced in my veins when I spied the coiled malice in her gaze, which was at odds with her words. It made me think of how she'd looked when she'd brought me before the Duchess of Suffolk. I knew in that instant she was lying, right through her teeth. She was misleading her own son.

"He hasn't forsaken you," she was saying, softly now, almost tenderly. "He simply thinks it wiser if we see to Mary first. After all, who can predict what she will do to damage our cause?"

I held my breath in the ensuing silence. Her deceit was like a knot in my belly. Why? Why would she want Robert away from Elizabeth? What could she possibly hope to gain from it?

Robert was staring at his mother as if he had never seen her before. It was clear he, too, sensed betrayal somewhere, but was at a loss as to how to decipher it. The hesitation cut like a blade between them before he gave a derisive chuckle.

"The only damage Mary can do is to make an ass of herself. Edward should have ordered her married off the moment he became king—to some Calvinist who'd beat some sense into that obstinate Papist head of hers."

"Be that as it may," countered Lady Dudley, "you must admit she poses a hindrance. She's free to roam the countryside and rouse sympathy. The rabble loves a lost cause. I, for one, would sleep easier knowing she's been dealt with. A day or two of hard riding, a few hours of unpleasantness, and it will be done. Then you can return to court and your Elizabeth. Surely, she won't spoil in the meantime."

I observed the play of conflicting emotions on Robert's face as his mother spoke, and wasn't surprised when at length he nodded, albeit in poor humor, and muttered, "Of course not. She's stubborn as a mule, that one, just like her sister. She'll stay put until all her questions are satisfied. I suppose that if I have to see Mary to prison first in order to get that idiot Council to heed reason, then I will. I'll bring her in chains to London if need be."

Lady Dudley inclined her head. "I am relieved to hear it. I will tell your father. He's deliberating with Lord Arundel. They'll want to send trustworthy men with you, naturally. Once the preparations are in order, you'll be informed. Why not rest till then? You look tired." The hand she set on his cheek should have invoked tenderness, but instead it made me feel ill.

"You are our most gifted child," she murmured. "Patience. Your time will come."

Then she turned and, with a swish of skirts, departed the room.

As soon as the door shut Robert grabbed one of the candlesticks and flung it against the wall. Plaster sprayed. In the ensuing silence, his panting was like that of a cornered beast.

Fighting back a sinking sensation in the pit of my stomach, I took a deep breath and emerged from behind the curtain.

Robert whirled about. "You!"

"Given the situation," I said, "I thought it best if I remained out of sight, my lord."

His eyes narrowed. "You were there? All this time?"

I dropped my gaze with what I hoped was appropriate contrition. "Forgive me, but I was so tired. All the free drink last night, the ride here . . . I fell asleep on my lord's bed. I implore your forgiveness. It won't happen again."

Robert's hunched shoulders slackened. He stared at me for a moment before he gave a tight laugh. "Asleep, were you? You'd best learn to hold your wine then, or drink less if you can't." He paused again.

I held my breath. It was a plausible excuse, but if he decided I posed a liability it could spell my doom. I could only pray he considered me little more than a dog who owed everything to the family who'd taken him in, who would never turn on the hand that fed him.

To my relief, Robert kicked the candlestick aside and stalked to the hearth. "To the Devil with my father. Just when I had matters well in hand. I'm beginning to think he wants to thwart me. First he sends me off to the Tower on some idiot's errand while he invites her to court, and now, once again, he has found a reason to delay his promise."

I made a sympathetic sound, trying to piece together what I'd learned.

First of all, the much-vaunted Dudley unity appeared to be cracking. Lady Dudley had said her husband no longer confided in her, though she'd always been his mainstay, the iron behind his steel. Whatever plans the Duke had in store for Elizabeth now excluded Robert, despite the repeated mention of a promise made to him. I could hazard a guess as to what this promise had entailed.

Moreover, Lady Dudley had mentioned the Suffolks as obstacles. Could it be they, as royal kin, were opposed to another royal union for a Dudley? That could explain why the Duke had elected to send Robert after Mary. Putting the heir to the throne in the Tower would prove a persuasive argument. Or was there a more sinister motive to the Duke's machinations?

I longed to delve further, particularly where the Suffolks were concerned. They had an important role here. The Duchess, in particular, was someone whose intentions I needed to know. Elizabeth's safety, and my own, could depend on it. But a servant who hadn't overheard anything shouldn't ask clarifying questions.

After careful consideration, I said, "My lord's initiative should be appreciated."

It was a tepid attempt, but like most people with a hurt to avenge, Robert seized upon it. "Yes, it should, shouldn't it? But my father apparently thinks otherwise. And my mother— God's teeth, I know well the only one she's ever cared about is Guilford. She'd see the rest of us dead in a minute if it came to his life or ours."

I let the moment pass. Then I said, "I've heard it said that a mother loves her children equally, regardless."

"Did yours," he retorted, "when she left you to die in that old cottage by our castle?"

The question was rhetorical and didn't require an answer. I stood silent as he went on. "She doesn't give a fig about me. Guilford's always been her favorite because he's the one she can control. She was the one who pushed to have him wed Jane Grey. Father said she even went up against Jane's mother when the Duchess refused to consider it, citing her daughter had the blood of kings in her veins, while we were upstarts with only the King's favor to commend us. Somehow, she got the Duchess to change her mind. Knowing my mother, she probably put a knife to her throat."

93

His words jolted me to my sinews. A knife at the Duchess's throat. Suddenly, I felt as I'd been snared in a dark and tangled web, one in which I had no defense.

Robert undid his doublet, threw it onto the bench. "Well, foul on her! Foul on all of them, I say. I've my own plans now, and I'm not about to give them up just because she says I must. Let her go after Mary herself if she thinks the Papist is such a threat. I'm not her lackey to be ordered about at will." He scoured the room. "Is there nothing to drink in this godforsaken hole?"

"I'll fetch wine, my lord." I went immediately to the door. I had no idea where to find it, but at least I could take some time to compose my reeling thoughts.

Robert stopped me. "Forget the wine. Help me undress. No use muddling my wits when what I need is rest. I'm going to find a way to see Elizabeth, whether my father approves or not. I'll see her and get her consent, and once I do, he'll have to agree. He can do nothing else."

I divested Robert of his breeches, chemise, and boots. From the saddlebag, I extracted a towel and dried the sweat from his torso.

"They'll have no idea of what hit them," he expounded, caught up in the fervor of his decision. "Guilford and my mother, especially. I can't wait to see the looks on their faces when I tell them the good news." He guffawed, spread his legs as I untied his points and peeled off his hose. "What? Have you nothing to say?"

Folding his undergarments and setting them on the coffer, I replied quietly, "I'm content to serve as my lord deems best."

"I certainly hope so, for if all goes as planned you will soon serve a king." He laughed. "Brash courage, Prescott, that's what it takes to survive this cesspit we call a court." He turned, naked, to the bedchamber. "Do as you like this afternoon. Just make sure you're back in time to dress me for tonight. And don't you dare get lost this time. I'll need to look my best."

"My lord." On sudden impulse, I reached to my jerkin. The die was cast. It would not do to have her messenger return to inquire why Lord Robert had failed to reply. "I found this on the table when I first came in," I explained, extending the paper. "Forgive me. In the ensuing excitement, I forgot I had it."

Robert snatched it. "Clever boy. It wouldn't have done for my mother to see this. It's a good thing you took a nap when you did." He ripped the letter open. Triumph flooded his face. "What did I tell you? She can't resist! She says she'll see me tonight, in the old pavilion, no less. She has a macabre sense of humor, our Bess. It's said her mother spent her last night of freedom in that pavilion, waiting in vain for Henry to come to her."

"Then, it is good news?" There was a vile taste in my mouth.

"Good news? It's the best bloody news I've had yet. Don't stand there like a simpleton. Fetch the ink and paper from my bag. I must send an answer before she changes her mind."

He scrawled his reply, sanding it and sealing the paper with wax. He thrust it at me. "Deliver this to her. She arrived hours ago, demanding her old apartments overlooking the garden. Take the corridor to the ward, cross to the stairs, and climb them to the gallery. You won't see her in person. She has a penchant for long afternoon rests. Her woman should be about, though, a juicy morsel named Carey who has her trust." He guffawed. "Whatever you do, don't give it to that dragon, Astley. She hates me as if I were Lucifer himself."

I slid the paper into my jerkin. "I'll do my best, my lord."

He gave me a cruel smile. "See that you do. For if all goes as planned, you could soon be squire to the next king of England."

CHAPTER FOURTEEN

As soon as I got out of the room and ran down the hallway, I turned a corner and stopped to examine the seal on Lord Robert's reply. I cursed. The wax was still wet. I'd destroy the paper if I tried to undo it. Thinking I could tarry until it dried sufficiently, I moved into the ward.

I reminded myself not to act precipitously, no matter how strong the urge. Anything I did could turn against me. Still, I couldn't deliver Robert's reply and simply wait for whatever occurred. The hunt had begun. If I was right in my assumptions, Elizabeth would become the first of the two royal sisters to end up in the Tower, especially when Robert learned she'd never consent to a plot that hinged on both her siblings' deaths. I wanted to march to Cecil, but I had no idea of how to reach the Secretary, nor had I thought to ask, which didn't say much for my fledgling skills as a spy.

I would have to warn Elizabeth myself, before it was too late.

I crossed the ward and entered a short passage leading to the stairs Robert had mentioned. I turned my attention back to the seal, about to worry it a bit when I caught a sudden movement out of the corner of my eye. For a second I couldn't move. Then I took my dagger from its sheath. I shifted around to a nearby doorway. The door was ajar. There was nothing there, although I could have sworn I had seen a figure moments before, watching.

My heart galloped. I inched forth, my dagger clenched in my fist. I drew short stifled breaths through my nose, but even these sounded too loud to my ears. Whoever waited for me could at this moment be drawing a more lethal weapon than the blade I brandished, readying to cleave my skull the moment I inched over the threshold. Or perhaps it wasn't my death he sought. He had stalked me through the streets of London and not taken me when he had the chance. He had come to Greenwich, presumably after me.

If it wasn't my death he wanted, I didn't care to consider the alternative.

A step from the door, I came to a halt. Cold sweat beaded my brow; as a drop slid down my temple, I found to my horror that I couldn't take that final step that would bring me inside.

Coward. Get in there. Face the bastard and be done with it.

I reached out to the door, every finger stretched taut, hoping to startle whoever lurked behind it. My fingertips grazed wood. With a simultaneous uplifting of my blade and savage push at the door, I leapt into the room, a half-cry on my lips.

A skeletal man stood there, dressed in black.

I stood rigid. "I could have killed you."

Walsingham returned my stare. "I doubt it. Shut that door. I'd rather we weren't seen."

I closed the door with a kick of my heel. "Why are you here?" I asked. He was the last person I'd expected to see. His presence made my flesh crawl.

The slight tilt to his lips might have been a smile. "I'm here for your report."

I bit back an inquiry after his absent henchmen. "What report?"

"For our mutual employer, of course. Unless you've returned your dubious loyalties to that pack of scheming traitors who raised you."

I returned his stare. "I don't answer to you," I said, my hands tightening at my sides.

"Oh?" he countered. "I believe you do. Master Cecil entrusted me with your welfare. Henceforth, you take your instructions from me." He paused, with marked intent. "Whatever you have to report, you will report to me."

In the starkness of the chamber he looked taller than I remembered, and so gaunt the light seemed to pierce his skin and skim the angles of his cadaverous face. His eyes were sunken, black and dull as cinders, the eyes of one who has seen and done things I could not imagine.

I forced myself to sheathe my dagger. I didn't trust him. He had an

97

air of immorality about him, a corruption he wore like a second skin. He was probably capable of doing anything to suit his purpose, without thinking about it twice. But he still had to answer to Cecil, and, in my current straits, I would oblige him. To a point.

With my other hand still clenched about Robert's note, I said, "I only just arrived."

"You've had plenty of time." His stare bored into me. "I do not relish the antics of callow boys, nor am I in favor of employing them. But I must accommodate, for now. Therefore, I'll ask you once more. Do you have something to report? Or shall I tell our employer he clearly expects more than you can deliver?"

I debated, prolonging the moment just enough to see his jaw edge. Then, with deliberate reluctance, I opened my hand and revealed the missive. "There is this."

He took it from me. He had peculiarly feminine hands, soft and white, and icy to the touch. He slid a long nail under the seal, and, with expert precision, unglued it from the paper. After reading the missive he re-folded it, pressed the damp seal back in place. "An ideal place for a rendezvous," he remarked, handing the paper to me. "Secluded, unfrequented, and close to the postern gate. Her Grace the Princess plays this game well."

The note of chill admiration in his otherwise passionless voice surprised me. "You approve? But I thought . . ." My voice trailed off into silence. I didn't know what I thought. I had been instructed to retain Robert's confidence, to listen and report, and facilitate, if instructed, the Princess's escape. I suddenly realized no one had hired me to think, and I felt exactly like what he had called me— a callow fool, my strings yanked by some master puppeteer.

Walsingham regarded me in cold boredom. "Did you think we had days in which to fine-tune our plan? Proof enough of how unsuitable you are. In matters such as these, success often depends on initiative. It is something an experienced intelligencer would understand."

"Look here," I said, and I heard an infuriating tremor in my voice. "I didn't ask to get involved in this. You forced me into it, remember? Neither you nor Cecil, I might add, gave me a choice. If I hadn't agreed to help, no doubt I'd be at the bottom of the river by now."

"We always have a choice," he said. "Anything else you care to remonstrate about?"

Again, I debated. I couldn't think of anyone I would less prefer to give my information to. But withholding it wouldn't help Elizabeth. She was what mattered now. The rest could wait.

"I overheard Lady Dudley and Lord Robert talking," I said. I kept my tone impersonal, not wanting to demonstrate any emotion, which he could interpret as another sign of my unworthiness. "His lordship wants to send Lord Robert to capture the Lady Mary. He has also refused Robert's request to see Her Grace and present what my master calls his 'proposal'. You should tell Cecil the Duke may have another purpose in mind for her."

I paused. Walsingham was expressionless.

My fists clenched at my sides as I continued, "It stands to reason it must be something he doesn't want his son to know about. Why else would he send Robert away?"

Walsingham still did not speak.

"Did you hear me?" Anger sparked in me. "Whatever the Duke plans, it cannot bring good to the Princess. You just said our success depends on initiative. Well, here's our chance. We should get Her Grace as far from here, and the Dudleys, as soon as we can."

Had I not known any better, I would have thought he couldn't have cared less. Then I detected a surreptitious gleam in his hooded eyes, a near indiscernible tightening of his mouth. What I had relayed was important. But he didn't want me to know it.

"I'll convey your concerns," he said at length, confirming my suspicion. "In the meanwhile, this note must be delivered, lest your master or Her Grace suspect our interference. After you do so, return to Lord Robert's side. If your services are required, you'll be advised."

I stared at him. "What about Her Grace? Aren't you going to warn her?"

"That is not something you need concern yourself with. You were told to follow orders."

To my disbelief, he started to turn to the door. I burst out, "If you don't warn her, I will."

He paused, turned back around slowly. "Are you threatening me? If you are, I should warn you that eager squires who inform on their masters are not irreplaceable."

The intimation was unmistakable. I met his eyes, held their gaze for a long moment before I slipped the note back into my jerkin. Then I heard a soft thud at my feet.

"For services rendered," he said. "I suggest you be prudent where you spend it. Servants eager to flaunt ill-gotten wealth often do end up at the bottom of the river."

Without another word, he strode out. I didn't want to touch the purse he'd flung on the floor, but I did anyway, pocketing it without examining its contents, and edging back into the passage.

I saw no sign of Walsingham. Turning into the passage, I made for the stairs.

If I had had any doubts before, now my mind was made up. I must warn the Princess myself. Robert couldn't be trusted for obvious reasons, and I was beginning to think that neither could anyone else. The purse in my hand might be small, but it contained enough to warrant my silence. Walsingham was Cecil's hireling, and truth be told, I had no idea what the Secretary's ultimate purpose might be. I suspected this matter was more complex than I'd been led to believe. Still, I found it difficult to believe Cecil would harm the Princess.

Perhaps it was Walsingham who played a false hand. I wouldn't put it past him. He hadn't seemed inclined to alert the Princess to the danger brewing around her, though she, of anyone, deserved to know. I also had no notion of how I might warn her. Maybe if I gave my name at her door and refused to budge, she would admit me. I'd leave her no other choice.

I climbed the staircase, my resolve like steel in my heart.

A gallery stretched before me, its airy width leading to a pair of imposing doors, the lintel boasting carved cherubim. To the right, recessed embrasures overlooked a garden. The panes were cracked open to admit the afternoon breeze.

Standing halfway between the far doors and me were three men in court velvets.

I didn't recognize them. Nor did I have much time to look, for as I started to take a step back a voice came at me from behind. "By the cross, where do you think you're going this time?" I swiveled about as a spry, curvaceous figure swept up to me and wagged her finger in my open-mouthed face. It was Elizabeth's attendant, the one I had first seen at Whitehall.

"Haven't I told you that the kitchens are not in this wing, you oaf?" she declared.

Up close, her curiously yellow-hued eyes were alive with an intelligence that belied her careless air. She exuded a heady scent, like crisp apples and gillyflowers. I didn't know whether to laugh or flee, until I noted the warning in her gaze as it met mine.

"My—my lady, forgive me?" I stammered. "I got lost, again."

"Lost?" She turned from me in a whirl of tawny skirts to the man who approached. "Horses may lose their way, but only mules are likely to return time and time again to the same empty stall. Don't you agree, Master Stokes?"

"I do." Master Stokes was of medium height, slim, his face too sly to be called handsome, his cheekbones accentuated by the light brown hair slicked back from his angular brow. On his hands were displayed various gemstone rings. From his left ear, dangled a glittering ruby pendant. It caught my attention. I had never seen a man wear an earring before, though I would later learn it was more a fashion abroad than in England.

"Speaking of which, is this servant bothering you?" His voice was languid with jaded menace. "Shall I teach him not to trouble pretty damsels, Mistress Carey?"

Stokes's insolent stare dropped to her cleavage as she flipped her hand, a trill of laughter reeling from her lips. "Bothering me? Oh, quite the contrary. He's just a poor servant, new to court, who seems to think we keep the kitchens under Her Grace's duvet!"

His corresponding laugh was equally high-pitched, almost effeminate. "If it will cure her headaches," he said. "As far as our mule is concerned—" His stare rose over her head to fix on me. "Perhaps I can see him on his way."

Mistress Carey sidled up to him. Though she kept her back to me, I could imagine the provocative look she treated him to. "Why waste your time on hired help? Let me see the boy back to the stairs, yes? I'll be but a moment."

"If you promise," said Stokes. For no discernible reason, the finger he briefly, sensuously, drew down her exposed throat filled me with dread.

He turned heel on his elegant boots and returned to where the other men stood grinning. Linking her arm in mine, Mistress Kate Carey drew me back into the passage.

The instant we were out of sight, she yanked me from the doors and into a recessed window bay. "What?" she said, all coquetry vanished, "do you think you are doing?"

Seeing as she'd foregone the pretense, I saw no reason why I shouldn't follow her example. "I hoped to see Her Grace. I bring important news she must hear at once."

She thrust out her hand. "Give me the missive, whoever you are."

"You know who I am." I paused. "Did I say I had a missive?"

I caught her off guard. She was an expert dissimulator, however, and before I knew what was happening, she'd stepped close, her apple-blossom scent taunting my senses. "I assumed," she said, "under the circumstances . . . You are, after all, Lord Robert's squire, are you not?"

"Ah, so you do remember." I, too, leaned close, so that our noses almost touched. "Not to mention that you must also be expecting a reply to the missive you just delivered."

She drew back as if I'd stung her. "I'm sure I don't understand."

"Oh? Then, that wasn't you in my master's chambers earlier? There is another lady at court who wears boots under her gown?"

She went still. I smiled to myself as I saw her withdraw her betraying foot under her hem. "You were there?" she said at length.

I nodded. "Behind the curtain. Now, if you don't mind, I'll find another way to deliver my lord's reply." I started to turn away. She gripped my arm again, with astonishing strength for so small a person.

"Are you mad?" she hissed. "You mustn't be seen anywhere near her. You are his servant. Their meeting is supposed to be a secret." She glanced to the gallery entrance before returning reproving eyes to me. "Give me his reply. I'll see that she reads it, have no fear."

I pretended to consider. Then I removed the paper from my jerkin. As she made a move to take it, I shifted my hand behind my back. "I must say, this is rather convenient, you being here at the precise moment I arrive."

Her fingers closed on air. Her chin lifted. "What, pray, is that supposed to mean?"

"Well, for one that I've seen you before. Last night at Whitehall. I was there."

"And?"

"And you didn't look too concerned for your mistress when she left the Hall, though she was clearly in distress. And earlier, I believe I saw you eavesdropping on her conversation, not to mention that you were also listening in on my unexpected introduction to Her Grace of Suffolk. I'd say that's one too many coincidences, Mistress. So, before I hand over my master's private communiqué, I'll need some answers."

She tossed her head, with practiced and, I must admit, rather charming indignation. "I've no time for this. You can keep your master's reply. I know his answer well enough." She started to step past me. I blocked her way. "I'm afraid I must insist."

She planted her hands at her hips. "I could scream for help. I am the Princess's lady."

"You are, and you could. But you won't. You don't want your admirer back there to catch wind of us." I squared my shoulders, drawing myself to full height, hoping my stance would prove intimidating enough. "Now, who told you I was coming? Was it Walsingham? I saw you in the Hall with him last night, as well. Are you his doxy? If so, Her Grace won't enjoy discovering her own lady-in-waiting, whom she entrusts with her personal correspondence, is being paid to spy on her."

She burst out laughing, then clapped a hand to her mouth. "You really are too inexperienced for this sort of thing," she said in a low voice. "I should send you on your way and not tell you a thing. But in the interest of time, I will say, no, I am not Walsingham's doxy. I simply know him because of Her Grace's acquaintance with Master Cecil. Or rather, I know of him. He's a professional informant. And, if rumors are to be believed, was trained in Italy as an assassin."

"Hence his gallant manner," I muttered.

Her smile was tart. "He's not the most brilliant conversationalist, either. He happened to be near me as Her Grace left the Hall. I assure you, we exchanged only amenities."

"I suppose you weren't listening in on her conversation, either?" I said dryly.

"Indeed, I was. She calls me her ears. I'm the reason she need not resort to outright gossip, which would be unbecoming in one of her rank. Before you ask, yes, I also tried to hear your presentation to the

Duchess of Suffolk. I reasoned Her Grace must have been curious as to why you were brought before the Duchess."

She paused, searching my face. All of a sudden, her entire manner softened. It was the first time since I'd set eyes on her that she revealed her actual person, not the fabrication she had perfected for court. Her look of compassion startled me with its sincerity.

"You have no reason to trust me," she said, "but I would never betray her. I am the bastard daughter of Sir William Carey, whose mother is Mary Stafford, sister to our late Queen Anne Boleyn. Her Grace and I are kin."

A pang went through my heart.

"Forgive me." I lowered my eyes. A lump formed in my throat. "I didn't mean to pry." My voice cracked. To my mortification, all of a sudden I couldn't control the rawness of my emotion. "God help me, I don't know who to trust anymore."

She was silent. Then she said softly, "You can trust Her Grace. That is why you are here, is it not? She told me you'd offered to help her, and she refused. Do you know why?"

I shook my head, blinking away sudden tears.

"Because," she said, "Her Grace would not see you harmed for her sake."

I hesitated another moment before I handed her Lord Robert's missive. She tucked it into her bodice.

It was then we heard the footsteps coming toward us. She froze, our eyes meeting in mutual panic. There was no time, or place, to hide. Without warning, she flung herself at me, with all the passion of a deprived lover. She took my astonished face in her hands, pressed her lips to mine. As she did, I managed to catch a fleeting glimpse of the figure that stalked right past us, followed by the three men, none of whom made comment at what we were doing.

For a paralyzing second I thought I must have imagined it.

Kate Carey melded her body to me, and I heard her breathe, "God save us. Don't move. Don't say a word."

I didn't. Only after the echoes of those heels had faded away did she draw back. "He just left her rooms," she said, passing a quick hand over her rumpled skirts. "I must go to her." She paused. "You mustn't say a word of this to anyone."

I stood immobile. "The Duke, he—he was with her? Why? What does he want?"

She shook her head. "I don't know. He arrived before you did, demanding admittance. She was abed, resting. She let him into her audience room and sent us away."

I didn't like the sound of this. "I must speak to her."

"No. It's not safe. He could return. Someone could see you. We cannot risk it. We cannot be exposed. If anyone should know . . ."

"Know?" I exploded under my breath. "Know, what?"

"You will discover all in time. I must go."

She turned away. I followed her to the gallery entranceway. As she made to enter, I touched her shoulder. "Then tell her this, from me. She's in danger. There's a plot afoot to arrest her sister. She must not meet with my master tonight. She must leave Greenwich, before it is too late."

From the gallery came a ringing: "Kate? Kate, are you there?"

The voice paralyzed us. Kate pushed me away from the entrance, yet despite her urgent whispered protest, I had to look.

Elizabeth stood silhouetted against those magnificent far doors, her hand clasping at the high collar of her crimson robe, her hair unbound. "Kate!" she called out again, and this time I heard the tremor in her voice. "If you're there, answer me, please."

"I'm here, Your Grace!" Kate cried back. She shoved me backwards to poke out her head. "I dropped something. I'll be right there."

"Hurry up," said the Princess tremulously. "I've need of you."

Kate moved forward. Something instinctual held me back. I had the perfect occasion to relate my suspicions directly and instead I said: "Tell her about her sister. Tell her she must leave, before it is too late."

"She won't listen." Kate met my uncomprehending stare. "She loves him, you see. She has always loved him. Nothing we do will stop her." She gave me a poignant smile. "Gallant squire, if you truly wish to help her, be at the pavilion tonight, with your master."

She left me standing there, incredulous.

I didn't want to believe it, though it made perfect sense. It certainly explained why Her Grace had insisted on remaining at court despite every apparent threat to her safety.

She loved him.

Elizabeth loved Robert Dudley.

CHAPTER FIFTEEN

I needed time to sort out my inner turmoil before I could return to Lord Robert. The palace was eerily still, devoid of the hordes of courtiers one might expect in the prelude to a nuptial celebration. I saw only a few menials going about their business, none returning my wan greeting as I wandered Greenwich's unfamiliar corridors.

I was adrift, a stranger in an unfamiliar and shadowy world.

A brooding heaviness engulfed my thoughts. I tried to tell myself that despite being the daughter of a king, she was still flesh and blood, and, as such, prone to error. Which could explain why she'd failed to see the depths of avarice and shallow ambition that constituted my master's inner heart. But then, she herself had admitted as much to me. She had said only last night in Whitehall that she'd needed to believe in him, that she'd never had cause to mistrust him, and wouldn't start looking for reasons.

Yet in the web being spun around her, anything less than the truth would bring about her doom.

I reached a grand hall, where servants were laying out carpets, setting up tables, and hanging silk garlands over a dais in preparation for the festivities. Those few that paid notice looked at me once and looked away.

I stopped, suddenly realizing what I must do.

Shortly thereafter I emerged onto a tree-lined promenade leading into the formal gardens that stretched to a loamy hill. Daylight faded from the sky, scalloping the bruised, low-hanging clouds in scarlet. It looked as if rain were on the way. I took Cecil's miniature map from my pocket, ascertaining my location. To my disappointment, the map didn't detail the gardens, and I didn't have much time before I had to make my way back.

Like most palace gardens, these followed an established pattern. Spacious and thoughtfully laid out for the court to amble and enjoy, wide gravel avenues bordered with topiary wound past the ubiquitous herb patches and flowerbeds before threading off in various directions. I took one of these narrower paths.

Thunder rumbled overhead. A drizzle began to fall. I stashed the map in my pocket, pulling my cap lower on my brow as I looked about. In the distance, I glimpsed what looked like an artificial lake girdling a stone structure.

My heart leapt. It had to be the pavilion.

It was further than it appeared. I found myself traversing the length of a forested mall into a wild and strangely haunting parkland.

Glancing over my shoulder, I spied fresh-lit candles in the hulking palace windows. I wondered if Elizabeth herself gazed out from one of them at this moment, deliberating on her encounter with the Duke. Or was she thinking only of tonight, and of what her rendezvous with Lord Robert would bring? I had never been in love, but from what I'd read, lovers pined and longed for each other when apart.

I suddenly wished I'd taken the opportunity to tell her everything I knew. I might not have relished the deliberate crushing of her romantic notions, but at least she would arrive at her rendezvous tonight fore-warned as to just how high my master aspired.

The rain grew stronger. Turning away from the palace, I shook away my brooding thoughts and quickened my pace.

Algid water surrounded the pavilion on three sides. A set of crumbling steps led up to it from the unkempt pathway where I stood. Once, it must been a lovely spot, an idyllic place to dally, before years of neglect had rendered it lichen-stained and decaying.

Exploring the area nearby, I located, as Walsingham had remarked, an old postern gate in an ivy-covered wall, leading to a dirt road and the sloping hills of Kent. This gave me pause. Horses could be tethered here, out of sight, and hearing, if properly muzzled and their hooves bound up in cloth, yet within easy reach. Had the Princess selected this place less out of a sense of irony, as Robert had supposed, and more because of its value as an escape route? The thought lightened my spirits significantly, until another, less appealing prospect occurred to me.

What if this was Cecil's plan? It could be he had decided to take advantage of her intention to lure Robert here, a place from which she could quickly, by force if need be, be spirited away. No matter what else the Secretary might be involved in, it couldn't possibly serve him to have Elizabeth fall prey to the Dudleys.

She was, as he himself had said, the kingdom's only hope.

I turned back to the pavilion, sunk in thought. Now that I considered it, what did Cecil plan for me? I had delivered my master's reply. Had I become a pawn to be discarded? Was there more to this elaborate subterfuge than met the eye, more lies within lies? I felt compelled to recall every word that had passed between Cecil and me, to search our verbiage for clues. Somewhere in our conversation lay the key to this riddle. And I'd best find it.

I came to an abrupt halt.

The tip of a blade pressed into my back, just below my ribs.

A nasal voice intoned, "I wouldn't resist if I were you. Take off your jerkin."

I slowly removed my outer garment, thinking of the map folded in my pocket as I let it drop at my feet. My assailant's blade was deadly sharp against my thin chemise.

"Now, the dagger in your boot. Carefully."

I reached to the hilt and pulled my knife from its sheath. A gauntleted hand reached around and took it from me. Then the voice, which I now recognized, said, "Turn around."

He wore a hooded cape, his features concealed.

"You have me at a disadvantage," I said. "I hardly call that fair play."

With that effete laugh, he cast aside his cowl. A face too sly to be deemed handsome, cheekbones prominent; in one earlobe, a ruby. His sloe eyes pierced me where I stood. How had I not recognized him earlier?

He's taller than you, but not by much, and has a pointy face, like a ferret.

"We meet again," I said, right before a burly henchman emerged from the shadows and hit me in the face.

I could barely make out the way before me, my left eye throbbing with what promised to be a magnificent bruise, my jaw aching from the blow as I was marched with my arms twisted behind my back past crumpled structures and through a ruined cloister into a passageway. Rusted iron gates hung like dislocated shoulders from doorways. We descended a steep staircase, went into another passage, and descended again. The passage we now entered was so narrow two men could not walk abreast. A lone pitch torch crackled in a peeling sconce on the wall.

The air smelled fermented. I had to breathe deep of it, reminding myself not to give into panic. I had to concentrate, observe and listen, and find some means to prolong my survival.

We came before a thick door. "I hope you'll find your accommodations agreeable," said Stokes as he slid back the bolt. The door swung outward. "We want only the best for you."

Inside was a small circular cell.

His ruffian shoved me inside. Slime coated the uneven flagstone floor. Skating on my boot heels, hands splayed before me, I skidded into the wall under a high, grated window. The smell was awful, the sticky moldering substance adhering to me like crushed entrails.

Stokes laughed. He stood under the flickering light of a nearby torch, his cloak parted to display his stylish costume. I saw a stiletto on a chain at his waist. I'd never seen anyone wear the Italian weapon before, and, unlike his earring, I assumed it was more than mere display.

"Tsk, tsk," he said. "I daresay no one would recognize you now, Squire Prescott."

With my shoulder smarting from where I'd hit the wall, sudden anger rushing through me with palpable force, I righted myself. I was surprised by the composure in my voice. "I see you know my name. Again, not fair play. Who are you? What do you want with me?"

"My, my. Aren't you the nosy one? No wonder Cecil likes you."

I hoped the jolt of fear I felt didn't show. "Cecil. Has this something to do with him?"

"Well, you certainly earned his interest in a short span of time, wouldn't you say? And as far as I know, boys aren't his specialty."

I didn't respond. I lunged. In a flash Stokes flung his arm, aiming the stiletto at my chest. "If I miss," he said, with a quivering laugh, "which is highly unlikely, my man won't. He'll slit you from sternum to bowel like a spring calf."

"You wouldn't be so cavalier if we were evenly matched," I replied, breathing hard. I inched back. What had gotten into me? I knew better than to incite an opponent with the advantage.

And incite, I had. Stokes's face darkened. "We'll never be evenly matched, no matter who you pretend you are, you miserable imposter."

Imposter? Did he mean, spy? I went cold. He was the Duchess of Suffolk's hiring, my mystery stalker. I was sure of it. How much had he overheard of my meeting with Cecil? If he'd learned enough to unmask the Secretary, then whatever escape attempt Cecil planned for Elizabeth could flounder. Or fail.

"I'm Lord Robert Dudley's squire," I said, seeking to gain time. "I have no idea why you'd think I aim to be anything else."

"Oh, I do hope you're not going to play the innocent." Stokes clucked his tongue. "It will not do, no, not at all. False modesty never impressed Her Grace. She knows all too well why you were brought to court, and why Cecil has shown such interest in you. She's not pleased. She does have that infamous Tudor temper, after all. But you'll learn that soon enough."

With theatrical flair, he waved his hand at me, "Now, don't go anywhere." He yanked the door shut. The bolt shot into place. Pitch darkness plunged over the cell.

In all my life, I had never been so afraid.

CHAPTER SIXTEEN

I closed my eyes, drew in a series of slow breaths. I let my vision adjust to the gloom. A patch of the night sky grew visible through the grate. Judging from the angle, I determined I had to be underground. In the silence, I could discern the distant murmur of water. Was I somewhere near the river?

I willed myself to creep around the cell. I didn't like what I found. Despite the algae on the floor and the overall unpleasantness of the place, there were no droppings or other signs of rodent life, though rats must infest Greenwich as they did any place where food could be found. I also discovered that though I could scratch clumps of mortar from the wall crevices, the stone underneath was solid, impervious to the pervasive chill that seeped into my bones.

My disquiet spiraled. I must be under the ruins of the medieval palace, perhaps in an old dungeon. But we'd come a distance from the lake, and not enough rain had fallen to explain all this moisture. Greenwich was built to celebrate the end of feudal warfare. It had no ramparts or defensive moats, as lords with armies of vassals were, allegedly, no longer a threat. Yet the slimy floor and moldering air indicated this cell had been inundated in a not too distant past.

None of which did anything to ease my anxiety.

After circulating the cell twice, I returned under the window to stare up. I thought I now knew exactly how a caged lion must feel. Stamping my feet to stir the blood in my legs, I squatted, coiling my muscles, then sprang up, as high as I could, arms and fingers straining. My attempts confirmed the sill was too high. Even if the mortar around it could be dug out, and the grate loosened or broken, I had no way to do so without something to stand on.

I was trapped, while in the Hall the festivities for Jane Grey and Guilford Dudley's wedding would soon begin, and the hour of Lord Robert's rendezvous with the Princess neared.

I sank to my haunches. I couldn't have said how long I sat there, waiting. At one point I slipped into exhausted sleep, and awoke, gasping, thinking I was drowning in a viscous sea. Only then did I realize that the smell permeating my skin was of river water, that I'd glimpsed no sign of any ground during my leaps toward the window, and that a muted clamor approached.

I came stiffly to my feet. An exasperated voice declared, "By the rood, Stokes, was there no other place to lock the wretch in?"

"Your Grace," said Stokes. The bolt slid back. "I assure you this was the only place I could find on short notice suitable to our needs."

The door opened. Torchlight flooded the cell, blinding in its intensity. Seeing only shadows in the doorway, I brought up a hand to shield my eyes. A bulk pushed inside, swatting about with a cane. Then it went still, peering. "Is that him?"

"It is, Your Grace."

"Bring in that torch," she commanded.

Stokes squeezed in behind her. The torch he carried illuminated what first looked to me like a mastiff swathed in carnelian, a ludicrous pearl-dotted coif perched on its oversized head. I blinked, forcing my eye to focus. The swollen one, by now, had completely shut.

Frances Brandon, Duchess of Suffolk, glared at me. "He looks smaller. Are you certain it's him? He could be someone else. That scoundrel Cecil is wily. He'd substitute his own mother if it would further his cause."

"Your Grace," said Stokes, "it's him. Let me call for my man. It's not safe."

"No! I am not some lily-livered girl. If he so much as looks at me the wrong way, I'll bash in his skull and be done with it." She blared at me, brandishing her stout silver-tipped cane, "You! Come closer."

I advanced as calmly as I could, making certain to stop far enough away to evade an unanticipated swipe at my head. "Your Grace," I began, "I'm afraid there's been a misunderstanding. I assure you I have no idea how I've offended you."

"No?" The end of her cane stabbed out, missing me by an inch. She guffawed. "Well, well. He has no idea. Did you hear that, Stokes? He's no idea of how he's offended."

"I heard, Your Grace," twittered Stokes. "An actor he most certainly is not."

The cane slammed down. "Enough!" She lumbered to me. I had to stop from flinching. During my wandering through Whitehall the night after Elizabeth left, I had come across a portrait of Henry VIII, his gross ringed hands on his hips, his bulging legs apart. Standing face-to-face now with the late king's niece, I found the familial resemblance daunting. "Who are you?" she asked.

I met her vicious stare. "Begging Your Grace's pardon, but I believe we were introduced. I am Brendan Prescott, newly made squire to Robert Dudley."

I choked on a cry. With savage accuracy, her cane slammed up between my legs. I doubled over as white-hot pain seared away my breath. Another whack brought me gasping to my knees, my groin shrieking in agony.

She stood over me. "That's better. You will kneel when I address you. You are before a Tudor. I am the daughter of Henry VIII's beloved sister, Mary, late duchess of Suffolk and dowager of France. By all that is royal in me, you *will* show me respect." She jabbed my concaved shoulders with her cane. "Again, who are you?"

I gazed up at her contorted visage, and felt a rush of uncontrollable hatred. Her mouth turned inward, like a venomous bloom. "Seize him." Stokes's henchman, who was broad as a wall and twice my height, lumbered in. He hauled me up, pinioned my arms. I didn't have the strength to struggle anymore, still limp from the pain of her blow.

Stokes asked, "Shall we start with a few kicks to his ribs, Your Grace? That usually tends to loosen the tongue."

"No." She didn't take her stare from me. "He has too much to lose, and Cecil no doubt paid him well for his silence. I don't need him to say anything. I have eyes. I can see. Some things cannot be counterfeited." She stabbed her hand at me. "Strip him."

Stokes handed her the torch, and leapt forth to tear off my chemise. He eyed me. "He has very white skin," he purred.

"Get out of my way." She shoved Stokes aside, thrusting the torch

113

at me. I tried to recoil, but the henchman's grip was a manacle on my wrists, his chuckling breath fetid at my ear.

Her eyes scoured me. "Nothing," she said, "not a mark. It's not him. I knew it. Lady Dudley deceived me. That she-wolf forced me to surrender my claim to the throne for nothing. Christ's soul, I'll make her pay for this. How dare she set her drunkard of a son and my own mealy-mouthed daughter above me?"

My blood congealed.

"Perhaps we should be thorough," Stokes suggested, and he told his man, "Turn him around." The henchman started to pivot me. As he did, to my horror, I felt my breeches slip a notch, over my hip.

A hiss escaped her. "Stop." She thrust the torch at me again. I clamped down on a cry as the flame singed my skin.

"Where did you get that?" she said, haltingly, as if she didn't trust her own eyes.

I hesitated, not knowing what she would want to hear. Then a spear of pain flew through my shoulders and across my upper chest as the henchman yanked up my arms. "Her Grace asked you a question. Answer her."

"I—I was . . . born with it," I managed to whisper.

"Born with it?" She reared her face at me, so close I saw the tiny broken veins threading her nose under her powder. "You were born with it, you say?"

I nodded, helplessly.

She met my eyes in a moment of dreadful silence. Then she hissed, "I don't believe you."

Tears of fury and pain smarted in my eyes.

Stokes peered. "Your Grace, are you certain? It does look like—"

"Yes, I'm certain. It's not him. It cannot be." She handed Stokes the torch, grabbed back her cane "If you want to save that pretty white skin," she said, her fist clenching about the silver handle, "you'd best tell me the truth. Who are you, really, and what has Cecil paid you to do?"

I felt nauseous. I had no idea what to say. Should I spill out the truth, as I knew it, or pretend to know something I didn't? Which was more likely to keep me alive?

"I am just a foundling," I finally uttered. "I was raised in the Dudley household, and brought here to serve Lord Robert. That is all."

My words sounded like lies, even to me, the hasty justifications of a man caught in an illicit deed. She, of course, knew as much. It was why I was here. Whomever she believed I was had frightened her enough to have ordered me followed, abducted, and, if I didn't find a way out of this nightmare soon, probably killed.

Nevertheless, I'd caught her attention. Her eyes narrowed to slits. "Just a foundling?" she repeated. "Tell me this, were you truly left in the priest's cottage near Dudley Castle?"

Without taking my gaze from hers, I nodded, a shard in my throat.

"Do you know who left you there? Do you know who found you?"

I swallowed, struggling for a calm that eluded me. A dull roar filled my head, like an ocean in my brain. I heard myself say as if from across a vast distance, "I don't know who left me. Dame Alice, the Dudley housekeeper and herbalist, she found me. She took me in."

I gleaned another flash in her eyes. "An herbalist?" Her stare was a physical instrument, a probing device in my sinews. "A small woman, with a merry laugh?"

I began to tremble uncontrollably. She knew. She knew Dame Alice. "Yes," I whispered.

The Duchess of Suffolk recoiled, and took a jerking step back. "It can't be," she panted. "You're an imposter, tutored by Cecil, and paid for by the Dudleys." Her next words issued in a scalding torrent. "Because of you, they forced me to hand over my daughter in marriage to their weakling puppet. Because of you, I am humiliated in my God-given royal right."

She paused, her voice terrifying in its resolve. "But I am not so easily fooled. I'll see this kingdom destroyed before I let that woman and her spoiled brat triumph over me."

I tasted bile in my throat. All of a sudden, everything made perfect, dreadful sense.

Stokes let out a gleeful twitter. "Why, Your Grace, he's gone pale as a maiden. I believe he speaks the truth. He truly has no idea what they are doing with him."

"That remains to be seen," she snapped. She angled her cane level with my eyes, clicked the handle. A steel sliver slid from the cane's tip.

"See how fine this is?" she said. "I can slide it between two sheaves of paper without leaving a mark. Or, I can cut through boiled leather."

She angled the cane down, until it grazed my groin.

I heard Stokes giggle again. Forcing back another surge of impotent rage, I met her stare. I had one last chance. "Your Grace, I do not know of what you speak. I swear it to you."

For a moment, a rush of doubt blurred her expression. Then the savage cunning returned, and I knew it was over. "You play the innocent to perfection, I'll give you that much. Maybe you are what you say, a wretched unfortunate she trained to use against me. Cecil could have told her the story, seeded the idea that would give her the weapon she needed."

She gave a shrewd chuckle. "He's capable of that, and much more. It's a devious little game they play, each to their own end. They'll pay for it by the time I'm through with them. They'll rue the day they dared cross my path."

She paused. The expression that now came over her face was unlike any I'd ever seen, a dark riveting mask lacking in any empathy or compassion. "As for you, it doesn't matter who you are anymore." She swerved to Stokes. "I've wasted enough time. When will it be done?"

"As soon as the tide rises. The court will be on the gallery watching the fireworks." Stokes snickered. "Not that they'd know. No one's been here in years. It reeks of Catholic vice."

I saw it then, in all its clarity, each thread a part of the whole. While the festivities in honor of Guilford and Jane Grey's nuptials distracted the court, Robert— deprived by his father of what he believed was his right to win a royal bride— would meet with Elizabeth. Deluded and misled, blinded by his overwhelming ambition, he had only empty words to offer her.

The Duke had no intention of giving him the Princess. Jane Grey was his weapon now, the perfect pawn, a helpless girl with Tudor blood in her veins, daughter of a niece of Henry VIII and wife of his malleable youngest son. Two hapless adolescents were to be England's next sovereigns, while Elizabeth and her sister Mary were slated for the Tower and a swift end.

The henchman swung out his arm, delivering a clout that sprawled me to the floor.

"No more of that," said the Duchess. "It must look as if he wandered off by himself. No wounds. I want no indication of foul play."

"Yes, Your Grace," Stokes said, as I staggered to my feet. My cheek was cut from the fall, blood hot on my bruised face. Through a blur I saw her lumber to the door.

"Your Grace," I called. She stopped. "I would know the reason for my death."

She glanced at me. "Because you were never meant to live. You are an abomination." She trudged out, the henchman behind. Stokes tripped to the door. He looked over his shoulder. "Don't forget to hold your breath."

The door slammed shut.

Alone in the darkness, I began to shout.

CHAPTER SEVENTEEN

I shouted until I had no voice left. I couldn't believe it would end like this. It was unthinkable. I wanted to roar the walls down into rubble, dig my way out with my bare hands, knowing now how a wounded animal must feel, waiting for the end.

Without realizing what I was doing I started to pace. It was astounding how much had fallen into place, astounding and appalling. My arrival at court must have been premeditated, orchestrated by Lady Dudley to force the Duchess into relinquishing her place in the succession. And if this was true, then Lady Dudley had to know something about who I was. She had taken me into her care *because* of it. The woman who had disdained and humiliated me, set me to cleaning her stables, and ordered me flogged when I sought to read a book, held the secret to my past.

Il porte la marque de la rose . . .

A wave of desperation overcame me. I struggled not to give in, reminding myself that everything could be an illusion, a manipulation. In my pain and anger, as I sought to make sense of the senseless, I didn't pay heed to the subtle changes in the air around me, to the slow mounting gurgle that signaled the beginning of the end, until I heard water splash on stone.

And turned to see a black torrent gushing through the window grate.

I stood, petrified. The flow of water grew stronger, faster, bringing a smell of rot and sea, pouring in with unstoppable force as the flooding tide funneled through forgotten underground conduits into the small cell. In a matter of minutes, the floor was awash.

I backed to the door. There was no latch or keyhole, and several furious kicks confirmed that breaking it down was not an option. Fear tightened like an iron band about my chest. The overflow from the river would keep pouring through that grate until it filled the room to the ceiling. I was going to drown unless I found a way out. Now.

For an instant, my body refused to move. Then I jerked forward and sloshed through a death trap rapidly vanishing under liquid. I acted on instinct. Coming under the deluge, water pouring down on my face like lacerations, I gazed up. Mustering every last bit of strength, I bent my knees, coiled my body, and with a whispered prayer, sprang up.

My left hand jammed against the sill. My right one connected with wet iron. I tightened my grip, resisting the burning tear of muscles as I maneuvered under the torrent, gaining a hold on the grate with both hands. I dangled off the floor. Glancing back into the room, I saw through the curtain of water that the door was three quarters submerged.

I pulled. Nothing. Tightening my grip, I pulled again. Rusted shards scraped my fingers.

"Move," I whispered. "Move. *Move!*"

With a crumbling crack, the grate gave way. My arms flew up to shield my head as I plunged into the pool below me. Gasping, spitting out a slimy mouthful, I clambered to my feet. The grate had twisted outward, a toothy maw, so that now two torrents gushed into the cell. I had no way of squeezing out.

The water continued to pour in.

I still couldn't believe I would die.

Scenes from my brief time at court drifted past me, so that I saw again the bedlam of London, the labyrinthine passageways of White-hall, the pallid faces of those I had met, who had become the architects of my own demise. I thought Peregrine, of all of them, might mourn, and, just as I could abide no more, I recalled Kate Carey's face as she grabbed mine to kiss. It was then that, unbidden, I beheld the twin suns in a princess's eyes.

Elizabeth

Molten blood pumped through my limbs. I could feel the water creeping upward, an implacable presence whose clammy fingers swam about my midriff. As I imagined that taste of death and silt filling my lungs, I swirled about and started hammering on the remaining top of the door with all my might. My cries erupted. I didn't care if anyone answered. I refused to succumb in silence.

As if from across a chasm, I heard the faintest of calls. *"Breeendaaan!"*

I paused, pressed against the door, straining.

"Brendan! Brendan, are you there?"

"I'm here!" I banged again on the door, scraping my knuckles raw. "Here! I'm here!"

My knees started to buckle when the muffled splashing footsteps grew louder, running toward me. "Open it! Open it!" Unseen hands seized hold of the bolt, and started yanking it back.

"Be careful," I shouted. "The room's flooded. Get back before—"

I was knocked off my feet. Propelled out on a wave, I crashed against the opposite wall, and slid to the floor, a boneless, sodden rag.

In the dripping hush, a frightened voice asked, "Are you alive?"

"If I'm not, then you must be dead," I muttered, facedown in a pool. Arms like blocks of solid marble hauled me up. Before me stood two figures; one was Peregrine. The other, massive, carrot-topped, square-jawed and his complexion marred by pimples, was a stranger.

Peregrine said, "What happened to you? You look awful."

"You would, too, if you'd been up to your ears in bilge." I looked at the stranger. "Thank you." He nodded, his freckled hands hanging big as bread panders at his side. I said to Peregrine, "How did you find me?"

"This." He lifted my crumpled jerkin. "We found it near the entrance. We started searching for you when Barnaby saw a man running away."

"These old cloisters and cells," added Barnaby Fitzpatrick, the King's childhood friend, "belonged to the Gray Friars until King Henry kicked them out. They've been abandoned for years. If someone comes here, most likely they mean trouble. The moment I saw that man, I knew something was amiss."

I put on the jerkin, grateful for something dry. I was chilled to my marrow.

"We didn't get a good look at him," Peregrine jumped in, excited now that he realized they had saved my life. "It was too dark, and he wore black. But he caught Barnaby's attention—he's got eyes like a falcon, this one. Lucky for you, he did. If we hadn't happened to find your jerkin, we'd never have thought to look here." He paused, regarding me with a newfound awe. "Someone must really want you dead."

"Indeed. There was no one else with this man?" I asked, though I didn't need to hear more. I knew who the man in black had been.

Barnaby shook his head. "He was alone. Strange thing, it was if he wanted us to see him. He could have gone any number of ways besides right within our eyesight."

This gave me pause. I passed a hand over my hair, which was plastered with silt, then accorded the muscular youth a bow. "You must be Master Fitzpatrick. Allow me to introduce myself. I am Brendan Prescott. I owe you my life, it seems."

He couldn't have been more than eighteen. Tall and built like a barbican, not uncomely despite his blemished complexion, with a shock of wiry red hair springing out from under his cap, he was not someone to disregard. Judging by the size of those hands and his drenched doublet, he must have been the one who unbolted and yanked open the cell door.

Barnaby Fitzpatrick said matter-of-factly, "Peregrine told me who you are. You're a Dudley servant. He also tells me you're a friend to Her Grace. She's like a sister to me, which is why I agreed to come with him and help you. But I must warn you, if you intend any harm on her"— he shook his massive fist — "you won't like the results."

I nodded. "Trust me, I intend her no harm. I would explain more, if we had the time. Unfortunately, we do not. We must make haste. She is in danger." I reached over and wrenched the ebbing torch from the bracket. Peregrine piped, "His Majesty is here, in the Secret Lodgings. Barnaby says he's been here for weeks. See? I told you I'd find out anything you asked."

My gaze shifted to Barnaby over the tarry smoky flame. His stare conveyed grim resolution. We started down the passage, sloshing through ankle-deep pools toward the steep staircase. I ventured, "Is His Majesty very ill, Master Fitzpatrick?"

"He is." Barnaby's voice caught for a moment. "Edward is dying."

I was silent. Then I said, "I am sorry to hear it. Not only for his sake, but because Her Grace so hoped to see him again. Now, I fear she never will." I paused. "I can only pray she'll heed me."

"She'll heed me," Barnaby replied, and the sober certainty in his manner I found comforting in the extreme. "Her Grace, His Majesty, and I were raised together. She and I often shared Edward's lessons. In fact, we first taught Edward to ride."

He smiled briefly. "Old King Henry would laugh out loud whenever Edward's tutors went running to him, squawking that we must be punished for putting His Highness at risk." He shifted his dark blue stare to me. His smile became a taut grimace. "She knows I would never leave Edward's side unless I was forced to. And she knows that, even in exile, I'd find a way to watch over him. She'll heed me, especially once I tell her about the mischief the Duke's been up to."

We reached the gardens. I'd never been more grateful for fresh air in all my life. Above the palace, fiery jettisons and wheels careened and exploded, showering multicolored glitter over rapt figures crammed together on the leads lining the hall windows.

I started to attention. "The fireworks! Quick, which way to the pavilion?"

Peregrine sprinted to the left. Crossing an overgrown thicket of what had once been sculpted hedges and topiary I saw the pavilion ahead. The lake's still waters reflected the artificial spectacle, so that it seemed bathed in glittery fire. As we approached, I spied a silhouette in black standing motionless at the balustrade. Another figure stood a few paces away, looking into the gardens.

My emotion pitched. "Give me a few moments alone with her," I said to Barnaby. "I don't want to overwhelm her at first." He nodded, and he and Peregrine crouched down as I walked forth into the splashes of moonlight and counterfeit fire.

The figure in black turned to me. I took the stairs into the pavilion and, coming before her, bowed. At her side, Kate Carey gave a startled gasp. I hadn't stopped to consider that besides my soiled clothing, I must look a mess of bruises and cuts.

To her credit, Elizabeth did not make a fuss, though her concern was plain to see. "Squire Prescott. Rise." She paused. "Isn't it rather late in the day for swimming?"

I smiled. "An unfortunate accident, Your Grace. It looks worse than it is."

"Thank God for that." Her eyes glittered. Her hair was seeded with pearls, coiled at her nape in a simple coiffure. She looked disarmingly young, the unadorned severity of her black gown, with its banded ruff and lace cuffs, emphasizing her willowy figure. Only her hands gave her away, those exquisite fingers twisting and untwisting a handkerchief.

"Well?" she said. "Will you not speak? I assume something must be amiss. Has urgent business again detained your master?"

"Your Grace, I'm afraid I bring news of His Majesty your brother. And of your cousin, Lady Jane." I paused, wet parched lips. Her eyes bore at me. In that moment I realized how fantastic, even ludicrous, my tale would sound, let alone lacking in proof. I also had the disquieting sensation she knew exactly what I was about to say.

"I'm listening," she said.

"His Majesty your brother is dying," I told her in a quiet voice. "The Duke keeps his mortal illness a secret so that he can set Lady Jane and his own son Guilford on the throne. He plans to capture you and your sister, the Lady Mary, and put you both in the Tower. If you stay much longer in Greenwich, I fear no one will be able to vouch for your safety."

I swallowed. Without taking her eyes from me, Elizabeth said, "Kate, is this true?"

Kate Carey stepped to us. "I fear so, Your Grace."

"And you knew about it? Cecil knew?"

"Not everything." To her credit, Kate did not seek to avoid my stare, though she now confirmed she had reported to Cecil. "But I do not doubt Squire Prescott's word. It would appear he has good reason for saying this."

Elizabeth nodded. "I don't doubt. Not for a second. I've suspected something of this nature was afoot from the moment Northumberland refused my request to visit Edward. I suppose I should consider myself fortunate I haven't been arrested yet." She paused, her gaze still on me. "Do you know why I haven't been arrested?"

I did not hesitate. "I believe his lordship does not dare risk it, lest word of it gets to your sister and prompts her to flee the country. It would explain why they've decided to go after her first. I've heard someone at court is feeding her information."

"I'm sure quite a few are," replied Elizabeth, with some asperity.

"We are talking about John Dudley, after all. By now he's made more enemies than she ever could."

"Then we mustn't press Your Grace's luck further," I said. "I've friends nearby who can help us get you away. Even His Majesty's close companion Master Fitzpatrick is—"

"No."

For a moment, the last of the fireworks popping in the distance seemed to pause.

"No?" I echoed. I thought I must have heard wrong.

"No." Her face set. "I'm not leaving. Not yet."

Kate Carey said quickly, "Your Grace cannot mean to stay after what we've just heard. It would be madness. We promised Master Cecil you would—"

"I know what we promised," she interrupted. "I said I would consider his advice. Consider, Kate, not comply. I have tried. But now, I must see this through. I couldn't live with myself if I did not."

"My lady," I ventured, and I received the full force of her stare. "I beg you to reconsider. You cannot change the Duke's course, no matter what you do, nor can you hope to save His Majesty. Under the circumstances, you must now save yourself, for England."

She drew herself erect. "I hear Cecil speaking now, and I like it not. Be yourself, Prescott. I prefer you that way—impudent, rash, and determined to do whatever it takes."

I might have smiled again, had the matter not been so serious. "Then, impudent as I am, I must emphasize how dangerous it would be to keep your appointment with my master. Lord Robert aims higher than Your Grace knows, and will deceive you in any way he can."

At the mention of Robert, her expression underwent a change. It was almost imperceptible, but I saw it, the tightening of the sensitive skin about her mouth, the flash of something livid in her eyes.

"And I," she said softly, as if it were a warning, "know best how to deal with him." She raised her chin. "Besides, it's too late. Here he comes now."

I spun about. Kate grabbed me, pulled me back. "Go," she hissed. "Hide!"

I scrambled over the balustrade, dropping with what sounded like a deafening crash into the hawthorn bushes. "Graceful," muttered

Peregrine. He and Barnaby had crept up unheard, each armed with dirks. Peregrine handed me one. I remembered my old dagger, which Master Shelton had given me. Stokes owed me, if only for stealing my knife. As for my cap, I had finally lost it for good.

Through the leaves, I watched Robert swagger down the pathway. He had asked me to make sure to return to help him dress tonight. Despite my absence, he had fared well enough, resplendent in an outfit of gold brocade studded with opals that must have cost an estate. He paused, removed his jeweled and feathered cap, and stepped up the stairs to the pavilion, his legs sheathed to his thighs in cordovan boots with gold spurs.

He dropped to one knee before Elizabeth, his head bowed. "I'm overwhelmed to find Your Grace safe and in good health." Even in the openness of the pavilion, the smell of his musk was overpowering, like the breath of a magnificent beast in its prime

She did not extend her hand for him to kiss, nor gave him leave to rise. Slipping her handkerchief into her cuff she said, "I can't complain about my health. As for my safety, that remains to be seen. This court was never a place of refuge for me."

He glanced up. She'd spoken lightly, almost off handedly, but even he could not have mistaken her tone. He reacted as if he had, however, replying with husky promise: "If you would let me, I will make this court, and all this realm, a place of refuge and glory for you."

"You would do so much for me, wouldn't you, sweet Robin? Since we were children, you always promised me the sun and the stars."

"I still do. You can have anything you desire. Ask for it, and it shall be yours."

"Very well." She stared down at him. "I wish to see my brother before he dies, without fearing for my life."

I saw Robert stiffen. Still relegated to his knees, he took longer than expected before he managed to utter, "I dare not speak of that, my lady. And neither must you."

"Oh?" She tilted her head. "Why not? Surely friends as we are have nothing to hide?"

"We do not," he said slowly. "But it is treason to speculate on such a matter, as you well know."

Her laughter rang out. "I'm relieved to hear someone in your family still has a conscience, my lord, and that my brother still lives. It would no longer be treason to speculate if he did not." She paused. "I thought you said I could have anything I desired."

"You toy with me." He sprang to his feet, overpoweringly robust against her slenderness. "I did not come here to play games with you. I came to warn you that your right to the throne is in danger."

"I have no right," she retorted, swift as a knife, but there was a weakening in her, a supple yielding like a vine before an inescapable sun. "My sister Mary is heir to the throne, not I. Thus, if you must warn someone, it should be her."

Robert guffawed. "Come now. We're not children anymore. We needn't see who can outwit whom. You know as well as I that the people will not have your sister for their queen. She represents Rome and the past, and everything they have come to detest."

"And yet she is their rightful— their *only*— heir," said Elizabeth. To my amazement she shrugged, as if the matter were beneath her. "Besides, who's to say? Mary could change her faith, as so many these days are apt to do. She's still a Tudor when all is said and done, and our family was never one to let religion get in our way."

Robert eyed her with a familiarity I found discomfiting. I hadn't thought about how much history can be collected in a mere twenty years, how much two children reared on a diet of intrigue and deception can come to rely upon each other.

"Do you take me for a fool?" he said. "You know Mary would defend her faith to the grave if need be. You know it, the Council knows it, your brother the King knows it and—"

"Your father knows it," cut in Elizabeth. "In fact, he knows best of all. You might even say, he anticipated it." Now, it was she who eyed him, with a calculated intimacy that made him look an amateur. "Is that why you wished to see me? Have we danced around each other these past two days only for you to warn me that my sister mustn't be allowed to take the throne because she, like all of us, reveres the Church in which she was raised?"

"God's blood!" He stomped his foot. "I came to tell you that in the eyes of the people, you, and only you, have the right to be queen. You are the princess they revere. You are the one they await. They would rise in arms to uphold you, if you would but say the word. They'd risk their lives in your defense."

"Would they?" Her voice was glacial, lowering to a cruel caress. "There was a time when they would have done much the same for Mary's mother. Then, it was Katherine of Aragon who was the rightful queen, and my mother the hated usurper. Would you have me step into a dead woman's shoes?"

He glared at her. The air between them was charged, the tension so palpable it set my teeth on edge. There was indeed history here, and far too much emotion. It was my first glimpse into a passion unlike any I had experienced, under whose shadow I would spend much of my life. A passion so deep, so unstable, that were it unleashed it would erupt with such violence as to sweep away everything before it.

"Why must you always banter words with me?" Robert's voice quavered. "You fear Mary taking the throne as much I do. You know it would mean the ruin of the Church your father built so he could wed your mother; the ruin of all hope for peace or prosperity. She'll set the Inquisition to burning us within the year. But not you; you have no desire to persecute. That is why you have the people on your side, and most of the nobility. And me. Anyone who dared question your right will suffer my sword."

She regarded him in absolute silence. From my hiding place I could almost feel her hesitation, her terrified understanding of all that was at stake, and all she might gain by it. My legs tensed like an animal's about to spring, imagining her struggle to justify a past smeared by her mother's spilt blood.

Then she spoke. "My right, you say? Is it my right, truly? Or, do you mean, ours?"

"It's one and the same," he said quickly, too quickly. "I live to serve you."

"Inspiring words. They might stir me, had I not heard similar ones before."

It was the first time in my life I had seen a Dudley struck speechless.

"Do you want to know from whom?" Elizabeth stepped close. "It was your father. Yes, Robin— your father the Duke offered me much the same this very afternoon. He even used the same arguments, offered the same blandishments."

Robert stood still, petrified to the spot.

"You can ask Mistress Carey, if you don't believe me," Elizabeth went on. "She saw him leave my rooms. He barged in— while I was abed, I might add— and declared he was willing to make me queen if I consented to marry him. He promised to get rid of his wife, your mother, for me. Or rather, my crown. For I would have to make him king. Not king-consort, if you please, but king in his own right, so that should I die before him, say in the childbed, as so many women do, he can continue to rule after me, and bequeath the throne to his heirs, regardless of whether they are my issue or not."

She smiled, graceful and unforgiving as a lioness. "So, you must excuse me if I don't react with the enthusiasm you might have hoped. I'm fresh out of enthusiasm where the Dudleys are concerned."

Like Robert, I was mesmerized by her performance. She hadn't breathed a word of this, though it explained why Northumberland had elected to set Jane Grey on the throne. An experienced courtier, he had a contingency plan, in case his first choice fell through. His declaration at Whitehall the night of Elizabeth's arrival— it had been his warning he was willing to proceed against her if she stood in his way. And she had done just that, refusing him and everything he contrived to obtain for her, and in return issuing her own declaration of war.

As Cecil surmised, the Duke had underestimated his opponent.

The disbelief spreading across Robert's face drained his sun-bronzed skin to a chalky hue. I actually felt sorry for him as I heard him say in a faltering voice, "My father offered . . . to marry you?"

"You sound surprised." She flipped a dismissive hand. "The seed is the same as the apple it came from, or so they say."

He stepped to her with such fury in his stance that without thinking, I started to lunge. Barnaby's vise-like grasp on my shoulder, coupled with a lightening glance from the otherwise motionless Kate, detained me. I clenched my jaw, closed my fist about my dirk handle. As I did, I saw Kate slip a hand into her cloak, for something no doubt equally sharp. It reassured me that, in this instance, she'd spoken the truth about her loyalty to the Princess.

Robert snagged Elizabeth by the arm so forcefully her hair broke loose and cascaded like flame over her shoulders, the pearls scattering across the pavilion floor.

"You lie! You lie, and play with me; and still, God help me, I want you!" He yanked her against him, crushing her mouth with his. With a stinging retort that echoed in the electrified air, she reared back and struck him across the face.

"Unhand me this instant, or by God I'll not be responsible for my actions!"

Her words proved more blistering than her blow. Robert backed away. They faced each other like combatants, their breath audible, heavy. Then the aggression crumbled from his face, and he gazed at her with something akin to grief.

"You're not considering it? You'd not wed him to spite me?"

"If you think that, you are more deluded than he," she retorted, but her voice was quivering now, as though she fought back an uncertainty that threatened to undo her. "As if I, a princess born and bred, would ever let a lowborn Dudley rut between my sheets. I'd rather die first."

He flinched. His face set like stone. It was a terrible moment, sounding the death-knell on years of trust and childhood affection. No woman had outmaneuvered Robert Dudley. Any woman he had wanted, he'd undoubtedly had. But he, despite all his guile, desired only one woman, and she had rejected him with a callous resolve aimed like a spear at his heart.

He drew himself erect. "Is that your final word?" he asked, his voice like steel.

"It is my only word," she replied. "King or commoner, I will be no man's pawn."

Robert flinched. "What if that man should declare his love for you?"

She let out a chuckle. "If this is a man's love, I pray God to spare me any more of it."

He exploded. "So be it! You will lose it all, country, crown: everything. They'll take it all from you and leave you with nothing save your infernal pride. I loved you. I still love you, but seeing as you will have nothing to do with me, you leave me with no other choice but to do as my father commands. I must go and arrest your sister, and see her to the Tower. And as God is my witness, Elizabeth, when he next sends me out at the head of a company of soldiers, I cannot promise it will not be to come knocking at your door in Hatfield."

She lifted her chin. "Should that come to pass, I'll be grateful for a familiar face."

Robert bowed furiously and turned heel, storming down the steps toward the palace. The night swallowed him. The moment he was gone, Elizabeth swayed. Kate hurried to her.

"Oh, God," I heard the Princess whisper. "What have I done?"

"What you had to," Kate told her. "What Your Grace's dignity required."

Elizabeth stared at her. Then a shrill quiver of a laugh escaped her. "Squire Prescott!"

I rose, brushing dead leaves from my damp breeches as I came before her. In her eyes I glimpsed an anguish she would never admit to, not even in her most private moments.

"You told me I am in danger of my life. It seems you were right. What shall we do now?"

"Leave, Your Grace," I said promptly, "before Lord Robert confesses to his father. Once he does, they will have to take you. You know too much."

"Robert won't say a word," she said, as Kate removed her cloak from the balustrade and draped it about her thin shoulders. "I've hurt him in the one place he'll not forgive or forget, but he'll never seek revenge on me through his father. No. He will do as he said and hunt Mary down like a prize doe. His pride of manhood demands it."

"Whatever the case, we can't wait to find out." I turned to Kate. A lesser woman might have flinched at the marked, impersonal tone in my voice. "Any plans we need know about?"

She said softly, "I am to take Her Grace through the postern gate. There is transport waiting for us on the road. But you weren't supposed to be here." She paused, looked away. I had the feeling that, like me, Kate had been told only as much as was deemed necessary. She had no idea of how deep this treachery ran.

Elizabeth broke into my thoughts. "I am overwhelmed by the concern, but I've no desire to leave my Arabian, Cantila, here for the Duke's use. He's far too valuable a friend." Her lips curled. "Speaking of which, didn't you say you had friends nearby?"

In answer to her query, Peregrine bounded up out of hiding. "I'll fetch Your Grace's horse!" Behind him Barnaby offered stiff genuflection, shreds of leaf in his hair. "My lady," he said with the warmth of years of familiarity.

"Barnaby Fitzpatrick. I am glad of you." She leaned to Peregrine with a wry smile. "Don't you work in the stables at Whitehall? Where is my dog?"

Peregrine gazed in unabashed adoration. "Urian is safe, Your Grace. He is here, stabled with Cantila. I'll fetch him too, if you like. Anything you need. It would be my honor."

"He means it," I added, with a mock look of indignation at Peregrine. "My horse Cinnabar is also here, my friend, in case you've forgotten. And my saddlebag is under the straw."

Peregrine glanced at his feet, flustered. Elizabeth said briskly, "Peregrine here will fetch my dog and the horses, and meet us at the southern gate. I've a friend of my own outside Greenwich, where we can take refuge lest the Duke sends troops after us. I don't think it wise to return to Hatfield quite yet."

She paused. A chill went through me as I saw her tense. Even though I anticipated her words, they still took me off guard.

"But before we leave, I will see my brother."

CHAPTER EIGHTEEN

There was a deafening hush. I marveled that I should feel any shock at her words. It wasn't as if she were behaving in an unexpected fashion. I also wondered why I tried to convince her otherwise, even as I said, "Your Grace, that's impossible. We couldn't possibly get inside. His Majesty's rooms will be too well-guarded."

Elizabeth regarded me stonily. "Maybe we should ask Master Fitzpatrick, who's slept at the foot of my brother's bed these many years. He will know how impossible it is." She turned to Barnaby. "Is there a way for me to get into Edward's apartments without being seen?"

To my disbelief, Barnaby nodded. "There's a secret passage to the bedchamber. In times past, His Majesty your late father used it. Last time I checked, the Duke hadn't set a guard there. But I must warn you, should he do so, the only way out is through the apartments and they're infested with his minions."

"I'll take my chances." Elizabeth returned her gaze to me. "Please, don't seek to detain me. If you wish to help me, do so. If not, you can meet me at the gatehouse. I must do this. I must see Edward before it is too late." She paused, faltered. "I have to say goodbye."

I felt her words tug at my soul.

Barnaby stepped forth. "I will take Your Grace." He shot me a look. "I'll see her to His Majesty's rooms and back to the gatehouse safely."

"Thank you, Barnaby." She didn't take her gaze from me. I finally conceded defeat with a sigh, lifting my own gaze past her to the palace, and the rows of glowing windows. The firework display had ended. Furtive storm clouds leaked a fragrant humidity. The festivities would reach their apex soon, with the court imbuing free claret and dancing in feverish delight in front of the morose couple ensconced on the dais. The Duke would be obligated to stand attendance, and keep close watch on the nobles, seeing as the King had not made his promised appearance to bless the nuptials. If ever there was a time to sneak into the royal apartments, this was it. Why, then, did I feel this terrible presentiment?

"Kat Astley has orders to tell anyone who asks that I'm indisposed," said Elizabeth, misinterpreting the reason for my silence. "My assorted stomach complaints and headaches are notorious, as is my temper when I am disturbed. Unless they decide to break down my bedchamber door, no one will dare intrude on me, at least not tonight."

"Not while His Majesty lives," I countered. I paused, met her eyes "Your Grace has rejected the Duke's suit. Once the King is gone, you cannot expect mercy from him."

"I never did," she replied. "You are bold, nonetheless, to remind me."

I looked to Barnaby. "Are you sure it's safe to use this passage?"

"Providing it isn't still guarded, and someone stands watch while we're inside, yes. Only the King's favorite Sidney is with Edward now. He'll not raise warning against us."

"I'll stand guard." Kate withdrew a dagger from within her cloak. I repressed immediate protest. We weren't so many that I could afford to disdain help; and we did need someone to stand watch.

I assented. "Peregrine will come with us. If all looks well, he can then proceed to the stables. Your Grace does realize your visit must be brief?"

She pulled up her hood. "Yes," she said softly.

With Kate and Peregrine flanking her, I motioned to Barnaby. "Lead the way."

We edged past the façade of the palace, a stalwart company of five, avoiding the taper light spilling from the loggias and windows. Laughter, uninhibited and slightly frenetic, tumbled from open panes.

I wondered if the Duke had been obliged at the last minute to let more courtiers into the palace. I fervently hoped so. The more distractions the Dudleys had to contend with, the more time it would give us to get in and out of Edward's rooms. Elizabeth's absence from the nuptial celebration had surely been noted. There might even be guards at her doors at this moment. Much as I disliked the thought, we had to be ready for any eventuality.

I stole a glimpse at Barnaby. If I ever found myself in a brawl, he was someone I'd want on my side.

"Barnaby," I said in a low voice. "Will you promise me something?"

"Depends on what it is."

"If something goes wrong, will you do whatever you must to see her safe?"

Barnaby's teeth gleamed. "Did you think I'd leave her to that pack of Dudley wolves? I'll see her safe all right. Or die trying. Either way, they'll never get hold of her."

We passed into an enclosed ward, fronted by the palace. An odd, derelict-looking tower rose at one end. I smelled the aroma of the river nearby, swollen and rank.

Barnaby halted. "The entrance is in that tower." He went still. I likewise came to a halt, an unspoken curse on my lips. The others also paused. In the silence, I heard Elizabeth draw a sharp breath between her teeth.

"Sentries," she whispered.

There were two of them before the tower, which squatted among Greenwich's soaring tiers like a medieval toadstool. The guards, sharing a wineskin and muttering in conversation, were not keeping an eye toward whoever might approach. They probably didn't expect anyone to approach, not on a night like this, with the Duke's son's wedding afoot. It explained why they were probably half-drunk and surly. They had been left out in the cold to watch over a doorway few knew about, while the court fattened itself on roast and frolic.

"I thought you said it was safe," I hissed at Barnaby. He grunted. "It usually is. I guess my lord the Duke isn't taking any chances. He's never had the entrance watched before."

I glanced at Elizabeth. Inside the hood of her cloak, her face was an icon, the toll of her encounter with Robert hidden within her eyes.

"There are only two," she said in response to my unvoiced question. How could I have thought she'd say anything else? "We'll have to find a way to distract them."

Before I could reply, Kate shifted to me. Her apple-tinged fragrance made me acutely aware of how much she had begun to affect me.

"I have an idea. Her Grace and I have played similar games before, albeit with a different caliber of gentlemen. But men are still men, and these two have drunk more than their share." Her pretty teeth glimmered in a wicked smile. "If you and Barnaby are amenable, I believe we can accomplish this task with a minimum of effort."

I stared, momentarily speechless. Barnaby grinned. "There's a lass." Even as I struggled for a reasonable refusal, Elizabeth tugged her hood further over her head, concealing her face. I reached for her arm, bringing her to a halt.

"Your Grace." I ignored her barbed glance at my offending fingers. "Please, think before you do this." I shot a look at Kate. "You could both end up confined."

"I have thought of it," Elizabeth said. She calmly reached down and pried my hand from her sleeve. "It is all I have thought about since I came to this miserable court. I must do this, my friend. Are you willing to see me through?"

I met her fixed stare, nodded. Kate muttered instructions, such as they were, then flipped back her hood to expose her face. With that deliberate sway, she sauntered over to the two men as they passed the skin between them.

"Time to fly, my friend," I said, and Peregrine fled into the darkness.

I gripped my blade, watched with my heart in my throat as Kate and Elizabeth neared. The sentries had come to their feet, startled, but not suspicious. The random light cast by the waning full moon, and reflections of candles in the palace's upper windows, were enough to show the intruders were only women, who had somehow wandered into these gardens.

The larger of the two men lumbered forth, a lasciviously expectant grin on his face. Kate was in the lead. Elizabeth lingered a few steps behind, her elegant stature made more pronounced by her hooded cloak. I doubted the sentries would bother to notice that the cloak's lush velvet was prohibitively costly, but should her face be revealed by some mishap I had no illusions as to whether or not she would be recognized. There couldn't be another face like hers in all England.

"Be on the ready," I told Barnaby. He bared his teeth in response.

The guard's voice carried into the night. "And what are you pretty damsels doing here?" He was already reaching out with a grubby paw to Kate, and my fist closed convulsively over my dagger hilt. Barnaby murmured, "Easy, lad, easy. Give her a moment."

Kate effortlessly evaded the man's inept grope. Cocking her hip and head in a disingenuous display, her right hand hidden within the folds of her cloak, where I knew she'd stashed her blade, she said, "My lady and I thought to escape the air of the palace. We were told there was a pavilion nearby, but alas, we seem to have lost our way."

She paused. Though I couldn't see it, I was certain she was gracing the man with one of her artful smiles. Peril not withstanding, her sheer audacity made my unwitting admiration of her only increase. She had the heart of a tigress. No wonder Elizabeth trusted her so.

"A pavilion?" The guard guffawed to his companion, who stood, gazing warily. The less drunk of the two, I thought, and therefore the one to watch. "Did you hear that, Rog? These ladies were looking for a pavilion. Ever heard of the like?"

The one called Rog didn't answer at once. I saw Elizabeth tense under her cloak, her shoulders involuntarily squaring. It wasn't so much the gesture that alerted the man as the manner in which it was done. With that one movement, she exposed herself as someone of import, unaccustomed to being questioned by menials, and Rog reacted accordingly. He strode to them, his chin thrusting forward in the universally belligerent display of men with little power.

"There's no pavilion in these parts that I'm aware of. I must ask you ladies to give us your names. This is no time to be wandering about alone." He cast a pointed stare at Elizabeth. "I would see you returned to the palace and the Hall, my lady."

Kate laughed; to my ears, she sounded taken aback. "Surely this palace poses no danger, what with all these celebrations going on. But I see we were misled. We would, welcome an escort, if you gentlemen would be so obliging."

It wasn't the plan, but she was doing what she could, trying to dissuade further questioning and secure us the cover we needed. And it would work, if she could lure them to the wall where Barnaby and I lurked at the ready. The thick shadows of the tower would serve almost as well as its interior.

Rog, however, wasn't taking the bait. He had not removed his suspicious glare from Elizabeth; and just as I felt the situation had become too volatile and that Barnaby and I would have to act, Rog suddenly, with a thrust of hand as swift as it was inescapable, yanked back the Princess's hood.

Dead quiet fell. Elizabeth's pale skin and fiery tresses glowed like a beacon. The larger guard let out a strangled gasp. "God's bones, it's—she—"

He didn't have time to finish. Kate threw herself at him, her knife raised in a blinding scything arc. Barnaby and I simultaneously rushed forward, fleet as hounds. I hadn't thought we might have to murder these two men but in the heat of the moment, with my own knife raised and readied, I understood it was exactly what our survival might require.

I reached Kate as she grappled with the guard, his fist closed about hers, fending off her knife and guffawing as he did it. Grabbing her by the shoulder, I whirled her away and slammed my own fist as hard as I could into the man's astonished face. I felt my knuckles connect with bone. The guard went down with an audible smash onto the cobblestones.

Panting, I spun around to see Barnaby dodging the sword Rog had yanked from his scabbard. Elizabeth rushed toward the tower. Even as I realized Barnaby's dagger was no match for the sword, and it was only a matter of moments before Rog delivered a lethal blow, I caught sight of a blur of movement, a swish of dark cloak. Then a long white hand came up.

I heard a wet crack. Rog stood perfectly still. His sword wavered, dropped clattering. He swayed, half-turning in disbelief to his attacker. A thin line of blood seeped down his forehead.

Then he, too, fell, face forward.

I met Elizabeth's eyes. The stone she held dropped from her fingers. A speck of blood spattered their tapered perfection. Kate ran to where the Princess stood like a statue. "Your Grace? Your Grace, are you hurt?"

Elizabeth managed a wan smile. "Scarcely. I'll wager, however, that this one will awake with a headache he won't soon forget." She paused, looked at the man sprawled at her feet. She lifted her eyes to me. As I stepped to her, Barnaby checked the man's pulse in his throat.

"He lives," Barnaby pronounced. Elizabeth's entire posture sagged. "Merciful God," she breathed. "They were only doing their duty."

"That, and a bit more, I'd say," said Kate. She pushed disheveled hair from her brow, her color high in her cheeks. "What a pair of louts! Can Northumberland find no better to do his work?"

"Let us hope not." Barnaby took the unconscious Rog by his wrists and started hauling him toward the tower doorway. I gestured to Kate. "Come, help me."

Urgency overcame us. With Kate and Elizabeth lending assistance, we dragged the larger guard through the door, into a small round room, such as might be used for storage. A rickety set of stairs spiraled up toward a concave ceiling.

We lay the guards side by side. I went back to retrieve the sword. When I returned, Barnaby was using his tunic's belt to bind the inert men's wrists together, palms facing each other. He took the handkerchief Elizabeth gave him, ripping it in half and stuffing the pieces of cloth into the men's mouths. "Not much of a hindrance if they really want out," he said, "but it should hold them otherwise."

"I'll see they don't stir." Kate took the sword from me. "If they so much as breathe too loud, I'll skewer them like a Mayfair swan."

Elizabeth had started moving to the staircase. Barnaby stopped her, "No, this way." He walked around the stairs to the seemingly solid wall. He reached down to lift a flagstone. I watched, amazed, as he pressed a concealed lever with his foot.

The wall opened in the shape of an arch before our eyes. Beyond, another narrow staircase wound upward into cobwebby gloom.

Elizabeth paused, glanced from Barnaby to me. "It's very dark."

"We can't risk any light," Barnaby said. She nodded, went to the stairs. I motioned Barnaby to follow. "I'll be right behind you."

Then I turned to Kate. "Are you sure you want to do this?" I tried to keep my tone neutral, taken aback by the concern I felt for her, which only a few minutes earlier had driven me at the guard with the intent to kill. I didn't want to leave her here, alone, where anyone might overpower her.

She gave me a teasing smile, "Are you still suspicious of me?" Before I could respond, she set a finger on my lips. "Be still. I owe you an explanation, but as you may have noticed I can use a blade for more than peeling leeks."

I had no doubt she was good as her word, and still I hesitated. No matter how well she could defend herself, she'd be no match for these two fools should they decide to break their bonds. The possibility raised unpleasant consequences.

"You're not to harm them." I looked her in the eye. "They're the Duke's men. The punishment would be severe. If it comes to that, run. Make your escape. Find Peregrine and meet us on the road. We'll find another way to get her out." I paused. "Promise me."

"That's most gallant of you. But I fear this is no time for doubt. Go. You've more important things to fret about."

Bowing my head, I turned away and moved into the suffocating darkness.

The passage containing the secret staircase was impossibly narrow, the ceiling angled low, barely high enough to accommodate a child. With my knees bent and shoulders hunched, my hair brushing cold stone, I wondered how the enormous Henry VIII had ever navigated it. An unwitting gasp escaped me as the sense of space behind me was cut off. Kate had depressed the lever and closed the false wall.

I started up the steps, though it was more like moving up a tunnel. My eyes gradually adjusted to the gloom. Rats perched on the steps, eyeing me without any fear.

I came up behind Elizabeth and Barnaby on a landing. We resumed the climb single-file, losing sight of the other at each turn in the pike, the clammy air wringing sweat from our brows.

We reached a third story. A small wooden door was visible in the wall to our left. Barnaby paused here. "Before we go in, Your Grace should know that His Majesty is not the prince we knew. The illness and the treatments have taken a terrible toll."

"I understand," she said, and she edged closer to me as Barnaby rapped on the door.

In the hush, Elizabeth inhaled a stifled breath.

Barnaby rapped again. I gripped my dirk.

The door cracked open. A sliver of light cut across our feet.

"Who goes there?" stammered a frightened, hushed voice.

"Sidney, it's me," whispered Barnaby. "Quick. Open up."

The door swung inward, a covert entry masked by the wainscoting of a small, well-appointed chamber. The first thing that struck me was the heat. It was stifling, emanating from scented braziers set in the corners, from the fire burning in the recessed hearth, and from the tripod of candelabra illuminating the scarlet and gold upholstery of the chairs, the curtains at the alcove, and the damask hangings shrouding a tester bed.

A young man with lank blonde hair faced Barnaby, his fine features haggard with fatigue. "What are you doing here? You know his lordship ordered you away. You must go." The young man's protest choked. His blue eyes went wide.

Elizabeth stepped around Barnaby and cast back her cowl. "Henry Sidney, I have come to see my brother. Where is he?"

I was behind her. Beyond the breath-quenching heat I detected another smell in the air— something faint, fetid, scarcely masked by the medicinal fumes from the brazier.

Elizabeth noticed it, too. "God's teeth," she murmured, as Sidney dropped to his knees. She stepped past him. "There's no time for that," she said faintly, moving to the bed. On a crosshatch a falcon watched her, its ankle tethered, candle flames reflected in its opaque pupils.

"Edward?" she whispered. She reached out. "Edward, it's me." She parted the hangings. A hand flew up to cover her mouth. She gagged, staggered back.

I rushed to her side. When I saw what she stared at, I went still.

The stench I had detected in the room came from an unrecognizable figure lying supine on the bed, the flesh of its emaciated legs and arms blackened, festering with sores. Propped on the pillows like a decaying marionette, only the rise and fall of his chest indicated the King's heart still beat. I could not believe anyone in such a state could be conscious.

Then Edward VI's gray-blue eyes opened, and I saw in his anguished gaze that he was fully aware of his own torment, and that his sister stood before him. He opened bruised lips, struggled to mouth unintelligible words.

Sidney hastened to his side. "He can't speak," he told Elizabeth. She did not move, her face pared to transparency.

"What is he trying to say?" she whispered.

Sidney leaned close to his royal master's mouth. Edward's talon-like fingers gripped his wrist. Sidney looked up sorrowfully. "He begs your forgiveness."

"My forgiveness?" Her hand crept to her throat. "Blessed Jesus, it is I who should beg his. I wasn't here. I didn't stop them from doing this to him."

"He is beyond such concerns," said Sidney. "He needs you to forgive him. He had no power to gainsay the Duke. I know. I've seen everything that transpired between them."

"What— what do you speak of?"

"Of the choice, Your Grace, the terrible choice they forced on him. He was beset with fevers. He knew his end was near and he had made his peace with it. He'd also made his decision about who must succeed him. But then the Duke brought him here and ordered his physicians dismissed. He was at him night and day, without respite. His Majesty signed in desperation, because he could abide no more, because they had promised him relief."

"He was forced to sign something?" Elizabeth's anger flared. "What? What did they make him sign?"

Sidney averted his eyes. "A Device," he said, "naming the Lady Jane Grey as heir. The Duke made him disavow your and the Lady Mary's claim. He made him," Sidney's voice lowered to a whisper, "declare you both bastards."

Elizabeth's entire countenance darkened. She whirled about, took a furious step toward the apartments' main door, as if she intended to confront the Duke then and there. "Your Grace," I warned. She paused where she stood. "What now?" she asked, her voice taut.

"Listen." I moved in front of her.

The dragging sound grew steadily louder, coming closer and closer. As Barnaby leapt to the wall by the door, I drew Elizabeth behind the alcove curtains. I shielded her with my body, the dirk in my hand feeling suddenly like a toy. I tightened my hold on it, watched the door open.

A stunted woman limped in. Her ankles contorted inward, displaying livid scars.

She paused in the center of the room.

"It's only the herbalist," Sidney gasped, in relief. Barnaby sagged against the wall.

I looked close.

And felt my entire world keel.

I emerged from behind the curtains. I knew it without needing to ask a single thing, like a nail driving in my heart. All the blood in my veins seemed to empty. I saw no recognition in the withered face framed by its old-fashioned wimple—a leathery shrunken face, lashed by crevices. Even as I paused, suddenly, horribly, doubting, the scent of rosemary, of my childhood, overcame me.

He has someone to care for him. She came here to fetch one of his spaniels.

I regarded her for an endless moment. Her eyes were bovine in their resignation. I raised a trembling hand to her cheek, fingers poised over desiccated flesh. I was terrified of touching her, as if she were a mirage that might dissolve to dust at my feet. My heart hammered in my ears. If I hadn't known it was true, I would never have believed this was happening. Not now. Not here.

Not after all these haunted years.

Behind me Elizabeth whispered, "Do you know her?"

And I heard myself say, "Her name is Dame Alice. She . . . she cared for me when I was a child. I was told she was dead."

Silence ensued. Barnaby shut the door and planted himself in front of it.

I couldn't tear my eyes from her, couldn't reconcile this aged, brittle figure with the quick-witted matron enshrined in my memory. She'd always been spry, fleet of word and gesture, and her eyes had been discerning, bright and merry, not these sunken hollow orbs.

She had left Warwickshire on a trip to Stratford, as she did every year. A day to come and go, she'd said. *Don't fret, my pet. I'll be back before you know it.* But she hadn't come back. Thieves had beset her on the road. Master Shelton told me. I didn't weep, didn't ask to see her or where her body lay. The pain was too deep. It hadn't mattered. She was gone. She was gone and she would never return to me. That's what I'd been told. That's what I believed. I was twelve years old and bereft of the one person in the world who had loved me. Her loss became an incurable wound I hid within. Now, the question burned inside me, building with the force of an eruption.

Why? Why did you leave me?

But as I took in her appearance, I knew the answer.

Those scars on her ankles, I'd seen much the same on horses and mules condemned by unfeeling masters to a lifetime of hobbling about with an iron manacle.

I let my hand trail to her jaw, as I might soothe a frightened mare. Like a mare she understood. She opened her lips. Her mouth was dark inside. Defiled.

They had cut out her tongue.

A scream curdled in my throat. I choked it back as I heard Elizabeth say, "Would someone please tell me who this woman is and what she is doing in my brother's room?"

From the bed Sidney replied, "Lady Dudley, she brought her here to tend His Majesty. He was in terrible pain, and . . . her treatments seem to help him. She mixes draughts. I think. . ."

"What?" Elizabeth snapped. "Spit it out, man. What do you think?"

"She's helping His Majesty die," I said quietly. "Dame Alice is a master herbalist. She cured me of many illnesses in my childhood."

Elizabeth pointed at her brother. "You mean to tell me this horror is her doing?"

Dame Alice's misshapen hand tugged at my jerkin. I looked into her eyes. The lump in my chest turned molten. Barnaby acknowledged my warning glance as I turned to where Elizabeth stood.

"She didn't cause his illness. By the color of His Majesty's skin, I believe he's been given tiny doses of arsenic. I know something of this. Arsenic can prolong life for a time, but will cause intense suffering. The Duke must have ordered it done, to keep His Majesty alive, and gain the time he needed to set his plans in motion."

Elizabeth was staring at me, her eyes black in their scrutiny, impenetrable.

"Dame Alice would never have done it willingly," I added, a catch in my throat. "She has always revered life. She's trying to put an end to it, probably through a powerful narcotic, an opiate of some kind. His Majesty will die. Your Grace cannot do anything to save him."

She hissed, "I won't leave him to die. Get him out of that bed. He comes with us."

"I'm afraid I can't do that," I said, and she took one look at my face and stiffened. "Your Grace," I said, "we really must go. We have run out of time."

She glanced at Barnaby. Her hand crept to her throat. "I don't hear anything," she said, and I answered, "Neither do I. But Dame Alice

143

does. Look at her."

Elizabeth did. Dame Alice had shuffled to the secret door and was motioning to us with unmistakable agitation. Her hands, I saw, were unbearably twisted, like a hundred-year old crone's. Whatever tortures she had endured had stolen years from her life. She was not yet fifty.

I swallowed against the barb in my throat, returned my attention to Elizabeth. She met my stare. Then she turned away and made for the door without a backward glance.

Barnaby followed behind. Sidney bolted to a coffer and flung open the lid. He yanked out a jeweled-hilted sword sheathed in leather, tossed it to me. "Edward has no need of this anymore. It's of the finest Toledo steel, a gift from the Imperial ambassador. I'll try and delay them while you get away."

I caught the sword in mid-air. I knew instantly from the feel that it had been fashioned for someone light of build and weight. I could never have bought such a sword on my own.

Dame Alice started purposefully to the bed. "See that Her Grace gets out safe," I ordered Barnaby and I kicked the secret door shut in his face. Sidney was at the main door. He froze. "Where are you going? They're here!"

I moved to where Dame Alice hunched at the bedside table, rummaging through a wooden chest— her medicine chest, which she'd stashed on the kitchen shelf, out of my reach. She had always taken it with her, even when she traveled.

Nothing in there for a big-eyed curious lad; no secrets for him to see . . .

She turned, gazed at me as if she were seeing me for the first time. Tears leapt in my eyes as I felt her take my hand. With quivering, gnarled fingers, she set something wrapped in thin cloth in my palm. She folded my fingers over it. I was captivated by the tenderness that came over her face then, as if she had at long last found redemption.

Then the door opened and Sidney was thrust back.

With her offering in one fist, and the sword in the other, I pivoted to meet my past.

CHAPTER NINETEEN

She wore a court gown the hue of armor. Of all those who might have entered through the door, she was the last person I had expected to see, though it made perfect sense that it should be her. Behind her came Archie Shelton, his scarred face impassive. At the sight of him, I had to stop myself from vaulting forward in fury.

There were voices in the antechamber. "Wait until I call for you," she said over her shoulder, and Master Shelton closed the door. I registered Sidney's slow retreat out of the corner of my eye. At my back Dame Alice had gone still. I outstretched an arm as if to shield her, even as I recognized how futile the gesture was.

"I see you failed to heed the one cardinal rule of the loyal servant," said Lady Dudley. She regarded me without a hint of surprise in her cold stare. "You failed to recognize your proper place." She glanced at the panel in the wainscoting that concealed the secret door. "How clever of you to find that entrance, and how daring." Her voice hardened. "Where is she?"

Aware that Barnaby and Kate must be rushing Elizabeth to the gate where Peregrine waited with the horses, I said carefully, "I came alone. I wanted to find out for myself." I met her eyes. "Why? Why have you done this?"

Her aristocratic features twisted. "You know why. So does that red-haired harlot you brought here with you. It will serve her nothing to flee. No matter where she goes, we will find her. She'll lose that feckless head of hers just like her mother before her."

She motioned. "Move away from the bed. Oh, and drop that—sword, is it?" She laughed coldly. "My son Henry and our retainers are outside, eager for better sport than toasting Guilford's fortune in the Grey virgin's bed. One word from me and they'll flay you alive."

I threw the sword onto the rug between us and took a step forward. I didn't deign Master Shelton with a glance. The steward stood before the door, in the same stance Barnaby had affected, powerful arms folded across his barrel chest.

Bastard. I hated him in that moment as I had never hated anyone in my life, as if it were venom in my blood, poisoning my breath. That he could have participated in such a horrific deed, stood by as they stole Dame Alice away, feigning to care about my future even as he lied to me all these years.

I wanted to kill him with my bare hands.

If she had remembered how, Lady Dudley would have smiled. "Dame Alice, you can mix His Majesty's draught now. It is time we relieved him once and for all of his torment."

Dame Alice began to remove dried herbs from the chest.

I found it almost impossible to maintain calm. *She* had done it, all of it. She had mutilated Dame Alice and set her to poisoning the King. She had always been efficient, whether she was organizing her household or ordering the autumn slaughter of the pigs. Why should this have been any different? Understanding now what had been kept hidden from me all these years, I marveled at how I could have missed it, how I had failed to sense the ghastly deception.

It had been Lady Dudley who had schemed to provide the kingdom with an alternative heir to the two Tudor princesses. Implacable and relentless, she had woven a web aimed at exalting her favorite son, and had used everything at her disposal. She'd even divined a weakness in the Duchess of Suffolk's past and made a devil's pact to one end, and one end only—preserve the Dudley power.

The Duke had repaid her in false coin. He had gone along with her plans, even as he in turn contrived to take Elizabeth for himself. But Lady Dudley had found out. She had discovered the truth. What else did she know? What else had she hidden, all these years?

As if she could read my thoughts, her bloodless lips curved. "Twenty years. That's how long it's been since you came into our lives. You were always too clever for your own good. Not even the Duchess's ploys could finish you off. Perhaps I should keep you alive a while longer, in case she reneges on her promise. I still need her compliance until Jane is declared queen. She thinks you dead now. I let her have you that night in the Hall, but I could use you again."

Sweat broke out on my brow, and in my fist clutching the piece of cloth. Without betraying my spiraling fear, knowing my life was at stake, I said, "I might prove even more useful if your ladyship told me everything. I do have questions."

Her plucked brow lifted a fraction. "Questions?"

"Yes." My chest felt tight, as if I were short of breath. "I was brought here for a purpose, was I not? At Whitehall, your ladyship told the Duchess I bore the mark of the rose."

"You heard that, did you? I hadn't known you counted a fluency in French among your talents. Interesting."

The sweat trickled down my face, pooled in the hollow of my throat. The salt stung the bruises on my cheeks. "I taught myself," I told her. "I am clever, yes. If I knew who it is she thinks I am, I could further the game. I'm amenable to an arrangement that will serve us both."

It was a pathetic deceit, born of desperation. Her startling laugh showed as much. "Would you, indeed? I must say, you're not as clever as I'd supposed. Did you think I'd be stupid enough to trust you, after I know you've joined forces with Anne Boleyn's whelp and her lackey Cecil? But you have solved my dilemma. Shelton, watch him while I see to His Majesty."

She glided past me to the bed. I stealthily tucked the cloth into my tunic pocket, pushed it down against the inside seam as I braved a glance at the steward. Master Shelton avoided any eye contact, his eyes fixed on an unseen spot. It seemed strange that for someone as attentive as he usually was, he didn't notice Sidney shifting away from the alcove where he had retreated.

In his wake, the curtains stirred.

I turned my attention to the bed. Dame Alice had finished mixing the herbs in a goblet. Edward didn't stir, didn't lift protest as Lady Dudley reached down to smooth his coverlets and rearrange his pillows. He stared fixedly at her through his pain-laced eyes as she took the goblet from Dame Alice and, with one hand under his head, propped him up.

"Drink," she commanded, as if she offered a remedy for a cold, and Edward did. She smiled. "Now, Your Majesty can rest. Rest and dream of angels."

His eyes closed. He seemed to melt into his pillows. Turning away, Lady Dudley set the goblet on the bedside table and reached into the chest. She brought up something, made a sudden movement. Steel slashed. There was no sound. A gush of scarlet sprayed from Dame Alice's breast, splattering the carpet and the bed. Still without a sound, before my horrified eyes, my sweet nurse and friend, crumpled to the floor.

"Nooo!" The wail erupted from me like an animal's wounded howl. I sprang forth. Master Shelton rushed me, seizing my left arm and yanking it behind my back. My cry was cut short, the pain searing.

"I told you not to meddle," the steward hissed in my ear. "I warned you. Now, be still, lad. You cannot stop it."

I panted in helpless rage, watching, paralyzed, as Lady Dudley dropped the bloodied scissors and stepped over Dame Alice's convulsing body.

"Kill him," she ordered Master Shelton.

I kicked back with all my strength. I felt my heel slam into the steward's shin, and rammed my elbow into his chest. It was like hitting a granite wall, yet with a surprised grunt, Master Shelton released me.

Sidney scooped up the sword and thrust it at me as I dove for the alcove curtains, where a draft now blew. I heard Lady Dudley cry out, heard the door open, heard furious shouting, but I didn't pause to see how many were coming after me.

Something whined and popped. I ducked as the ball flew past and embedded itself in the wall. Someone, perhaps one of the Dudley retainers with Henry, had a firearm. The weapon was costly, and difficult to manage. I knew it would take a good half a minute to re-load and ignite the matchlock. That was all the time I had.

I leapt onto the windowsill, squeezed through the open window. With sword in hand, and my heart in my throat, I dropped into the night.

I hit the stone leads of the story below with teeth-rattling impact. The sword flew from my hand, clattering off the edge into the courtyard below. Sprawled out, my head reeling, the agony was so intense I feared I had shattered both my legs. Then I realized I could move, despite the pain, and glanced up to the window through which I'd just leapt, in time to see a long-nosed hand-pistol belch smoke.

I rolled. A ball struck the spot where I'd lain, and ricocheted against the palace wall.

"A pox on it," I heard Henry Dudley curse. "I missed him! Don't worry. I'll get him yet."

The pistol disappeared for reloading. I forced myself upright. Standing as flat against the wall as I could, I looked to either side. I felt a sickening drop in my bowels. The leads weren't leads at all. Instead of a walkway, there was an extended parapet with a decorative balustrade, punctuated by stucco nymphs and running parallel with an indoor gallery. At the far end I could see a mullioned casement. At any moment someone above me would realize the same and race downstairs to finish me off.

I made myself not think of what else I had left above, of Dame Alice's life's blood staining the floor of that room of horrors.

To the left was the moldering roof of the tower housing the secret staircase. To the right ran a fluid expanse. I began edging in the direction of the casement, away from the light spilling from the window above. I didn't know much about firearms but Master Shelton did, having served in the wars. He had told me they were a primitive weapon, infamous for not igniting when lit, for missing targets despite perfect aim, and backfiring due to poorly packed powder. It was too much to hope that Henry might blow his own face off, but for the time being, instinct urged me to put as much distance between us as I could.

Instinct proved correct. I froze as the pistol fired again. This time Henry displayed remarkably improved marksmanship, the ball spraying grotesquerie above my shoulder. Not until I felt the warm trickle of blood did I realize the ball had grazed me as well.

"I think you got him!" Henry guffawed. Someone else had fired the shot. I continued my precarious advance. My escape must have addled their wits. I was surprised whoever had the gun hadn't realized they could just as easily, and far more effectively, shoot at me from the gallery.

The pistol was pulled back. I quickened my step, nearing the casement. I prayed there wouldn't be shutters, locks, small leaded panes I couldn't smash. Between the pain in my legs and the throbbing in my shoulder, I was starting to feel faint. Another pop came, the ball razing the air above my head.

I struggled forward, at one with the wall.

All of a sudden, the casement swung open. I halted, my blood icing over as I saw a figure step onto the parapet with feline stealth. It paused as the shot rang out and pinged a nymph, sending plaster flying. It turned. In the moonlight, I caught the gleam of eyes.

Then the figure started moving. Toward me.

My entire being clamored warning, even as I stood transfixed by the sight of the man approaching me in complete disregard for his own safety.

Two distinct impressions went through me in those crucial seconds. The first was that he moved as if he'd been tripping over rooftops all his life. The second was either he'd come to finish the job the Dudleys seemed unable to do, or he sought to rescue me.

When I spied the curved blade in his gloved hand, I knew I couldn't wait to find out. Hopefully I had come close enough. If not, I wasn't likely to regret my error.

I sprang forth, with all the strength I had left.

And leapt over the leads into nothingness.

CHAPTER TWENTY

I plunged into the river. The water was like slate, pummeling the air from my lungs in a single, terrifying moment. I gasped, flailing to the surface. The brackish taste of salt mixed with dregs and mud clogged my nostrils, my throat, my ears. I coughed it out like bile, trying to gain control of my floundering body.

The river flowed all around me, a swift liquid passage flooded by the tidal influx, its inky back littered with branches, leaves, and the bloated corpse of a drowned animal, bobbing and sinking and resurfacing. Caught up in the current, I was like so much flotsam, dragged along while I struggled to stay above water.

My left shoulder had gone numb, as had my arm. Gazing upward at the dwindling palace, I envisioned my would-be assassin staring in disbelief. I also understood just how far a leap I'd taken. It was amazing I had survived at all.

I was beginning to develop a definite aversion to water.

I struggled to swim toward a distant cluster of trees on a shore, evading the putrid corpse. I couldn't ignore how dire my situation had become. I'd been shot, or at least, skimmed by a ball, and must be losing blood. The cold had also begun to congeal in my lungs, making it difficult to breathe and move at the same time. Even while my heart and head roared defiance, somewhere deep within, in that dead dark place where nothing has consequence, I wanted to stop, go completely still, drift and let it all pass.

The shore wavered before me, distant as the desert. Submerged in what now felt like an icy, suffocating cocoon, I stared toward it with faltering eyes, my arms inexorably ceasing their futile movements. In a rush of panic, I thrashed my legs, seeking to quicken my blood. Nothing moved. Or I didn't feel anything move. I kicked again, in desperation. There was something twined about my ankles.

"No," I heard myself whisper. "Not like this. Please, God. No."

It seemed as if an eternity passed. Then, as I tried to bring my legs up to my unfeeling hands and untangle whatever had wrapped about me, I noticed I was feeling better. A strange warmth welled under my skin. The cold had ceased its stinging assault.

I sighed. It was just a skein of riverweed, or an old rope . . .

That was the last thing I thought before the water closed over my head.

Rain, intermixed with what sounded like fistfuls of gravel being flung against a rooftop, was the first sound I heard, the first sound that told me I was, miraculously, somehow still alive.

Cracking open a grit-sealed eye, I tried to raise my head. The pounding in my temples, and nauseous wave of dizziness told me I'd best stay put.

After the spinning in my head started to ebb, I tentatively lifted the sheet covering me. I appeared intact, though my torso was a mass of contusions. I was dressed in a linen undergarment, my bruised chest bare. When I tried to move my left arm, a sharp pain coursed through my bandaged shoulder. I looked up. I was in an unfamiliar room, submerged in gloom. Sprawled in slumber across the rushes near the bed was a silver beast.

"Some watch dog," I muttered.

As I drifted back into sleep I thought the dog looked remarkably like Elizabeth's.

When I next awoke I didn't know if it was hours or days later. Delicate sunlight drifted in shafts throughout the room. The dog was gone. I also found, to my relief, I was both less stiff and sensitive, and could in fact sit up, albeit with much clumsy maneuvering. Easing a pillow under my head, I reclined against the daub wall and prodded my wounded shoulder. It was still tender to the touch. Oily salve seeped through the linen bandage. In addition to tending to my obvious bodily functions, someone had taken the time to dress and treat my injury.

Lying on the bed as the afternoon faded into dusk, I glanced from the room's door to the half-shuttered window. I heard water dripping from gutters. The slant in the ceiling led me to deduce I was lodged in a garret. I wondered when whoever had brought me here would make his or her appearance. I could recall plummeting through an airless abyss, the crash into black water. I even had a faint recollection of trying to stay afloat, and of swimming for a time against a sweeping current. After that, there was nothing. I had no idea how I'd ended up here.

My eyelids started to droop. I blinked. I couldn't be certain what I'd find upon awakening. Despite my best efforts, I slipped off again, only to be jolted awake by the creaking of the door. I struggled upright, wincing. When I saw the figure who walked in, bearing a tray, my entire being quickened.

"I'm pleased to see you up."

I could only stare in astonishment as she pulled up a stool by the bed and set the tray beside it. She wore a russet gown laced over a chemise. Tendrils of lustrous hair curled about her face. I couldn't believe how, given my state, my loins could still react with such vigor to her proximity.

She uncovered the tray, releasing the aroma of hot bread and soup.

Water flooded my mouth. "God," I said, in a hoarse voice. "I'm starving."

"You should be." Kate unfolded a napkin and leaned over to tie it about my neck. "You've been lying here for three days. I feared you might sleep forever."

Three days.

I averted my eyes. I wasn't ready yet to delve into everything that had transpired.

"And you've been here," I ventured, "all this time, caring for me?"

She broke the bread in chunks over the soup, ladled a spoon, and cooled it with her breath before lifting it to my lips. "You needn't fret. You haven't anything I haven't seen before."

Was I so bruised then, that the birthmark on my hip had gone unnoticed? Or was she simply being tactful? A closer look at her expression didn't reveal anything, and I was too flustered at the moment to ask.

"This soup is delicious," I said.

"Don't change the subject." She narrowed her gaze. "What on earth possessed you to stay behind in that room, when you could have followed Her Grace and Barnaby? I'll have you know we risked our own lives waiting for you at the gate. Her Grace refused to budge. She kept saying you'd arrive at any moment, that you knew the woman attending His Majesty and had tarried to question her. It was only when we heard gunshots, and saw the Duke's retainers start coming out from every doorway, that she agreed to leave. She wasn't happy about it, though. She said it was nothing less than craven of us to abandon you."

"But she did go? She's safe now at her manor?"

Kate refilled the spoon. "Safe is a relative term. Yes, it's been given out that she's at Hatfield, where she's taken to her bed with a fever. Illness can be a useful deterrent at times like these. Of course, so can the cellars of numerous neighboring houses in Hatfield's vicinity, any one of which would gladly shelter a princess should the Duke's men be spotted on the road."

"And you?" I asked, guarding my tone so as to not reveal my interest in her reasons for being here. "How is it you're not with her?"

"I stayed with Peregrine, of course. He insisted we look for you."

"Peregrine found me?"

"He did, on the riverbank. He told us he used to fish the Thames for bodies." Kate paused. A slight tremor crept into her voice. "He said we had to keep searching, regardless. And he was right. You'd been swept downstream by the high tide and washed up near where the river bends to London. You were soaked through, wounded, and delirious. But you were alive."

"And you nursed me back to health," I said, and I heard the lack of gratitude in my voice. It had become second nature to me to doubt even my good fortune. "May I ask, why? After all, you did lie to me about not working for Cecil, did you not? Why would you care if I lived or died, so long as your master's orders were fulfilled?"

Her lips pursed. She set down the spoon, reached over and removed the napkin. She dabbed my mouth and chin clean. When she finally spoke, her voice was composed.

"I didn't tell you the entire truth, and for that I apologize. But I never meant to put you in danger. My loyalty is with Her Grace, though she can be far too headstrong, and often needs protection, whether or not she cares to admit it. When Walsingham told me Master Cecil felt it best if we got her far from Greenwich, I agreed to help. I didn't tell you because he said you had your instructions. You were to deliver the missive, which I would intercept, and return to Lord Robert. He said you had been paid. I didn't expect to see you again."

I observed her face as she talked and saw only sincerity. I also realized she must care for me to have stayed here, perhaps even as much as I cared for her. But as I willed myself to recall the events of the past days, an implacable pain and anger rose in me. I wasn't prepared for the complications she presented, for the vulnerabilities and potential heartache. Falling in love, in truth, had never been a part of my plan.

Suddenly I burned with the need to push her away, to make her dislike and forget me.

"Walsingham did give me instructions, yes," I said. "And I was certainly paid." My words were cold, unyielding. "But I also knew that allowing Her Grace to go ahead with her insane plan to meet with Lord Robert could put her in more danger than she incurred already. I'm surprised no one else seems to have shared my concern."

"What would you have had us do?" If she had detected the deliberate harshness in my manner, she didn't let it show. "Her Grace insisted on questioning Robert about her brother and wouldn't hear anything to the contrary. None of us could have known the Duke intended to woo her himself, or put Jane Grey on the throne if she refused him."

It did make sense. How could they have known? I had to rest my suspicions, at least as far as Kate was concerned. She had not been involved in plotting harm against the Princess.

"I suppose the horses were on the road, then," I said, "just like Walsingham said?"

"Yes." She raised gentle eyes to me. "Of course they were, gallant squire."

She plucked a chord in me, much as a hand plays a lute. In a ham-handed attempt to hide my discomfort I said the first thing that came into my head. "It's not fair to insult someone you've seen without their clothes on."

She laughed. "You've managed well enough thus far."

I wanted to embrace her and weep at the same time. In some ways, she reminded me of Dame Alice, of the garnet-cheeked, honest girl that she, too, must have been. And as I thought of this, I saw again the look in Dame Alice's haunted eyes when she'd turned to me by the King's bed, the sense of triumph in her regard. She had been trying to impart something to me, something precious. But what? I would never know now.

I met Kate's gaze. "I thought I was going to die on that parapet," I said quietly. "I thought that fiend Henry Dudley would shoot me." I faltered. Suspicion and fear surged again in me, like a torrent, without warning, inundating me in darkness.

"Where are we?" I asked in a taut whisper.

"In a manor, not far from Greenwich town. Why?"

"Whose manor? Who is here with us?"

Kate frowned. "Her Grace owns the deed, privately; but the house is leased to a friend. Besides Peregrine, you and me, Walsingham comes and goes. He was here earlier, in fact, wanting to know how you— Brendan, what is it? What ails you?"

I hadn't realized I had recoiled, until I saw the hurt on her face. "That's who I saw on the leads. Walsingham. He had a dagger. That's why I jumped. I remember it now. Cecil arranged Her Grace's escape, but he wanted me dead. He sent Walsingham to kill me."

To her credit, Kate didn't lift protest, didn't attempt to reassure. In a level voice she said, "Walsingham was there to help you. We would never have known where to look had he not told us he'd seen you jump from the leads into the river. He even fetched your sword from where it had fallen into the courtyard."

"Maybe he thought he had no other choice," I countered angrily. "The sword was evidence I had been in the King's rooms, and I might survive the fall, as I did."

"You still wouldn't have been found. Brendan, the current washed you downstream. You had a wounded shoulder. There was rope and riverweeds wrapped about your legs. By all rights, you should have drowned." She paused. "Cecil entrusted Walsingham with your welfare. He's been watching over you the entire time. That's why he ended up on those leads. When we failed to show up at the postern gate, he followed our trail."

I let out a harsh chuckle. "I wonder where he was when the Duchess of Suffolk and her henchman locked me in an underground cell and left me to drown." Yet even as I spoke I thought of my jerkin, which I'd left by the pavilion and had inexplicably materialized near the ruined cloister entrance, where Peregrine found it. What had the boy said?

If we hadn't happened to find your jerkin, we'd never have thought to look.

"Peregrine told us about that," said Kate. "At the time you were taken, Walsingham was readying the horses we never took. Surely, you can't fault him?"

"Not unless you take into account that everyone I've met at court, not to mention everyone I've known since childhood, has proven me false," I retorted. The instant the words were out, I regretted it. Kate bit her lip. "I'm sorry," she murmured. She stood.

I caught hold of her hand. "No, Kate. I'm the one who must apologize. I didn't mean it."

She looked down at our twined hands, lifted her gaze back to me. "Yes, you did." She unhooked her fingers. "I understand. That woman in the King's room . . . Barnaby said she was an herbalist brought by the Dudleys to poison His Majesty. He said you knew her, and they had lied to you about her death. How could you not be angry?"

My throat knotted. I looked away, tears burning in my eyes. I didn't see Kate reach into her pocket, only felt her set something into my limp hand. When I saw what it was, I went still.

"I thought you might want it," she said. "I found it in your jerkin pocket. I took the liberty of polishing it. It's a strange thing, but pretty." She took up the tray, went to the door. "I'll be back in a few hours with your supper. Try to get some rest."

The door clicked shut.

I gazed at the delicate gift Dame Alice had given me. It was an ornamental gold petal, its jagged edge indicating it had once formed part of a larger jewel. On its tip, set there like a perfect dewdrop, was a ruby. I had never seen anything like it before. It was the last thing I would have expected her to possess.

I enclosed it in my hand and stared forward sightlessly, as dusk faded into night.

When the grief finally came to claim me, I did not try to fight it.

CHAPTER TWENTY-ONE

K ate returned as promised, with a bundle of clothes under one arm and her tray heaped with meat in trenchers and sauced vegetables. Peregrine tripped at her side, bright-eyed and grinning. He carried a folded table. After he set up, he left and returned with my saddlebag, and, to my surprise, the King's sheathed sword, which I'd last seen clattering off the leads at Greenwich. I immediately opened the bag and examined its jumbled contents. I sighed in relief when I found the stolen psalm book still there.

I turned my attention to Kate. She had changed into a rose velvet gown that enhanced the muted gold in her hair. As she busied herself setting the table and lighting candles about the room, I became aware of a longing to draw her into my arms and caress away the last of my lingering mistrust. But Peregrine demanded all my attention, dancing about like a precocious imp, Elizabeth's silvery hound at his heels.

"You look rather pleased with yourself," I told Peregrine as he helped me to my feet and manipulated my uncooperative limbs into a robe. "If I'm not mistaken, isn't that my sword and Her Grace's hound? Have you been stealing again?"

"I have not," he replied. "Master Walsingham said he found the sword. And Her Grace left Urian here with us, so we could track you. He's the best tracker in her kennels, she said. She knows her beasts. He was the first to smell you on the riverbank." He paused, his nose crimping. "What is it with you and water? You've done nothing but get wet since we met."

I burst out laughing. It felt wonderful, and unfamiliar. I took Peregrine's hand, made my slow but steady way to the makeshift dinner table. "Unrepentant as always," I said, easing onto a stool. "I'm glad of you, my friend." I looked at Kate. "And of you. I thank God for both of you. You saved my life. It's a debt I can never repay."

The brightness in Kate's eyes might have been tears. She brushed them aside with her sleeve, and Peregrine perched next to me as she started to serve.

"I'm not helpless," I said as Peregrine handed me my plate. "I can feed myself."

Kate wagged her finger. "He's not there to feed you. You've had quite enough pampering, I'd say. Peregrine, either you tell that dog to get its paws off the table this instant or you can both go eat in the kitchens."

Amid laughter and candlelight, we dined and spoke of innocuous matters. Only after we'd wiped up the last of the sauce with our bread, and Peregrine had recounted how he and Barnaby employed Urian's olfactory skills to track me, did I breach our camaraderie.

Leaning back with a sigh, I said as casually as I could: "And where is Fitzpatrick?"

The rustle of Kate's skirts as she stood emphasized the sudden silence. She began stacking the empty platters. Peregrine reached down to caress Urian.

"Well, don't all tell me at once." I glanced at Kate, who didn't return my searching look. A subsequent glance at Peregrine confirmed what I already knew.

"The King is dead, isn't he?"

Kate paused. Peregrine said, "It's not been officially announced yet, but Master Walsingham told us that Edward died yesterday. Barnaby returned to court as soon as we found you, to be at his side." He added sadly, "It's said that at the hour of his death, Heaven wept."

The rain. I had heard it.

As the memory of that sixteen year-old youth rotting away in a fetid room surfaced in me, my gaze went to the sword on the bed.

My voice tightened. "And the herbalist? Did Walsingham say anything about her?"

Kate said quickly, "Brendan, please, let it be. It's too soon. You're still weak."

"No." I raised my eyes to hers. "I want to know. I need to know."

"Then I will tell you." She drew in a deep breath and came to sit at my side. Her hand set on mine. "She is dead. Sidney told Walsingham. Someone took her body away. No one knows where. The Dudleys threatened to kill Sidney, as well, for helping you, but by then word had gotten out that Elizabeth had escaped and the palace was in an uproar."

I came to my feet. Resisting the dizziness that came over me, I paced to the window and stared out into the night. My stalwart Dame Alice was dead and gone forever this time. Lady Dudley had slashed her open as if she'd been some barnyard beast. I couldn't think of it. It would drive me insane.

"What about Jane Grey?" I asked at length. "Has she been declared queen?"

"Not yet. But the Duke has removed her and Guilford to London. And there are rumors he will send men after the Lady Mary."

"I thought he already had. I thought he sent Lord Robert after her."

"It seems he decided to delay. We think that after he discovered Elizabeth had fled Greenwich, he wanted first and foremost to get Lady Jane somewhere safe, in case someone came and stole her away. She is all he has now."

She didn't try to pacify the situation with false assurances, which I appreciated. At a gesture from her, Peregrine said good night and exited the room, Urian padding behind.

Kate and I faced each other from across the room. Then she stood and turned to pick up the tray. "We'll talk about this tomorrow," she said. "Until then, it can wait."

I stepped to her. "I agree. Only . . . don't leave." My voice broke. "Please."

She came to where I stood, helpless as a child, and touched her hand to my bearded cheek. "It's so red," she said. "And thick. I wouldn't have thought you'd have such a rich beard."

"And I," I told her, "would never have thought you'd care."

She regarded me steadily. "Neither did I. But there you have it."

I brought her to me, held her close as though I might meld her to me forever.

"I've never done this before," I murmured.

"Never?" She raised her eyes to me in genuine surprise.

"No," I answered. "I've only ever loved one woman. But not as I would love you." I stroked her cheek. "Are you free, to love me, that is?"

She smiled. "Suitors have been begging for my hand since I was a babe."

"Then you may add my name to the list." The words did not disconcert me as much as I would have supposed, seeing that I'd never given thought to marriage before. It seemed the most natural thing in the world; and so I added, "Once I've earned enough to buy a parcel of land and build you a proper house, I would like to make you my wife."

She stared into my eyes. "Must it wait that long?"

She took my hands in hers, guided them to the lacings of her bodice. I undid them. The bodice slipped to the floor. Moments later, she was stepping out of her skirts and, without taking her eyes off me, shrugging off her chemise until she stood nude, patterned in candlelight and slivers of the ebbing moon outside, desirable as no woman before her.

I gathered her up, burying my face in her breasts. She gasped involuntarily as I carried her to the bed, where she reclined and watched me cast off my robe before sitting up on her knees to help me pull my shift over my head. My shoulder ached. She frowned at the fresh spotting of blood on the bandage.

"It, too, can wait," I said against her lips. As I drew back her gaze traveled down my torso, resting for a moment on the blemish on my hip. Then she brought her gaze lower.

"I said you didn't have anything I hadn't seen before, but I believe I was mistaken."

I chuckled as I lay down beside her. Her tempting air didn't deceive me. Under my hand I could feel her pulses racing and knew that if she had explored the ways of the flesh to a certain extent, in the end she had remained shy of the ultimate act.

I soon discovered that I, too, was innocent, in every way a man can be. As I pressed her splendid length against me and we tasted each other with fervor, I realized I could not hope to compare this luxury to my rambunctious couplings with simple Annabel. I worshipped as I might at a temple, until the desire in Kate's eyes turned to flame, and she was shuddering beneath me, rising to meet my ardor. Only once did she cry out, softly.

161

After we were spent, and she cradled in my arms, I whispered, "Next time, there'll be no pain. I promise you."

She laughed shakily. "If that was pain, I never want to know anything else." She spread her hands over my chest, on my heart. "I don't need land or a proper house. All I want is here."

I smiled. "Be that as it may, I will make an honest woman of you."

"For your information," she replied, "I'm of age and no longer considered chattel. As for honesty, what I do, I do of my own accord."

I suppressed a chuckle. "I should at least request Her Grace's blessing. You are her lady."

"Yes, I suppose you should." She sighed. "I wish my mother still lived. She would have liked you, I think, and you, her."

I detected an old pain in her voice. "I probably would," I said gently, "if she were as pretty and willful as you."

Kate smiled sadly. "She was pretty, yes. I suppose willful, as well, for one born to the kitchens. She was too young when she had me, only fourteen, a year older than my father."

She paused, sought to keep the emotion from her voice. "It wasn't a love affair, you understand. My mother's parents were also servants, who died in the same outbreak that killed my grandmother Mary Boleyn's first husband. My grandmother re-married and became Lady Stafford. Together with her son from her first marriage— my father— she came to Stafford manor, where she took a shine to my mother. She invited my mother into service and taught her to be a ladies' maid."

"This Lady Stafford," I interposed, "she was sister to Queen Anne Boleyn?"

"Yes." Kate sat up, shook the hair from her eyes. "She had none of her sister's haughtiness, though, God rest her soul. When my mother became pregnant, her morning sickness soon gave her away. She was mortified; she feared she'd be dismissed, but Lady Stafford understood. She had been Henry VIII's mistress before Anne caught his eye and experienced firsthand the hardships women endure. Without remonstration, she bundled my mother up and sent her to the Cecils, under her friend Lady Mildred's care. That was where I was born."

So, this explained her connection to Cecil. She had dwelled under their roof; Cecil and his wife had been her mother's benefactors. It also explained why she would have trusted Walsingham, a man in Cecil's pay.

"I gather Lady Stafford didn't know who your father was," I ventured.

"No," said Kate quietly. "My mother kept it a secret. She was afraid they'd take me from her. It didn't matter that my grandmother now lived a retired life, as no one cared to be reminded of the Boleyns after Queen Anne's fall. A nobleman's child, even a bastard one, can be of use; and my mother wanted to raise me herself. And so she did, with Lady Cecil's help, of course."

She paused, her eyes turning wistful. "I had a good childhood. I was loved and cared for, and provided for in ways others in my position never enjoy. I even received an education. I'm one of the few women in Her Grace's service who can read and write. That's why she has me run her private errands. If a message need be destroyed, I can memorize it."

"Yes, I see why she'd trust you." I hesitated, my fingers twining the lush auburn hair spilling over her bare shoulders. "How did Lady Stafford find out her son was your father?"

"My mother confessed it on her deathbed. She caught an ague in her lungs. When she realized she was dying, she said she wanted my father to have the chance to meet me. Lady Cecil approached my grandmother, who immediately welcomed me as family. Lady Stafford is a warm-hearted soul, surprisingly unafraid to love. As for my father . . ."

Kate's brow furrowed. "He's married now, with children of his own. One of his daughters is also called Katherine. He isn't sure how to behave with me, though. Not that I mind. I've lived most of my life without him. He did allow me his surname, out of respect for my mother. He never forgot her. They say a man never forgets his first love."

She smiled, a bit sadly. "Your turn. Tell me about your mother."

It was out before either of us realized what had been said. In the following instant, as she took in the look on my face, she flinched. "Forgive me," she said, looking away. "I sometimes speak before I think. Your mother is dead, isn't she?"

I cupped her chin, brought her face up to mine. "I want no secrets with you. The truth is, I don't know who my mother was. Or my father, for that matter. I am a foundling. I was abandoned as a child. Dame Alice raised me."

"You're a foundling?" she echoed. I nodded, waited for her to collect her thoughts. At length, she said, "Then this Dame Alice . . . she was the woman in the King's room?"

"Yes. She saved me." As I uttered these words, I felt an overpowering need to tell someone, to leave her memory in someone other than myself, so she would never be forgotten.

"I was left in the priest's cottage near the Dudley Castle," I went on, "presumably to die. I was later told it happens often enough. Unwanted babies dropped off on noble thresholds like livestock, in the hope the rich will take pity on what the poor can't afford. I would have none of it; according to Dame Alice, I made enough fuss to wake the dead. She heard me wailing all the way from the slop pit, where she was dumping leavings, and went to investigate."

My voice caught. I steadied it, took Kate's hand for strength. "In truth, she was the mother I never knew. When she died—or rather, when I was told she had died—I never forgave her for not saying goodbye."

"Is that why you did it?" she asked. "Did you agree to help Her Grace, because you understood she needed to say goodbye to her brother?"

I nodded. "I wouldn't let anyone suffer what I did. I know what it is like to lose someone unexpectedly, without reason. I believed Dame Alice had died. Peregrine mentioned a woman caring for the King, and for a moment I felt the strangest sense of hope. But I never thought it was she. I couldn't. Even when I saw her, I . . ."

I paused, released her hand, and righted myself on the pillows. My voice turned cold.

"I scarcely recognized her. They had cut out her tongue, done something to her legs that hobbled her. Master Shelton, their steward, whom I'd always looked up to, who had told me of her death and took over her care of me, he did nothing when Lady Dudley stabbed her. She lay bleeding on the carpet by the King's bed, and he did nothing."

The recollection was like shards in my gut. I had been a fool to ever think Master Shelton would choose anything over duty. To be a loyal servant, in everything it entailed, was all he had known. I might have pitied him for his stolid, meaningless life, had I not burned for vengeance.

There was a long silence. Kate's hair draped like a curtain about her face. She raised brimming eyes. "Forgive me for the way I told you about her death. It was selfish. I didn't want you to hurt anymore."

I kissed her lips. "Sweet Kate, you must always speak the truth to me. You couldn't have prevented my pain. It happened long before I met you. I lost Dame Alice on that day they stole her from me. The woman I met in His Majesty's chamber, she wasn't the woman I knew. Now, at least, I have the truth. I know she didn't abandon me. Lady Dudley must have ordered her taken on the road and made up the story of her being waylaid by thieves. Master Shelton was her willing accomplice."

"But why would they do such a terrible thing?"

"Because of what she knew. I am certain of it now. Dame Alice knew something about me. About who I am."

Kate went still. "Does this have something to do with that piece of jewelry?"

In response, I rose, padded naked from the bed to my crumpled robe. From the pocket, I withdrew the little jewel. The ruby caught the moonlight filtering through the window as I handed it to her.

"I think it's the key to my past." A shudder ran through me. "Dame Alice gave it to me because in that moment when I went after her, she recognized me. I don't think she knew me before. She had suffered too much. But she kept that gold petal with her for a reason. It means something. It has to."

Kate gazed upon it, marveling, in her hands. "Yes, but what?"

I took it back from her, ran my fingertips over the fragile veined gold. "Dame Alice never had much use for anything save her herbs. She didn't hoard material things. She used to say they took up too much room. Yet, she kept this object hidden in her medicine chest for God only knows how many years, when she might have pawned it or used it as a bribe to gain her freedom."

I looked past her to the window. "Lady Dudley used my existence to force the Duchess to agree to wed her daughter, Jane Grey, to Guilford. The Duchess said as much when she held me in that cell. Whatever secret this petal represents, it must be powerful enough to have warranted my death. It might even be the weapon I need to stop the Dudleys for good."

She crossed her arms over her breasts, as if she felt a sudden chill. "You want revenge for what they did to her."

165

I returned my somber gaze to her. "How can I not? She was everything I had in the world, and they stole her from me. They held her against her will, tormented, and maimed her, and then used her, after years of imprisonment, to slowly poison the King. Yes, I want revenge. Even more than that, I want the truth." I leaned to her. "Kate, I need to know who I am. Surely I deserve that much."

"Yes," she said, "you do. It's just that I'm afraid, for you, for us. This secret can't be good if the Duchess of Suffolk sought to kill you to keep it quiet. And If the Dudleys used it against her, they too must know who you are."

"Not every Dudley," I said, and she stared at me. "Only Lady Dudley knows. I don't think she told the Duke. She must have suspected he would betray her, as he in fact tried. She wasn't about to entrust him with the only weapon she had that might keep him in line—her ability to coerce the Duchess. Without her coercion, without this secret, I believe the Duchess would never have agreed to give her daughter to a—"

"Low-born Dudley," Kate mused. She went quiet, regarding me thoughtfully. "Why don't you tell Master Cecil about this? He knows many important people. Maybe he could help you."

"No." I grasped her hands. "Promise me you'll not breathe a word of this to anyone. Northumberland is still in power, perhaps now more than ever, and Her Grace may still need our help. It's best I carry this burden on my own for now."

I silently asked forgiveness for the lie. I couldn't risk exposing her to that frozen hatred I'd seen in Lady Dudley's eyes. Nor did I want the murderous Stokes stalking her on the Duchess's behalf. I would become a hunted man once it was discovered I was still alive, and whatever happened Kate must be kept safe. Still, what I must ask of her next would hurt.

"I need you to do something for me," I began, and she met my regard without flinching. "I need you to promise you'll return to Hatfield and stay there."

She arched an eyebrow. "And if I refuse?"

"Then I would remind you that Her Grace still needs you. None of her servants have your skills, which she may require in the days to come. You know it as well as I. Just as you know, but haven't yet said, that Cecil

166

has an assignment for me. That's why Walsingham has been coming and going from London, returning my sword and inquiring after my health. He can't possibly be that solicitous."

"I don't care," she whispered. She thumped the mattress with her fist. "Let them find someone else. You've risked enough. Not even Her Grace would dare ask more of you."

"Yet, I would do more—for her. So would you. How can you not? You love her."

"And you?" she asked, haltingly. "Do you love her?"

I pulled her to me. "Of course I do, but only as my princess. She deserves that much, I think, especially since a love such as we have found may always elude her."

Wrapped in my embrace, Kate murmured, "They say her mother was cursed. Sometimes, I wonder if Elizabeth carries it in her blood. Lord Robert threw himself at her feet. So did the Duke. Yet when she denied them, they turned on her like wolves. Can it be that the spell she weaves can just as easily turn men to hatred as it can to love?"

"For her sake," I said, "I pray not." I let the moment pass. "Will you go?"

She sighed. "I will. And may God look after us all."

CHAPTER TWENTY-TWO

When I awoke the next morning, refreshed and renewed, it was to an empty bed. I was taken aback at first. Then I chuckled, passing a hand over my tousled hair. The trestle table had been dismantled, the stools set in a row against the wall. Folded in a pile by the bed were the clothes she'd brought me, freshly laundered. Otherwise, it was as if Kate hadn't been here at all.

I started to slide out of bed when the door opened. She appeared with towel, basin, and a small coffer—once again in her russet gown, her hair under a caul, neat and clean as if she'd spent an uneventful night. I hugged her as she set the articles down, drowning out her feigned protest with my mouth. She clung to me for a moment before she firmly pushed me away.

"You must stop," she chided. She went out to retrieve a tray. "Walsingham is here. He wants to see you as soon as you break your fast."

"That's what I was trying to do." I smiled, reaching out to grab her again.

She pranced away, elusive as dandelion seed. "You'll have to content yourself with the meal I gave you last night, my lord, for that's all I plan to cook until you put a ring on my finger and a roof over my head." She tossed the towel at me.

I laughed. "This from the wanton who assured me she had all she wanted last night."

"A woman can always change her mind. Now, behave yourself whilst I wash you."

I affected a penitent stance, though it took concentration as she cleaned me from head to foot, lathering and rinsing without discrimination. Only when she undid my bandage to replace it did I react with a wince. "Does it hurt?" she asked.

"A little." I glanced at the wound. It was as ugly as I'd expected. "Infected?"

"It was. But you're fortunate. The ball shredded, and took a few layers of skin, nothing more." From the coffer she took out a jar and proceeded to swab green salve over my shoulder. "It's a French recipe: rosemary, turpentine, and rose oil. It hastens healing." With expert fingers she applied a fresh bandage, tucking it under my armpit. "That will have to suffice. It will be uncomfortable, but I assume you're not about to stay in bed a few more days."

I pecked the tip of her nose. "You know me well."

She helped me into my clothes—shirt, new leather jerkin, breeches, and a belt with a pouch. I was surprised when she produced soft kid boots in almost my exact size.

"Peregrine bought them," she explained. "He's gone for a cap and cloak, as well, after I dissuaded him from sneaking back to court to fetch yours. He's determined to be your manservant once you get rich."

I chuckled. "He's got a long wait. Maybe he'll be content to mind our chicken coops, instead." I turned about. "Presentable?"

"A veritable prince." She served bread and cheese and dark ale, which we consumed in companionable silence, though I could sense her anxiety.

"Does Walsingham bring bad news?" I finally asked.

"By the looks of him, it's always bad news." She started to clean up. "I've no idea what he brings. He didn't say anything other than ask that I fetch you." She made a face. "Now that I'm no longer required, I've reverted to being another ignorant woman in his eyes. Never mind that I'm as able as any hooligan he could ever hire, or can pick locks and spy with the best of them."

"Not to say, you've a temper to match. If I were him, I'd watch my step."

"You're the one who needs watch his step." Kate stopped to face me, hands on hips as she'd done that afternoon—it seemed ages ago—in the gallery at Greenwich.

"Didn't you assure me that he helped save my life?" I reminded her.

"I did. That doesn't mean I trust him with it. He's a snake, that one, out for his own advantage. I don't think even Cecil can control him." Her voice cracked. "Promise me you'll not agree to anything dangerous. I know I said I'd go to Hatfield, and I will, but I don't want to spend all my time sick with worry for you."

I nodded. "I promise. Now, show me the way."

She pointed to the door. "Down the stairs and to your right. He's in the Privy Closet off the hall." She turned away. "I'll be in the garden, hanging sheets."

The image brought a smile to my face as I took the stairs to the ground floor and moved through the country house, which was simple, sparsely furnished, and a refreshing change after the spiked opulence of court. Outside the hall I paused before a door and took a deep breath.

I pulled it open and strode into the closet-room.

Like Kate, I likened Walsingham to a serpentine presence. His alleged contribution to my survival had done nothing to change my impression. Rather, it was unnerving to know that the man had been ghosting me since Whitehall, watching but not interfering, until that night on the leads. I wasn't convinced of his motives but I hid my discomfort at the sight of his gaunt figure seated at the desk, Urian's head resting on his thigh.

"Ah, Squire Prescott." Walsingham's spidery hand caressed Urian with hypnotic repetition. "You've recovered with remarkable alacrity, I see. The vigor of youth is a marvel."

Something in his arid tone indicated he knew more of said vigor than I would have liked. I had to force myself not to order Urian away, appalled by the dog's utter lack of discernment. "I was told you wanted to see me," I said in as neutral a tone as I could manage.

"Ever to the point." The bloodless lips twitched. "Why waste time on the superfluous?"

"I trust you weren't expecting a friendly chat. If so, you'll be disappointed."

"I never expect anything." His hand paused in its stroking of the dog's ears. "That's what makes life so interesting. People never fail to surprise me." He gestured to a stool opposite his. "Pray, sit. All I require is your attention."

Because my shoulder was starting to pain me, I obliged. As I sat, that vague feeling of unease I now recognized as a warning revisited me. Cecil and his men seemed to carry the shade of doom about them like others carried disease.

"Lady Jane Grey and her husband Guilford Dudley have been taken to the Tower," he announced. "It's traditional for a sovereign to lodge there before the coronation."

"I see." My voice tightened. "So, they're going to do it. They're going to force the crown on that innocent girl's head, regardless."

"That innocent girl, as you call her, is a traitor. She usurps another's throne, and now awaits her coronation with all the dignitaries of the court at her side. Thus far, the only compunction she's shown is her continued refusal to allow her husband to be crowned alongside her— to the collective Dudley fury."

I contained my revulsion. Of course, Walsingham would deem Jane Grey a traitor. It was always easier to view the world through the prism of convenience. "By another," I said, "I assume you mean the Lady Mary. She's still considered King Edward's legal heir, is she not?"

"Of course. Any change in the succession requires the sanction of Parliament. I don't think Northumberland has gone so far as to request official approval of his treason."

I paused, deliberating. "But the Council," I ventured, guarding my tone. "They have agreed to uphold Jane as queen? Northumberland doesn't act alone?" I was thinking of the Duchess, of her threats to bring down the Dudleys. If she raised protest against the usurpation of her rights, it could buy both princesses the time they needed.

Again I received that unblinking stare. "What exactly are you asking, Squire?"

"Nothing. I just seek to clarify the situation." I watched him fold his hands at his chin. Deprived of his caresses, Urian lay down on the floor with a dejected sigh.

"The Council would agree to anything to save their skin," Walsingham said at length. "The Duke has badgered them to submission with his threats that he has enough ammunition in the Tower to crush any revolt in Mary's name. He's also garrisoned the surrounding castles. Still, our sources indicate not a few of his so-called associates would as quickly see him hang than give him further rein over England. He's made more enemies than is safe for any man in his position. He may also soon face significant opposition from the Lady Mary herself."

It was the longest speech I had heard from him and despite my antipathy, I had to admit I was impressed.

"Significant?" I echoed. "It was my understanding that her Catholicism and doubtful legitimacy made her anything but."

"It would be wiser not to discredit her quite yet," said Walsingham.

"I see. What is it you want of me?"

"The Duke has not officially announced Edward's death; however, with Jane Grey in the Tower awaiting her coronation, it can't be long in coming. Mary has let it be known she's at her manor of Hoddesdon, from where she continues to issue demands for information. We suspect someone at court is warning her to stay away. She has no resources to draw upon, and few will risk themselves for a princess whose own father and brother declared her a bastard and whose faith is at odds with their own. There is the possibility she'll flee the country, but we think it more likely she'll head for the northern border and her Catholic strongholds."

As if it were the most ordinary circumstance between us, Walsingham withdrew an envelope from his sleeve. "We want you to find her, and deliver this."

I eyed it. "I assume that isn't her safe conduct to Spain."

"Its contents," he replied, "are of no concern to you."

"I beg to differ. Its contents could be my death, judging from past events. I'm as loyal as the next man, but I do have my limits. I'll need to know what it says."

He deliberated for a long moment. "Very well," he said, with a mocking incline of his head. "It's from a few select lords of the Council. An explanation of their predicament, if you will. It offers Mary their support, should she choose to fight for her throne. They would prefer she not abandon England, an absent queen being even less desirable than an illegal one."

"Hedging our bets, are we?" I allowed myself a short laugh. "She must have become significant, indeed." By the look on his face, Walsingham was not amused.

"You may accept the job or decline," he said stiffly. "It makes no difference to me. We can hire a dozen couriers."

Cecil was behind this, naturally; he had seen the way the matter could go. I had no illusions as to whether he wanted the Duke's puppet or a Catholic daughter of Henry VIII on the throne, and I took my time to answer, smiling and patting my knee, enticing Urian to my side.

Walsingham's stony black eyes narrowed.

After enough time had elapsed to establish I was no longer his for the taking, I said, "Since our last engagement, my rate has gone up."

It pleased me to note that he visibly relished the introduction of cash. It put us in his terrain, where everything was open to negotiation. He removed a leather pouch from his doublet. "We are willing to double your fee, with half in advance. If you do not deliver the letter, or Mary is captured, you forefeit the other half. Would you like me to put it in writing?"

I took the pouch, and the letter. "That won't be necessary. I can always take care of any misunderstandings when I next see Cecil." I stood. "Anything else?"

He stared up at me. "Yes. As you may know, time is of the essence. You must get to her before the Duke's men. We also don't think it wise for you to use your real name and have therefore provided you with a new one. You are now Daniel Beecham, son of Lincolnshire gentry. The persona is real enough. Cecil patronized the family before its demise. Daniel's mother died in childbed, his father in Scotland. The boy himself was under Cecil's care until his own death six years ago. Your beard should help with the disguise, so don't shave it off. Daniel Beecham would have been two years older than you were he still alive."

"So, I'm finally a dead man," I remarked. "My enemies will be pleased."

"It's for your protection," he said, with a lift of his brow.

I smiled thinly. "Yes, I've been told how protective you are. I heard about your ill-timed venture to the stables while I was otherwise engaged, and of your aborted intervention on the leads." I paused. "I can't help but wonder about the time before, when I was trapped in the monk's cell. It was you who found my jerkin by the lake, wasn't it? You found it and dropped it at the entrance to alert Peregrine and Barnaby. A rather passive rescue, but I suppose I shouldn't quibble." I straightened, despite the jab in my shoulder. "Now then, am I free to go?"

173

"In a minute." Walsingham's eyes flicked to Urian, who sat attentively at my feet. "I thought you might be interested to know that a Dudley didn't fire the ball that hit you."

I didn't shift a muscle. "What does that mean?"

"It means Steward Shelton had the pistol at that time. I saw him aiming from the window. I thought you should know. He is, I believe, someone you trust."

"Trusted," I corrected. I met his stare, hating him more in that instant than I had thought possible.

Turning heel, I strode from the closet with Urian at my heels.

In the hall, a scullery girl emptied the hearth of cinders. With a shy smile she indicated the way to the garden, which I found enclosed by walls and windswept with the scent of apples.

Kate was doing just as she'd said—hanging sheets on a line to dry. I crept up behind her, wrapped my arms about her waist. "Did you scrub them yourself, wench?" I breathed in her ear. With a gasp, she let a pillowcase fly from her hand. Urian barked in delight, jumping up to seize it in mid-air. He trotted off with his trophy, tail held high.

Kate turned on me. "I'll have you know Holland cloth doesn't come cheap on our wages. Unless you indeed plan on getting rich, we've a household to economize for."

"I'll buy you a hundred pillow cases, in Egyptian silk, if you like." I pressed the pouch in her hand. As she felt its weight, her eyes widened. She searched my face. Before she could voice the question that hung between us, I pulled her to me. Limp in my arms, she whispered, "When?"

I replied softly, "As soon as I can let go of you."

CHAPTER TWENTY-THREE

W hen did you say she'd arrive?" said Peregrine, for what had to be the hundredth time.

"I didn't." I suppressed my impatience as I peered through the ragged opening in the bushes, where I crouched with a crick in my back and legs gone numb below the knee. A star-spattered sky displayed the last of the moon. A breeze rustled in the woods behind us, where we'd tethered and muzzled the horses.

"She left her manor some time yesterday. Seeing as she didn't head to London, as she'd have been arrested by now, we can only hope she took this road. She could be anywhere."

At my side, in a heavy blue wool cloak that matched the one he'd brought me, Peregrine pursed his lips. "Well, bite my head off, will you? I was only asking. If I'd known you'd be such a grouse, I'd have gone to Hatfield with Mistress Carey and Urian."

I forced out a chuckle. "Sorry. Camping in a trench at the side of a road isn't my idea of fun, either. I'd rather be with Kate and Urian, as well."

"I should think so," he mumbled. "I saw how you looked at her when we said goodbye. You love her, don't you?"

The discordant blend of envy and longing in his voice gave me pause. He had been nothing if not resourceful, not to mention tenacious. I knew all about how, while we had crept into Edward's chamber, Peregrine had slunk past several guard posts in order to reach the stables, where he then avoided the night watch, and had saddled, bridled, and led three somnambulant horses out to the gate.

He had waited, feeding the beasts tidbits of those crabapples he seemed to grow in his pockets, keeping them quiet until the Princess, Kate, and Barnaby arrived. According to Kate, when they heard the pistol and saw the Duke's retainers racing out, Barnaby had to haul Peregrine onto Cinnabar. As soon as they reached the house, Peregrine demanded they turn back to search for me. He would have gone then and there, were it not for fear the Duke had sent troops after them. As it was, Peregrine did not stop pacing the room where they hid. When Mistress Astley and the men sent by Cecil arrived to spirit the Princess away, he had exclaimed with relief that now he could go find me.

This same unwavering devotion had prompted his refusal to let me undertake my latest mission without him. He'd cited, not without reason, that, as I had a penchant for tripping into disaster, it would be best if I took a friend. I had made the mistake, however, of viewing him as he wanted to be seen—as a comrade, forgetting he was in fact still a lad. Now, as I saw the trepidation in his eyes, I said softly, "Yes, I love her. We are pledged to marry. But you will always have a place with us. I promise you that."

Peregrine kneaded his cloak. "You do?" he whispered.

"I do." I reached over to rustle his hair, when I heard a faint rumble coming toward us.

We froze amid the overgrowth. I unsheathed my new dagger, having entrusted the sword to Kate rather than risk losing it again. Peregrine pulled out his knife.

The clangor of iron-shod hooves striking the road increased. I whispered, "Remember, we mustn't show ourselves until we know for certain it's her. The Duke could have sent out a hundred decoys to flush out her supporters."

He nodded, his eyes wide. It sounded as if an infantry were coming upon us, yet when I looked out, I saw only a company of horsemen, their lathered mounts flinging up clumps of dirt. Dark cloaks billowed about the riders. They carried no torches, but as they thundered past, the leader glanced at the bushes where we lurked. Despite his unadorned black cap, I immediately recognized that flash of dark eyes.

My heart was in my throat. I half expected him to yell a halt and turn on us. When the contingent continued down the road, I sagged onto my haunches. "That was Lord Robert."

Peregrine stared. "*The* Lord Robert?"

"The same." I sprang to my feet. "Come!"

We raced to the woods. Cinnabar and Peregrine's mount (which had the odd name of Mouse) had dozed off. They snorted at the rude awakening as we leapt onto the saddles and yanked them about. "We'll ride parallel with the road," I said. "Hopefully, we can find a quicker route."

The hem of the night was lifting. Though still a few hours away, dawn approached. Cantering at the forest edge, using the trees as camouflage, evading or jumping fallen trunks that could snap a horse's leg, I thanked God for the scant moon. I couldn't see far ahead, which was unfortunate, but it also meant Lord Robert and his men might not see us. I knew that if we were spotted we'd be hard pressed to make our escape.

How had Robert caught the scent so fast? It was not unexpected that the Duke would send his son after Mary, but Walsingham had said he would ride for her manor first, which was miles from here. Somehow, Robert had discovered she was on her way north and determined to run her to ground, employing that same ruthless purpose he'd shown in pursuit of Elizabeth. Only this time, it was a warrant, not a ring, he carried in his pocket.

Peregrine broke into my thoughts. "They're stopping."

I slowed Cinnabar to a walk, straining my eyes toward a fork in the road. "Go further in," I told Peregrine, "and wait there. If something should happen, don't be a hero. Ride to Hatfield without pause."

I picked my way to the group. Cinnabar had a remarkably light step, but even that couldn't stop the occasional crackle of twigs underfoot or jiggle of harness. At every sound, no matter how subtle, I cringed. I'd hunted with the Dudleys in our youth, before the cruelty of the sport turned my stomach. I had seen the delight Robert took in tracking his prey. How much more would he enjoy hunting that squire who'd betrayed his trust?

But no one heard me, probably because they were too engrossed in their own vociferous debate. Sliding from my saddle, I continued on foot, drawing close enough to overhear, but not so close I wouldn't have a fighting chance if I were seen.

I counted nine men. Among the clash of voices Robert's was the loudest.

"Because I say so. God's teeth, am I not the leader here? Is it not my head that stands to roll if we fail to capture that papist bitch?"

"Begging your pardon," retorted a gruff voice, "but we all stand to lose here, my lord. None of us wants to see a Catholic queen setting the Inquisition over us, which is why we shouldn't have left our soldiers at King's Lynn. What if she has more retainers than we think?"

Robert scoffed. "You heard her steward at Hoddesdon. At the most, she has six: her treasurer, her secretary, her chamberlain, and three matrons. We don't need a host of soldiers to catch her. They'll only slow us down."

I had to smile. Out in the middle of a road, in the middle of nowhere, and still they trembled in their boots over what one embattled spinster might achieve. It was good to hear that, like her younger sister, Mary Tudor had a reputation for mettle.

Then my entire being went cold as I heard a voice drawl, "Perhaps we should come to an agreement, gentleman, before she sets sail for Flanders and returns with an Imperial army at her back. We'll need more than soldiers then, I can assure you."

It was Stokes. He was here, riding with Robert's men.

In that instant, I wanted to leap out, seize him by the throat, and throttle him until he gasped out the secret he carried.

Robert declared, "Master Stokes is right. We can't afford to waste time. She fled Hoddesdon and has been riding nonstop. All the signs indicate she's on her way to Yarmouth. She has to take refuge somewhere, if only to rest her horses. Most likely, she'll seek out a sympathizer. Now, I ask you, how hard can it be to track down one old woman and a pack of cowering servants on their way to Norfolk?"

"Hard enough," muttered the gruff voice. "Considering we've not seen hide or hair of them. I still say we should head west into Suffolk."

"And I say I've had enough of your bloody dissension." As Robert slammed his fist on his thigh, I detected the unwitting panic in his cry. My former master was scared, and that gave me reason for hope. "You've set us by our ears since we started out," he snarled, "and I, for one, am starting to wonder at your purpose. Are you with or against us, Master Durot?"

I watched this Durot swing about on his horse, a large, muscular figure clad in a quilted doublet and oversized cap, equipped with sword, short-bow, and arrows. "If you're questioning my loyalty," he intoned "and, by implication, that of my master Lord Arundel, I can always head back to London to report on your progress, my lord. I've no pressing need to continue on this particular goose chase."

Robert glared. "You might not, but your master the Earl has every need. He's made a fortune off the pillage of the abbeys. I don't think he'll appreciate having to explain himself to Queen Mary. I suggest you follow my orders, lest you'd rather hang from a gibbet."

Durot didn't respond.

Satisfied, Robert swerved to the others. "Anyone else have cause for complaint? Best speak now. I'll not tolerate it later." When none spoke, he added, "We'll head east. This area is infested with Catholic landowners. She could be hiding with any one of them. If we have to search house by house, thatch by thatch, then we will." He flung his next words at the silent Durot. "Lest we forget, she's but a woman."

No one argued the point. Digging spurs into horse flanks, they charged off.

I slipped back to Cinnabar. Peregrine waited at the crest.

"To Suffolk," I told him.

We rode at unflagging pace, the hours slipping past as dawn drenched the sky in mauve. Though I trusted my instinct, seeing the countryside resolve into a placid vista of rolling vales and hills, I began to wonder if I had relied too much on it and not enough on harsh reality.

Could Mary have gotten this far on her own, with only a handful to assist her? Or was she at this very moment being marched out of her hiding place at the tip of a Dudley sword, bound for the Tower? Rather than chasing her, shouldn't I be rushing to Hatfield to warn Elizabeth, fetch my beloved Kate, and make for the nearest port before the Duke destroyed us all?

I wiped a hand across my chin. My beard felt strange against my fingers. Tugging off my cap, I let my matted hair tumble to my shoulders, and glanced over at Peregrine. The boy sat half asleep on his saddle. We had to stop soon. Even if the horses held out, we couldn't.

A half hour later, I spied a manor ahead, nestled in a vale among orchards, a veil of bluish smoke hovering over chimney and courtyard.

Otherwise, from the distance, it almost looked deserted.

Taking in the sight, I sighed. "Peregrine, wake up. I think we've found her."

The boy started, raised bewildered eyes. "How do you know?"

"Look at the courtyard. There are horses, seven to be exact."

We rode into the courtyard with our cloaks thrown back over our shoulders to expose the sheathed blades at our belts, our hands free, and heads uncovered. I instructed Peregrine to remember my new name and refrain from appearing perturbed, while I, in turn, feigned a calm I did not feel, as the servants preparing the mounts froze in mid-buckle of stirrups. One of three men overseeing the operation lifted a firearm. The other two advanced. Both were men in their middle years, dressed in yeomen's costumes, their bearded faces haggard.

The elder of the two, who had the dignity of a steward despite his attempt to appear common-born, barked, "Who are you, and what is your business here?"

"Who I am doesn't matter," I replied. "My business is a missive for the Queen."

"Queen? What queen?" The man guffawed. "I see no queen here."

"Her Majesty Queen Mary. The missive is from the Council."

The men exchanged terse looks. "Go fetch Lord Huddleston," the older one directed and the other ran off. "Jerningham, keep that arquebus aimed," he ordered the man with the gun. The servants didn't shift an inch. "Dismount," ordered the man. Peregrine and I obeyed.

A moment later, a harried, portly gentleman I assumed was the aforementioned Huddleston bustled out. "I advised her not to, Master Rochester," he said in a worried tone, "but she says she'll see them in the hall, providing they come unarmed."

The man Rochester turned a stern eye on me. "Your lad stays here."

Detecting the lingering scent of roast as I was escorted into the hall, my stomach rumbled. Rochester was at my side, the armed man Jerningham at my back, and Huddleston ahead. At the entrance, Jerningham backed into the shadows, from where I had no doubt he would continue to aim the gun. Rochester and Huddleston led me forth.

A slight figure clad in bucolic dress stood before a table. The men bowed low. Dropping to one knee, I glimpsed a map on the table, alongside quill and paper, flagon and goblet.

A brusque voice said, "You may rise," and I came to my feet before Mary Tudor.

Had I not known it, I would never have thought her sister to Elizabeth. Indeed, Mary more closely resembled their cousin, Jane Grey—short and quite thin, with a hint of red-gold in the graying hair under her coif.

Unlike Jane, however, Mary's age and suffering were written on her face, etched in the crevices on her brow, the webs cradling her lips, and crepe slackness at her chin. Her thickened hands were clenched at her girdle, each of her fingers ringed. Only in her eyes could be discerned that indomitable Tudor strength—forceful dark gray eyes rimmed in shadow, meeting mine with a forthrightness that imparted she was a royal being, far superior to myself.

"I'm told you bring a missive." Mary thrust out her hand. "Give it to me."

I removed the envelope from my interior pocket. Turning to the light, she tore it open and peered. Her frown deepened. She looked at me. "Is this true?"

"I believe, Your Majesty, it is a genuine offer of support."

"You *believe*?" she echoed. "Have you read it, then?"

"Your Majesty, I would not be much of a messenger if I failed to memorize so important a missive. Such letters, if fallen into the wrong hands, can prove dangerous."

She gave me a long, appraising stare. Then she paced to the table with brisk, mannish steps. "This dangerous letter," she declared, with a hint of asperity, "is from none other than my lords Arundel, Paget, Sussex, and Pembroke; all of whom served my lord brother the King, and now inform me that while they have no desire to see me deprived of my throne, their hands are tied. The Duke's hold, it seems, is too powerful for them to resist. They say they fear they must uphold my cousin's claim, though Jane Grey has expressed no desire to rule. What say you?"

Her request for my opinion took me aback. Though she hid it well, I sensed her trepidation. Thrust into notice after years of obscurity, forced to flee within her own realm, the Lady Mary emanated the agitation of a persecuted animal. She had been hunted before, too many times in fact, for her to trust in anyone's promises, written or otherwise.

I understood. I'd not heard anything positive about her, from anyone. On the contrary, the possibility of her accession was rife with fear and turmoil, so much so it had spurred the Duke to plot her destruction. Yet in that moment I felt only empathy. She was at an age when most women had wed, borne children, and settled, for better or worse, into their lives, while here she stood in someone else's manor, a princess and a fugitive, marked for death.

She stared at me. "Will you not answer? You were hired on their behalf, were you not?"

"Your Majesty, if you'll pardon my insolence, I would prefer to reply in private."

"Absolutely not," growled Rochester. "The Queen of England does not entertain strangers. You're lucky we haven't clapped you in a dungeon for conspiring with her enemies."

"A dungeon?" I inquired mildly, before I could stop myself. "In a country manor?"

There was a stunned silence.

Then, to my relief, hoarse laughter rang out. "At least, he doesn't mince his words like some." Mary clapped her hands. "Leave us. I think we can safely assume he is not an assassin."

Rochester marched to where the shadowy man with the gun lurked, Huddleston behind him. Mary motioned to her flagon. "Drink. You must be thirsty."

"Thank you, Your Majesty," I said, and her terse smile revealed bad teeth. She had not had much occasion to smile in her life, I thought. I poured a goblet, drank deeply of the warm ale. She waited.

I ventured, "Your Majesty, my companion, he's just a boy. He'll not be harmed?"

"No, no." She made a hasty gesture. "He's breaking his fast as we speak." She faced me now without trepidation. "Tell me honestly, and I promise I'll not seek reproach on you. My brother King Edward: is he dead?"

I met her stalwart gaze. "I am afraid so."

She was quiet. Then she said, "And this letter from the Council, is it a ruse, or can I trust what these lords assure me?"

I measured my response, as she would not take well to either rude bluntness from an inferior or fawning subservience. "I haven't been at court long, Your Majesty, but I would say, no, you should not trust them." As her face tightened, I added, "However, you can trust their letter. The Lady Jane Grey is indeed the Duke's pawn. She would never have taken your crown had she been allowed the choice."

She eyed me. "I must say, I find it difficult to believe you. She did, after all, marry Northumberland's brat."

"Your Majesty can believe in her innocence if you believe in nothing else. The Duke has devised this situation to secure his own power. He is the perpetrator. He—"

"He should be drawn and quartered, and his head stuck on a pike," she blared. "How dare he contrive to steal my realm, which is mine by divine right! He will see I am not a lady to be trifled with—he and every other lord who dares exalt my Grey cousin over me."

The fervor of her declaration animated her person. Mary might not possess her sister's magnetic lure, but she was still Henry VIII's daughter, willing to fight for her rights.

"I gather Your Majesty intends to do battle for your crown," I said.

"To the death, if need be. My grandmother, Isabel of Castile, led armies against the heretic Moors. Nothing less can be expected of me."

"Then Your Majesty has answered your own question. The Council's offer is trustworthy only as much as you make it so."

Her eyes turned cold. "I see you've mastered their art of double talk."

I felt a prickle of fear in my belly. Her face was drawn, closed. I didn't know what to say.

Rochester strode in. "Your Majesty, we found this cur lurking outside." He stepped aside, revealing three others dragging another between them. As they threw him face down on the floor, his cap slipped off his head.

Moving to him, Mary prodded him with her foot. "Your name, knave."

I could not contain my relief when the man lifted his face.

"Some call me Durot, Your Majesty, but you would know me as Fitzpatrick."

CHAPTER TWENTY-FOUR

There was a brief silence. Then Mary said, "Barnaby Fitzpatrick, my brother's servant?" and from behind her I interjected, "Your Majesty, he's been working to keep the Duke's son Lord Robert from you. Whatever news he brings must be important."

Barnaby came to his feet. Streaks of his natural hair color showed through his walnut-juice stained mop. At Mary's nod, he said, "Robert Dudley and his men are fast closing in. I was sent ahead as a scout, upon the word of a local sheepherder who swears he spotted you riding in this direction. Your Majesty has less than an hour to make your escape."

Rochester said, "Where is your proof?"

"My lord steward," said Mary, before Barnaby could reply, "Master Fitzpatrick served my late brother loyally for many years. I don't require further proof than his word."

She returned to the table, Huddleston at her heels. She gathered her map and papers, thrust them at him. "We leave for Framlingham. It's a Howard seat, and they have always revered the True Faith. If God is with me, I'll gather supporters there. Otherwise, it's not far to the coast. My lord Huddleston, you'll come with us. Your house is no longer safe for you."

White as the papers he clutched, Huddleston hastened after Rochester and the other men, who bolted from the hall shouting orders. As the manor erupted in pandemonium, Mary called out, "Clarencieux, Finch!" and two women emerged from the hall's recesses, bearing a cloak and small valise. "These are my faithful servants," Mary said, as the women draped the cloak about her. "You must defend them with your lives."

She did not ask us how we felt being entrusted with this duty. A queen already in her mind, she simply assumed we would obey.

We followed her into the courtyard where servants stuffed saddle-bags with last-minute articles. Peregrine held our horses' reins. His eyes snapped wide as he saw Barnaby dart around the side of the manor and return on his cob. While Rochester assisted the Queen and her ladies to their mounts, Huddleston and Mary's other menservants jumped onto theirs. Barnaby eyed Peregrine and me. "We may need someone to defend us with their lives, 'ere this day is done."

"Or maybe not," I said. "Lord Robert looked none too fresh last I saw him."

Barnaby chortled. "I thought I heard a rat in the brush. By the way, the beard suits you."

"A precaution of the trade. In case anyone should ask, my name is Daniel Beecham, of Lincolnshire." I reached over to thump his back. "That was quite a voice you used, Durot. And the hair—it's an accomplishment, indeed. How did you manage to get yourself into Robert Dudley's company?"

"Let us say, I was accosted by a certain earl who offered me the opportunity to avenge my king. The rest was easy. I made myself Robert's bane from the start. If I'd said she was in France, he'd have gone looking in Brussels. He was only too pleased to send me off ahead. He probably hoped some Rome-loving sniper would rid him of me for good."

"You are bold. And you've helped save me twice now. I shan't forget it."

"Just pray you don't need a third," Barnaby said. His expression turned somber as he looked up. He lifted his voice. "Your Majesty, the hour isn't getting any longer."

Swiveling in the saddle, a sickening lurch went through me. Horse-men rode down a distant hill, toward the manor.

"This way," Barnaby shouted. Sandwiched between her servants, Mary galloped onto the road, hard after him as he led us to a ridge of purple hills. Robert Dudley and his men appeared too far off to pose an immediate threat, but as we climbed the path single-file, the sun wringing sweat from our brows, we discovered we weren't moving fast enough.

A gasp escaped the women. Behind us rose a plume of thick black smoke. The manor we had just left was being torched.

At Mary's side Huddleston went white. "My house. Oh, no."

"Let it burn," she said. "I'll build you a better house. You have my word as your queen."

Huddleston's dismayed expression indicated he wasn't taking her promise to heart.

I motioned Barnaby aside. "We're too easy a target. We have to do something to divide their pursuit."

Barnaby assented. "What do you suggest?"

"You proceed with Her Majesty and three of her people. Let Peregrine take the others along a different route. That way, Lord Robert and his men will have to separate. The less there are after her, the better her chances are of reaching Framlingham alive."

"Good plan." He paused. "What are you going to do?"

I gave him a grim smile. "I've an overdue appointment to keep. I'll need your bow."

Peregrine kicked up a storm before he was convinced of the necessity of sacrificing personal preference in order to serve his queen. To my surprise, Rochester supported my proposition, and Mary, too, agreed, insisting I come to her once I had scouted the lay of the land, which I cited as my reason for staying behind. The two parties galloped off in opposite directions, the Queen's escort headed further into the hills, while Peregrine's party turned toward the road to Essex.

As I scrambled up an incline and set Cinnabar loose to graze, I offered up a prayer for their safe deliverance, especially the queen, whom I found I liked far more than my employer would prefer.

I located a cluster of boulders to hide behind and turned my focus to the winding path, notching an arrow in anticipation of my prey.

It didn't take long. As an influx of scudding clouds smothered the sun, four men charged up the path, soot-faced and sweat-soaked. Robert wasn't among them. I soon found out why. The men dismounted a stone's throw from my hiding place, unhooked wineskins from their saddles, and proceeded to resume an argument that apparently had been going on for some time.

"He's as full of the devil's pride as his father," one of the men groused. "I've had enough of these upstarts lording it over us. Why didn't Lord Robert let someone else go back for the soldiers, I ask? Because he doesn't want to sully his hands, lest Mary wins the day and he finds himself at her mercy. Well, I say leave him to it. Papist or not, bastard or legitimate, she's still our rightful queen, no matter what the Dudleys say. Remember, old Henry beheaded the Duke's father for treason. Treachery runs in their blood."

The other two men grunted agreement, glancing at the trim figure who stood apart from them, sniffing the air as if he could scent the way Mary had gone.

"What say you, Stokes?" asked one.

The Duchess's man turned with a swirl of his velvet cloak, revealing a glimpse of scarlet lining. "I think we must each act as our consciences bids, Master Hengate. But I'll wager you're not the first to question the Dudleys' authority."

Behind the boulder, I repressed a derisive chuckle. Trust him to ensure his mistress's neutrality. She was Mary's paternal cousin; her daughter was about to don Mary's crown. Lady Suffolk stood to lose a great deal should Mary triumph, including her head.

Hengate stared at Stokes. "And you? What would you do if we decide to return to our homes and wait to see how it all falls out?"

Stokes shrugged. "I'll go home myself, and inform my lady that the Duke needs a new hound. The one he sent has obviously lost its skill."

At this, the men guffawed. Hengate hesitated before he went to his horse and swung into the saddle. He swerved to Stokes. "If you betray us, you should know my master Lord Pembroke's arm is long. He will find you, no matter whose skirts you care to hide behind."

"I'm no informant," Stokes replied testily. "I've no stake either way in what befalls the Dudleys. Neither does my lady."

"Good," said Hengate, as his accomplices mounted. "In times like these, it's the pliant man who survives." Digging heels into his horse, he and the others thundered off, leaving Stokes to wave a fastidious gauntleted hand before his nose, as if to dispel a noxious smell. He started to move to his own idling steed when my arrow hissed over his head.

He whirled about and froze, staring with narrowed eyes.

I stepped out from behind the rocks, extracted another arrow from the quiver strapped to my back, and fitted it to the bow. It was one of the first times in my life I had the chance to put my years of weaponry practice to action. I wasn't disappointed in Stokes's wary recoil.

"What do you want?" he said, with far more arrogance than I'd have expected from a man in his position. "Money?" He unhooked a small purse from his belt, threw it on the road between us. "That should be enough."

I pushed back my cap, to better show him my face. "Don't you recognize me, Master Stokes? It hasn't been that long."

He stared. "It . . . it can't be," he said, in a stunned whisper.

I adjusted the bow, aiming the arrow between his legs. "I'm thinking if I shoot you there, it will take you a few hours to die." I leveled the bow upward. "Or, I could just shoot you between the eyes and be done with it. Or, you can start talking. Your choice."

He snarled, yanked his sword from the scabbard at his waist.

I let the arrow soar. It struck Stokes in the thigh, brought him howling to his knees. He grasped the protruding shaft, blanching with shock. There was little blood. I walked to him, readying my weapon. I pulled the bow taut again, ignoring the flare in my shoulder from the ball wound. As I took aim, Stokes reared a vicious face. "Coward! Whoreson! You'd kill a defenseless man in cold blood!"

I paused. "There's a start. Whore's son. Is that what I am?"

"A murderer is what you are. I'm going to bleed to death!"

"Not if you let that arrow be. You'll need an experienced surgeon to extract it. The tip is barbed. Without the proper care, the wound could become infected. Still, you've a better chance of survival than you gave me." I lowered the bow. "Back to my question, was my mother a whore?"

"I don't know," he retorted, but he was quivering.

"I think you do." I squatted in front of him. "The Duchess seemed to know. She saw the birthmark on my hip, and was willing to kill to get rid of me. Why? Who does she think I am?"

"Exactly?" Stokes said, and then he flew at me without warning, bowling me back and crushing the quiver of arrows under our combined weight. My head struck the path. For a second, the world melted away. I rammed my knees into his ribs, clawing at the arrow shaft. His scream and the ensuing gush of blood were enough. I rolled, throwing

Stokes off. Springing up, I kicked the bow out of reach. Unsheathing my blade, I leapt onto Stokes's back and pinned him in the dust. I pressed my blade against his throat, pushing the side of his face into the dirt.

"Shall I do it?" I hissed in his ear. "Should I cut you here and now, and leave you to bleed to death? Or will you tell me what I want to know?"

"No!" he wailed, "No! Please!"

I released him. Stokes panted, blood seeping from his maimed leg.

I yanked him over, onto his back. Positioning the dagger at the site where the arrow protruded, I said, "I promise you, it will hurt. When I start cutting out that shaft, it will hurt more than you can imagine. But it might hurt less if you don't forget to hold your breath."

I punctuated the words with an icy smile. A dark rage erupted in my heart, a sudden uncontrollable thirst for vengeance. In my soul's eye, I saw again a slash of steel, the slow terrible crumpling of a mutilated form, and I stood swiftly, went and retrieved the bow.

Stokes was staring at me through distended eyes when I located an intact arrow, fitted it, and wheeled about.

I shot with precision. The arrow sang through the air and thumped into the cloak rumpled about his head, missing his ear by a hair's breadth.

He writhed and tore at the cloak, trying to get away from the arrow that held him fast. "You win," he shrieked. "I'll tell you anything you want. Just cut me loose, damn you to hell!"

"Answer my question."

He suddenly let out a feral giggle. "You deluded fool. You've no idea, do you? We were going to drown you, toss your body in the river, and you'd never have known why."

I clenched my jaw. "No, but you're going to tell me. Now."

"Very well," he said. Pure malice gleamed in his sloe eyes. "You are the last born child of Mary of Suffolk, also known to her family as the Tudor Rose. The mark you bear—it is one her babe inherited, a mark she too carried. The only ones who would have known of it are those intimate with the late duchess's person."

My breath came in stifled bursts. A dull roar drowned out the sounds around me. I stared at the man sprawled before me and recalled in mind-chilling procession the events that had led me to this unthinkable moment.

I forced back the bile in my throat. "Are you saying the Duchess thinks I . . .?" I faltered. I couldn't say it.

Stokes sneered. "I told you what you wanted. Now, set me free."

Feeling as if I were tumbling into an endless void, I raised my fingers to my lips and whistled. Cinnabar trotted down the hill. From my saddlebag, I removed Kate's salve and the linen she'd packed for my shoulder. With passionless efficiency I tore back his bloodied breeches, cut the arrow at the hilt, applied the salve and dressed the wound. Then I wrenched the second arrow from the cloak.

I looked at his ashen face. "You'll need a surgeon to remove the tip. See that you get to one as soon as possible. Otherwise, the wound will fester." I held out my hand. "Come. I'll help you onto your horse."

He gaped. "You lie in wait and shoot arrows at me, and now you want to help me onto my horse? It must be true. You are one of them. You're mad as old Henry himself."

"Don't. Not another word." I took hold of Stokes and yanked him up. He yelped as I held his stirrup and hoisted him onto his saddle. He gathered his reins, hauled his horse's head upward and swiveled about.

I met his malicious regard, knowing he prepared to inflict a far deeper wound than any arrow of mine could deliver.

"Your mother," he said, with undeniable glee, "her mother—she delivered you in secrecy before she died of childbed fever. The midwife conspired to tell my lady you were stillborn. No one asked to see you. My lady ordered your body disposed of, the birth covered up. Had she known that you lived, she'd never have rested until she found you. You could take everything away, you see, the estate and title, her place at court, and in the succession. You are the son her father wanted, the heir to the Suffolk earldom. Think of that next time you're mucking out a stable. You could have been a prince."

I looked up. My voice was cold. "Next time, I give no quarter."

"Neither do I," he spat at me. "Make sure there is no next time. If she finds out you're still alive, it'll go far worse for you than me. I'm not the one she wants dead."

He whirled about and galloped away.

Left alone on a road splattered with blood, I sank to my knees.

Framlingham

CHAPTER TWENTY-FIVE

E*very man, no matter how humble, should know from whence he came.*

Cecil's words echoed in my head as I rode in silence. By nightfall, I had to pause to allow Cinnabar to rest. I chose a clearing in a forest, beside a shallow stream. Loosening the saddle and removing bridle and saddlebags, I patted him. "At ease, my friend. You've earned it."

While my horse slumbered, I crouched in the bracken, opened my saddlebag, and brought out the ruby-tipped jewel Dame Alice had given me. I almost couldn't bear to look at it, knowing now its significance, the reason she had hoarded it all these years. I wanted to throw it away, forget it had ever existed, though in my soul I understood I couldn't delude myself anymore. If it were true, there was no turning back. I must discover all that I could, come to terms with something that was still too vast, too far-reaching, to accept. I owed it to myself, to the many times I had lain alone as a child and wondered. More importantly, I owed it to the woman who had saved me: to Dame Alice, who had somehow known who I was.

In the palm of my hand, the gold petal shimmered.

A Tudor. I was one of them, a son born of the younger sister of Henry VIII, a brother to the bestial Duchess of Suffolk, an uncle to Jane Grey, and cousin to Queen Mary.

And Elizabeth. We, too, shared the same blood.

Tears burned in my eyes. What had she looked like, this mother I had never known? Had she been beautiful? Had I inherited her eyes, her nose, her mouth, her voice? Why had she borne me in secrecy? What had she feared, that she had not let my existence be known?

And what would my life have been like had she lived?

The Tudor Rose . . . the mark of the rose.

I arched my trembling arm over my head. I should fling the petal into the stream, never speak of this to another living person. Suddenly, I thought it better to be a common stable hand, a bastard and foundling, yes, rather than become some nebulous being borne in secrecy and consigned to oblivion, a haunted soul, condemned always to shadows and the fear of discovery, to a lifetime of hiding and of keeping others, always, from the truth.

My fingers would not let go of it, though. The petal had a truth of its own now, inextricably entwined with mine.

I returned it to Kate's scented handkerchief and put it back in my bag. As I did, my fingers brushed the thin volume of psalms I had taken from the Dudley library, bringing a momentary smile to my lips. I carried another memory of Dame Alice with me, as well, one that made me think of her as she had been.

After I finished the last of the stale bread and cheese Kate had packed for me, I lay down on the forest floor and closed my eyes. But I couldn't sleep. I kept seeing a shriveled hand on mine, setting in my palm a gift of unimaginable import.

When dawn finally broke over the horizon, I mounted once more, to ride through fields dotted with golden iris. I tried not to think until I reached the River Orr.

There, on the other side of its banks, atop a great mound, was Framlingham Castle.

Its thirteen towers and immense ramparts overshadowed three moats. In the hunting park glittered an ocean of steel. As I forded the river and neared, I saw hundreds of men hauling cannon and firearms, stockpiling boulders, felling and stripping trees. I gave rein to Cinnabar's canter, the horse sensing stables, oats, and a well-deserved respite.

Guards stopped me on the road. After a rough barrage of questions at sword point, I was obliged to dismount, give my name, and wait under their watch before word came that Rochester bade me to the castle. Shouldering my bag, I took Cinnabar by the reins and trudged to the looming edifice, which swallowed half the sky. Few men paused to mark my passage, the majority engrossed in labor, their ribaldry interspersed with barking dogs and the lowing of livestock, tended by urchins and women.

Despite everything, I felt my spirits brighten. A makeshift city had sprung up around Framlingham, practically overnight, composed of ordinary people and retainers of local lords who had come to defend their queen. In less than seventy-two hours, Queen Mary had amassed her army. At least here, things were as they should be.

The main bailey was thronged with men and animals. Rochester strode to me, sweating profusely but otherwise a completely changed man. He clamped my hand in his. "Master Beecham! I failed to recognize the name. You're fortunate your friends informed me of it. Leave your horse to the grooms and come with me. Her Majesty is eager to speak with you."

Looking past Rochester, I laughed. Peregrine and Barnaby, both stripped to the waist and as filthy as they could be, waved at me before they returned to the arduous task of pushing a cannon into a forger's shed for repairs. I returned my gaze to Rochester.

"I'm pleased to see you are all safe," I said to him, smiling with genuine relief.

"We might not be, had it not been for you. We owe you much. After we separated, Robert Dudley's men chased the others for miles before he realized his error. He then turned and came after us. Praise God he's since been apprehended."

My smile slipped. "Apprehended?"

"Yes. But, of course, you wouldn't know." Rochester steered me toward an incongruous red brick manor flanked by timber lodgings, all situated inside the castle's curtain wall. "It seems that when he discovered where we were headed, Lord Robert decided to go for reinforcements. He must have thought we'd have no means of defending the castle once he set siege."

Rochester chuckled. "To be honest, we never expected to find old Norfolk's son waiting here with his retainers. But, here he was, and by nightfall, another five thousand had arrived. Word of Her Majesty's plight has swept before her, and a call to arms gone out. Men are arriving from all over England. It's as if God Himself watched over her."

"Indeed," I said quietly. "You were saying about Lord Robert?" I wasn't sure why I still cared. Perhaps because he had been the closest thing I'd ever had to a sibling; and though a Dudley to his marrow, he was also, in some ways, a victim of his family's ambition.

"He made it as far as King's Lynn," Rochester said. "By then, several of his men had deserted him. When he got there, he found his soldiers had also deserted, and he was forced to flee. He sought refuge in Bury St. Edmund's and sent urgent word to London. His messenger got away, but he didn't. Baron Derby arrested him shortly after, in the Queen's name. Fitting justice, you might say. He's being held in the ruins of the abbey his father helped destroy."

"What will happen to him?"

Rochester sniffed. "Her Majesty will decide his fate, once she claims her throne. It shan't be enviable. At best, a cell in the Tower for the rest of his days. At worst, the axe, along with the rest of his traitorous kind. I vote for the axe, myself. Ah, but Her Majesty will be pleased to see you. She's asked about you several times."

The last of my brief exultation faded. Like Rochester, I should be rejoicing in this blow to the Dudley cause. Without Robert, the task of apprehending Mary became all that more difficult. Yet all I felt was my fatigue falling over me like a mantle. I wanted only a hot bath, solitude, a cot, and to shut out the world for a time.

We entered the manor and climbed a staircase to a rustic upper hall. Mary, dressed in a plain dress and antiquated headdress that looked too heavy for her thin shoulders, paced back and forth as if its weight were of no account, dictating in a stern voice to a harried secretary whose quill couldn't possibly scratch fast enough to record the torrent issuing from her lips.

"Wherefore, my lords, we require and charge you, as your rightful sovereign, that for your honor and the surety of your persons, you employ yourselves forthwith upon receipt of this letter to proclaim us queen in our capital city of London. For we have not fled our realm nor do we intend to do so, but will die fighting for that which God has called upon us to defend."

Rochester cleared his throat. I bowed low. "Your Majesty."

She swirled about in an abrupt manner, peering. She was, it

seemed, severely near-sighted.

"My friend," she exclaimed, upon recognition. "Rise, rise. We're about to declare war on Northumberland!"

"Your Majesty, that is indeed good news" As I righted myself, I took note that despite her vigor, which was in no small measure instilled by the spontaneous demonstration of loyalty she'd received, Mary looked strained about the eyes and mouth, and too gaunt for her age.

"Good? It is more than good!" Her laughter was curt, derisive. "Our proud Duke is not so proud now. Tell him, Waldegrave."

She swerved to her secretary, her ringed hands clasped, beaming like a school teacher as the man dutifully recited: "Six cities garrisoned by the Duke have vowed allegiance to Her Majesty, offering artillery, food, and men. Her Majesty has also sent a proclamation to the Council, demanding—"

Mary couldn't stop herself from interrupting. "Demanding to know why they have yet to acknowledge me in London. I also demanded an explanation as to why they dared bestow my crown on my cousin. Do you know what they replied?" She grabbed a paper from the table. "They say my brother authorized a change to the succession before his death, denying my claim to the throne because of serious doubts concerning my legitimacy."

She flung the paper aside. "Serious doubts!" This time, her laughter was tinged with a darkness that stirred the hair on my nape. "They'll soon learn how well I take to such. Heretics and traitors are what they are, to a man, and thus shall I deal with them when the time comes."

Silence followed her outburst. Her eyes shifted from face to face before fixating on mine. "Well?" she said, in abrupt suspicion. "You are said Council's courier. Have you no opinion?"

It was a similar inquiry to the one I had faced in Huddleston's manor, only this time I felt sure Barnaby would not be dragged in. As though in confirmation, Rochester took a prudent step back. A pit opened in my belly. It seemed impossible that after everything that had occurred, I might still have to prove my loyalty. But then, how could she know where my ultimate allegiance might lie?

"Your Majesty," I told her, "may I have your leave to examine this letter?"

At her gesture, I retrieved the paper, scanned down to the appended signatures and seals. I met her stare. "Those lords whose letter I first conveyed, are they represented here?"

"They are not, as you can see." Though her voice remained terse, her rigid posture eased somewhat. She moved to me, saying over her shoulder to the others, "Leave us. I would speak alone with our friend."

I had passed her test, though it did nothing to ease my apprehension. The Council had persecuted Mary without mercy because of her faith. My association with them, however tenuous, had put me at a dangerous disadvantage.

She paused at the table. "I'm beginning to wonder about you," she said. "You come out of nowhere and neglect to give us a name. Then, you risk your life to help us escape. You're considered reliable enough to carry confidential letters, yet you feign ignorance of matters you should, in fact, know a great deal about."

"Your Majesty," I said, measuring each word, "I assure you I did only what I was paid for. As for my risking my life, you should know Lord Robert's men had already decided to abandon him. And you must know by now that my name is Daniel Beecham."

"I do, though not by you." She fingered a quill. "Why were you chosen to deliver the Council's missive? There are others they might have sent, men I would know personally."

I mustered a smile. "Your Majesty knows how such matters go. I'd done a few errands in the past, and was asked to convey it for a fee, the lords being disinclined to travel."

She snorted. "What you are saying is that you are a man for hire?"

"Aren't most men, Your Majesty?" I replied, and she stared straight into my eyes.

"I've little experience with men, Master Beecham. What little I do possess tells me there's more to you than you care to let on. Life has taught me a thing or two about hidden motives." She held up a hand. "There is no need to say anything else. I will not query further. Barnaby Fitzpatrick speaks highly of you, and you have proven your fealty. You will, of course, be welcome at my court once I'm proclaimed queen. For make no mistake, queen I shall be. Not even the Duke can prevail against those God protects."

"I pray it will be so," I said. I believed in her conviction. Mary Tudor was no coward.

With a brittle smile, she retreated to a chair, putting more than mere distance between us. Her next words were spoken with the remoteness of a woman with more important concerns to attend to. "As I'm sure you can appreciate, I'm not in the position to reward you at this time. You have my solemn word that you will be compensated as soon as I secure my throne. Until then, if you require anything, let Rochester know."

Resisting the sudden desire to retreat, I ventured, "I expect no reward for having served my queen, but there is something Your Majesty might help me with."

"Oh?" She set her hands on her lap.

"A few questions, is all. An indulgence." I paused. Though I knew it wasn't visible, I could feel myself start to tremble. "Your father, King Henry VIII, had two sisters. The Duchess Mary of Suffolk, was she the youngest?"

"She was. Margaret Douglas, dowager of Scotland, was the eldest."

"I see. Your Majesty, I don't mean to pry, but was your late aunt Mary of Suffolk also known as the Tudor Rose?"

She regarded me with that unwavering stare I now knew stemmed less from an innate perspicacity, such as Elizabeth possessed, and more from a basic goodness of nature tainted by years of corrosive mistrust. At length she said, "It's not widely known, but yes, thus was she called within the family. How is it you know of this?"

My throat knotted. I wet my lips. "I heard it once, at court. In idle talk."

"Talk, you say? Yes, my aunt always did lend herself to talk." She went still, her eyes distant. "I was named after her. She was like an angel, both to look at and in her heart. I adored her. So did my father. It was he who called her the Rose."

The sorrow was like a flood in my chest, filling me to burst. An angel, beautiful to look at, inside and out . . .

"This interest in our history," said Mary. "It is unusual for one of your class."

Despite the tears burning behind my eyes, the lie rolled off my lips as if I'd practiced it a thousand times. "An amateur enthusiasm, Your Majesty, nothing more."

Her smile was infused with warmth. "I commend it. You may proceed."

"I know of the late duchess's surviving daughter, of course," I heard myself say, and it was though I stood apart, listening to someone else. "Did she ever have a son?"

"She did, indeed. My cousin, Henry Brandon. He died of the Sweat in 1534, a year after her own death. It was a tragedy for his father. Only a few years later, Suffolk also lost his twin sons born of his second marriage."

"Did they, too, perish of the Sweat?" I asked, and my chest tightened in anticipation.

She paused, considering. "I believe so, though babes are apt to die of so many things. I seem to recall my cousin Frances helped care for them during their illness. She'd had the Sweat before and was immune to contagion. Their deaths were hard on her. She is the eldest, with two younger sisters. To lose one's own brothers must be a terrible burden."

Resisting a horrified burst of laughter, I looked down at my feet. The Suffolk male heirs had all perished in childhood. This was how the Duchess had inherited her estate!

"And Mary of Suffolk?" I asked at length, my voice muted. I had to know for certain. I had to be sure, no matter how much pain it might incur. "How did she die?"

"Of a fever," said Mary, in a distant tone. "I was told she'd been ill for some time. She was only a year older than I am today. We hadn't seen each other in years. She deplored the state in which my father had chosen to live, and retired from court to her manor in East Anglia." Her brow tightened, as if the memory caused her discomfort. "Few took time to mourn her. It was June, and everyone awaited the outcome of the Boleyn's pregnancy."

She was silent. Though she didn't say it aloud, the hatred struggling within her was apparent. Here, lay that seed of discord between her and her younger sister.

She collected herself. "I remember the details because a few weeks after her funeral, Charles of Suffolk's squire came to see me. A stalwart man, very proper. He had a terrible wound running from temple to cheek. It looked raw, and I asked him about it. He said he had had an accident while practicing with his sword. Poor man. He seemed most affected by his mistress's death. He brought me a piece of a jewel Mary had bequeathed to me in her will. I still have it. A leaf from a golden artichoke given to her by that rogue, Francois I, who conspired to wed her to Charles Brandon after her first husband Louis of France died."

As she spoke, I battled to preserve my disintegrating composure.

She chuckled. "It turned out well enough in the end, but for a time after their return to England my father threatened to throw them both in the Tower for their presumption. My aunt often said that jewel represented the best and the worst in her life, both the sorrow and the joy." She leaned forward. "Master Beecham, are you sure you are well? You look pale."

"I'm a bit tired, is all," I murmured, scarcely trusting myself. "Thank you for indulging me. I cannot begin to tell Your Majesty how much it has meant."

"I enjoyed it. It has been too long since I thought of my late aunt. Perhaps one day, you'll pen a family history for me. I'd happily commission it." She wagged her finger. "I daresay it would keep you from other, less reputable sources of income."

"I shall have to consider it, Your Majesty." I forced out a smile, glad of the dimness in the room. "I should like to retire awhile, by your gracious leave."

"Of course." She held out her hand. As I bowed over it, she said, "I believe I owe your current employers an answer. Come back tomorrow, and let's see if I can arrange one."

"Yes, Your Majesty," I said and I kissed her dry, bejeweled fingers.

Rochester led me to a building off the bailey. There was a trough in the quadrangle where I could bathe, and a room upstairs with the essentials. I stripped to my hose, careful to keep these above my hips as I washed in the moss water, then went up and closed the door.

A cold meal waited on the table. I had no appetite, and wondered if I ever would again. Still, I tied back my damp hair and ate my fill. The needs of my body cared nothing for the desolation in my heart.

After eating, I sat on the edge of the straw-filled cot and removed the jewel from my bag again. In the room's rustic surroundings, it shone like a fragment of a star. I marveled that I could have mistaken it for anything else. I ran a fingertip along a sculpted vein, as if it were alive, knowing now how far it had traveled to reach me, across the Channel from France, through a cherished lifetime. I looked down to my concave groin, and to the left, to that hip which bore my own mother's stigmata.

"The only persons who would have known of it are those who were intimate with the late duchess's person . . ."

"Charles of Suffolk's squire came to see me. A stalwart man . . ."

I closed my eyes. I had to rest. I slid the jewel into my cloak lining and lay down, pulling the coarse linen sheet over me.

As I drifted off to sleep I thought Kate would be as surprised as I had been when I told her it was not a petal, but a leaf.

CHAPTER TWENTY-SIX

I dreamed of angels. To the echo of a soaring chorus, I opened my eyes and found the room submerged in night. A fiery glow flickered from the open window. I sat upright. The singing came from outside. Then I saw the figure in the room with me.

"Barnaby? Is that you?"

"Yes. I hope you don't mind. I let myself in." He stood with arms wrapped about his chest, staring out. Though in partial shadow, I could see his features were somber. "Did you make your appointment?" he asked, without looking around to me.

"Yes. I brought your bow back." I paused. "Where's Peregrine?"

"Fast asleep. He eats like the famished, and drops like a stone. Come, look at this."

Pulling on my breeches, I padded barefoot to the window.

Indigo sky canopied the castle. An improvised altar had been set up in the bailey, draped in faded crimson sporting threadbare gold crucifixes. Before it stood a white-robed figure, holding aloft a chalice. Banked about the altar were beeswax tapers, their wavering flames casting incandescent light upon the uplifted faces of common men and women, kneeling in rapt silence. Perfumed smoke gusted from censers. The refrains of a hymn rose upwards from a choir of children assembled on crates.

I saw the Queen seated on a chair, a garnet rosary twined in her hands. The gems captured the candlelight, scattered it like blood drops across her dress.

"By God, she is secure of her victory," said Barnaby. "We can only hope this is all she'll make us suffer of her Papist rites."

Mesmerized by the scene's eerie strangeness, I said, "I've never seen the old ways before. They're quite beautiful, in truth."

"For you, perhaps. To those of us who've seen heretics burn in France and Spain, it's not so pretty a sight." Barnaby turned into the room. There were no shutters or pane on the window, so I could only turn about as well, and watch him pace.

"I don't like it," he said. "I want to do her honor as my queen, but already she brings out altars and burns incense, just as they warned she would." He looked at me. "Word came tonight that the Duke is assembling an army against her. If he fails, her way to the throne stands open."

"As it should," I told him. "It is, after all, her throne."

"I know that. But what if . . . ?" He glanced at the door, lowered his voice to a whisper. "What if we're wrong? What if her devotion to Rome proves more compelling than her duty to England? Edward was terrified of this very thing. He sought to alter the succession because he believed she would yank us back into superstition and idolatry."

I started. "What exactly do you mean? Philip Sidney said something to that effect, the night we were in the King's rooms. He said Edward had been forced to sign something. Earlier today, Her Majesty told me the Council had said she'd been disinherited because of doubts about her legitimacy."

"That's the excuse. In truth, Edward didn't think Mary was a bastard, but he also never thought she should be queen." Barnaby paused. "What he signed, barring her from the throne, he did willingly. I thought you knew."

"No." My mind worked fast to absorb this unexpected development. "I thought the Duke had forced Edward to sign an alteration, naming Jane Grey as his heir. Are you saying he had plans of his own, before he fell ill?"

"Yes. He wanted Elizabeth to rule. He was going to tell her himself. That's why Northumberland went to such lengths to refuse her permission to visit. He didn't want Edward and her to meet and hatch a plot against him."

I'd suspected there was more to this tangle of half-truths and lies.

"How do you know this?" I asked quietly.

Barnaby frowned. "How else? Master Cecil told me. He approached me shortly after Edward suffered his first serious collapse. He said the King and I were like brothers, and therefore I would understand his concern."

Again, I felt that sharp twist in my gut. "Concern about what?"

"That the Duke aimed to safeguard his own power, regardless of Edward's desires." He went to the lone stool in the room and perched. Clasping his hands, he regarded me thoughtfully.

"Edward had been ill for three years. He knew he might not live long enough to marry and sire an heir. By right of succession, Mary stood next in line to the throne. Edward was against any rapprochement with Rome, so he invited Mary to court to sound her out. Her refusal to accept the Reformed Faith convinced Edward of her unworthiness. According to Cecil, he decided to disinherit Mary in favor of Elizabeth. He told Cecil as much, and asked him to help draft the necessary documents so he could present his decision to the Council. But he developed a terrible rash and fever and, soon thereafter, collapsed. The Duke took over his care. That was the last anyone from the Council saw of him."

"Wait a minute." I held up a hand, the seemingly disjointed pieces of the puzzle falling like knives into place. "Edward wanted to present his decision *without* the Duke knowing of it beforehand? Why? Northumberland shared his concerns about Mary. Why hide it from him?"

Barnaby shrugged. "Edward could be tight-lipped when the occasion warranted. Once he decided against someone, he rarely changed his mind. I think he took a dislike to the Duke when he realized how much control Northumberland held over him. In any event, after his collapse, he was denied access to anyone without the Duke's leave, including Cecil."

"Which is when Cecil came to you." Had I not been so outraged, I might have admired its sheer audacity. Our Master Secretary had been far busier than anyone had imagined.

"That's right," said Barnaby. He looked perplexed. "He told me he feared the Duke might hasten the King to his death, and turn the axe on anyone who tried to expose him."

"And you believed him." As I spoke, I recalled that dapper figure with its modulated voice, which could exude such sincerity, even as his gaze remained indifferent.

"I had no reason to doubt," he protested, spreading his massive hands. "He wanted me to watch over the King and report anything unusual. He didn't know the Duke would dismiss me from service. I kept watch all the same, especially after I discovered Northumberland had also dismissed all of Edward's physicians."

I found it suddenly difficult to draw breath.

Barnaby went on. "You must know all this. You work for Cecil. When you helped Her Grace, it was by his orders. That's what Peregrine told me. It's why I agreed to help you."

I made myself move from the window. I felt cold, numb. "Half-truths and omissions," I mused aloud, "that's how he functions." I looked up. "He knew everything, all the time."

Barnaby stared. "He knew what the Dudleys were doing?"

"I think so." An implacable fury rose in me. "Without Edward to protect him, Cecil stood alone. He knew that if the Duke succeeded in his own plots, he wouldn't survive. He knew too much, and Northumberland had grown too powerful. Even if a lone assassin could do the deed, there were still the Duke's sons and wife to contend with. That's why he had to do more than bring down Northumberland. He had to destroy the entire Dudley clan."

I drew a shuddering breath. "I never saw it. I never would have, had we not spoken tonight, though it was staring me in the face from the moment he asked me to spy for him."

Barnaby stood. "But if Cecil was going to destroy the Dudleys, why didn't he warn Her Grace away? All he had to do was tell her Edward was dying. Why risk her life?"

"I'm wondering the same thing." I retrieved my chemise from the floor and slipped it on. "I intend to find out."

"I wish he were here!" Barnaby hit a fist into his palm. "I'd make him explain it, the snake."

I met his gaze, saw the grief and anger, and shook my head. "We've been cruelly used, my friend. None more so than you, whose devotion to your king became fodder for his game." I took a moment. "I have one more question," I said. "Did you tell Cecil about the herbalist?"

He averted his eyes. "I did. It seemed odd. Why would Northumberland dismiss the royal doctors only to bring in an herb witch? When Sidney saw Lady Dudley in Edward's room one evening, giving the herbalist orders, I recalled Cecil saying he feared the Duke might hasten

Edward to his death. What better way than poison? It seemed right to tell him."

My heart felt as if a giant hand gripped it in a vise. Drawing a steadying breath, I put on my jerkin and boots, and took up my battered cap.

"Where are you going?" asked Barnaby, as I fastened my bag's straps and shouldered it.

"To ask the Queen for leave. If she grants it, I've urgent business in London." I looked at him. "Promise me you'll look after Peregrine. I don't want him to think I've abandoned him, but I can't bring him with me. I can't risk them finding out what he means to me."

"By them, you mean Cecil."

"Among others."

"Let me come with you. I've a score of my own to settle with him."

I clasped his stolid hand. "I'd like nothing better. But you'll be helping me more if you keep Peregrine safe, and support the Queen. She may not share your faith, but it could be that with men like you at her side she will learn to rule with temperance."

We embraced, as companions and comrades, then I drew back and slipped away.

I had Cinnabar readied by the time her summons came. Rising from my crouch in the shadows to follow Rochester, I made certain my expression conveyed only dutiful concern. My sudden bid for departure was bound to incite suspicion.

She waited in the hall, her thinning hair in a net at her nape. Without her headdress, she looked tiny. The rosary hung at her waist, its scarlet stones muted against the array of rings on her fingers. She was a woman who in all other respects seemed impervious to vanity, and I found her fondness for jewelry inexplicably disturbing.

"Rochester tells me you wish to leave," she stated, before I righted from my genuflection. "Are our accommodations not to your liking?"

"Your Majesty, I assure you I've no wish to return to the road so soon, but I understand the Duke makes plans to march against you. I think it best if I conveyed your reply to the lords sooner rather than later—that is, if Your Majesty still wishes to reply."

I held my breath as Mary shifted her gaze to Rochester, who gave a slight nod.

"I do," she said. "I need all the support I can get, even from your treacherous lords."

The bite in her remark carried a warning. She wasn't an easy woman to know, nor, it seemed, to please. Whatever she had endured in her youth had marked her for life, warped her personality in some irreconcilable way.

"Your Majesty," I ventured, "with the Duke about to take the field against you, the lords will be even better disposed to your cause."

"I don't care what their disposition is. They'd be wise to do as I say if they wish to keep their heads." She went to her table, retrieved and thrust two folded and sealed parchments at me.

"The sealed one is in cipher. Anyone with experience will know the key. Tell your lords they're to follow it without deviation. The other is a letter for my cousin, Jane Grey. Memorize it. It's a private message meant for her alone, so if you can't find a trustworthy way to convey it to her, destroy it. I don't want it falling into the wrong hands."

"Yes, Your Majesty," I murmured. It was more than I'd hoped to perform. Getting one letter into the proper hands would prove dangerous enough, much less delivering two.

"I don't expect a reply from either one," she told me. "I should be in London soon enough. But, if you uncover any news that might influence my course, favorable or otherwise, I demand to be informed. Your loyalty to those who've hired you should not supplant your allegiance to your queen. Do you understand?"

"Yes, Your Majesty." I started to bow over her hand. She withdrew it. Glancing up, I found her looking at me as if she no longer knew who I was.

"Give my regards to Master Cecil," she said. "Though it's not in my instructions, tell him from me that he knows what he must do."

I pocketed the letters, and backed from her presence without a word.

London

CHAPTER TWENTY-SEVEN

Mist wreathing off the Thames formed a wavering veil. The day already promised to be hot, the mid-morning sun casting a luminescent chimera upon the thrust and sprawl of London.

It had been a short ride, a mere day and a half. I'd not taken much rest. I avoided whatever main thoroughfares existed and skirted all townships. A few discreet inquiries of passersby had revealed every town was jammed to the rooftops with the Queen's supporters, gates shut and manned in anticipation of the Duke. As with any situation that might result in anarchy, the streets were also teeming with riffraff. A lone man on a horse was an easy target, so I sought refuge in the woods, awakening before dawn to resume my ride.

I sat atop a hill, a vantage spot from which to view the place where it had all started. Was it only a week ago I'd beheld this same city with the awe-struck eyes of a boy eager to cull his fortune? The sight of it made me feel hollow inside. All of my life, I had longed to know who I was and where I came from. Now that I knew, there was a part of me that longed to turn about and lose myself in an ordinary life, to forget a world where sons born to royal women were forsaken and men sacrificed innocents to their ambitions. Whatever answers I had come to London for were not anything I wanted to hear.

Fortune often smiles upon those least favored.

I chuckled humorlessly. It seemed fortune had a sense of humor, for

I, the least favored, had more than my share of responsibilities; and one of them drew near even as I sat in the stillness, contemplating becoming a fugitive from my own truth.

I waited until I heard the telltale rustle, then I said without looking about, "No use hiding anymore. I've known you were behind me since Bury St. Edmund's."

A muffled clop of hoof preceded Peregrine's wary approach. He wore his hooded cloak. I took in the strips of homespun fettering his horse's hooves, the reins, bridle, and stirrups, even his dirk in its scabbard—in short, anything that might make a sound. The lad had more tricks up his sleeve than an artifact peddler.

"You can't have known," he said, eyeing me. "I made sure to stay at least fifteen paces behind you at all times, and Mouse has a light step."

"Yes, and by the looks of it should have been as quiet as his name. But you forget that horses, especially those who've ridden together, make all sorts of signals when they sense the other near. Cinnabar practically bolted away last night toward that glen where you were resting. You should have joined me. I had rabbit for supper."

"Aye, and, with that fire you made, you're lucky every poacher in the county didn't drop by to sample it," retorted Peregrine. He paused. "You're not mad at me?"

I sighed. "Disappointed. I did ask Barnaby to watch over you."

"Don't blame him. He did his best. He told me that under no circumstances was I to follow you. He said you had private business to attend to, and we must honor your decision."

"I'm glad you paid such close attention." I raised my hand to my brow, scanning the road. "I'm surprised he isn't behind you. You two must think I'm incapable of tying my own points, what with the way you fuss and fret."

"I wasn't going to let you leave me behind again." Peregrine squared his narrow shoulders. "You need all the help you can get. I told you before we left Greenwich. You're no good on your own. You get into too much trouble."

"Is that what Barnaby thinks, as well?"

Peregrine nodded. "He was going to be the one to come after you. I convinced him to let me do it, instead. No one would miss me, while Barnaby would have had to ask leave of Rochester, who isn't about to let a brawny lad get away from the Queen's service, not with the Duke hot on her trail."

"True. But you still should have heeded him. You've no idea what you risk."

"I don't care." Peregrine's eyes were earnest in his grimy face. "I'm your body servant, remember? I go where you go, no matter what. I have to earn my keep."

I couldn't keep the smile from my face. "By God, you're stubborn as a pit bear and smell almost as bad. How did I end up with such a tenacious mite?"

Peregrine scowled, about to retort when a startled flock of pigeons caught my eye. I turned back to the city. When I saw a cloud of dust snaking toward us, I hissed, "To cover!" and we spurred our mounts into the nearby fringe of bushes and beech.

We slid from our saddles and held the horses close, hands on bridles, barely breathing. A militant thunder came closer and closer. It reminded me of the night we'd sat at the roadside and watched Robert Dudley and his men gallop past. Only this time, the noise was like that of some great lumbering creature, composed of hundreds of metallic hooves striking the road. Its approach vibrated the air around us, sent the dust rising in billowing gusts.

The standard bearers came first, carrying banners emblazoned with the Dudley bear and staff. The cavalry followed on leather-caparisoned horses, swords and bows strapped to saddles. Then came the foot soldiers, line after line in chain mail, interspersed with oxen and mule-drawn carts. I detected the bulk of cannon under tarps, and assumed the carts must also contain a supply of equally lethal weaponry.

Then, I saw the mounted lords. Each wore quilted battle gear and rode solemnly behind the Duke, who, defiant at their head, was distinguished by his audacious crimson cloak. He wore no cap, his dark hair framing his granite face, which, even from my distance, appeared to have aged years in a matter of days.

At either side of him were three of his sons: Henry, Jack, and Ambrose, outfitted in a martial splendor. For the first time in all the years I'd known them, the brothers I had feared and hated, envied for their camaraderie, weren't laughing. Like Robert before them, they understood they now confronted the ultimate challenge, one that would either end in triumph or tragedy for their family.

In tense formation they marched past, this army assembled to defeat Mary Tudor. I waited in silence after they'd disappeared down the road, grappling with unexpected remorse. The Dudleys had never cared a fig for anyone but themselves. They'd gladly see both princesses, and all who tried to help them, to their deaths. There could be no room for pity in my heart, even if the Duke and his sons were innocent of the one crime I most burned to avenge. With Northumberland gone from the City, I had an opportunity I must not ignore.

I mounted Cinnabar, spurred him back onto the road, where the dust wafted in the air like tattered veils.

"Where are we going?" Peregrine asked as we cantered toward London.

"To see an old friend," I replied. "By the way, how do we get into the Tower?"

"The Tower!" Peregrine exclaimed, as soon as we cleared the checkpoint at Aldgate, which had required distribution of most of the gold angels from the purse Walsingham had given me. "We can't get inside there. It's a royal fortress, in case you hadn't noticed."

"What a shame. You see, I really must get inside. I've a letter to deliver."

Peregrine blew air out of the side of his mouth. "The strongest fortress in England, and you have a letter to deliver? Why don't we just knock on the gates? It'll have the same result. Or haven't you heard the old saying? Once in, only your head gets out. I'm beginning to think you're as much of a unicorn as Kate says."

I paused. "A what?"

"A unicorn. A fabled beast. A lunacy."

I threw back my head and laughed, with genuine, belly-heaving mirth. I suddenly felt much better. "I've never heard that before. I like it."

"I wager you'll like it less if you end up trussed in a dungeon with your horn cut off. We can't get inside the Tower without proper leave, so forget about even trying. Any other wretched place you'd like us to try instead?"

"No. But you've given me an idea." My smile lingered as we rode into

Cheapside. The streets were eerily quiet. Shuttered windows had turned taverns into bastions. Except for a lone beggar too wasted to crawl away from the doorway where she huddled, there were no people to be seen. The populace had gone underground, as if to await a calamity.

"We should stable the horses and take to the river," Peregrine said. "We're too obvious. There's no one around but us."

"You'll have to excuse my aversion to water at the moment," I replied as we rode single-file down to the riverbank, where we might better avoid the conduits and refuse heaps, if not the ubiquitous sewage.

When I spied Whitehall's jumbled turrets in the distance, I reined to a halt. "Which way to Cecil's house?"

Peregrine looked leery. "Do you think he'll still be there?"

"He's there." My voice hardened. "You're to do exactly as I say from now on. Do I make myself clear? If you make a nuisance of yourself, I'll truss you up. This is not a game, Peregrine. One mistake and we could both end up dead."

"I understand." He gave a servile whirl of his hand. "This way, lord and master."

He led us back into the labyrinth of crooked streets. The feeling of impending disaster was palpable here, a presence stalking the dark pockets where the houses staggered into each other like drunkards. I was glad when we emerged onto a wider street that went through the palace, though even here it was remarkable how still and deserted everything was, like a kingdom in a fable, frozen in time.

When we neared our destination, I left Peregrine with the horses and strict orders, and proceeded alone.

A high wall enclosed the house's façade. I tried the postern gate first and found it unlocked. Moving toward the front entrance, I unsheathed my dagger. It would serve me little in a pitched confrontation, but the bow Barnaby had left strapped to Cinnabar's saddle was too cumbersome for indoor fighting.

I glanced up at the windows. The house appeared as uninhabited as the rest of the city. A small gate opened to the side. I vaulted it, landing on soft turf. I stood in the garden, which sloped toward a private landing quay screened by willows. As I suspected, a barge was moored there, the boatman hunched at the fore, swigging from an ale skin.

I turned to creep around the house. I found a coffer propping the back door open, as if someone had been coming and going in haste. Beyond was the mullioned window of Cecil's study. Flat against the wall, I inched forth and craned my head upward to peer within.

When I spied the figure inside, taking ledgers from the desk and stuffing them into a valise, I returned to the door and slipped quietly into the house.

The interior was submerged in gloom. I eased toward the far, open doorway with caution, looking to either side. The wood floor creaked under my weight. I froze where I stood, anticipating thugs with knives and fist. Then I crept forth, until I was close enough to look inside.

Cecil stood with his back to the door, clad in plain breeches and doublet. A traveling cloak was tossed over his chair. He had the valise on the desk, about to close it when he went still. Without looking around, he said, "This is a surprise."

I stepped forth.

He turned, glanced at the dagger in my fist. "Have you come to kill me, Squire Prescott?"

"I should," I replied. Now that I was face-to-face with the man who had played and outmaneuvered everyone with the skill of an expert puppeteer, my heart beat impossibly loud in my ears. I looked about the room. "Are you alone? Or do I have to deal with your assassin first?"

Cecil gave me a thin smile. "If you're referring to Walsingham, I assure you the situation has become too precarious for a man of his staunch persuasions. I imagine he's on his way to Dover by now, to book passage to the continent. I'd have gone with him myself, had I not my family's welfare to consider."

"What? Queen Mary getting too close for comfort?"

Cecil's smile didn't waver. "Entirely. In fact, I was about to take my barge to the Bridge, and hire a mount to Hertfordshire. It's not far from Her Grace's manor at Hatfield." He paused. "Would you care to join me? She'll be happy to receive you, I should think. She may even reconsider your request to enter her service, after everything you've done for her."

My anger, held too long under check, blazed. "Don't dare play with me, not after everything *you've* done."

He regarded me. "It seems you've a bone to pick with me. Let us sit and discuss it like gentlemen." He leaned to his valise, as if to shift it aside.

I didn't hesitate. Leaping forth, I pressed my dagger to his ribs, hard enough to be felt through his doublet. "I'd be careful if I were you," I whispered. "I don't need another reason to make you regret ever having met me."

He replied, "I would never regret that. May I, at least, sit? I have a touch of the gout, and my leg pains me."

Despite everything, I had to admire his restraint. I even found myself hoping I wouldn't be forced to act. Truth be told, I wasn't certain I could carry out my threat, particularly now that my initial blinding rage had started to ebb into something more manageable. I wasn't like him. I didn't relish these elaborate subterfuges, nor did I have the desire to harm anyone. I also needed his cooperation, if I was to discover the truth.

"I'm not sure what I've done to offend you," he began, his hands draped on the armrests as if he addressed an inopportune guest. "I am no more a traitor than any other councilor obliged to support the Duke against the Queen."

I met those cool, appraising eyes, which had been my first indoctrination into his perfidious world. "My business with you is private. I'll leave Her Majesty to ordain whatever punishment she deems best."

"Ah. I must say, you stay remarkably true to character. You believe Mary has been wronged and I had a hand in it."

"Would you deny you provided information they needed to pursue her? Was it a coincidence Lord Robert happened to be on the same road as I was, at almost the same time?"

Cecil leaned back in his chair, crossing his trim legs in their dun-colored hose. "I won't deny I nudged him in the right direction. I also did not lift protest when I heard Lord Arundel had put Durot—or rather, Fitzpatrick—in Lord Robert's company, though I knew he could confound the chase. You see, I'm not entirely her enemy."

I likened his voice to a siren's song, soothing, melodic, and all too convincing. A few days ago, I would have been lulled.

"You're lying. Mary is the last person you wanted on the throne. You've worked against her almost as avidly as you've worked against the Duke. You wanted her taken on the road, or better yet, killed as she fled. It's what you planned. Fortunately for her, she proved less gullible than you thought."

"I've never hidden where my ultimate allegiance lay." He eyed my hand as it tightened on my dagger hilt. "You might be interested to know that, regardless of what you may think, Her Grace will have more need of me than ever before. She and Mary have never been close, not as sisters should be."

He reached again for his valise. I snapped, "Stay away from that."

He paused. "I shall need my spectacles and cipher wheel. I assume the letter you bring is written in her usual code? You must have impressed her. She never entrusts her missives to strangers."

I had the unsettling sensation I was dueling with someone who exceeded any ability I had to thwart him. I struggled to make sense of what I felt, of what I saw and heard; to pry it apart and search it for the unspoken meaning within. When I finally did, I nearly guffawed aloud at my own naïveté. That I could have ever have believed I'd found out all there was to know about this subtle, lethal man.

"It was *you*," I breathed. "I overheard Lady Dudley telling Robert someone at court was feeding Mary information. Walsingham said much the same. You were the one who warned Mary away. You let Robert go after her, but you protected yourself first by sending her advance notice. She told me at Framlingham you would know what must be done. I thought it was a threat, but it's not, is it? She will spare you because she thinks you helped save her from the Duke."

A touch of amusement laced Cecil's voice. "I can hardly take all the credit. I'm told her cousin, the Duchess of Suffolk, also sent her a communiqué, detailing all types of sordid goings-on. It seems Madame Suffolk had her own axe to grind against the Dudleys."

I was not surprised to hear of the Duchess's involvement. She had vowed to wreak her fury on the Dudleys. What better way to achieve it than to feign compliance with them, while secretly inciting her royal cousin to action?

But there was, of course, the other matter involving her, the primary reason for my being here. I watched Cecil closely as he added, "As I've said, I'm not entirely Mary's enemy. Oh, and she always uses the same cipher. I've advised her several times to devise a new one, but she never listens. One of the few qualities she shares with her sister."

He reached again to his valise, drew out a pair of silver-framed glasses. He held out his hand. "The missive, please?"

I gave it to him. A chill surety began to seep through my veins. He was indeed a master of opportunism, an expert in courtly games of deceit. Whatever I thought he had done, or was about to do, only revealed another layer underneath.

He read Mary's letter in silence, glancing now and then at the key wheel in his other hand. When he was done, he removed his glasses, and set the paper and wheel aside.

"Well?" I said. I felt a subtle shift in the air.

"She, too, stays true to character, I'm afraid." He raised weary eyes. "She orders that before the Council thinks of asking clemency, they must see to it that she's proclaimed queen to the exclusion of all other claimants. She also warns that those who failed to offer her support should remove themselves at once. Those who stay must show proof of their constancy by taking the Duke and his sons into custody, as well as Jane Grey. She promises the usual array of punishments if her orders are disobeyed. Not that they will. We all know when the die is cast."

"You'll be safe enough," I pointed out, but I found no satisfaction in the barb. There was an awful tingle in my belly, a growing awareness I had made an error in my assessment of him.

"Do you truly believe that?" He offered me a rueful shake of his head. "I may have helped her to stay one step ahead of the Duke, but don't think for an instant she's forgotten I served the man. There'll be no place for me at her court. No matter. Country life suits me well enough."

"She would banish you?" I felt a keen disappointment. Cecil was not someone a wise monarch should disdain.

"Not in so many words, but she gives me no other choice. She'll never trust any of us who served the Duke or her brother. I'm simply luckier than most, in that I needn't soil my hands by putting my former master in prison."

And those hands, I noticed, had changed. The ink stains under the nails were faded, as if he had already started to slough away the skin of his prior role.

Cecil went on: "Had it gone differently, we'd have seen her to the same prison quick enough. Those, like me, who are merely banished, should count themselves fortunate indeed, considering not a few heads will roll before this matter is done."

His play for empathy was a mistake. I smiled coldly. I had been wrong. She had not disdained him. She had seen through him. The time had come to cast my own die.

"But not yours," I said. "You made sure no one would know the extent of your duplicity."

This time, I was pleased to see the skin about his mouth tighten.

"Unless you've been filling Mary's ears with nonsense, yes," he answered dryly.

"I would never stoop so low. Difficult as it may be for you to imagine, Her Majesty is an innocent when it comes to men like you."

"We'll see soon enough how innocent she is. You mustn't let her virginal righteousness blind you. She's an enemy to our faith, and her accession a tragedy to all those who've labored these many years to bring a greater glory to England."

"To England? Or to Cecil? Or are they one and the same to you?"

"I assure you, I've sought only to serve Her Grace."

Without warning, my anger returned, virulent as a fever. Lies and more lies—with him, they never stopped. I had no doubt he would lie his way to the tomb.

No more. I would make him speak the truth.

"Is that why you let her come to court?" I advanced on his chair. "Though you knew she risked her life? Is that why you failed to warn her away? Because you sought to serve her?"

There was no mistaking the change in the air.

"You forget I did advise her to leave," he said, in a measured tone. "I warned her several times of the danger she courted." He did not move, did not rise in alarm, though I stood so close I could have pierced him with my blade before he had time to cry out.

"You manipulated her," I hissed. "You manipulated her just as you manipulated me. You've been playing a game with all of us from the beginning."

Cecil smiled. "And what, pray tell, did this game of mine entail?"

I had to shift back, lest I went too far and didn't stop until he lay in a sprawl at my feet. It had all become crystalline clear, the truth surfacing as if a cloth had been wiped across the tarnished glass of my mind.

Everything was more horribly real than I had imagined.

"To see Elizabeth made queen instead of her sister—that was your game. The Duke's time had run out. After years of watching him exercise control over Edward, you decided never would the likes of Northumberland and his clan rule again. When the time came, they would fall, all of them, no matter the cost. And they would take Mary with them."

I drew a shuddering breath. "But then, something happened. Something you didn't anticipate."

"Is that so?" Cecil folded his hands at his chin. "Do go on. I find this all . . . fascinating."

"Jane Grey happened," I said. "You had no idea what the Duke planned, did you, that night Elizabeth arrived at court? All you knew for certain was that the King was dying, and Northumberland wanted the Princess for himself. By the time the Duke announced Jane Grey's marriage to his son and you understood how far he was willing to go to secure his grip on the throne, it was too late. So, you decided to put Elizabeth to the test, and, if all went as planned, dispose of your rivals."

His thin smile revealed nothing.

My voice rose, despite myself. I flung my next words at him as if they could humiliate, bruise, maim. "Northumberland posed no threat. You knew she would never have him. But Robert Dudley was another story. Only he had a claim on her more powerful than your own. Only he might have curtailed your influence over her. And it was that, more than anything else, which you could not bear."

"Careful, my friend," he said softly. "You go too far."

I'd finally struck a nerve. I should indeed be careful, for the only thing more dangerous than his friendship was his enmity. In that moment, however, I no longer cared.

"Not as far as you. You knew the moment the King died, the Duke would put an end to you, because of what you knew. His Majesty had confessed to you that he wanted Elizabeth as his heir. Putting Jane Grey on the throne might prove a deadly error, but it was possible the Duke would succeed, that Mary would escape, or the lure of power would prove too great and Elizabeth would succumb to Robert. If any of these occurred, you would disavow yourself completely."

I paused. His pale eyes were fixed on me.

I stabbed my finger at him, my breath coming fast. "You were willing to abandon her, to turn coats and feign support of whoever won—including Mary, though in your heart, you loathe and fear her more than the Duke himself."

At this, Cecil yanked his fingers across the chair arms. "You insolent pup! You dare insinuate I would betray my own princess?"

"I do. But no one will ever know, will they? No matter what, your hide is safe."

He came to his feet. Though he was not a tall man, he seemed to fill the room with his presence. "You should be an actor. The profession would benefit from your flair for the dramatic. I should warn you, however, that before you entertain Her Grace with this preposterous tale, you might consider she'll require more than unsubstantiated charges."

My every muscle tensed. I was right, and it stunned me. I had not thought to be so taken aback, so shocked, by what I'd uncovered. In some part of me, I had held on to the desperate hope that it might not be true.

"She is no fool," I told him. "It's clear to me, as it will be to her, that you let her, and her sister, walk into a quagmire of lies, completely unprepared for what might befall them."

An odd light flickered in his eyes. The violence I had glimpsed had vanished, replaced by disturbing levity. Uncoiling his hands, Cecil started to clap. The sound was rhythmic, reverberating against the oak paneled study. "Bravo. You have exceeded my highest expectations. You are everything I had hoped you would be."

I stared. "What do you mean by that?"

His regard was all encompassing, and merciless. "In a moment. First, let me say you've a rare gift for deciphering intrigue. You are correct. I did want Mary dead and Elizabeth on the throne. She is our last hope, the only one of Henry VIII's children worthy to inherit his crown. I may have failed in my goal, but it is an untimely delay of the inevitable. She was born to rule. When her day comes, nothing—*nothing*—shall compete with her destiny."

"Not even love?" I breathed. A hard lump filled my throat.

"Especially not love." His voice was matter-of-fact, as if he spoke of a color she must never wear. "That, above all, would be disastrous. She may have been born the wrong sex, but in everything else she is the prince her father longed for. She has his strength, his courage, his drive to conquer each obstacle thrown in her path. She must not give in to the weakness in her blood, the weakness of her mother, who was ever one to indulge herself. I'll not see her wreck herself for that Dudley knave, whose virility is his sole asset, and ambition his overriding vice."

"She loves him," I shouted, my hands clenched. "She's loved him since they were children! You knew that, and you deliberately set out to destroy it. Who are you to dictate her fate? Who are you to say where she may or may not give her heart?"

"Her friend," was his reply, "the only one with the stomach to save her from herself. Robert Dudley would be her downfall. Now, she need never be tempted. Even if he can survive Mary's wrath, which is unlikely, he's lost Elizabeth forever. She'll never trust him again. It is a reward which, in my estimation, more than compensates for her suffering."

"You're a monster," I whispered. "Did you ever stop to think that in your grandiose plan to put a crown on her head, you might break her spirit? Or, that Jane Grey, who never wanted any part of this, could lose her life because of it?"

Cecil's gaze riveted me to my spot. "Elizabeth's spirit is more resilient than you give it credit. As for Jane Grey, it wasn't my idea to make her queen. I merely sought to benefit from it."

I wanted to leave him there, with his papers and his machinations. Nothing he could tell me now would bring me anything other than revulsion and despair.

And yet I stayed, transfixed.

His smile was like slivered steel. "Have you nothing to say? We have reached the crux of the matter, the reason for why you are here. So, ask me. Ask what else I've been hiding from you. Ask me about the herbalist, and the reason Frances of Suffolk had to surrender her claim to the throne to her daughter."

He let out a small sigh. "Ask me, Brendan Prescott, who you really are."

CHAPTER TWENTY-EIGHT

You know," I whispered. "You have known from the start."

"Not from the start," he said. "I did hear the rumor. I heard it years ago, in fact, when I was younger than you. It was another of many scandals overhead in passing, like so much at court. I wouldn't have paid it any mind, had it not concerned Henry VIII's sister, the French Queen, that headstrong princess who'd risked a scandal when she wed his friend Suffolk, yet whose death caused nary a ripple."

"It was June," I said. A terrible cold enveloped me.

"Yes. June 1533, to be exact. King Henry had crowned Anne Boleyn in her sixth month of pregnancy, proof that God had blessed their union, and the turmoil they'd wrought on England. Little did they know that the child they awaited would signal Anne's doom."

Cecil lowered his gaze, paced to the window, where he stood staring out into his garden. Silence descended, like the hush of a tomb.

"I was thirteen years old, serving an apprenticeship as a clerk, another lad among thousands, working my fingers to the quick. I got around. I was nimble, and knew how to keep my mouth shut. Thus, I heard a great deal more than my appearance might suggest." He smiled faintly. "I was a little like you, in fact, diligent, well intentioned, and eager to find an advantage. When I heard the rumor, or rather, the story, it struck me as a sign of the times that the King's favorite younger sister had died alone, after months of seclusion in her manor at Westhorpe, where she'd lived in terror that Anne Boleyn might discover her secret."

The cold infiltrated my veins. "What secret?" I said in a near inaudible voice.

"Why, that she was with child, of course." Cecil turned back to me. "You must remember many believed Anne Boleyn had employed witchcraft to win her crown. The people hated her. She'd threatened to send Henry's own daughter to the block, and many of the King's oldest friends had already lost their heads because of her. She'd staked her entire future on the fact that Henry's first marriage was incestuous and he had no legitimate heir. But until she gave him a son, his sisters' children stood next in line to the throne.

"She therefore had every reason to fear Mary of Suffolk. Mary had witnessed Henry's break with Rome with horror and been a staunch ally of his first queen. She'd also given birth to a son and two daughters. Any child of hers posed a threat, but one born in those precarious months when Anne awaited hers— well, let us say, she would not have suffered it to live. In fact, it's said Anne's enmity was why Mary stayed away from court. At least, it was the reason Mary wanted everyone to believe."

My hands hung limp at my sides, my dagger pointed at the floor.

"Then she died," I said, without inflection.

"According to the story, she died shortly after giving birth. She'd hidden her pregnancy from all save her most trusted women, fearing Anne would find out and poison her. She was buried with some haste. In any event, Henry didn't mourn. He was too excited about his queen's impending confinement. So was everyone else. By the time Elizabeth was born, few remembered Mary of Suffolk had ever lived. In the next three years, her widower Charles Brandon married his pubescent ward and sired twin sons before his own demise. Anne Boleyn went to her death, and the King wed his third wife, who died after giving him his coveted son. In our world, nothing is as quickly forgotten as the dead."

"Mary's child?" I asked thickly. "What became of it?"

"Some said it was stillborn; others that it was hidden away, at Mary's dying request. Certainly, Charles of Suffolk never mentioned a child, which he would have, had he known."

"Maybe he didn't know." I wanted to bolt, to get as far away as I could. I didn't want to hear anymore. I didn't want to know. Once I did, there would be no peace for me, no rest. I would search for each missing thread till the end of my days.

Cecil nodded. "It's possible. Suffolk was abroad for most of that year. He might not have questioned her appearance when he did pay her the occasional visit, as it had been given out she suffered from dropsy. But why would she keep such news from her own husband? By all accounts, theirs was still a love match, despite the monotony that comes with years of marriage."

I averted my eyes. Just as I heard him take a step toward me, I pulled the words up out of my aching, bewildered soul. "Maybe," I whispered, "he wasn't the father."

Cecil stood still, so close, we might have embraced. His face looked ancient, the stigmata of worry, of ceaseless statecraft and insomniac nights, engraved upon it.

"Maybe," he said, and he reached out. "We will never know."

Before he touched me, I shifted away, though it felt more like lurching, so leaden were my limbs. "How did you find out?" I asked, and the chamber closed in around me, shot through with random afternoon light and long, stark shadows.

"Quite by accident." His voice was subdued. "Henry VIII's will stipulated that after his children and their heirs, his sister Mary's issue was next in line, so when I learned the Duchess had renounced her claim in favor of Jane, it gave me cause for thought. Frances of Suffolk has never renounced anything in her life. On the contrary, a more rapacious soul you would be hard-pressed to find. Northumberland said his wife had offered Guilford as a spouse for Jane, in exchange for Frances's acquiescence. I decided it was time to investigate. It wasn't long before I learned that Lady Dudley had threatened Frances with something the Duchess couldn't ignore."

I gave him a hollow smile. "Me."

"Yes, though I didn't know it at the time. I kept close watch on Lady Dudley. Once I learned she had appointed a squire for Lord Robert, I made the usual inquiries. Routine. One never knows what one will find. That is how I found out about the babe left in Warwick, whom the Dudleys had raised and set to clean their stables. That didn't surprise me. Orphans are, alas, all too common, as are exploitative patrons. But, when Fitzpatrick told me of the herbalist Lady Dudley had brought to treat Edward, I began to hunt in earnest. The answer, when I knew what it was, proved irresistible."

I was floundering, fighting against the unraveling of my self.

"And it was . . .?" I managed to say. Silence ensued. For the first time, Cecil wavered, as if he debated whether or not to continue.

The cruelty of the game finally unhinged me.

"TELL ME!" I leapt forward, my dagger clattering to the floor as I grabbed him by the doublet and rammed him, hard, against the wall. "Tell me this instant! Tell me, you miserable liar, or I swear by God, I'll kill you with my bare hands!"

In a choked whisper Cecil said, "The herbalist, Dame Alice—she had been in service to Mary of Suffolk. She was at Westhorpe in 1533. Lady Dudley, also, years before, had served Mary in France when she went to marry King Louis. All three women knew each other."

With a strangled sound that was part-moan, part-sob, I released him. I staggered back, as if I had been flung back to that day, years ago, when Lady Dudley had taken the book of psalms from me. I saw its frontispiece in my mind, with its scrolling dedication in French. I had not put it together, though it, too, had been with me all along.

A mon amie, de votre amie, Marie.

I had my mother's book. It had belonged to her, and she had bequeathed it to her friend—a favored lady who had accompanied her during her brief time as queen of France, someone she had confided in.

Lady Dudley.

Grabbing hold of the nearest chair, I threw it across the room. I wanted to tear the roof down about our ears, scour the walls to ashes, and rip off my own skin.

"You knew," I gasped, the words scalding my throat. "You knew who she was, and you kept it from me!"

He didn't shift a muscle. "You can blame me if you want. But it won't return the years lost to you. I may be guilty of many things, but not this. I didn't take your identify from you. Lady Dudley did. She concealed the truth, and murdered your Dame Alice."

I was beyond hearing reason. "She loved me," I bellowed at him. "She sought to protect me, to keep me safe, and they cut out her tongue! They mangled her, and kept her tethered like some beast, only to use her and kill her in the end."

"Yes," Cecil said quietly. "They did. And she endured all of it for love of you. She took you from your dying mother at her request, from the sister who wanted you dead, and brought you to the one place she thought would shelter you. She couldn't have known that she in fact was giving her new mistress a sacrificial weapon. She did take steps to protect you. Your name alone shows as much."

I thrust out a trembling hand. "No more. I cannot bear it."

"You must." Cecil shifted from the wall. "You must accept the treachery and the lies, and you must overcome them. Otherwise, it will be your undoing." He paused. "She named you Brendan not because of her reverence for the saint, but because it is the Latin form of the Irish name *Bréanainn*, which is derived from the term 'prince' in ancient Welsh. She knew who you were and she feared she might not be able to tell you herself. So, she gave you your legacy from the beginning. It was there with you, all the time."

"It doesn't matter," I said, and a lone tear slid down my cheek. "I may not know who I am anymore, but I know this much: I'll never be your pawn again. You have no proof. There is no proof. I intend to keep it that way." I met Cecil's eyes. "If you ever tell another living soul about this, as God is my witness, I will kill you."

"You can't imagine how relieved I am to hear it." He adjusted his rumpled doublet, walked past the broken chair to his valise. "Because if you ever did decide to declare yourself, it would be most unfortunate."

My laughter burst from me, an explosion of raw bitter mirth. "Is that why Walsingham was on the leads with a dagger? With all this uncertainty surrounding the succession, I must have posed a terrible hindrance!"

"You were never a hindrance. A bit too ingenious perhaps, but that's all." Cecil draped his cloak about his shoulders. "I had no intention of letting you die in my service." The gravity in his tone gave me pause. "If you consider the facts, you will see that when you first arrived in court, all I had was a story, a rumor, and the existence of an herbalist who'd served Mary of Suffolk in the year of her death. I can't possibly have known you were the alleged child."

As if I were back in Whitehall the night of Elizabeth's arrival, I heard that cryptic whisper: *He bears the mark of the rose.*

I couldn't rage anymore, couldn't fight. I met his steady gaze, saw myself reflected there and said, "No, not until someone confirmed it for you. That's why you had Walsingham follow me. You knew Lady Dudley had coerced the Duchess. You also knew about Dame Alice. Then I came to court. You must have been overjoyed when Walsingham told you about my introduction to the Duchess in the hall. After that, all you had to was wait and see how matters went."

He inclined his head, as though I had offered him a compliment. "I stand condemned. I have no further secrets from you."

I went still. "Hardly. But at least I'm no longer your fool."

"Indeed. And we can now work together for a cause greater than both of us—the cause of Elizabeth, which will soon face a challenge far worse than any Dudley."

"I never said I wanted anything more to do with you," I told him flatly.

He smiled. "Then why, my dear boy, are you still here?"

CHAPTER TWENTY-NINE

I t was late afternoon when we emerged together from the house. Having never been on a barge before, I had to concede it was indeed the preferable way to travel when in London. Though riddled with flotsam I didn't care to examine too closely, and exuding an acrid aroma, the periodic tides that washed in ensured the Thames remained cleaner than any city street, and infinitely more navigable. I was amazed by the speed with which the hired boatman, half-drunk as he was, propelled us toward that great bridge spanning the river, which carried the road from Canterbury and Dover into London.

The cake-like structure perched on twenty-one cramped piers, ornamented with a southern gatehouse and roofed with teetering tenements. As I gazed up at it, Cecil said, "Some people are born, live, and die without ever leaving it. When the tide is full, shooting it can be quite the experience, if you survive it."

The boatman grunted, displaying a toothless grin.

The barge rose and catapulted with nauseating force through a narrow vaulted arch. I gripped the edge of the bench on which I sat, forcibly lifted off my seat, my belly in my throat. Catching a churning swell on the other side, the barge reared up and down like a leaf caught in a maelstrom. I swallowed vomit.

I'd stick to my horse henceforth.

We entered swift but steady water, sailing toward a breathtaking view of a mirror-still tidal pool, where anchored galleons swayed against the lowering sky. The Tower brooded at the far end, guarding the city approach. Though I couldn't see them, I was certain that cannons protected every inch of those river-lapped walls. In the waning sunlight, the weathered stone looked tinted with rust and blood, a foreboding place no one would willingly enter.

Cecil said, "You needn't do this in person. There are many ways to deliver a letter."

I stared at the central keep, mortared in white, its four turrets tipped with standards. "She deserves this much, and you owe it to me."

Cecil sighed. "Ingenious *and* headstrong. I hope you know we can't overstay our welcome. I've no idea what to expect after I relay the Queen's orders, and in a few hours curfew will be upon us."

The barge docked. Cecil stood. "Pull down your cap," he instructed. "Whatever you do, don't speak unless you have to. The less they see and hear of you, the better."

"You'll get no argument from me," I muttered.

We mounted the water steps, turned past an open field to a gate-house, where an alarming number of guards patrolled the entry into the Tower. I heard the muted roar of lions, lifted my hooded gaze to the edifice before me. Crenellated battlements studded with barbicans thrust into the sky, shielding the central keep.

A guard stepped forth. Cecil swept back his hood. The man paused. "Sir William?"

"Good day to you, Harry. I trust your wife is doing better." Cecil's voice was smooth as the tidal pool shimmering below us. I hunched my shoulders, watching the guard from under my cap, which I'd yanked down about my ears. I was glad for once for my small build and moderate height. I did not stand out in any particular way.

"She's on the mend," the guard replied, in apparent relief. "I thank you for asking. Those herbs your lady wife sent served her in good stead. We are indebted to you for your kindness."

I had to smile, not withstanding my suspicion of Cecil and his wiles. Trust him to have sowed a debt in the Tower by offering medical assistance to a guard's wife in need.

I heard him say, "Lady Mildred will be pleased to hear her panaceas worked. She's ever tinkering with her recipes. By the way, Harry, I forgot to collect some papers when I was here yesterday." He motioned casually to me. I bowed. "This is an apprentice clerk of mine. Would you mind letting us through? We'll only be a moment."

"I'm afraid I can't, Sir William," said Harry, with some discomfort. He glanced over his shoulder at his companions, who were engrossed in a game of dice. "My lords Pembroke and Arundel gave strict orders to let no one enter the Tower without their leave."

His voice dropped. "A missive from the Lady Mary arrived this morn. My lords left at once for Lord Pembroke's house. Rumor has it she threatens to put the lot to the block if they don't declare for her by tonight."

"Indeed?" remarked Cecil, as if this news were of no particular account. "Rumors say so many things these days. One doesn't know who or what to believe anymore."

Harry chuckled uneasily. "Indeed. What with all this talk of mutiny at Yarmouth, and the Duke's army up and deserting him, the speculation's rife." His tone adopted the nervous conspiratorial confidence of a lackey with his better. "Before they left, the lords even ordered Lady Jane and Lord Guilford confined to their apartments, for their own safety. Lady Dudley was beside herself with rage. She threatened Lord Arundel with a dire end when her husband returns. My lord wasn't exactly civil in return, if you get my meaning."

He paused, searching Cecil's face. "I've heard that his lordship of Northumberland cannot win. Now, I'm not one for gossip, Sir William, but, if it's true, I'd appreciate fair warning. I've my own to see to, as you know, and truth be told, I'm only following orders."

"Naturally," said Cecil. "I don't think we should be discussing this in the open." He drew Harry into the gatehouse shadow, where they conversed out of my earshot. I saw him slip Harry one of his perennial pouches.

When Cecil returned, I hissed at him, "What is he talking about? What missive? I gave the Queen's letter to you!"

"It appears yours wasn't the only one she sent." He smiled thinly. "I had to bribe Harry for more information, and to let us through, so save your questions for later."

He walked forth in the brisk manner of a man who hasn't time to dawdle, nodding to the other guards, and forcing me to quicken after him like the menial I was supposed to be.

We passed under the raised iron portcullis, into the outer ward.

Cecil halted, pretending to adjust his sleeve, his valise clutched in one hand. In a hushed tone he said, "Mary has learned a thing or two, after all. She dispatched a duplicate of her orders via another courier, along with the news that she has amassed thousands to her cause. She prepares to march on London. The more sensible on the Council have retreated to debate her reception. Suffolk went with them. More telling, his wife the Duchess has departed for their country manor. In other words, all those involved save for Lady Dudley have abandoned Jane and Guilford to their fate. Both are here, in the same rooms where they were to await their coronation."

He looked about, drew a quick breath. Again, I was struck by the turns and twists of these past few days that I must now rely on the man I'd considered my foe only hours ago.

Unexpectedly he said, "I believe the Council will declare for Mary by this evening at the latest. As soon as they do, anyone inside these gates stays inside. Are you certain you want to proceed? I, for one, would rather not take the chance."

I regarded him. "Are you afraid? I didn't think you capable of it."

"You'd be afraid, as well, if you had an ounce of sense in that head of yours," he replied tartly. He squared his shoulders, assuming his suave aura of invincibility as if it were a well-worn coat. "Come, then. Let's get this over with."

We strode onward toward the keep.

I barely had time to reflect on the fact that I was in the infamous Tower of London. The murmur of the Thames at the numerous water gates echoed throughout the inner ward, magnified by the breadth of unrelenting stone. Guards, pages, and functionaries went to and fro, attending to their duties with nary a smile to be seen among the lot, their sullen presence adding to the claustrophobic air.

Cecil didn't acknowledge anyone. In his unadorned hooded cloak and flat velvet cap he could have been any one of the numerous clerks looking for their shifts to end. Indeed, any of said clerks could have been other than what they appeared. I scanned the ward. For a heart-stopping moment I thought I glimpsed a familiar figure pausing to mark us. When I focused, however, there was no one there.

I felt my nape prickle. It couldn't possibly be Stokes. I was tired. I was letting my fatigue get the best of me. And I must be mad to have insisted on this errand. Impregnable walls surrounded me. Below my feet lay miles of pits and dungeons, where men suffered the most agonizing of torments. Death on the scaffold was preferable to the array of devices inflicted on those imprisoned here, some of which were so demonic in ingenuity that many ended up shrieking for the mercy of the rope or axe.

Fear scrambled in the pit of my stomach. I concentrated on maintaining an impassive expression when we were detained at the keep's entrance. Again, Cecil parlayed his credentials and astonishing recollection for first names and familial details, not to mention a discreet use of coin, to gain us admittance.

Inside, torches shot out tongues of flame. The hall we traversed was damp, cold, for the sun never penetrated here. We climbed a turnpike staircase to a second floor roofed in timber, where two stern-faced yeomen in uniform, snub-nosed dags at their belts, stopped us.

"Master Cecil, I regret to say no one is allowed to see her," a burly fellow informed us, though not without an apologetic note.

Cecil took immediate advantage. "Ah, yes, Thom. I was told the lords had ordered her confined for her own protection." He removed Mary's letter to the Council from his pocket, the broken seal showing. "This man brings news from the Lady Mary. I don't think we should interfere with family business, do you?" he added, in an amiable tone. "We might soon find ourselves having to explain our own rather insignificant roles in this unfortunate affair. I assure you, he needs only a moment. "

Good Thom didn't need to be told twice. Motioning brusquely to the other, he had the door unlocked. I waited for Cecil to move forward. Instead, he stepped aside. "I do have some papers to fetch," he said. "You've a few minutes. That's all."

I stepped inside.

The room was small but not unpleasant, much like a bower, hung with tapestries. Fresh rushes cushioned my feet. I gazed to figure seated in a chair positioned at the casement window, which offered a circumscribed view of the city.

Without looking around Jane Grey said, "I'm not hungry and I am not going to sign anything, so put whatever you have on the table and go."

"My lady," I said, and I bowed low. She stood. She wore a fustian gown, her hair parted under a coif. In the gloom of the chamber, where premature dusk had already begun to settle, I could discern bruised shadows under her eyes. She seemed tiny, a child in adult garb.

Her voice caught in her throat. "I . . . I know you."

"You do, my lady. I am Squire Prescott. We met at Whitehall. I am honored you would remember me."

"Whitehall," she whispered, and I saw her shudder.

I ached to embrace her. She looked as if she hadn't known an hour's peace in weeks, as if nothing save tragedy would ever touch her again.

"I've little time," I said. "I've come to tell you not to despair." I removed Mary's second letter from my cloak. "Her Majesty sends you this."

She recoiled, as if she'd been struck. "Her Majesty? Is it over, then?"

"It will be soon. By tonight, the Council must declare for her. They can do nothing else. The Duke's army is abandoning him. It is a matter of time before he must surrender."

"Praise be," she said. "God knows in His Wisdom, I never desired this. The Duke and his wife, my parents, and the Council forced it on me. They wed me to Guilford, and made me do their bidding. Thus shall I tell Mary, if she ever can find it in her heart to forgive me."

"She already has." I took a step closer. "Her Majesty knows how grievously you've been used."

Her voice was as firm as the hand she held up, detaining my advance. "Pray, do not seek to lighten my burden. She is my cousin. In assuming her throne, I committed treason. There is no other remedy than to suffer the punishment she must impose. I will not shirk my duty, not even for my life."

My tears felt perilously close. I extended the letter to her. "Her Majesty won't wish you to suffer anything. As soon as she's seen to the true culprits in this affair, she will release you. You will go home, my lady, to your studies and your books."

"My books . . ." Her voice quivered. "To be a queen is a terrible thing, I've discovered. It brings neither reward nor comfort."

I could resist no longer. I strode to her and engulfed her in my arms. She sagged against my chest. Though she didn't make a sound, I felt her begin to weep.

Ebbing light slanted through the window. In that moment, I

wanted to tell her everything I had discovered, so that she would know she was not alone, that she would always find in me an uncle who cared for her.

But the words stuck in my throat. I could never tell her the truth. It would only heighten the terrible guilt she carried. I also realized that though I might one day come to forgive the Dudleys for their sins, perhaps even understand the rapacity that had driven them to such cruel acts, I would never forgive the devastation they had wrought on this fifteen year-old girl's soul.

She drew back. She was composed, the wet trails on her cheeks fading as she took the crushed letter from my hand and slipped it into her gown pocket. "I'll read it later," she murmured. From outside, came the sudden, disquieting toll of bells.

"You must go now," Jane said, "before they come. You cannot be found here. It would not go well for you."

"My lady," I said, "if you ever find need of me, you need only send word."

She smiled. "Not even you can save me from the path God has ordained."

I bowed again, went to the door. As I reached for the latch, I glanced over my shoulder.

She had returned to her vigil at the window, twilight gathered about her.

Cecil rose from a stool in the passage. Thanking Thom, who locked the door once more, he took me by the arm. "I was about to come in after you. Did you hear the bells? We must leave at once. In an hour at the most, the Tower gates shall close in Queen Mary's name. Henceforth, it will be her prison."

I shook his hand away. "God speed, then. I still have unfinished business."

Cecil leaned close. "You cannot. I know what you're thinking, and I tell you, it is madness. She is not a prisoner. She is free to move about and tell anyone she pleases that you didn't perish from that fall from the leads."

I met his penetrating stare. "She won't. She'll be too busy trying to save her precious son. Besides, I have no proof. I'm no longer a threat to her, if, indeed, I ever was."

"Be that as it may," he countered, and for the first time since we had met I believed he felt genuine concern, even worry, for me. "Would you put your life in her hands? Think well before you do this. I will not be held responsible for whatever may befall you."

"I never expected it of you. I instructed Peregrine to wait for me in the fields outside the city with our horses. If I'm not there by nightfall, he's to proceed to Hatfield. You can meet him and ride off to be with your family. But I must stay. She has something I need."

Cecil's jaw worked under his beard. He considered me for a long moment, then drew his cloak about him and tightened his hold on his valise. "May you find what you seek," he said tersely and he went down the staircase without a backward glance.

I resisted the claw in my belly, where the fear multiplied like vermin. Turning to meet the guards' curious stares I said, "If one of you might indicate the way to Lord Guilford's room?"

The yeoman Thom said, "I'll take you to him."

CHAPTER THIRTY

I climbed worn stone flags to the uppermost story, Thom ahead of me. Despite my icy bravura, I feared the upcoming confrontation more than I cared to admit. I could understand the primeval malevolence of the Duchess of Suffolk more than I ever would Lady Dudley. Frances Brandon had done what she had out of base greed. She was savage, heinous, but still motivated by recognizable emotion, warped as it may be. What Lady Dudley had done went beyond humanity as I defined it. She'd demonstrated an unforgiving brutality that had shattered my existence, caused the death of the one person in my world who'd loved me without reserve.

We came to a narrow closed door. As Thom spoke with the guards, I debated whether to leave. I could still catch up with Cecil, who was another kind of monster, yes, but one I'd prefer to deal with any day. I could meet Peregrine. By tonight, I could be in Kate's arms. I could live the rest of my days in ignorance, and most likely be the better for it. Whatever lay beyond that door could only bring me more pain.

Even as I thought this, my fingers strayed to the hidden inner pocket in my cloak, seeking the almost intangible object I had secreted there. The touch of it steeled my nerve. I had to do this, for Dame Alice's memory, if nothing else.

"Five minutes." Thom handed me his weapon. "Be careful. She's rabid as a dog, that one."

He unbolted and pulled open the door. Shoving the pistol in my belt, I stepped inside.

A large leather coffer sat in the middle of the room, heaped with clothing. Upon the floor were piled papers and books. Two figures labored in a corner, hauling a wooden chest from the wall. Near identical shades of fair hair mingled damply, the lean bodies under sweat-stained clothing molded of the same rib and bone.

At the sound of the door opening, she reared to face the intruder. At her side Guilford likewise looked up, and froze.

"It's about time you deigned to—" she began. She stiffened. "Who are you? How dare you barge in on us!" Her voice was strained, almost frantic, so unlike the woman I'd always known I couldn't formulate a word. Then I recalled my beard and cap.

I removed the cap. "I thought I'd be recognizable to you, of all people, my lady."

Guilford yelped. Hissing breath through her teeth, Lady Dudley stalked to me, her unbound hair showing streaks of silver, framing her gaunt, infuriated features.

"You," she said, "you are supposed to be dead."

I met her empty eyes. I could see now that she was ill. She'd been ill for years, both in mind and in spirit. She'd kept it well hidden under her glacial facade, against which nothing had seemed to penetrate. All the while, it had been eating at her like a canker, her husband's betrayal after years of dutiful marriage exposing the raw creature she had become. Like any woman faced with abandonment after a lifetime of self-sacrifice, she had lashed out with all the cunning at her disposal. Lethal as it was, in the final say, she had acted out of unbearable grief.

It brought me scarce comfort.

"I'm glad to disappoint you," I said.

Her mouth twisted. "You always did enjoy making a nuisance out of yourself." She reached up a hand in a phantom's gesture of her previous elegance, pushed back tendrils of hair from her brow. "How tedious. I had thought to be rid of you."

"Oh, you'll be rid of me. As soon as you answer my questions."

She stared at me. From behind her Guilford cried, "You stay away from us!"

"Be quiet," snapped Lady Dudley, without taking her cold, appraising gaze from me. "Let him ask whatever he wants. It will cost us nothing to hear him waste his breath."

I flipped back my cloak, revealing Thom's dag. I saw her eyes widen. "I may not be the best shot," I said, "but in such a small room, I'm bound to hit something. Or someone."

She stepped before me. "Leave my son out of this. He knows nothing. Ask your question and be gone. I have pressing matters to attend to."

For once, she spoke the truth. When the bells had begun to toll, she'd been in the middle of packing valuables. Like Jane, she'd understood what those bells signified; and she and Guilford had started dragging that coffer to the door in a futile attempt to block it. She knew the Council would soon arrive to put him under arrest—Guilford, her beloved child, the only one she had ever cared about. Her hunger for revenge was equaled only by her devotion to the one soul she could mold to her will.

She was human, after all. She could love, and hate.

"You cannot save him," I told her. "Those bells ring for Queen Mary. You've lost, my lady. Guilford will never wear a crown. In fact, he'll be lucky to keep his head."

"I'll tear you to pieces for that, you bloody cur," snarled Guilford.

Lady Dudley let out a macabre laugh. "I never wanted a crown for him! It's my husband who will lose his head for this, not my son. I'll save him myself, even if I have to beg for his life on my knees. Guilford will not pay for John Dudley's vile ambitions."

She took a step closer, her breath acrid. "It is *you* who have lost. Dame Alice is dead, and you'll get nothing more from me. Dead or alive, you don't exist anymore. You never did."

I took her measure, with deliberate indifference. "I know about Master Shelton."

She went still.

"Archibald Shelton," I continued, "your devoted steward. I know he was the one who shot at me that night in Greenwich. Rather poor aim for a man considered an expert marksman during the Scottish wars, wouldn't you say? I believe he was trying to spare me when he aimed at the wall. The ball just happened to ricochet. I also heard from none other than Her Majesty herself that before he came to you, Master Shelton was in service to Charles of Suffolk."

She threw herself at me, keening like an animal. Her attack threw me off balance. As I fended her nails from my face, the door flung open and the guards charged in. They grabbed hold of her, hauled her off me as she flailed and screamed obscenities.

"No!" I yelled. "Wait, leave her! I have to—"

It was too late. Two of the guards dragged her away, her shrieks rebounding against the walls. I knew then, as I'd known little else, that it would be a long time before I stopped hearing that unearthly sound in my dreams.

The echo faded to silence. Thom stood on the threshold. "It's time you left. They're shutting the gates at the Council's command. You don't want to spend the night in here."

I nodded numbly, moving toward the door when I heard a muffled sob. I looked over my shoulder. Guilford had slid to the floor, his face in his hands. I tried to find some compassion. It saddened me that all I could muster was disgust.

"Where is he?" I asked.

Guilford raised tear stained eyes. "Who?" he quavered.

"Steward Shelton. Where is he?"

Fresh tears choked Guilford's voice. "He—he went to fetch our horses."

Wheeling about, I bolted from the room.

Night had fallen. In the bailey, torches exuded smoky light, limning the stone walls. Bells rang out in discordant spontaneity, as more than one local pastor took to his steeple in an excess of joy. Outside the Tower walls, all of London had emerged in celebration for their rightful queen, while inside pandemonium erupted, as those still loyal to the Duke recognized their folly and sought to escape, even as ramparts were manned and gates shut.

Rushing down the stairs out of the keep, I came to a breathless halt. My heart pounded in my ears. I could scarcely draw breath as I scanned the crowded bailey for that figure I'd seen earlier, which I now knew had not been a figment of my overwrought imagination.

It had been Master Shelton in a black cloak. Master Shelton, who'd been fetching horses to aid Lady Dudley and Guilford in their escape, and seen Cecil and me going to the keep. He had to be close by. Lady Dudley had been expecting him. He wouldn't abandon her until he'd determined he could do nothing more. Master Shelton had always fulfilled his responsibilities with an impeccable sense of duty, no matter what. But he had served Charles of Suffolk before the Dudleys. He had known, and apparently grieved, my mother. That was why he loathed Elizabeth, daughter of the witch-queen who had driven the late Duchess to hide her pregnancy. Did he blame Anne Boleyn and her unborn child for my mother's death? Did he think she would have lived had Anne Boleyn not been queen?

Or was there more?

I had to find him. I had to know why he had, in his coarse way, sought to protect me.

I cursed, peered into a flickering darkness filled with cloaked figures. I'd never find him in this jumbled mess. I should make my escape while I still could, before they locked the gates, and I was trapped inside.

I started to turn to where the majority of those in the bailey were headed. As I did, I caught sight of a shadow lurking at the wall opposite me, where the night crept, inky thick.

A hood shielded its face. It stood still as a column. As I paused, every nerve on alert, it lifted its head. For an electrifying instant our eyes met. I sprang to him, just as Master Shelton whirled about and ran, pounding on powerful legs, into the crowd hastening from the ward.

I crashed headlong into the onslaught, trying to wedge my way forward. Master Shelton was ahead, distinguished by the bullish width of his shoulders. The cobbled causeway narrowed, forcing the fleeing officials and menials into a bottleneck. The portcullis was shut, a maw of teeth impeding their escape. From behind us, the ringing clangor of hooves signaled the arrival of mounted patrols on steeds, accompanied by scores of guards in steel helmets and breastplates.

I watched in horror as the soldiers began pulling men with seeming randomness from the throng, their staccato question—"Whom do you serve? Queen or Duke?"—accompanied by the sickening thrust of pikes through flesh. Within seconds, the stench of terror and blood thickened the air. At the portcullis, men clawed at each other in a frenzied scramble, stepping on heads, shoulders, ribs; breaking and crushing flesh and bone.

My stomach clenched. Master Shelton was trying to pull back, to fight his way from the madness that had erupted. He had spared my life at Greenwich. He also had served the Suffolks, and held the final key to the secret of my birth. If a guard or someone else identified him as a

Dudley servant, chances were he'd be arrested. Or killed.

A blood-flecked guard on a massive bay approached, forcing the crowd to part. Several unfortunates were forced off the causeway into the churning moat, where others swam and drowned. I rammed forward with my shoulders, as hard as I could, pushing those behind Master Shelton. The steward whipped his head about, the puckered scar across his face starkly visible.

He glared when he saw the guard coming toward him. I started to shout out a warning just as the crowd lurched into motion. The portcullis had been forced up. Men scurried under it in a frenzy to escape.

Master Shelton vanished. I started shoveling and elbowing, battling to stay afloat in the stampede. I staggered over the inert bodies of those who had fallen underfoot and been trampled. As I was dislodged along with the rest of the horde onto a landing quay, I looked about, desperate.

There was no sign of him.

Behind me I could hear the charge of the guards on horseback, followed by those with their pikes. Scattering like terrified beasts, many of the men began leaping off the quay into the river, preferring to risk the tide than be caught and skewered alive.

"NO!" I roared, even as I, too, ran forward. "NOOO!"

I kept roaring as I plunged into the swelling Thames.

Hours later, dripping and reeking of sewage, I reached the fields outside the city. Above me the bonfire-lit sky blazed. Behind me, London reverberated with clanging bells.

I had swum to a set of crumbling water steps on the south side, avoiding the river depths, where whirlpools gnawed the surface. I'd also avoided the sight of those sucked under by the pools' vortex, and those clambering back onto the quay like drenched cats, only to find the soldiers waiting.

I tried not to think of Master Shelton, who I doubted had ever learned how to swim.

Even more painful was the thought of that young girl who, as of this hour, had become a prisoner of the state, dependant on the Queen's mercy. Instead, I focused on putting one sloshing foot in front of the next, dragging the sodden length of my cloak behind me as I slogged to the road. I had no idea of how far it was to Hatfield. Maybe I could hitch a ride on a passing cart after I dried off

When I thought I was at a safe enough distance, I sank to the ground to search my cloak. I extracted the gold leaf in its drenched cloth, removed it to my jerkin. I was squeezing the excess water from my cloak and rolling it into a bundle to carry on my back when hoof beats came galloping toward me.

I crouched by a hawthorn bush, which was no place to hide. Fortunately the night was moonless, providing some cover. Perhaps whoever it was would ride by.

Huddling into myself, as close to the ground as I could get, I held my breath as two horsemen neared, both in caps and cloaks. When one came to a halt, I cursed my luck.

"It's about time," said a familiar voice. With a weary smile, I stood.

Cecil looked me up and down. He rode Mouse. At his side, on Cinnabar, Peregrine exclaimed, "Finally! We've been searching for you for over an hour, wondering what kind of trouble you'd gotten yourself into this time." He chuckled. "Another dip in the Thames?"

I gave him a sullen stare.

"Indeed," said Cecil. "Did you find what you were looking for, Master Prescott?"

"Almost." Tying my half-bundled cloak to the saddle, I swung up in front of Peregrine. "It wasn't a pleasant experience."

"I imagined as much." Cecil followed my gaze back to the Tower's silhouette. "The rabble's gone wild," he said quietly. "They clamor in the streets for Northumberland's blood. Let us pray Queen Mary proves worthy of it." He returned his regard to me. I met his eyes in tacit understanding. Enemies we should have been; indeed, should have remained.

The times demanded differently of us.

"To Hatfield, then," said Cecil.

We parted ways hours later, as dawn spilled over the horizon. Cecil's manor lay a few miles away. He gave me detailed directions to Hatfield, and then there was an awkward moment when I spoke my gratitude that he had stayed behind to help Peregrine, "Though I did tell the rascal not to wait for me," I admonished.

Cecil smiled. "There is still something to be redeemed in me, it seems." He inclined his head. "Pray, give my regards to Her Grace, and to Mistress Carey, of course," jolting me with a knowing sparkle in his cool eyes before he turned rein and cantered off.

I looked after him. Too much had gone between us for a true friendship to ever develop, but I reasoned that if Elizabeth must have an amoral champion, she would find none better.

Peregrine slouched behind me, half-asleep. "Hold tight," I told him. "I'm not stopping till we get to Hatfield."

I spurred us forth under a lightening sheet of a sky, over summer meadows and through copses of beech, until we came upon the red-brick manor nestled amid towering oaks, the floury scent of baking bread rising warm in the morning air.

I slowed Cinnabar to an amble. As we neared, I saw that Hatfield was a working manor, with enclosed pasture for livestock, orchards of fruit trees, a dairy, and other outbuildings. I knew, without seeing them, that the gardens would be lovely and slightly wild, like their mistress.

Peace stole over me. Here was a place where I might heal.

When I saw the figure that ran from the house onto the road, auburn hair tumbling about her shoulders, I lifted my hand to wave, in joy and relief.

I was home, at last.

Hatfield

CHAPTER THIRTY-ONE

I did not dream.

Awakening to the chamber where Kate had brought me in a state of exhaustion, I lay under rumpled linen sheets, absorbing the scent of lavender coming from a wreath on the wall, mingling with the linseed polish of the chair, the clothes press, and table.

Stretching bruised limbs, I rose. I stepped past a pewter pitcher and basin, peered out the mullioned window to the vast parkland surrounding the manor. I did not know how long I had slept, but I felt refreshed, almost whole. I turned back to the room, began searching for my clothes, which I seemed to recall Kate peeling off my inert body as I dropped into bed.

Without so much as a knock, the door banged open.

Mistress Astley bustled in, carrying a tray. "Breakfast," she announced, "though in truth it should be supper. You've slept away most of the day. So has your little friend. He's in the kitchen, devouring a lamb."

I gasped, my hands shooting down to cover myself.

"Oh, don't mind me," she chuckled, to my astonishment. "I have seen a man in his skin before. I may seem a bit long in the tooth, but I'll have you know I'm a married woman."

"My—my clothes?" I said, stunned. The last time I'd seen Mistress Astley, she'd scoured me with her eyes in mistrust. I barely recognized this stout partridge of a woman, with her cheery voice and convivial manner.

"Your clothes are being laundered," she said, whipping the linen off the tray to reveal a platter of manchet bread, cheese, fruit, and salted meat. "There's a fresh shirt, jerkin, and breeches in the press. We tried to match your weight and height to one of the grooms. Nothing fancy, mind you, but they'll do until we have you properly fitted."

She eyed me matter-of-factly. "You needn't fret. Mistress Carey found your things in the lining and has them safe. She's in the garden now, picking herbs. It's down the stairs, through the hall, and out the doors to your left. You can meet her there once you've eaten and shaved." She paused. "I do hope you'll want to shave. You're too slight for a beard. There's water in the ewer, and lye soap in the basin. We make the soap ourselves. It's as good as any you'll find, including that silly perfumed stuff from France."

She marched to the door, then stopped, as if she'd forgotten something. Turning back to me as I whipped the rumpled sheet from the bed and flung it around my waist, she said, "I believe we owe you our gratitude. Mistress Carey told us how you helped Her Grace visit with His Majesty her brother, God rest his soul, and then escape the Duke's clutches. Were it not for you, who knows where she would have ended up? Northumberland never wished anything but harm on her. I did advise her not to leave here to start with. But she didn't listen to me. She never listens to anyone. She thinks she's invincible. It'll be her undoing one day, mark my words."

She babbled, like a brook! Who would have guessed?

I lowered my head. "I was honored to be of service," I mumbled.

"Yes, well," she retorted, "serving her is no charm, I can assure you. I should know. I've been with her since she was yea high, and you never met a more contentious soul, even in her leading strings. Always did have to have her way. Still, all of us in this house love her as if she were our own. She has a way of making you care, even when you know you shouldn't."

Mistress Astley smiled. "Well, I'll be off. You've the two of them waiting on you, and I'd be hard-pressed to say who is less demanding. Wash yourself well. Her Grace has a nose like a bloodhound when it comes to odors."

The door closed. I descended on the fare with gusto. After I'd eaten my fill, I bathed and took out the clothes from the press. I was glad to find my saddlebag there. Gently, I removed the leather-bound volume, which was a little more battered for the wear; opened it to that front page, and the hand-written inscription in faded blue ink.

Votre amie, Marie.

I caressed those slanted lines, penned by a hand I had never known. I set the book on the bedside table. Later, I would read Dame Alice's favorite psalm, and remember.

I was able to shave using lather from the soap, my knife, and a sliver of cracked mirror from my bag, and my days as a Warwick urchin. Though I couldn't see myself well in the reflection, what I did glimpse as I washed away the hair-flecked spumes brought me to a halt.

The face looking back at me was still slightly bruised, pallid, and more angular than I remembered, its youth tempered by hard-earned maturity. It was a face not yet twenty-one years of age, a face I had lived with all my life; and it belonged to someone I did not fully know.

I turned away and dressed. The clothes were indeed a remarkably close fit.

Passing through the great hall with its impressive hammer-beamed ceiling and Flemish tapestries, I proceeded to the open oak doors and into a lingering dusk that drifted over eglantine and willow like a velvet rain.

Kate stooped ankle-deep in an herb patch, a straw hat on her head as she bundled fresh-picked thyme into a basket. She glanced up at my approach, the hat slipping off to dangle on ribbons at her back. Gathering her in my arms, I indulged my starved senses.

"I assume you slept well," she whispered at length, breathless against my lips.

"I'd have slept better if you'd been with me," I said, my hands at her waist.

She laughed. "Any better, and you'd have needed a shroud." Her laughter turned husky. "Don't think to tempt me. I'll not give in to any tom cat that decides to wander home."

"Yes, I like that about you," I growled. We kissed, after which she drew me to a bench. We held hands, gazing to the diminishing sky.

Presently Kate said, "I have these." From her skirt pocket, she brought out the leaf and, to my surprise, Robert Dudley's silver and onyx ring.

"I'd forgotten about this," I murmured, slipping the ring on my finger. It was too big.

"Do you know what's happened?" she asked.

"Last I heard, the Duke marched on Framlingham."

She nodded. "Word came late today. He never reached it. The moment the Council proclaimed Mary queen, Arundel and the others rushed to grovel at her feet. Arundel then marched off to arrest the Duke, Lord Robert, and his other sons. They're being taken to the Tower. Guilford Dudley, of course, is already there. Rumor has it Mary will order all of them executed."

My fingers closed over the ring. "One can hardly blame her," I replied. My mind flew back to other times, long past times, when a bewildered boy crouched in an attic, trembling, fearing discovery, yet envying the tribe of sons who would not accept him.

I felt Kate's hand on mine. "Do you want to talk about it? You still have the petal. Did you find out what it means?"

The memory faded.

"It's a leaf." I shifted about to meet her gaze. Opening her palm, I set the golden leaf in her hand. "I want to tell you. I want to tell you everything. Only, I need more time to sort it out. And she is expecting me. Mistress Astley said she waited on me."

I noticed the subtle stiffening of her posture. I knew she couldn't help her jealousy, which we would have to learn to cope with if we were to build a life together. Elizabeth had become too much a part of us to ever relinquish.

"She is," Kate said at length. "She had another of her headaches this afternoon, but she asked to see you as soon as you were ready. I was gathering herbs for her draught. I'll take you to her now, if you like. She is taking her exercise in the gallery."

She started to rise. I pressed her closed hand to my lips. "Kate, you mustn't fear."

She looked at our twined hands with palpable sadness. "You don't know her as I do. A more loyal mistress cannot be found, but she requires your undying devotion in return."

"She has it already. But my heart belongs to you." I stood, cupped her chin, and kissed her lips. "Keep that jewel close. It's yours now, a symbol of our troth. I hope to soon match it with a ring, and a house."

I was warmed by the radiance in her eyes. Time enough later to prove nothing would interfere with the life I wanted to build with her—a life far from the tumult of these days and the malice of the court, a life in which the secret of my past would remain forever concealed.

I followed her to where Elizabeth awaited.

At the entrance to the gallery I paused. The slim figure I espied, Urian at her side, appeared taller, familiar and strange at the same time, arresting in its solitude. I drew in a quick breath to ease the tightness in my chest, then stepped forth and bowed. With an elated bark of recognition Urian bounded to me.

Elizabeth came to a halt. Silhouetted in the diffused sun slipping through the embrasures, her pale mauve gown caught the light like water, a perfect contrast to her mane of red-gold hair. She looked like a faun caught in a clearing, until she strode toward me with that quicksilver determination that was more a lion's than a deer's. As I rose, I noted a parchment clutched in her left hand.

I met her amber gaze. "Your Grace, I am overjoyed to find you safe."

"And in good health, don't forget that. What of you, my friend?"

"I am, too," I said, "as well as can be expected."

She smiled. "I'm relieved my sister didn't infect you with her dourness." She waved me to a window seat, its worn upholstery and stack of books to one side indicating it was a favored spot. I perched on the edge, taking the time I needed to adjust to her presence. Urian curled contentedly at her feet.

Elizabeth sat beside me, close but not too much so, her tapered fingers fussing with the parchment. I recalled those pampered hands using a stone to smash a guard's head, and wondered at this mercurial duality, which was as much a part of her heritage as her coloring.

As I pondered this, the reality of our situation struck me. How would she react if she found out who I was? Would she welcome me as a long-lost member of the family? Or would she, like her formidable cousin the Duchess of Suffolk before her, view me as a threat?

As if she could read my thoughts, she said, "You are comely. So lean, with those light gray eyes and hair like barley, it's no wonder Jane thought you familiar. My brother Edward might have looked a little like you, had he lived to your age."

Emotion welled in me.

Whether or not she could accept me as kin mattered little in that moment, as I understood that this was how it felt to be enamored of two women. For no matter how true I was to Kate (and I was true, and would be to the death) I had no doubt I was also in love with Elizabeth. How could I not be? Only, it wasn't the earthly passion I felt for Kate; and I was glad of it. Such a love for Elizabeth Tudor was far more demanding, took far more than it could ever give. To desire her as a man desired a woman was to condemn oneself to an eternal limbo, to yearn for what could never be. In this respect, I had only pity for Robert Dudley, whose physical prison could never equal the one she'd chained about his heart.

"Where have you drifted, Squire?" I heard her ask, and I pulled myself to attention.

"Forgive me, Your Grace. I was thinking."

"Indeed." She regarded me intently.

I removed the loose ring from my finger. "I believe this belongs to you. Lord Robert gave it to me in hope of better things. Given the situation, I think he'd want you to have it."

Her hand trembled as she reached out. "You risked much in order to get this to me. Some might say, too much."

"Some might, Your Grace."

"But not you." She raised her eyes. "Tell me, was it worth it?" As she awaited my answer, the regal distance in her evaporated. She reverted to what she was at heart, an achingly young woman, vulnerable and uncertain, fated always to dwell in certain loneliness.

I leaned to her. "Every moment. I'd risk it all again to serve Your Grace."

She gave me a tremulous smile. "You might yet find reason to regret those words."

She unfolded her other hand. The parchment she held was crumpled, brittle, but the broken wax seal was still visible. "Her summons to London," she said, to my unspoken question. "She expects me to join her at court to celebrate her victory. I may yet have need of your keen eyes. Mary and I, we are not like other sisters. There's too much pain in our past, pain she can never forgive or forget, though all I ever did against her was be born."

"I am here," I reassured. "So are others. We'll see to it that you come to no harm."

"From your lips to God's ears," she said softly. She slipped Robert's ring into her bodice. Mary's letter drifted from her hands to the floor.

With a glance at my somber face, she suddenly let out a clarion laugh. "So serious! Do you know how to dance, Brendan Prescott?"

I felt my eyes widen. "Dance, Your Grace? No, I. . .I never learned."

"Never learned?" She leapt to her feet, Urian springing up beside her. "We must remedy that. How can you expect to survive, much less enjoy, life at court if you don't know how to dance? It's the weapon of choice for every well-heeled gentleman. Much more has been done on the dance floor to save a kingdom than in any council room or battlefield."

My grin emerged, lopsided, as her clap of hands brought Kate and Peregrine into the gallery, my suspicion that they'd been lurking nearby, awaiting her cue, confirmed by the lute in Kate's hands.

Jaunting at her side, Peregrine was another boy all together, scrubbed to shiny perfection, his lithe form in a suit of jade velvet that matched his eyes. His smile looked to split his face in two when Elizabeth ordered him to beat time on one of her books: "Slowly, as if it were a kettle drum, or the hindquarters of an ill-tempered steed. And Kate, you play that pavane we learned together last week, remember? The French one, with the long measure."

Strumming the corresponding chords, Kate gave me a mischievous smile.

With a look that warned I would have my sweet revenge later, I surrendered to Elizabeth's hand as she led me into the dance.

END OF BOOK ONE

AUTHOR'S NOTE

I t is important to note this is a novel, first and foremost. It takes as its premise: *What if. . .?* and interweaves fact, rumor, scholarly deduction, and imagination in order to tell a story. I have tried to remain true to the historical period and limit my conjecture to a circumscribed realm of possibilities. For no matter how much we think we know about the 16th century, there's always something new to discover.

Because writing can be a solitary obsession, I'm grateful to those who remind me there's more to life. First and foremost, I owe immense gratitude to my partner, who has stood by me through thirteen wonderful years. This book is dedicated to him.

I must also thank our beloved dog, Paris, for her unconditional love and boundless joy, which teach me every day how to enjoy the most simple and precious part of being alive; my brother Eric and his wife Jackie, for providing early feedback; Linda, for reading it a hundred times; fellow aficionado and designer extraordinaire, Paula, for inspiration; Jean and Jean, Billy, LuAnn, and Jack of the Sunset Writers Group, for laughter and encouragement; my editor, Victoria, for always believing; my friends in McLaren Park for keeping it simple; Marie H., for tea and wisdom; the team at Two Bridges Press, for helping turn a potential loss into gain; the Historical Novel Society, for keeping the genre front and center; and all the independent bookstores, fellow writers, and many friends who helped me realize this dream.

Last, but never least, I wish to thank my mother, for giving me my first historical novel; and my father, for encouraging me to write.

Without them, this book could never have been.

The Secret Lion

1. *The Secret Lion* takes place during the succession crisis of 1553. What did you discover about England at this time? Who were the major players in the crisis and what were their motivations?

2. Religion plays a crucial role in the conflicts described in this book. What were the main issues between Catholics and Protestants? Were their conflicts based on actual religious differences or larger political power struggles? Do you see any parallels to today's religious divides?

3. Brendan Prescott is a fictional character with a secret. Like many servants of the time, he is entrusted with his master's messages. What were some of the possible repercussions he could have suffered for his actions? If you had been in his place, what might you have done?

4. The jewel in the book is based on a real jewel featured in a painting of Mary of Suffolk. Why do you think the jewel was divided up? What message do you think Mary was trying to send?

5. Lady Dudley has secrets of her own. What are they? Did you understand her reasons for doing what she did? What does her character tell us about the roles of noblemen's wives in the 16th century?

6. Brendan carries a clue to his past with him all along. Why doesn't he understand its significance until the end? What part of his past does he fail to solve?

7. The death of Edward VI remains shrouded in mystery. Do you find the author's hypothesis plausible?

9. Elizabeth Tudor is one of history's most popular and enduring figures. Why do you think she continues to exert such fascination?

8. Who was your favorite character in the book, and why?

ABOUT THE AUTHOR

C. W. Gortner holds an MFA in Creative Writing, with an emphasis in Renaissance Studies. He has taught courses on, and lectured about, the 16th century in a variety of venues. He has written about the history behind this novel in the Historical Novel Society's *Solander* magazine.

In addition to *The Secret Lion*, he is the author of *The Last Queen*, a novel about Juana the Mad of Castile. He is currently at work on the second book in "The Spymaster Chronicles", as well as a new historical novel about the life of Catherine de Medici.

He divides his time between San Francisco and South Lake Tahoe, together with his partner of fourteen years and their Welsh Pembroke Corgi, Paris.

Visit him at: www.leonibus.com

Printed in the United States
107999LV00002B/136/A

9 780972 394710